The
Wish
List

RUBY
HUMMINGBIRD

bookouture

Published by Bookouture in 2019

An imprint of Storyfire Ltd.
Carmelite House
50 Victoria Embankment
London EC4Y 0DZ

www.bookouture.com

ISBN: 978-1-83888-092-7
eBook ISBN: 978-1-83888-091-0

Previously published as
The Wish List of Albie Young

For Andrea – a warm, wonderful and inspiring woman

Prologue

She didn't remember much of the days and weeks and months after it had happened. She had moved through the flat, unseeing, time simply passing – daytime, night-time, all blurring into one long, terrible grey day.

The weight fell from her and when she looked in the mirror she saw a skeleton of her past self: cheeks hollow, eyes deadened, fine grey hairs appearing at her temples.

Nothing would ever be the same.

She had stopped answering the door, let the post mount up, left the telephone off the hook. Then she would regret the silence, crave some other noise aside from the relentless sound of the sea as it rolled in and out, rhythmic, unstoppable, reminding her of time passing and of the world moving on while her whole life had stopped, reminding her of that night: that terrible night.

MONDAY – Weekly shop
TUESDAY – Blow-dry
WEDNESDAY – Laundrette
THURSDAY – Albie
FRIDAY – Ironing
SATURDAY – Buy TV listings
SUNDAY – Church

Chapter 1

Maria padded back into her bedroom with a coffee. On other days she had a different routine – her usual one – but Thursdays were decadent. She climbed back under the duvet, settled herself back on the pillows and took a sip from the mug: it was like drinking satin. Instead of picking up her book on the bedside table, she ran through her morning's preparations, pretending not to feel the fleeting flutter of butterflies in her stomach. It was the caffeine, she told herself.

Closing her eyes, she ignored the strain of sunshine on the back of the thick cream curtains, not yet ready to pull them back and leave her cocoon. She loved Thursday mornings. She glanced at her beloved photo frame on her bedside table and smiled at it fondly. Everything hurt less on Thursdays.

Setting the mug down, she enjoyed a few more moments of peace: the gentle tick of the alarm clock, the slight hum of traffic moving along the road below and her own breathing, slow, steady. The digits of the clock changed: it was past breakfast time, really. She'd skipped it, as she did every Thursday. She didn't like to overindulge on Thursdays as she didn't want to feel bloated for the day – she liked to have plenty of room for their treat in the café. It was time for a bath.

But first, it was time for her to select music for it. She chose a piano concerto by Mozart and set up her record player, the needle needing a tiny blow to remove the dust that had built up over the last week. The sound of the instruments swelling in the small space, the decisive notes on the piano, loud and fast, reminded her how quiet her apartment was the rest of the time.

Stepping into the bathroom, she headed straight to the cabinet. She pulled down a dark blue bottle and tipped a few drops of oil into the water, swirling it with her hand. The oil was expensive but she could make it last for weeks and the bath wouldn't be the same without it. The small room immediately filled with the scent of lavender, the yellow liquid making the water silky and inviting. Stepping in carefully, gripping the side bars of the bath, she lowered herself slowly, feeling every muscle sing as it hit the warm water. Wiggling her toes, resting herself back on the folded hand towel underneath her head, she slowly closed her eyes again: decadent. It was a wonderful ritual. She reached for the book she had brought in and lost herself in the pages until the water grew tepid and her skin became even more wrinkled than usual.

The LP had stopped a while ago and as Maria emerged from the bath, the small mirror steamed up, she was grateful only to have a glimpse of blurred pink cheeks and the damp grey tendrils sticking to her neck. She still had time to transform. Plenty of time on Thursdays.

She rested her hand on her stomach and moved back to her bedroom, sliding open her wardrobe and staring at the clothes hanging on their hangers. She had watched the weather forecast last night after the nine o'clock news and knew there was a small chance of rain but, dash it, she could risk it: the sun still brightened her curtains.

Pulling out a pair of black Capri trousers and a silvery-grey jumper with a lace collar, she lay them carefully on the bed. She had worn the jumper seven Thursdays back – she hoped he wouldn't remember – and he had commented on the detail at the neckline. The memory of his words made her blush just as she had at the time, as if he was right here in her bedroom, saying it again.

Now that she had chosen her outfit it was time for her to move across the room and open the curtains. She pulled them back, securing them on their ties and letting the sun flood into the small bedroom, highlighting the dancing dust motes in the air and bouncing off the dressing table mirror, leaving squares of light on the cream walls. She made the double bed, tucking in the patterned bedspread and plumping the pillows.

Sitting at the dressing room table in her dusty pink towel she couldn't help sigh at the sight in front of her. Sometimes on Thursdays she hoped to see a younger, smoother-skinned version of herself sitting there but she knew she was just being silly.

You're being silly, she chastised, knowing talking out loud to oneself was probably one of the first signs of madness. *A silly old woman.* Then she poked her tongue out at her reflection, making herself giggle. Reaching for her face cream, she began the weekly ritual. Powders, brushes, eyeshadow, concealer, pale pink lipstick. She took her time, relishing every stage, watching the potions and lotions transform her usual look into something a little more appropriate for Thursday.

As she carefully lined her lips with a soft pale liner, she thought of the television programmes she had recorded or watched that week. She had selected a couple she knew he might have seen too: he had a fascination with the Second World War and Channel 4 had aired an excellent documentary about Operation Mincemeat. She probed her own thoughts: had she enjoyed the documentary? Had it kept her attention? She looked forward to asking him his opinion. Then there was the Sunday night period drama they both enjoyed – the last episode had ended on something of a cliffhanger and she was keen to hear his prediction about what might happen this week. He was always rather good at it. She enjoyed watching his face, animated, as he constructed the possible outcome. He had such imagination.

Then there was her book. He had recommended it a few Thursdays ago and she was almost at the end. She wished there were slightly fewer lengthy descriptive passages – were there really that many ways to describe the weather? Still, she was interested to ask him his thoughts on the reveal in the middle – she hadn't seen it coming and wondered if he had been as surprised as her. She imagined not, she had always been terribly thick when it came to anything like that. Her ex-partner had called her 'too trusting', just one of his many complaints.

With a last flick of mascara, she was finished, tilting her head from side to side to check for powder clumps or streaks from the foundation. Then she began on her hair, picking up the very expensive hairdryer she had been persuaded to buy after a visit to the salon earlier in the year. She tried to copy the method used by her lovely regular hairdresser Mandy, lifting the separate chunks of damp hair at the back and firing the hot air at the roots for a little lift. Her silvery-grey bob started to become smoother as she worked around her head, taking care, enjoying spending time on it. With a spritz of perfume on her wrists and neck, she was ready. She had become Thursday Maria – the best of the Marias!

It was now she had another cup of coffee – decaf though, she didn't want to be jittery when they ordered the tea. She would have to leave soon. Pulling on the clothes she had selected, careful not to get make-up on the collar of her jumper, she gave herself one last appraising glance. She looked confident, happy, and the silver of the jumper, the slick of mascara made her eyes twinkle that little bit bluer. Or was it the thought of the afternoon ahead?

Maria liked to walk to the café, happy that the sun was shining, peeking intermittently out behind puffs of white cloud. With the slight chill in the air, she was glad to be wearing her light pink coat. He had once said that it had reminded him of candy floss, a wistful expression on his face as he spoke about the fairs he had visited with his father as a boy. She liked looking like candy floss.

The side streets in Brighton were busy with people moving, distracted with their everyday activities. Two screeching seagulls swooped overhead, no doubt heading to the beach less than a mile away, but a lifetime of distance for Maria. She hadn't been to the pebbled beach for years, wouldn't go. She stared up as one stretched out his wings, seeming to hover on the breeze before diving out of sight. The smell of petrol and the sea filled her nostrils: as the sound of bicycle bells, idling cars and chatter jangled in her ears. She was glad to arrive outside the café, push the door and hear the familiar tinkle of the bell that always made her heart skip.

Glancing quickly around the room she realised she was early this week and felt a small smile spreading in anticipation. The waitress nodded in recognition and Maria quickly nodded back. The table along the furthest wall, *their table*, was empty: the surface recently wiped down, a single red carnation in a small vase in the centre, two chairs opposite each other. She would take the seat facing the door and spend the next few minutes guessing what he might be wearing. Was it cold enough for the thin green scarf that made his eyes even deeper? Would he be wearing a shirt and a coat or a shirt under a jumper? Would he have combed his hair carefully to the left, the still-damp hair a hint that he had showered recently? Silly thoughts, but ones that made her move quickly and lightly to the table, remove her coat and place it on the back of the chair.

The waitress, Amrit, approached. She'd been working here for more than a year now. She was a saxophonist in a jazz band – he had asked her that once. Maria felt her eyes dart away as Amrit approached, always less confident when he wasn't sat opposite her, ready to make strangers feel at ease.

'Hello, I thought you might be along.' The small blue jewel in her nose flashed as she smiled at Maria. 'Do you want anything different today?' She held a small white pad in her hand and had a pencil stuck in her dark brown hair, which was tied back and streaked with strands of hot pink.

'I'd love a slice of the marble cake, two forks please and a pot of tea: just English Breakfast, nothing fancy.'

'Your turn this week then?' She smiled again, not writing anything on the pad.

When Maria didn't reply, simply offering a small nod, the waitress gave a slight wave. 'I'll go and get it.'

Maria looked around the small space, at the faded red gingham tablecloths, the scuffed skirting boards, the walls punctured with old holes from where pictures had once hung: so tired but so familiar. She couldn't think of a place that made her feel more content.

The bell on the café door jingled and Maria looked up expectantly, her eyes already widening, her throat clearing ready to say hello. A young woman pushed inside with a pram and Maria felt a flicker of disappointment. She folded one hand over the other on the table, realising as she did so that she had forgotten to paint her nails the usual colour, a pinky-grey like the inside of an oyster shell, good for distracting from liver spots and lines. *Silly old woman*, she thought again but still she removed her hands from the top of the table.

Amrit returned with a tray, a pot of tea and a large slice of marble cake, along with a small side plate – an extra thought – and Maria was grateful to her.

'Thank you,' she said, watching the waitress unload the items.

'Not at all. You were lucky too, this was the last slice. Good job you only ever order one to share, I suppose.'

Maria felt tongue-tied in the usual way, biting on her bottom lip. 'Thank you,' she repeated, aware she sounded like a broken record. Amrit had a hundred other far more interesting customers to serve though, she mustn't keep her.

'You just shout if I can get you anything else. Chef's just started making chocolate peppermint slices and they are incredible. Better than se— well, they're just really delicious,' Amrit said, tugging at her collar.

Maria felt a giggle escape and swallowed it down quickly, adding, 'Just this for now but thank you.'

She normally waited for Albie to pour the tea and slice into the cake but as the time wore on, Maria couldn't let the pot sit there much longer: it would get cold. She could ask for a refill perhaps. She glanced at her small, round watch and frowned. It wasn't like Albie to be this late.

She reached for the teapot and placed the strainer over her cup, the liquid a little darker perhaps than she liked. Next, she picked up her fork, her hand hovering over the marble cake. She placed it down again, took a sip of her tea.

More people left and arrived through the café doors, bell tinkling, and she could see the waitress glancing across at her at intermittent moments. Feeling self-conscious, she pretended to be enormously interested in the pictures on the walls. They were painted by a local artist, small red stickers below them showed a price. Albie painted. Nothing was ever 'orange', 'red' or 'blue' when he looked at them: the salt shaker was 'burnt umber', the tablecloth 'scarlet', her eyes were 'cerulean blue'. She wished she had the courage to ask him to show her his paintings, the question often on the tip of her tongue.

She couldn't help looking at her watch. A half an hour had passed and Maria picked up the fork again, carefully cutting the slice of cake in two with the edge. A small seed of worry planted itself as she placed the first morsel in her mouth. It didn't taste quite the same: perhaps a little dry today, not so sweet. She took another sip of her tea, long past hot. She wondered where he had got to.

Time went on and Maria had stopped looking up every time the bell rang out. She had finished her half of the cake, topped up her tea, drank it, the taste tangy and wrong as she wondered for the hundredth time where he had got to.

She glanced at the door, the bottom of the glass steamed up, the net curtains drawn back on both sides. The letters on the outside were reversed from her angle, spelling out 'S N O C A E D'. People moved past in the street beyond, fast blurs. No one with neatly combed-down grey hair, no one holding a rolled-up newspaper, no one wearing a green scarf.

She felt something tighten in her stomach, her muscles clenching. Had he forgotten? It seemed hardly likely, he was normally prompt and had kept their arrangement religiously for the last four years. Had he been deterred by some crisis in his life? She cast her mind back over the nuggets she had gleaned from their previous conversations, realising as she did that he rarely spoke of family members or the private details of his life. Had he fallen on his way here? Become waylaid by some drama?

She realised she had no way of contacting him. All she could do was wait at this table, alone.

She felt the eyes of the waitress on her as she sat there. If only she had brought her book, she could stay longer then, without looking preposterous. She should leave. But something stopped her getting up, some fear held her to her seat. She realised she didn't care if she looked silly. She stared at his half of the cake, her half sitting solidly in her stomach, weighing her down, her mouth dry as she imagined swallowing more.

The baby in the pram had been lifted out and had now started wailing. The woman was jiggling him up and down and patting him but the noise was getting inside Maria's head, making the room a little fuzzy. Someone dropped something in the kitchen behind her, a clang of saucepans on a hard floor, and she started in her seat. She felt a creeping sense that something wasn't right.

She sat frozen, repeatedly placing one hand over the other, an old habit she had started doing years ago, after everything had changed. She needed to get up and visit the Ladies' room but she didn't want to leave the table. What if he turned up now and assumed she'd left?

The woman with the pram left, more people came and went. The waitress lingered by her table, cloth in hand, as Maria averted her gaze. She knew she had to leave. She'd been sat there far too long. With alarm, she felt tears push behind her eyes as she prepared to stand up. Something had changed today. Thursday's shine was well and truly dulled.

The weather seemed to reflect Maria's mood as she left the café in the direction of home: the sun sat stubbornly behind a bank of thick grey cloud, the street mostly in shadow, pigeons pecking at detritus on the ground. A knot of worry was tightening in her stomach as she wandered, unseeing, down the road, and gave a jump as a cyclist rang his bell, swearing under his breath as he passed her, too close to the kerb. *Careful.*

Albie hadn't done this before, he had always been prompt. More often than not he was the one sat there with the tea and cake waiting. She liked the days when she beat him to it, paid for them both, she liked seeing his face, the mock exasperation. Something twisted inside her as she recalled that familiar expression. His heavy brows drawn together, his normally dancing eyes rolling at her, the twitch of his lips. She found herself coming to a complete stop on the pavement, a woman behind her almost barrelling into her.

'I'm sorry,' Maria muttered as the woman skirted round her with a small huff of annoyance.

Where to go now? Home? She imagined herself in the apartment, her careful make-up, her hair, the floral scent of the bath she had sunk into that morning. Normally, Thursday evenings were a relaxing joy: a small supper, a chance to replay the conversations from the café, a warmth in her stomach that made her rifle through her LP collection, choose something upbeat. She'd open a half bottle of rosé and take the glass out onto her small balcony on a warm evening. But not tonight. Tonight, she knew the knot would get bigger and tighter until it filled her up entirely. Where was he?

She blinked: it couldn't be? Had all her thoughts conjured him? Ahead of her, through a thin crowd of people, she glimpsed a beige check flat cap, brown tweed shoulders. She started walking again, eyes on the hat, not wanting to lose it moving in between passers-by. Apologising as she weaved her way between people, feeling her hands slippery on her handbag, she could see grey tendrils of hair curled over the man's collar. The hat had stopped and Maria held her breath as she gained on it. Then, in slow motion, he turned, glancing over his shoulder before crossing the road. This man had paler skin, thinner eyebrows, a straight nose, no familiar bump where Albie had broken his playing squash years ago.

She felt her whole body sag at the sight. Someone else muttered behind her, a car horn blared, a child called out to its mother. The sounds of the street were loud around her, everyone busy, busy, no time, looking at smartphones, chatting, quick footsteps. Maria had never felt more alone.

Perhaps he had forgotten their usual arrangement or had just arrived at the café and she hadn't waited long enough. Why hadn't she sat there another half an hour? She wavered for a few more moments, feeling utterly undecided. Should she have left a note for him in the café perhaps? Should she go back there? She imagined Amrit's kind face, would she understand?

The sun seemed to break through the cloud for a moment, a streak of light slicing the road in front of her, and Maria suddenly recalled a napkin Albie had once handed her: a napkin with his home telephone number written on it. He had told her to call him if she ever needed to postpone their tea and cake. She had never rung him, had never found the excuse to do so. She certainly would never have postponed their meeting. She must find that napkin.

The thought made her footsteps lighter, a renewed purpose now, something to cling to. Her legs were aching as she pushed her way into her apartment block and started up the first flight of stairs. Her hands fumbled with the key to her front door and she cursed uncharacteristically as it slipped out of her grip.

Flustered, she moved through her apartment to the side table in the hallway, past leaflets about takeaways, local restaurants she had never frequented, a florist, an electrician. No napkin. She tapped at her teeth, hair mussed up, make-up slipping. She knew she looked a mess, didn't care. In the kitchen she removed the stack of paper from the side, a place she used for the things she would recycle. With a sinking feeling she knew the napkin wouldn't be there. What had she done with it? *You silly old woman, think, don't start losing your memory now*. She would have wanted to have kept it safe. She would have put it somewhere safe. The mantelpiece was empty, the bedside table in her bedroom was empty bar the single photograph in the frame. She didn't want to look at that now.

Slumped on her sofa, she put her head in her hands, feeling completely hopeless. Tears pricked her eyes. She didn't want to cry but she didn't understand how the day had taken this terrible turn. Thursdays had been her refuge for so long. How could she have misplaced the one thing that might help her uncover what had happened to Albie: her Thursday friend, her only real friend?

She pressed her two hands to her eyes, leaving mascara marks on her palms, and swallowed. A long evening ahead. A long evening of wondering, worrying. And then, from across the room she saw it: her small bookshelf, her books arranged haphazardly. And she remembered: the napkin, the book she had taken that day. She sprang up, feeling fifty years younger in that second, and crossed the room. She was already scanning the titles, her eyes narrowed slightly – she didn't have time to fetch her glasses from her handbag. It had been a midnight blue, she thought, as one finger moved over the spines. There! She pulled the book out, her heart racing as she turned the cover over to reveal the small square napkin nestled like a precious bookmark in its folds. His name and the digits of his phone number, centred neatly in his slanted hand: *Albert Young 01273 890572.*

She wanted to kiss the napkin but hugged it to herself instead, not wanting to smudge the numbers with her lipstick. She returned to the sofa and pulled the small round side table nearer to her, the large telephone on top of it. With a shaking hand she dialled the number written on the napkin, feeling nerves leaping and jittering in her stomach, excited to hear his voice, the hint of his West Country accent in his vowels. The ringtone sounded and she licked her lips. Why hadn't she fetched a glass of water? Too late now, of course. She cleared her throat, the ringtones continued. Another, and another. No answer, no one picking up. Then a click and the voice she had been waiting to hear, but this time it was a pre-recorded voice: an answerphone.

'You've reached the answerphone of Albert Young, I can't get to the phone right now but please do leave a mes—'

With a jolt Maria replaced the receiver.

Albie wasn't home.

And with a horrible certainty she knew something must have happened to him.

*

She always smelt of apples and the outdoors and I loved her so much, sometimes I thought my heart might burst with it. One night she had appeared in the doorway to my bedroom, dragging her cream blanket in one hand and holding a book in the other.

'Rabbit book,' she had demanded, moving across the room to me lying on the bed.

I struggled up on one elbow. 'Again?'

She nodded solemnly, her round eyes enormous in her tiny, smooth face.

I laughed, my thoughts fading as they always did when she was there. 'Come on then, darling, hop up here.'

'Like a rabbit,' she said delightedly, bouncing over and managing to drop the book in her enthusiasm.

Scooping it and her up, I settled her on my lap, relishing the scent of apples and baby shampoo, her wispy hair tickling my chin as she rested back on me. I loved the feel of her tiny body against me, completely trusting.

I opened the book, seeing the familiar inscription 'From Dad' and felt a twinge of pain. Hastily moving to the start of the book, I began, 'One day there was a rabbit, a very special sort of rabbit…'

She was sucking her thumb, the blanket drawn up to her face, our hearts beating at the same time. Sometimes I felt sick with love for her, all-consuming. I carried on reading as she snuggled next to me.

Where had those days gone?

Chapter 2

Maria didn't sleep well, an old dream nudging at her, forcing her eyes open in the dark, the thin outline of the moonlight at the edge of her curtains. She wasn't a big dreamer and the details of this one were just out of reach, but she felt colder lying there in the darkness, pulling at the covers.

Friday.

She woke far too early, staring at the swirled textured ceiling of her bedroom, the round beige lampshade. She felt a weight on her chest as she thought of the day ahead. Friday was when she liked to catch up with her domestic chores, clear the ironing, wipe down the apartment. Normally she didn't mind these activities, spaced them out throughout the day, enjoying watching the tiny transformations of the apartment: the sparkling glass of the bath, the gleaming taps in the kitchen, the neat pile of clothes waiting to be hung back up. Today though it all seemed insurmountable, even getting out of bed seemed an effort. If only she could lie here and pretend, pretend it was yesterday and there was nothing gnawing at her.

Friday.

She started her day in the usual way, barely tasting the toast and jam, the coffee tepid by the time she remembered to drink it. She rested her hands flat on the table in front of her, the tick of the clock loud in the room, reminding her that she was alone. She didn't move across to her LP machine, she didn't bustle and fuss with the paltry amount of washing-up; she just sat there and stared at her hands. Her fingernails were still bare, her cuticles ragged, the ends in need of filing. She couldn't summon the energy required. She didn't even get up when she heard the buzzer go downstairs, the familiar clatter as the postman dropped off parcels and letters and pamphlets to the residents of the block. Her own letterbox opened and closed – normally she might be there, attempting to summon up a nice word for him, but today she could do nothing more than stare at her hands.

Moving back through to her bedroom she glanced over to the wire basket to see that an envelope and a leaflet had been pushed through the letterbox. Automatically, she took them out, hoping for a brief second that the envelope might contain some kind of answer, but of course she was being silly and it was just from her bank. The leaflet was for gym membership, lots of people on indoor cycling machines looking focused and content. The tagline shouted 'NEVER GIVE UP' and she held the piece of paper in her hand, didn't take it across to the recycling pile, but stared at the words instead. 'NEVER GIVE UP'… Something jolted within her and she realised the slogan was the sign she needed to wake up, to *really* wake up.

She phoned him again, didn't hesitate, didn't pause, just dialled, her heart in her mouth, her hand slippery on the receiver. *Come on*, she muttered, *come on*! The click of the answerphone again: of course, it couldn't be that easy.

She cleaned her teeth and she pulled clothes out of her wardrobe, located her most comfortable shoes. She'd start back at the café; she couldn't stay here ironing and cleaning and pretending that nothing had changed. She had to do something, had to know he was alright.

She left her bedroom, a quick glance back to the photograph that stood on her bedside table: a photograph that always filled her with mixed emotions. Today, the face seemed to be willing her on.

It was a different waitress today, the taller, older woman Pauline, who often left her knitting on the stool behind the counter: she seemed to have a never-ending stream of baby hats, jumpers, cardigans to produce, but Maria had never been brave enough to ask probing questions. Albie of course had no such compunctions and Maria always watched in proud amusement as he would make Pauline open up, share her life story: an upbringing in East London, one of six children, a husband in the Navy, their retirement to be by the sea, his death only two months into retirement, the opening of this café.

Pauline obviously couldn't help but glance at the clock, unused perhaps to seeing Maria at this time, on this day. She greeted her warmly though and moved behind the counter, a cake stand of scones, plump and golden, on top.

'Can I help?'

Maria opened her mouth to ask her and then panicked, feeling silly, closed it again. Pauline looked enquiringly at her, her eyebrows lost in her thick ash blonde fringe. *Just ask her.*

'A scone please,' Maria said in haste, pointing to the cake stand.

Pauline bent to reach under the counter. 'They're fresh this morning. I'll just get a plate.'

'No,' Maria said in a loud voice, which startled Pauline enough to shoot up straight, 'to go please.'

Pauline nodded slowly, a slight frown on her face as she tore off a paper bag and took up the tongs.

Maria took a long, slow breath in and out. 'I was wondering,' she muttered, not quite able to meet Pauline's eye, instead watching as she dropped the scone in the bag, 'I was wondering if Albert, my companion, the gentlemen I am usually here with on a Thursday afternoon, I was wondering if you'd seen him?'

Pauline looked up, replacing the tongs. 'I weren't working yesterday, I'm afraid. I can ask Amrit? She was on yesterday.'

Maria's eyes darted to Pauline's face and away, 'Oh yes, I know. I was here, you see – Amrit was kind enough to serve me. I was wondering, since then, well, obviously not,' the words were tied and twisted on her tongue, 'you would have said. So you haven't…' She was rubbing her fingers together distractedly.

'Sorry, no, I ain't seen him. If I do, I can let you know though, you could leave a number? Or let 'im know you're looking for him?'

'Oh no, oh, that's fine,' Maria said, feeling herself flush. What must Pauline think? Some crazed old woman running around town, searching for a man? She made herself look her in the face. 'I'll catch up with him, I'm sure. There's no need for any trouble.' She forced a smile.

The café bell rang and a young man moved inside to stand behind Maria at the counter.

'It's no trouble,' Pauline said, placing the bag down and reaching for a pen.

Should she leave her number? Where was the harm really? And yet she didn't want to cause a fuss and Albie might think it strange. She was aware of the other customer waiting behind her, his light cough. 'No, really,' Maria said, backing away, a wave of a hand, an attempt to look nonchalant.

She was just turning to leave when Pauline picked up the bag. 'Your scone.'

'Oh,' Maria replied, spinning round, feeling her whole body warm now. 'Oh yes, of course,' she said, stepping towards the counter and fumbling with her handbag, 'the scone, how lovely. What a treat!' She knew she was overcompensating.

'It's £1.80,' Pauline said slowly, opening the till.

'How lovely,' Maria repeated handing over a two-pound coin. 'Do keep the change and thank you for the help. I'll see you soon.' She scooped up the bag and placed it inside her handbag, one side already shining with a slight grease mark.

'See you then,' Pauline smiled, the till sliding shut.

Maria was already at the door.

Stood on the street, just around the corner from the café in case Pauline could see her, Maria stopped. What next? She didn't know Albie's exact address – only a rough area – and they didn't have any mutual friends she could call on or telephone. She couldn't just wander the streets of Brighton, shouting out his name. And anyway, she reminded herself firmly, he could be absolutely fine, this could all be in her head. Maybe he was simply away: he'd been to Scotland on a painting holiday last year, perhaps he had simply forgotten another one? Maybe she *should* go home and do the ironing and stop working herself up into this strange hysteria.

Then she thought back over their conversations and she made another decision: she could try and see whether he was at the other places he had mentioned to her. Albie loved to fix things up and he often explained his projects to her: his carpentry, making dovetail joints and the such. Maria had learnt an awful lot over the years, admiring his ability to do things for himself. Whenever anything broke in her apartment she found herself dialling the management company, grateful for the tradespeople and their expertise. Albie had mentioned the shop he visited regularly and she knew it wouldn't be too far, perhaps a small bus ride and a little walk, but it was still early and the ironing could definitely wait. She felt a renewed sense of purpose and set off, her head up, her handbag bashing against her thigh as she strode.

The bus conductor was a wiry man behind a glass panel. Maria smiled shyly at him as she paid for her ticket, the destination vague, just a part of town.

'Thanks, love,' he said, his voice cheery as he dropped the change back with a clatter. She didn't tip bus conductors but she wondered if she should offer him the scone? She wasn't hungry and it seemed such a shame to waste it. Too embarrassed to ask, she shuffled past him and squeezed into a window seat, bag on her lap, eyes roving avidly for familiar sights as the bus chuntered into life.

They turned left at the end of the road and she felt her breath catch in her throat as she made out a sliver of navy sea ahead. Closing her eyes, she turned away from the sight, hoping they would soon turn back inland. She didn't want to think about the beach – she couldn't. She licked her lips and tried to feel reassured by the thought that she knew where she was headed. Perhaps he would be buying paint, batteries or bulbs? Perhaps he would simply be browsing, enjoying walking down the aisles, taking in the smell of the place?

Stepping off the bus, she moved down a side street with a few shops, hoping the one she was looking for would be obvious. With a small thrill she saw it up ahead: brooms and mops propped up outside, buckets and rows of plants, a wheelbarrow, a barrel filled with wire hanging baskets. Her pace quickened and soon she was inside, the smell of turpentine and sawdust all around her. A man in blue overalls walked past her with a can of paint, another was stacking shelves in the corner. She started on the left of the shop, working her way down each aisle – past extension leads and Tupperware, a row of cards, lightbulbs of every size – her eyes roving for his familiar face. No one in the first two aisles at all, a younger man in the third one, a woman browsing seed packets in the fourth. Maria started to feel the disappointment building. Only one aisle left.

There was a cluster of people at the end of the aisle staring at different-sized tools hanging from hooks on the wall. The glint of an axe, screwdrivers and hammers. One man, the same height as Albie, was obscured by an enormous man in a black puffer jacket. She held her breath as she made the slow walk towards them, her eyes taking in the shorter man's build: the same width shoulders, his clothes a little less formal, but perhaps that was what he wore on other days, not Thursdays? It was a DIY shop and not an evening heading to the Proms. Then the man turned and Maria froze: the profile all wrong, the downturned mouth, the cheekbones too pronounced. *Not Albie.*

She turned on her heel and went to leave the shop. Then, at the door she wavered, not wanting this to be the last place. She knew this was his local area and she wanted to linger a while longer.

'Can I help?' a young man in paint-smattered overalls appeared at her side.

'Oh,' Maria said, her mind racing with excuses already. 'No, I'm fine, I'm...'

'Were you looking for anything in particular?'

Yes, yes, a man, about yea high, a few years older than me but you'd never know it, with a cheeky half-smile often playing on his face, a soft voice, slight West Country burr, kind eyes...

The man in overalls was still standing there, waiting for a response.

'I was just looking at your, um, weed killer,' Maria whispered, spotting an enormous bottle of the stuff on a nearby shelf.

'Right, well, this is the brand we do. This'll do the job, works wonders. Do you want the two litres or the four?'

'Oh, um… two is fine,' Maria said on automatic. What could she do with two litres of weed killer? She lived in an apartment, didn't even keep window boxes: weeds were not a concern in her life.

The young man had already taken it off the shelf, was walking over to the till. 'Needing anything else?' he called behind him.

'Oh, um… oh no, just, just that,' she replied, scuttling across.

'Green fingers, eh?' the man said.

Maria was a second behind, her mind still working out how she could get out of buying the weed killer but also somehow remain in the DIY shop searching for her friend. 'Green… oh…' she said, staring at her hands, 'Yes, yes. Ha!'

She paid for the heavy bottle, watched him place it in a carrier bag. She saw some batteries behind the till. Why hadn't she asked for batteries? They were small, light, everyone needed batteries at some point.

The man pushed the heavy bag across to her and said, 'Receipt's in the bag.'

'Lovely,' Maria whispered as she wrenched the bag off the counter, practically dislocating her shoulder as she did so. She paused for a second at the door: this was it. The young guy in overalls was still watching her as she bit her lip and turned back to the door, pushing her way outside, the heavy bag already cutting into her palms and no sighting of Albie to take the pain away.

She wandered then, ignoring two buses that would have taken her back in the direction of her apartment, not yet ready to leave. She stopped in a card shop, a newsagent, accumulating more and more items in her handbag, things she knew she would never use or need: bubbles, a birthday card, a new jotter. The small high street supermarket was bustling with people and the doors slid open as she approached. And yet amongst all those people there was no sight or sound of Albert Young.

It was time to go home. Heading towards the bus stop, she tried to convince herself that it had been a silly idea, a whim. *It doesn't mean anything*, she reassured herself, something still leaving a taste in her mouth: stale.

Glancing to her left before crossing the road, she almost missed it: an electrical shop. She was taken back to a conversation with Albie gushing with such enthusiasm about his new television: a flat screen television with something like an enormous forty-inch screen. It had seemed impossibly big to her and she had laughed along, swept up in his energy. He had told her about high definition and assured her that the *Planet Earth* documentary was incredible when watched on that scale. Now, here the shop was in front of her, gleaming electrical items in its windows. She found herself wandering in, her footsteps automatic, the bus stop forgotten.

The two walls were lined with glossy screens, some playing, some switched off, buttons seemingly hidden, wires leading to power sockets. Smaller items – camera, phones, sat navs – were sat on shelves beneath them and the whole place seemed to hum with electrical energy. She was not at home here. They wouldn't stock LP players, she was fairly sure. A sleepy-looking young man with shoulder-length black hair headed her way. He was wearing a deep purple shirt that seemed to shimmer under the overhead lights and various reflective surfaces around him. A badge announced he was called 'Gareth'.

'Everythin' alright?'

She nodded, her heavy bags making her arms ache. 'Just looking, at, well, things,' she said, realising immediately that no other customer was in the shop, that Albie wouldn't be here anyway as he'd already bought his television and of course now she was stuck having to extricate herself from another store. For a moment though she felt comforted by the fact that he had been here once, that he had bought a television, browsed these walls, that he might have spoken to Gareth too. She felt a gossamer-thin link to Albie, a flash and then, as Gareth started to rub at his nose, flick his eyes to the left, she realised that link had gone.

'I… was just…'

Fortunately, she was saved by the door opening and a couple bustling into the shop. Gareth seemed relieved, as the couple were at least forty years younger than Maria and would understand terms like High Definition without needing them explained.

'I'll let you look then,' he said, sloping away to accost the new customers.

She didn't stay long, leaving with a leaflet and only narrowly avoiding paying a deposit on her own flat screen television with high definition when an older salesperson had emerged from a curtain at the back and tried to drag her off to a heavily discounted screen. The weight of the weed killer was a reminder to her that she must not engage. Two litres of the stuff she could handle. An LED fifty-inch screen with Smart TV, three HDMI ports, Bluetooth and wireless technology, she could not.

She breathed a sigh of relief as she found herself back on the pavement outside. She caught the bus back, her bags sat on the seat beside her. Perhaps he was visiting a friend? Perhaps he had forgotten to tell her? Perhaps it was alright after all and she would never have to tell him what she'd been up to.

She repeated the words as she ironed. She repeated the words as she nibbled at a thin ham sandwich, as she sat on her balcony sipping at her tea, as she watched the cars move slowly past her on the road below. She repeated the words until she started to believe them.

The mask slipped momentarily and she found herself trawling the local Yellow Pages, dialling the local hospital, just in case.

'Hello. Good afternoon. I was wondering if an Albert Young has been admitted?'

Beeps, shouts, a rustle, she could barely hear the woman on the other end of the line, 'Are you a relative?'

'Yes,' Maria said quickly, 'his sister, three years younger.' She didn't know why she felt the need to embellish the lie. What next? Tell the receptionist about their fake childhood growing up in Devon? The fake time Albie had pushed her too high on the swing and she had fallen and chipped a tooth?

'Nothing under that name, I'm afraid.'

She had hung up before the receptionist could continue.

Stop this, Maria, she thought, scolding herself. *Stop this. You'll just have to wait and see. There will be a perfect acceptable reason.*

Of course, she didn't forget it. She wasn't sure how she got through the days, how she found herself getting ready for bed on Wednesday evening. How she had lain there hoping the last few days were this strange blip, that they would laugh about her worries. She imagined Albie already sat at a table in the café, the marble cake in front of him, ready to tell her a new story, another adventure. The image seemed impossibly real and she fell asleep with a small smile dancing on her lips. It was Thursday in a few short hours, she would see him again.

*

Her pudgy hands were squeezing my cheeks, her little body lying on top of me. 'Mummmmmmmeeeeeeee.'

I was laughing, my whole body shaking with it, which made her laugh too, delightedly giving my cheeks another squeeze. 'Mummmmmeeeeeee, ddddooooooonnnnnn'tttttt laugh at me, it's not kind.'

'You're right,' I wriggled into a sitting position, 'But you know you've got something on your face?'

I wasn't sure how she'd managed it, but she had drawn a thick black line right across her face so that it looked like she had an enormous black monobrow.

'I use make-up like Mummy.'

'I can see that.' I laughed, spitting on a finger to rub at her face.

'Noooooooooooo, Mummmmmmmeeeeeeeeeeeeeee,' she squealed, covering her face with both hands. 'I wear make-up.'

'I'm not sure Mummy wears it just like that,' I said, my voice gentle, hoping to coax her.

She was stubborn, arms folded as she stared me down, 'Want make-up.'

'But we have to be at school in half an hour…'

She stared me down again and I shrugged and got out of bed. 'Your choice.'

'I do your make-up?'

'Absolutely not.' I laughed again, reaching to tickle her until she squealed and rolled off the other side of the duvet, only just missing the bedside table. 'Be careful,' I said through my laughter.

We left the house shortly after, me in my skirt and jacket ready for a long day ahead, bag bursting, her small hand squeezing mine, the solemn expression on her face made more severe by the insane black eyebrow. Passers-by craned their necks to get a second look.

'What, Mummy?' She grinned, clearly forgetting what she had done to her own face.

'Nothing, darling,' I said, pulling out my Polaroid camera and snapping the shot, 'Just one for the album.'

Dropping her at school, with a shrug at her Year One teacher Mrs Kimble, I sloped away. Throughout the day I found myself grinning every time I thought of her.

Chapter 3

She didn't lounge in bed with the curtains closed this Thursday. She didn't bring her coffee back to bed. She couldn't seem to force herself to do what she had always done. Instead, she had all this energy. She swept aside the curtains, stared out at the gloomy sky, her window peppered with raindrops, the pavements slick with a thin layer of water.

She ran her bath, poured in the lavender oil, and yet the aroma didn't feel soothing as it wafted around the small space. The water was too hot, so she turned the cold tap and yet she couldn't get the temperature right, didn't wait for the bath to fill to its usual level. She felt she was faking everything, wanting to fall into her usual routine but just wanting the clock to speed round, for her to get to the café so she could finally relax.

Her breakfast was dry and she had forgotten to put a record on her LP machine so all she heard in the space was the crunch of her cereal, the tick of the clock. She was early as she settled down at her dressing table, pulled the pots and pencils towards her and started on her face. She tried to take real care but she rushed everything, had to wipe at her cheeks because she'd piled on too much blusher, her hand shaking as she messed up her lipstick, tried to draw a thin brown eyeliner along her lashes, smudged her mascara.

The clothes she chose were ones Albie had seen before but not for a while: a plum roll-neck jumper and a grey skirt, tights and black suede boots that she hoped would survive the rain. She added a thin silver necklace and stared at herself in the reflection. She was early, she was very early. She set about blow-drying the back of her hair again, the heat making the skin on her neck prickle. She sat on the foot of her bed wondering what to do with the spare time – she didn't want to be too early.

She moved through to the living room, knew she had to fill the hour ahead, stared at her book. Turning the page, she was aware she had no idea what she had just read. Instead, she pictured him getting on a bus, if that was how he got there – she'd never asked – walking along the street towards the café. She thought of him settled at a table, wondered what excuses he would come up with for his absence a week ago. Perhaps a tan would give him away? Or a cast on one arm? She pictured every scenario as the words blurred in front of her.

Finally, she could leave, taking a small umbrella with her, her hands fumbling with the buttons on her beige mac.

Just before passing the window of the café she paused for a second, relishing this last moment before she saw him. Taking a breath and plastering a smile on her face, she moved to the door, put a hand out and pushed her way inside, the bell tinkling, and glanced slowly around the café. His face had been so familiar in all the thoughts she had conjured that morning that it took a few seconds to realise he was not in the room, not at the table they shared. She felt a pain start in her chest, an ache.

Another couple, about twenty years younger, were sat at the table, *their* table, along the furthest wall. It didn't mean anything, Maria thought, sometimes people did sit there, it wasn't a sign. She stepped briskly across to a different table. He was just late. That was fine. She had been earlier than him before. It didn't mean anything.

The café was reasonably full with people lingering over lunch, the smell of jacket potatoes and warm bread in the air. A nearby chalkboard announced the 'Soup of the Day: Minestrone'. Maria took it all in. It felt similar to last week and her stomach churned. Amrit was there, brown hair still streaked with pink, bent over her notepad as she spoke to the young couple. Maria reached out and repositioned the small vase of flowers on the table, her hand nudging the bowl of sugar cubes. The bell went and her hand slipped, upending the bowl completely so that it clattered in the small space, sugar spilt all over the table.

'I'm so sorry.' Maria had already started to pile them back in the bowl, disappointed that the new arrival was a middle-aged woman shaking out a leopard-print umbrella.

Amrit wandered over with the same outfit, the same hair, the same kind smile, but a different coloured jewel in her nose: purple. 'I'll sort that out, don't worry. Nice to see you.'

'You too,' Maria whispered, her throat closing.

'Same as usual. I'm glad you're back, I was a bit worried last week.'

Maria bit her lip, not quite trusting herself with the words. She wished he had been there first, had ordered, sat poised to cut the marble cake in half, the steaming teapot beside the plate.

He was just late, he would be here.

'Marble cake and tea please,' Maria said, not quite meeting the eye of the waitress.

Amrit took a while longer to produce it and as the minutes dragged by, Maria's stomach seemed to get heavier and heavier. Five minutes, ten, fifteen… The customers were filing out, tables emptying, a few people arriving, but most on their way out. The marble cake sat in front of her, the other empty plate accusatory. She could feel Amrit's eyes on her as the tea went cold, untouched. Twenty, twenty-five, thirty…

Tears swam in Maria's eyes, she had bitten away her lipstick, her head bowed at the table, no more curiosity if the bell rang. Amrit wiped a table next to her. Maria saw her wait, her heavy boots pointed in her direction, a small sigh and then she moved behind the counter.

Thirty-five, forty… For a terrible moment Maria thought she might be sick. Instead she stood on wobbly legs and left a ten-pound note on the table.

'Don't be silly, you haven't touched it,' Amrit said, appearing at her arm.

Forty-five minutes, fifty…

Maria didn't trust herself to respond, simply whispered a goodbye and headed to the door, clutching her bag like a shield.

She didn't remember walking back to her apartment, and her hair was flattened and dripping – she had left her small umbrella under the table – as she turned the key in her lock.

She moved to lower herself on her sofa, no more pretence that things were alright, that Thursdays, or any day, would ever feel the same again. The silence of the apartment was oppressive, the darkening sky through the window making everything feel worse. A roll of thunder from somewhere far away and Maria let the tears fall, marking tracks through her powdered cheeks, dripping into her lap as she sat, shaking, on her sofa.

Sitting back, she felt drained, hollow. It was still early, the rain trickling down the panes again, dark, but not yet evening. Something in the corner of her eye was blinking at her. A small red light: her answerphone. She hardly ever had any messages, not even cold callers since she had made herself ex-directory. She found herself moving across the room, legs heavy, staring down at the handset. She picked it up slowly, brought it to her ear.

Pressing the button, she heard a female voice chime in. 'Hello, this is a message for Mrs Birch, it's Becky Leonard from Clive & Sons. I am calling regarding Albert Young…'

Later, she wouldn't know why she slammed the receiver back down, why she backed away from the counter, breathless, and sat back on the sofa, staring at the now unlit answerphone.

She just knew that she didn't want to hear the rest of the message, somehow she had realised: it was over. That she would never see Albie again.

*

I found a note from her in the folds of a book, stuffed there without thinking – why hadn't I framed every last thing? The words enormous, jumbled and sloping down the page.

'You are the best mummee in the whole world. I love your smell and that you are bootiful, helpfull and kind.'

I felt a stone settle in my stomach, so heavy, filling up the space, forcing me to drop to the floor and stay there.

Chapter 4

What else could she have done but try and go about her usual week? At times it had seemed things were just happening, as if to someone else. She lost hours in the launderette, the enormous glass bowl spinning in front of her: blurred colours, soaked clothes, the smell of detergent. The drum had long since fallen silent, but still she sat there, not registering.

'Excuse me,' a man in a khaki green jacket said, 'I think it's done.'

She mumbled as she got up and pulled at the door, removing the dripping items and taking them across to the dryers. The sound persistent and loud, drowning out her thoughts. The clothes were hot to the touch as she bundled them back into her cotton laundry bag and set off for home.

Another few days passed and then, Thursday. She didn't leave the house, didn't speak to another soul. Where would she go? There was only ever one place on a Thursday and she couldn't go back there without him. She sat in her living room, forgot to open the curtains, remembering just as it was getting dark again. Something on the television, an old episode of *Columbo*, maybe two – not that she was able to follow the plot anyway.

Friday and the ironing was completed before she had thought to have breakfast and picked at her dry cereal, the milk on the turn, but she'd had no energy to head to the shops, had thought she'd survive.

Another day with just the sound of her own breathing, the chatter from the television, which she had left on as if it could be a companion. She sat in her chair, her book slipping into her lap, picking at a nail, feeling the exquisite pain as she pressed it, reminding her she was still there. The curtains were open, the sky thick with grey cloud, blank. She looked away again, picked at her nail.

Still there.

Saturday morning, and she had a shock leaving the house, as if all the trees had lost their leaves overnight, the air nipping at her face and hands, the exposed skin at her wrists. The walk to the newsagent was hard going, the wind pushing her backwards as she bent her head into her chest. She felt the cold seeping through her coat, into her very bones, as if nothing would warm her again.

The bell rang out and she hurried to the counter, snatching up the newspaper for her weekly TV listings, not that she had the energy to circle anything in its pages. She remembered how she would scan its pages with her biro, circling programmes, underlining others, how she had learnt what he liked over their meetings. And the feeling forced her to place a hand on the counter, the pain immediate and intense, as if she'd been stabbed in her chest.

'You fine there, Mrs?' The familiar voice enquired from behind the counter.

She caught her breath again, not trusting herself to speak. Normally, she would ask after Mr Khan's grandchildren, he kept photographs of them sellotaped to his till: grinning, toothy pictures of children dangling from playground equipment, ice-skating. One of the girls had her first competition on the ice last month. The questions froze on her tongue as she handed over her five-pound note.

'Regan's asked me for tap shoes for Christmas. Tap!' He had a throaty laugh that emerged from a face covered in an enormous beard.

Maria found her reply stuck somewhere inside her. It didn't help that she hadn't said a word out loud for more than forty-eight hours. She wondered then if it mattered at all if she ever spoke again.

'Clackety clack, my daughter's told me it'll drive her up the wall but you know Regan, she's headstrong…'

This is a message for Ms Birch…

Regan and her tap-dancing. Another fad, Maria was sure. Would she give up ice-skating? Try a musical instrument next? Why should Maria care? She felt bone-tired as she took her change.

It's Becky Leonard from Clive & Sons…

'How nice,' she croaked, the words flat. The sound didn't seem like her voice.

I am calling regarding Albert Young…

'Is everything good with you, Mrs?' His eyebrows were drawn together, his black eyes pools of concern.

Maria nodded curtly. Was it that obvious? Couldn't she just not be interested in someone else for once? Couldn't she be allowed to be left in peace? Her hand closed tightly over the coins, her knuckles strained white.

'Did you see my new Harry and Meghan mug? It's the Wedding Edition.'

Mr Khan was fiercely patriotic, carrying a strong love of the country that had adopted his parents, the shop ceiling criss-crossed with British Flag bunting, tins of Scottish shortbread, Brighton rock and mugs with the royals on display next to the usual fare. Maria had a Queen Elizabeth II mug to mark the 50th anniversary of her coronation.

She glanced in the direction he was pointing and gave a small grunt of acknowledgement. His frown deepened as she opened her handbag and deposited the change in her purse.

'Is that all? Nothing sweet?' He pointed to the newspaper on the counter in front of them with his laugh again but this time it made her muscles stiffen. He was right, of course – normally she added a chocolate bar to the mix, a Fry's Chocolate Cream or a Daim if she was feeling brave and her dentures could take it. Today, she didn't feel like it, didn't even really feel like taking the newspaper although she did, folding it underneath her arm. Habit.

'That's all,' she finished, feeling her face move but knowing the smile was stuck somewhere inside her.

His voice wavered as she pushed her way back down the aisle.

'You sure everything's—'

She didn't wait for the end of the sentence, not wanting his pity or his questions, feeling a strange bubble of heat inside her that threatened to spill over. She didn't deserve anything. Everyone should just let her go about her day and leave her alone.

She didn't feel the cold as she walked back to her apartment, back up the stairs, barely noticing the smell of her flat – the unwashed surfaces, abandoned mugs of congealed tea, rumpled bedding.

The newspaper stayed on the kitchen counter, still folded in two, showing the top of a young girl's head, her eyes staring at the ceiling. What had happened to that girl? Maria felt a flicker of her old curiosity before it was extinguished. She didn't have the energy to unfold the paper and find out: no doubt it would depress her further and what did she want with that? She returned to her chair and spent the rest of the day and evening slumped in it, only getting up to go to the bathroom.

She skipped church the next day, not ready to face the perky female vicar with her energetic sermons, the jaunty hymns, the beaming congregation. She spent the day back in her chair, didn't even change out of her nightdress and dressing gown: there was really no point at all.

On Monday, she was still in the same place, as if she had lost an entire day. She was starting to feel as if it could be any day, any time, her usual markers fading. Today, she should be doing the weekly shop. She opened the fridge and smelt the milk, now long gone. A wedge of dried-out cheese, a shrivelled lemon, an out-of-date steak and kidney pie, a pot of soured cream and one wrinkled yellow pepper. She needed eggs, milk, fresh bread at the very least and yet she found herself returning to her chair, staying in her nightdress and staring back out at the strip of window, the clouds today parting with weak winter sunlight.

The phone rang. She left it.

It rang again. She ignored it.

On the third attempt, she reached for the receiver. It was bound to be a cold caller, even ex-directory – some still got through. She felt the sudden urge to give them a piece of her mind.

'Is that Mrs Birch?' came the voice.

'Ms,' she snapped.

'Oh, I am sorry Ms Birch, it's Becky Leonard from Clive & Sons. I've been trying to get hold of you for a while now.'

'I've been…' Maria looked around her apartment at the dirty dishes left in piles next to the sink, her dressing gown abandoned in a pool on the floor, a half-eaten sandwich curling on a plate, soil from a plant pot that she'd spilled trodden into her cream carpet. Neglected, sad,

stale and yet even this glimpse didn't make her want to clean it up. '…
busy,' she finished lamely.

It's Becky Leonard from Clive & Sons…

'It's a busy time of year!' the voice said.

I am calling regarding Albert Young…

'Well, if it would suit you, we would be grateful if you could pop
into the offices at your earliest convenience, please.'

No, no, no! Maria looked down at the stray crumbs on her lap, a
yellow stain from some tea she had spilt. 'Well, I'm not sure I'm…
You see…'

She didn't say another word as the voice continued, 'It's about
Albert Young's estate.'

*

Our baby girl had a tuft of blonde hair and the smoothest skin I'd ever seen.

*We brought her home from the hospital and spent the first evening just
staring at her as she slept, fists curled tight, both arms flung above her head.*

*'She's perfect,' he whispered as he pulled me in close, stared down at
the tiny bundle.*

*Everything ached, everything hurt, but in that moment, everything
was also perfect.*

'I know,' I whispered back. 'I know.'

Chapter 5

She nearly cancelled the appointment – it was absurd to be getting a blow-dry when she hadn't even changed into clean clothes, wearing her nightdress for three days straight.

Albie's estate.

Albie was dead.

Albie was dead and his solicitor wanted to talk to Maria.

Maria hadn't known. She had spent three days going over every second of their meetings. Had he looked like a dying man? Had she missed the signs? He had complained of a sore neck a few weeks before, had been so grateful when she had given him a pack of paracetamol and a wheat-filled neck cushion he could heat in the microwave.

'So thoughtful, Maria, so thoughtful,' he'd said, his eyes crinkling as she'd handed it over.

A neck cushion and some over-the-counter pills and he'd been dying.

Hardly thoughtful. She must have missed so much more. He'd lost a little weight earlier that year. She'd commented at the time, remembering the heat flooding her cheeks as he'd teased her for noticing.

'I last wore this jacket in '72!' he'd laughed proudly.

He'd told her he'd been walking more. Had that been a lie? And she had simply nodded and thought ruefully of her own body, sucked in her stomach as she'd stood to head to the Ladies' room.

What a fool she'd been, thinking of herself.

She didn't know how it had happened, hadn't asked the solicitor, hadn't managed to get the words out. Wouldn't the solicitor assume she should have known? She had simply agreed a time, hung up, a hand reaching out before her knees had given way.

It had rained overnight and the street was spattered with droplets, some patches slippery underfoot from the frosty weather. She pulled her coat tight around herself, feeling the sting on her cheeks. Passing a homeless man in a doorway on the high street she averted her gaze, not wanting to be seen to be staring at him. Her breath was a puff of cloud in the air as she headed past the café, keeping her eyes fixed straight ahead, not wanting to see the familiar faded red-and-white checked tablecloths that Albie had never liked – 'too cheap-looking for a lovely place like this' – the warm bustle of customers inside, the loaf-shaped marble cake presented on the counter in a glass-covered stand.

Albie Young is dead.

Her pace quickened until she was stood outside the glass-fronted building, chest rising and falling with the effort. Stepping inside the salon, she caught sight of herself in the mirror to the side: pink cheeks, red-rimmed eyes and windswept hair. Her shoes squeaked, the white floor recently mopped, a small yellow sign warning of potential danger.

'Maria!' Mandy was straightening magazines on the low coffee table by the entrance, 'You're right on time.'

Maria was always surprised how someone so pocket-sized could contain all that energy. Mandy bounced over, wearing a low-cut black top and leopard-print leggings, her shoulder-length blonde hair a halo of curls around her face. 'Let me take that,' she said, whipping off Maria's coat and hanging it in a cupboard to the side. 'Nina,' she called over to a woman with a thick brown fringe and black-framed glasses who was folding towels, 'Maria's here.'

Nina abandoned her task and came straight over, her eyes almost hidden by her blunt fringe – 'bangs' she had called them before.

'Hi, Maria,' she said, holding out the thin black fabric for Maria to put on, tying it at the neck. 'Follow me,' she added, leading her over to the row of sinks.

'Massage?' she asked as Maria settled back in one of three leather chairs.

'No, thank you.'

Maria always said no. No fuss.

He's dead.

Shoving the morbid thought out of her head, she let Nina get to work, answering automatically that the water was fine – it could have been warmer – and the new conditioning treatment sounded good. The strains of a pop song she didn't recognise piped through speakers set up in the corners of the room and Maria let the music wash over her as Nina kneaded and rinsed her head. Normally, she might ask Nina something, enjoyed her quiet conversation but today, she found she didn't have the energy for it, closing her eyes as the girl got to work.

'All done! I've used a conditioning treatment today, it's a new brand and I hope you like it,' she said with a small smile. 'Can I bring you anything?'

'I'm fine,' Maria replied.

'You sure?' Nina asked, knowing Maria nearly always wanted a magazine and a sweet tea.

'I am,' Maria said, staring at the old lady sat in the mirror opposite, a towelled turban wrapped around her head, small, red eyes, grey skin. This blow-dry wouldn't touch the sides, she thought as Mandy appeared behind her.

Gone. And she hadn't noticed a thing.

'Good to see you, Maria. We were just talking about you the other day. You missed an appointment and we wondered if you'd gone somewhere nice. It seemed strange without you in here.'

Maria didn't really know what to say, seeing Mandy's expectant face, surprised they had noticed when she hadn't appeared. She hadn't bothered to cancel it, the days after she'd found out about Albie a blur of nothingness.

'No, I wasn't away.'

…about Albie Young's estate…

Mandy was distracted as she removed the turban, comb gripped in her teeth: 'You want Nina to get you a tea? She keeps trying to make people try this new liquorice-flavour stuff. It's properly disgusting, but she seems to love it.'

'I'm fine, thank you,' Maria said primly, normally enjoying the buoyant warmth, the atmosphere of the lively salon, the blasts of the hairdryer, the conversation. She always left feeling better: more attractive and less alone. Today, though, she regretted coming – exhausted already by the well-meaning questions, the attention.

'…Been up to anything interesting? And how is your gentlemen friend? Albert innit?' Hairdryer cocked at her hip, Mandy smirked.

The question made Maria start, her eyes darting around the room. What should she say? How could she even begin to…?

'He's well… yes, well,' Maria mumbled, not able to get the words out.

Maria felt the room close in on her, her breath growing shallow, wishing she had ordered her usual sweet tea, could distract herself by taking a sip of something.

It's Becky Leonard calling from…

Fortunately, at that moment Nina appeared, pulling Mandy away to deal with a delivery man at Reception. 'Sorry 'bout this, Maria,' she called.

Nina stood, a shy smile on her face. Maria hadn't known what to say to Nina when she'd first started working there five or so years ago, but over a few visits she'd noticed her through the open door to the backroom, engrossed in a book. That had given Maria the confidence to start up a conversation the first time. Today, talk of books froze somewhere inside her.

'She telling you about the coin?' Mandy asked, pointing her comb at Nina.

'I hadn't…' The blush crept up Nina's neck.

Maria frowned, every response slower.

Mandy removed the towel and started combing Maria's hair. 'She's been on and on about this coin she found at the weekend, could be Roman or from the fifteenth century or the third century or some time ages ago… There could be more of them…'

'It's not Roman,' Nina muttered, a small smile flickering on her face. 'But—'

'I don't pretend to understand it,' Mandy said, cutting in, 'Spending her weekends out with a beeping pole and a little trowel. Still, she tells me she likes it,' she added, as if Nina wasn't standing right there.

Maria knew Nina had a metal detector; she'd inherited it after she had chucked out her long-term boyfriend after seeing 'sexts' on his phone. Maria remembered because she hadn't heard the phrase 'sexts' before and had never giggled so long and hard at the hairdresser's. Mandy had had to stop that blow-dry for her to catch her breath. The memory of that moment almost made her mouth twitch into a smile, a second of feeling something other than this strange, dream-like misery.

He's dead.

The smile stayed deep inside her.

'Still, best thing you got out of that relationship, if you ask me. Could make you wealthy, unlike that no-good layabout,' Mandy said, shouting to be heard above the blast of hot air.

Nina reddened further before moving away to greet a customer at the door.

The rest of the blow-dry was spent listening to Mandy, who was telling Maria more about her latest foray on the dating scene. She had been married but it had ended when he'd run off with someone he met on a cruise Mandy had saved for a year to go on: 'I wish he'd got that Norovirus half the ship went down with.'

'So, I tried this new online site but the photos, Maria, are something else. Then you meet them and it's like you're meeting their larger, hairier, older brother. And the descriptions of the women they want,' she scoffed, tugging on a strand of hair as she met Maria's eye in the mirror, 'always thirty-five to forty-five despite the fact they look like they've been round the block and then round it again...' She moved the hairbrush through Maria's hair, drying as she went. 'Made a mistake describing myself as generous of bosom, of course. Attracted some right sorts, had to change it to curvy... And hobbies... Oh, don't get me started... I started talking to a man who described himself as a "gamer", a gamer, Maria, like he's a twelve-year-old boy with a PlayStation. Honestly, that's not a man's hobby, am I right? Where are the carpenters, the metal workers? PlayStation!' She huffed, cocking her head to one side as she inspected her work.

Maria listened, grateful to try and switch off the thoughts in her own head for a moment, focus on someone else. Before she knew it,

Mandy was standing back to inspect Maria's refreshed head of hair. The woman in the mirror looked a little lifted, her grey bob now styled and smooth, the new conditioning treatment giving it some added gloss under the salon lights.

'That looks good, you like it?' Mandy asked, unplugging the hairdryer.

Maria patted one side. 'I do,' she said, knowing she could probably sound more enthusiastic. The thought of leaving the comfort of the salon, the taps running, hairdryers blowing, the chatter, the background music, to return to her empty apartment and wait for the next part of her life to happen filled her with a sudden dread. She had never normally minded being on her own, had grown used to it, but since Albie, it was like she was frightened of her own head.

Maria got up from the chair, shrugging off the black gown and handing it to Mandy.

'You're quiet today, Maria. All fine with you, is it?' Mandy asked, rolling the gown up into a ball.

Maria answered quickly, her eyes sliding to the side, 'Fine, fine, just...'

Just what? She tailed away, not sure what she was.

Mandy kept watching her, her mouth parting as if on the verge of asking more, then with a friendly pat on her arm, she said, 'That's good then. We'll see you next week and I'll let you know how it goes...'

Maria gave her a blank look.

'The date! The electrician... the Harry Potter enthusiast, bloody Ravenbore or something, I haven't read them... Were you listening at all?'

'I'm sorry, I was, I just...' Maria whispered, alarmed to realise she felt like weeping. She tried to laugh, give Mandy a reaction. It seemed to work.

'Hey, don't you mind a thing! I know I bang on.' Mandy smiled, waving to her next customer, 'You take care of yourself alright?'

Maria shuffled towards the reception desk, removing her purse as Nina approached. 'I will,' she whispered, seeing the rest of the day stretching ahead of her: empty and purposeless. 'Thanks,' she added and left the shop and Nina's curious gaze behind.

Only one person ever commented on her hair.

He's dead.

*

He left in the day. I had taken her in to see the secretaries at the office and he was gone when we returned.

I had set her down on the floor and called his name. She didn't crawl away, perhaps realising something wasn't quite right too.

The cupboard doors in our bedroom were all open: his side empty. His other things had gone, only my toothbrush in the enamel mug. He'd taken our toothpaste.

I returned, numb, to the kitchen. She started wailing almost imme-diately, red-faced and tearful, still wearing her pink crocheted winter hat with the bow under the chin. He had taken the television too – the one thing that might have given me some company, a distraction, another voice. There was an envelope on the countertop and I moved across to pick it up. We'd been rowing but was this really it? Maybe he was just gone for a few days? He wouldn't leave me to do all this on my own, would he? We were going to marry when things were calmer. We were going to... I tore at the envelope. Why put it in one at all? The note wasn't long.

'I'm leaving you. Sorry. Tell her I will love her always.'

So, he wouldn't be back.

I balled up the note, her screams now piercing the air as if they were inside my head.

I wouldn't want him back anyway.

Red-faced, the screams more urgent. She was pulling herself up on my leg, her face tipped towards me.

I scooped her up, soothing and sshhing and whispering into her hair, realising this was it now: we were on our own.

Chapter 6

Maria felt embarrassed as she fretted over what to wear to the solicitor's office, but it was almost a relief to feel something other than the aching misery. Why was she seeing the solicitor? 'The estate,' the woman from the solicitor's had said. Had Albie left her something in his will? She prayed for a small token, something she could treasure and keep safe in the apartment, look at, admire, polish. Then she wondered if she would one day hurl it against the wall in a fit of despair. How could he be gone? She pressed her hands against her eyes in the small square bedroom, distracted for a second from the agony of choosing the black wool skirt or the green wool skirt. Would the solicitor even notice?

Still, she dressed herself slowly and carefully, wanting to make a good impression, wondering for a moment if there would be others there. If she had been summoned to the office, surely others would have been too? A man like Albie had people in his life, he didn't push them away.

The solicitor's office was a converted Victorian terrace house in a part of town she had frequented when she'd worked as a big shot herself, a lifetime ago. She had marched into plenty of offices, shoulder pads and heels her uniform, but now she was fidgeting with nerves as she pressed a buzzer.

'Ms Birch for Ms Leonard,' she croaked into the small grey box to the side of the door.

'Do come in.'

A long buzz sounded and Maria pushed open the door, stepping into an open-plan room, immediately self-conscious as two faces glanced up. A woman at the back returned to her phone call.

'Can I help you?' A man with the smoothest black skin and a toothy smile approached her from the nearest desk.

'I'm here about Mr Young,' Maria said. 'Ms Leonard called me, asked me to come in.'

The man's smile didn't fade. 'Well, that's Becky, she's on the phone right now,' he said. 'But can I get you anything while you wait?' He pointed to a pair of plush armchairs set at an angle in the corner. On the small round glass table between them Maria could make out a range of leaflets, all with the company logo at the top.

'Oh no, I'm fine, thank you,' she said, not wanting to be a bother. Her throat was a little dry from the bus ride and walk, but it was too late to make a fuss.

'Well, do take a seat Mrs... Young, is it?' He widened his eyes in a gesture of encouragement.

'No,' Maria whispered after a too-long pause. 'It's Birch... Maria Birch.'

He raked a hand over stubbled hair. 'Mrs Birch, I'm sorry. Well, as I said, do take a seat.'

Fortunately, the woman on the telephone had finished her call and was approaching them both.

'Ms Birch, is it?' she asked. 'I'm Becky Leonard.'

She was impossibly young. Maria supposed everyone felt impossibly young these days – as if none of them could possibly be qualified to do anything. She had poker-straight blonde hair that fell to her shoulders and her hand was fiddling with an engagement ring – the solitaire diamond had slipped around the side of her finger, she kept straightening it. Maria wondered if she was recently engaged. She found herself staring at the ring, a lump forming in her throat at the thought that this woman was in love.

'Thank you for coming in. Shall we go and talk in the conference room? Jerome, have you asked Ms Birch here if she'd like a drink?'

She spoke with such authority Maria found herself interjecting on Jerome's behalf, 'Oh, he did, he's been very attentive. I'm fine, thank you.'

Becky Leonard beamed and Jerome relaxed a little.

Maria followed Ms Leonard through the office, past an empty desk stacked high with paper, a metal filing cabinet, beaming photographs sellotaped to the side, and into a small side room which contained a round table and four chairs that she had to suppose was the grandly titled conference room.

'Please do take a seat, I'll just fetch the relevant documents.' Ms Leonard turned and left Maria sat there, staring at the walls of the room: a print of Degas ballerinas tilted at a slight angle on the wall opposite. She wondered if Albie had liked Degas, or the Impressionists. Just another thing she would never know, had never asked and then it was too late. She felt the all-familiar lump stick in her throat once more.

Ms Leonard had obviously been talking to her when Maria finally snapped to attention. 'I'm sorry,' she said, shaking her head, trying to concentrate. It seemed so very hard these last few days to concentrate, time dragging interminably or speeding up so that she seemed to skip hours.

'…him well?'

Maria found herself nodding along as Ms Leonard sat in front of her, a strand of blonde hair sticking briefly to her lip gloss before she smoothed it behind her ear. She was using words Maria didn't understand: 'executor', 'portfolio'.

'A substantial amount…'

Nod.

'…Properties.'

Nod.

'…not inconsiderable amount of shares.'

Nod.

'Ms Birch, he's made you a very wealthy woman.'

Nod.

Silence.

Nod.

She felt she had been nodding for ever and now Ms Leonard was simply looking at her, arms on the table in front of her, twisting her ring once more.

'You'll need it resizing, I imagine,' Maria found herself saying.

'I'm sorry?' Ms Leonard's forehead creased.

'The ring,' Maria said, biting her lip, 'It's a little big.'

'Oh,' Ms Leonard blinked, self-consciously covering the offending hand. 'Oh, I'm not really used to it,' she said, her voice a little different, lighter as she continued, 'He only asked me last weekend. In the Lake District,' she blurted as if she couldn't help herself, the joy bubbling over for a second before she shifted in her chair, the professional once more.

Maria forced a weak smile. 'How lovely,' she replied, knowing it was an inadequate response. It *was* lovely. Ms Leonard seemed nice and she was young and in love and so incredibly lucky to have it all lying ahead of her.

'Ms Birch, I know it's a lot to process but I want you to know that I am here to advise you going forward, however we can help. I liked Mr Young, he was such a gentleman…'

'You knew Albie?' Maria couldn't help it: her voice raised as she leant forward now, desperate to talk about him, to hear more.

Ms Leonard nodded, 'I met Albert a month or so ago when he drew all this up. A lovel—'

'I'm sorry,' Maria knew she was interrupting, 'Was there a funeral? I didn't…'

She thought then of a funeral, mourners in black, gathered in a cemetery – everyone there, apart from her. Her eyes filled with tears, she swallowed hard.

'Albert informed me he had spoken with a funeral director already and had insisted on no service, just a simple cremation once he'd gone, which I'm told has been honoured. I have the details of where the ashes have been kept. The landlord of his apartment building registered the death too so that has been taken care of…'

'Ashes,' Maria whispered, the words washing in and around her. *Albie was ashes.*

Ms Leonard nodded, a sympathetic voice. 'He has specified where he would like them scattered.'

Maria swallowed. Albie had arranged for someone to handle everything when he was gone. Her head ached with the information, the room blurring. This was all so much.

'So, the logistics have been taken care of, and we…'

'How did he…?' Maria put a finger to her lip, tried to control her wobbling voice, 'I'm sorry…'

'Of course,' Ms Leonard said, 'are you sure you don't want a drink? Still? Sparkling water?'

'No, no,' Maria shook her head. 'I'm quite alright, thank you, it's just…'

She had so many questions, her head was crammed with them. She took a breath.

'How did it happen?' she finally managed to ask, 'How did he die?'

She looked up at the young woman, who couldn't seem to hide her surprise.

'Oh, I'm sorry, I had thought you knew.'

Maria shook her head miserably. No, she hadn't known. He hadn't told her.

It was the younger woman's turn to look flustered. 'Albert died of a heart attack, in his sleep,' she spoke quickly. 'He came to us after a diagnosis from a specialist a month or so ago. He had been warned it was most likely his heart would simply give out and he had been right, I'm afraid. I have included the coroner's report and death certificate in our pack. I'm ever so sorry to be the one to tell you.'

Maria stared at her hands, knuckles turning white as she clenched. Nodded once.

His heart. Sudden. Death certificate.

The solicitor was talking again, a softer, gentler voice, and Maria tried to pull herself back into the room. Why had he never told her about his diagnosis? Why?

'…We invited you in today to discuss Albert's estate…'

'Yes,' Maria whispered, barely able to focus. What token had Albie left her? What could she clutch to her body as she left this office with this new knowledge? She didn't want to be sat here anymore under the colourful Degas painting, opposite this nice young woman, her future sparkling on her finger.

'He was adamant that you should be the sole beneficiary. He obviously cared for you very much' – Ms Leonard blushed then – 'if you don't mind me saying.'

Maria looked up, didn't know what to respond to that. Had Albie cared for her? Yes, yes, she thought he had. How much she had never been sure, she'd never really dared to hope. But all this. No mention of any illness. If he cared for her, wouldn't he have told her?

'He did mention that you might be quite' – Ms Leonard cleared her throat – 'surprised by the sum.'

Maria was surprised by everything that day. She had assumed that Albie had left her a small item, something to remember him by. A book dear to him perhaps, or an ornament: a tea set perhaps? But suddenly the things Ms Leonard was saying started to filter in. The information becoming too much: the sole beneficiary, that Albie had been in this exact same room only a month or so before, the very fact he had known. He'd known he was going to die. And he hadn't told her. She blinked.

'So, we need to help transfer the funds across to you, and we can talk you through the various assets. We have the keys to his principal property, which now belongs to you of course...'

Suddenly the words were taking shape.

Property? Principal property? That suggested there was more than one. Sole beneficiary. That meant...

The whole room seemed to come into sharp focus: the livid scratch in the centre of the table, the black ink stain on Ms Leonard's right hand, the vivid colours of the Degas print.

'I'm sorry, are you saying' – Maria straightened in her chair – 'Are you saying that Albie left me things. More than—'

Ms Leonard cut Maria off before she could continue, a small half-smile on her lips. 'Ms Birch, Albie – Mr Young – he left you... everything.'

'Everything,' Maria repeated.

Now Ms Leonard couldn't stop the smile as she nodded, giving a tiny laugh, 'Everything. And it is a lot, if you don't mind me saying. The estate is worth over two million pounds.'

'Two million…'

There was a buzzing in Maria's head. Two million pounds. Albie. Two million…

'How, what…?' The rest of the words were muddled. 'But he…'

What about him? Why couldn't Albie be worth two million pounds? Maria found her whole head suddenly crammed with questions. How had he made the money? How had he lived? Had he really left it all to her? What would that mean? She hadn't even owned her own home before. Two million pounds was someone else's life. Maria Birch wasn't that person.

Ms Leonard was talking again, 'Obviously, the property is vacant now, and we can talk you through his share portfolio… he made some sensible investments… there is no mortgage on the property, you own that outright…'

Share? Houses? Mortgages? How was she meant to understand what all this meant?

But one question kept returning to Maria amongst all the buzz, all the words and her own confusion: why hadn't Albie told her?

*

She was sitting on the sofa, legs tucked up underneath her, wearing her pink flowered pyjamas, and sucking on one of those white sweets that looked like cigarettes.

'Mummmmmmmeeeee, look,' she said, removing the cigarette sweet and tapping the end, 'I smoke.'

She looked delighted at that, popping the sweet back in and pretending to suck on it. The empty open packet next door, where she had obviously eaten the other ones.

'I like Mummy,' she said happily, her tiny face lighting up at the thought.

'That's nice,' I said, her tiny toddler voice always filling me with a fierce love despite the stress of the last few months, despite Steve's departure.

'I like Mummy, I smoke.'

Oh, I realised, perhaps it was time to quit.

Chapter 7

She couldn't face returning home, the bus ride a blur, sat in a window seat clutching a tote bag stuffed with folders and paper from the solicitor's office, an envelope containing the keys to Albie's home a hard weight in her side. Outside, it had begun to rain. Droplets streaked the window as she stared, her body heavy and drooping. She was barely aware of the other passengers getting on and off. Then in a moment of clarity, she realised she didn't want to go home, she *couldn't* go home. She pressed the button urgently: once, twice and left at the next stop.

The café was around the corner and she found herself moving towards it, hungry for a moment of connection with Albie: their place. Pushing open the door, feeling the immediate warmth envelop her, the smell of cinnamon in the air, she felt momentarily lifted.

Pauline stood behind the counter, her fringe sticking to her forehead as she huffed over the coffee machine.

'It's broken,' she said, almost to herself as she jabbed at a long silver arm with a spanner.

Maria was slow to react. 'A pot of tea and a slice of marble cake, please.'

Pauline paused what she was doing, a small, brief frown on her face before she straightened up. Maria jutted her chin out – she didn't have the energy for more, simply couldn't summon any empathy for another human being. The coffee machine was broken, so what? That wasn't devastating. That wasn't life-changing. So, some people wouldn't be able to have their cappuccinos: big deal. She clenched her fists together, feeling an unfamiliar surge of heat course through her.

Pauline approached the counter, swiping at her reddened face. 'Of course. Everything alright?' she added brightly, something in her eyes making Maria unclench her fists.

'Fine, thank you,' Maria said in a tight voice, moving away to a small table set against the wall. It had two chairs. Maria realised with a terrible aching blow that she would never need a table with two chairs again. How could he leave her? She shot a hand out and righted herself before sinking into one of the seats. Why had she come here? she wondered as she watched Pauline reaching for the teapot, the cup, the saucer, all the while glancing over in her direction. Was she really behaving so differently?

Pauline set a small tray down on the table and unloaded the familiar items.

'Is the lovely Albert on his way?' she chirruped as she placed the plate with the marble cake in front of her.

Maria swallowed, an acid bitterness threatening to fill her mouth.

'No,' she said in tiny voice, 'No, he's not.'

'You tell him to get in 'ere soon. We miss seeing him, such a nice man.'

Maria felt her insides freeze. She couldn't even whisper a thank you as Pauline moved away. She should have told her, but then that would make it real. She hadn't uttered the words to anybody, not that there was anybody to tell.

She couldn't even do that for him: share the news with others. The envelope with the keys was heavy in her bag. She lifted them out, sliced a finger along the edge.

A slim piece of paper, folded once, was inside. She stared at it. A letter. From the solicitor? From Albie?

She eased it out with a trembling hand, smoothed it out.

To Maria,
The big key opens the main door, the Yale key my door.
Your servant,
Albie

She turned it over, needing to see more blue ink, sentences crammed over the surface: words, reasons, something... more.

There was only blank space.

'I don't...' She was talking aloud, felt her fists curl with a sudden flash of anger, the corner of the note crushed in her grip.

A woman at a nearby table looked up at her.

Was this his explanation? Surely not, surely he couldn't have left it in this way? Maria sat staring at the pot, at the cake, at her hands and her chipped nails, the old faded scar on her left knuckle: ugly hands. She had ugly hands, uncared-for hands. Albie had once complimented her on them, but he had always been too nice to her.

She thought back to the solicitor's office, to the moment when Ms Leonard had revealed the details of Albie's estate. It had floored Maria. Albie was preposterously rich: he had an apartment in Brighton, shares in companies she had never heard of and he had cash – quite simply, lots and lots of cash. And apart from a sizeable donation to the Macmillan Nurses it had all gone to her. She had inherited the whole lot. She, Maria Birch, was rich. Silly, what-she'd-dreamed-about-when-she-was-younger rich.

And yet now she felt devoid of any joy. She didn't want the house, the shares, the money. She didn't want to be rich. She wanted Albie.

Albie Young. She wanted Albie Young to walk through the café door, head straight to their table, pull out the chair opposite her, sit down and, with no ceremony, pick up his fork and start eating his side of the marble cake. Her whole body craved it. She was so filled with longing for it she couldn't stop herself looking up at the door of the café as if her desperate need was strong enough to end this whole thing, the need to bring him back to life.

No one appeared and she stared at the slice of marble cake, knowing for sure that she would never take another bite of that cake, the cake that would forever remind her of him. She thought then of all the questions she had for him, she thought of all the things she hadn't said. He hadn't told her any of this. Why had he left her to find out in this way? It wasn't fair, the whole situation wasn't fair. She could feel her fists clenching again, her body humming with heat. With a slow horror, she realised she was going to start crying hot, angry tears right there at the table, she could feel them building behind her eyes.

Across from her, unnoticeable until now, sat a young girl, a skinny teenager dressed in scruffy school uniform: a blue tartan skirt rucked up above the knee, a loose red tie, a white shirt and a V-neck black jumper slung over the chair behind her. She couldn't be more than sixteen years old. Maria had noticed her with a jolt, the tears stoppering in that moment. The girl was looking at her, her head tilted in a gesture of curiosity, and Maria found she couldn't look away as the girl got up out of her chair and walked towards her.

'Excuse me,' the girl said. She had a high voice, confident, and a smile behind her eyes, 'I was just wondering if you were alright?'

Maria swallowed slowly, licking her lips as she thought of a response. And then, unable to say anything more, she pushed back her chair, the scraping sound forcing the other customers in the café to look in her direction. Stumbling a little, she squeezed down the narrow hallway to the Ladies' and pushed her way inside. Resting her head back against the wall next to the hand dryer, she caught her breath. The three cubicles were empty, no one standing at the sinks, thankfully, and Maria allowed a few tears to fall.

A few moments later, the door opened and the young girl was there again, cheeks flushed. She scuffed her shoe along the ground.

'You left your tote bag at the table, and your coat, and your handbag. The manager's got them.'

It looked like she was turning to leave and Maria suddenly found herself pushing herself back from her position slumped against the wall.

'He died. My friend, my…' she choked on the word, 'my good friend, he died.'

She couldn't say his name.

The schoolgirl's eyebrows shot up and then she took a step towards Maria. 'That's terrible. I'm really, really sorry. How sad.'

Maria nodded, unable to tear her eyes away from this girl's face: her expression one of unadulterated pity. Maria needed to be around someone who cared, she needed to let this awful feeling out, even if it was to a stranger.

'Do you want to talk about it?' The girl swung herself up so she was sitting on the edge of the sink countertop, her feet, in her buckled shoes, dangling down.

'I…'

'I'm Rosie, I just thought… you looked like you needed to talk.'

Maria felt a warmth flood through her. She did need to talk, that was exactly what she needed. The schoolgirl had such an open, innocent face. Maria was desperate for her to stay, to be with her. She opened her mouth to speak: 'I do, I guess I do.'

She started with her trip to the solicitor's that morning, the revelation of what Albie had left her, the brief letter he had included. Then she worked backwards: the confirmation he'd died, the days of not knowing that had driven her to distraction, the guesses, the visits to his part of town, his first non-appearance in the café, the dread she'd felt.

Rosie simply listened, her presence a soothing balm, seeming to give Maria the strength to get the words out. Once she began, she found she couldn't stop, telling Rosie about their Thursday meetings, about Albie's crooked smile, the way he described the marble cake as 'lush' in his West Country accent. She told her what the solicitor had laid out for her, the shares, the property, the money.

At this, Rosie's eyes bulged. 'You mean you're a millionaire!' A high bark of laughter filled the tiny tiled space, the surprise so great, Maria stepped back, setting off the hand dryer, which caused both of them to collapse in helpless laughter.

In the midst of this chaos the door opened and Pauline's head appeared, eyes widening as she took in the scene. She stepped inside the room.

'Everything OK?' she asked, watching as Maria dried the tears from her face. She hadn't even realised she'd been crying. 'I've got your bags and coat behind the counter so you know.'

Maria nodded, 'I do.'

'I just thought I'd check where you'd got to…' Pauline continued, a sudden silence as the hand dryer finished. 'Are you sure you're alright?'

Maria looked across at Rosie, who was raking her fingers through her tangled mid-brown hair as if they were a comb. 'I'm better,' Maria said, a small smile lifting her features for a moment, 'a little better. Thank you for asking.'

*

We were in the supermarket and I turned my back for just a second. I was reaching for her favourite cereal, a box of Magic Puffs: she loved the tricks inside.

When I looked back around she was sat in the bottom of the trolley, blood dripping from her mouth, turning her white T-shirt scarlet, drops on the floor beneath the wire trolley.

I screamed and a woman with a headscarf and a wheeled trolley came straight over, a shop assistant in uniform heading our way.

'She's hurt, oh my god, she's hurt.'

Blood was still dripping from her chin as I scooped her out and cradled her in one arm.

'Where does it hurt?' I asked, trying to get her to open her mouth, frightened of what I might see.

Had she lost a tooth? Bitten her tongue?

She seemed fine… 'Such a brave soldier,' I said, over and over as if that might help.

'I'll call an ambulance,' the lady in the headscarf was saying. The shop assistant stood wringing her hands, young and panicked.

My daughter seemed nonplussed by the drama, looking at us all with large, round eyes.

It was only then that I realised she was clutching the roll of wrapped-up ground mince in her hand, blood dripping from where she had bitten right through it.

'It's yucky,' she said, her bloodied mouth twisting in disapproval as she dropped the mince to the floor.

I burst out into relieved laughter.

Chapter 8

As the days passed, she felt less and less herself, watching dispassionately from afar as she moved about her life. What was she meant to do with herself now? What was the point of any of it?

Someone's car alarm had gone off, the insistent wail permeating every thought.

'Bloody thoughtless, bloody selfish!' She never swore but she felt full of bad language, stamping around her apartment, twitching the curtain, staring at the offending vehicle, wishing bad things on the man who eventually ran over to put a stop to it. He looked up, perhaps feeling her intense gaze, and flinched at her expression. The flash of anger was white-hot, made her muscles tense, set her mouth in a hard line.

Childish shouts from the apartment below, crying, a woman's voice trying to soothe. How had she never noticed the sounds before? Someone was listening to music above her apartment. *Too loud, far too loud*, she thought as she stared up at her ceiling resentfully. They clomped around: bang, stomp, bang! Were they wearing clogs? The noise was ridiculous. She clamped her hands to the sides of her head and shifted in her armchair, the back uncomfortable, a spring sticking in her flesh. Why couldn't she get comfortable?

She wasn't hungry, would howl when she burnt her toast, chucking the two slices in the bin and going without. The fridge started to empty but she couldn't summon the energy to care enough to get to the shop. She opened a packet of powdered soup that had gone off three years earlier, spooning it silently into her mouth, swallowing the dry stuff that got stuck in her throat.

Tuesday arrived and she dithered over whether to go to the hairdresser. She hadn't been out and her hair was greasy and lank. Plus, she needed milk, so it would kill two birds with one stone. She grabbed her handbag and left, no need for make-up, a clean outfit, a hairbrush through her hair. Who was looking? What did she care what people thought?

The envelope was still in her handbag, the keys inside, the small slip of paper too. His letter to her.

It hadn't been a letter, barely a note, a sentence. He had left her everything and yet he hadn't offered her an explanation. Why? Did he have no one else? Had he wanted to say more? Had she missed another, longer missive? It had been so perfunctory: keys. No acknowledgement of the enormity of what he'd done, what he'd left her. A sentence as an accompanying note, written on a slip of paper from the solicitor's office.

She couldn't ask him any of this and that thought brought fresh surges of pain.

She couldn't face going to the address.

The hairdresser's was busy and she stood, foot tapping, near the door. A younger girl was sat reading a magazine. *It would have been nice if she'd offered her seat*, Maria thought. *Typical though, the arrogance of the young, like they own the bloody world.* The girl got up to get her haircut and Maria remained standing despite her aching legs. She almost turned and left but then Mandy was standing in front of her, taking her coat and offering her the familiar thin black shawl.

Maria let her put it on without saying a word, Mandy's prattle almost constant as she walked her across to a spare stool in front of one of the enormous mirrors. The spotlights around the edge were so bright – had they always been that bright? She couldn't stare straight at them, found herself scowling at her own reflection.

'All alright, Maria? I was looking forward to seeing you, wanted to catch you up on my date. Mr Ravenclaw, he was *so* short. I don't normally mind too much, I mean, you know people embellish a bit on their dating profile. I mean, I'm not exactly thirty-nine, but he was like an actual medical dwarf, tiny, he barely came up to the bar. It was so distracting. And he was nice, which was almost worse because I found myself rejecting him solely on his height, which basically makes me shallow, doesn't it?'

Maria couldn't keep up, zoning in and out. 'It does.'

Mandy frowned then readjusted her expression as she placed two hands on Maria's head. 'Well, what are we doing today? Usual blow-dry? Want to try a conditioning treatment? Your roots could do with a lift. And I could neaten up the cut?'

'Whatever you think,' Maria's voice was dull. Mandy was tugging on her hair. What did she want to do, pull the damn stuff out at the roots?

'We'll leave the cut for another time,' Mandy said slowly, then brightened, 'I'll get Nina to wash it, I need to see another client with her colour.'

Fine, palm me off, Maria thought. No time even to wash her hair. Why hadn't she stayed at home?

'Nina,' Mandy called, 'Maria's here, could you wash and try that new root revival treatment on her?'

Nina emerged from the room at the back, her fringe freshly cut in a line above her eyebrows, making her look even more severe than normal. 'Hi Maria, tea, coffee?'

'Nothing,' Maria said, wondering why she felt so cross, her skin bristling as Nina stepped behind her and flashed her a smile.

'So, shall we get you to the sink?'

Had she always patronised her? Maria wondered as she got up, moved over to the row of sinks. Someone had left the footrest up so she almost banged her calf: selfish and dangerous. She sat in the furthest-away chair, refusing the seat, the massage, just wanting it all to be over and done with.

'How have you been?' Nina asked as she started up the taps, the water too hot.

'Ow!' Maria pulled to the side, cricking her neck.

'Sorry, is it too warm?'

Almost burnt me, Maria thought, but didn't say anything, her lips set in a tight line.

She could have asked Nina some questions but today she didn't care what Nina had done with her weekend, didn't care about her metal detecting or whether she had found a whole golden cache of coins. She didn't want to ask questions and she didn't want to offer information: *Yes, I'm a millionaire now, by a man who didn't even tell me, who hid it from me and then died all of a sudden and left me in this confusing muddle.*

God, what a mess! What exactly was she meant to do now?

Nina was rubbing at her scalp and Maria felt the tug on her hair, the start of headache as she kneaded and pressed. The pressure was unbearable: had Nina always had such a grip, her nails scratching at her scalp? The towel she wrapped round her was loose and slipping, her neck exposed, strands of wet hair plastered to her skin. She didn't smile as Nina returned to the back room with a curious glance behind her.

Mandy ambled over, moments later. 'Dealt with your other client?' Maria's voice was acid and Mandy paused a second before her fuchsia-pink lips moved into a smile.

'She is getting balayage, I love a bit of balayage,' Mandy said, plugging in her hairdryer.

Unwrapping the towel from Maria's head, Mandy blasted the hot air at her scalp. Maria was grateful for the noise, the excuse that she hadn't heard any questions.

Mandy's voice drifted in and out, her familiar cackle of laughter now grating on Maria's nerves. Had it always been so high, so sharp? Maria dug her nails into her palms and waited for Mandy to peter out. The woman could talk.

'…So, although he lives in Petworth I suspect it's with his mother… I looked it up on Google Earth, it's enormous, I genuinely thought I'd seen peacocks. Anyway, I can't be doing with a mummy's boy so I think I'm just going to go for dinner and then make my excuses. We're going to Café Roma so I hope he doesn't think I'm all modern and want to go Dutch…'

She had been looking for a man for forever, why didn't she give up now? What was the point of trawling these dating websites and meeting these hopeless people? She would still be single, Maria was sure of it, no one could get that lucky. Maria hadn't deserved luck, and meeting Albie had been that. She hadn't been worthy of it, the karma from her past had finally caught up with her.

'…expensive, right, and I don't normally get a starter because it only prolongs it if it's awful but I've heard the goat's cheese salad is basically to die for so I can't say no, I'm a sucker for a starter. Nina can keep her sweet tooth, I'm all about cheese. Cheese for starter, cheese board for the end…'

Maria let the words wash over her, watching Mandy dry and tease her hair. She had to admit, the crown was glossy, the ends healthy, sitting just above her shoulders, the soft grey lovely under the lights of the mirror. Who was she going to see with hair like this? What a waste of time and money! Why had she come? It wouldn't exactly have made a dent in her new fortune – she could miss a thousand hair appointments and not do that. But that thought didn't comfort her one bit.

She answered Mandy in monosyllables and was glad to be paying and leaving, accepting her coat from Nina without a second glance.

'I hope everything's alright?' Mandy held out the change. Normally, Maria would wave it away for the tip jar, but today she found herself pocketing the money, making an abrupt goodbye.

'Of course,' Maria snapped back without a pause, watching in satisfaction as Mandy flinched.

Turning, she moved back across to the door, feeling Mandy's eyes on her as she stepped out into the street, a breeze buffeting her new hair, mussing it up. She felt uneasy, knowing she was being cold, unfair, yet still unable to turn and fix it all with a farewell smile.

She headed home, feeling empty, moving through an unfamiliar mini-market to buy bread and milk, not buying anything else, unable to think about what she needed. Toast and tea would suffice and what was the point of continually cooking meals for one person? She could get by, she'd buy multivitamins. Although they were probably a rip-off, who really knew what was in those tablets? Paying for her shopping and making her way home, she lingered over the resentment at paying 5p for a carrier bag, even though it wasn't like she couldn't afford it.

The day stretched ahead of her, with nothing to do. She was walking quickly, tutting at someone idling in front of her, a young Asian man who kept staring at his mobile. She didn't have a mobile phone, there had never been any point. Who would she have called? Albie had once asked her for her number, and for a moment she had wished she had had one. The man was still staring at it. What would happen, she supposed, if he didn't check it every minute? This generation were obsessed with technology. She found herself annoyed with all of them for that fact. She muttered as she passed him, noticing he appeared to be staring at a small map on the screen. Normally she might have summoned up the courage to ask whether he needed help with directions but she found the words frozen somewhere inside her. She didn't want to ask, didn't want to help. He would find where he was looking for somehow. No one needed her to hold their hand.

The café was up ahead, the large letters just visible, someone's face framed perfectly in the inside of the 'O', and she found herself heading there automatically. That was where it had all begun. She was stung again with the facts: the modest, joyful Albie she had known in that café not squaring with the wealthy benefactor who had kept his secrets to himself. She had thought she was close to him and yet this enormous, fundamental fact about himself, he had hidden. And now it was too late: he couldn't explain because he'd gone, he'd left her. She didn't want his money, she thought for the thousandth time, she didn't want to keep the connection, keep thinking about him. She had finally, after all these years, let someone in and they had left her too. She found she couldn't forgive him.

The place was quiet. Their table along the furthest wall was wiped down and empty and Maria stared at it. So many Thursdays sat in those chairs. She sat down quickly at the nearest table to the door, checking her watch, the hands seeming to drag. How interminably long could today be?

Pauline approached the table looking tired, bags under her eyes as she stepped over, a biro sticking out of her shirt pocket, a pad in her apron. 'The usual?'

'No, just a water.'

Pauline raised one eyebrow and didn't bother to write the order down. 'Are you on your own today?'

'It's quiet in here,' Maria said, pointedly changing the subject.

Why had she come here? What had she hoped for? The empty tables just acted as a reminder that he was no longer going to step through that door and join her.

'Thank god! Amrit's studying and Clive is off sick again, I swear that chef has had every illness going, twice. Hold on, let me grab that water.'

She returned with a glass half-filled with ice and a bottle of mineral water.

'So, are you well?'

It seemed Pauline might settle in for a conversation and Maria suddenly felt exhausted by the thought. 'I'll have the water to go, must get on.' She hadn't even removed her coat. She stood and rummaged in her handbag for coins.

Pauline tried to hide her surprise but it was clear she was thrown, handing over the bottle of water and accepting the money in return.

'Keep the change,' Maria muttered, not wanting to wait while Pauline moved behind the counter, opened the till, selected the right change.

As she left the café, the pavement spattered with raindrops and she looked up at the grey sky. What a miserable day it had turned into. The clouds were fat and brooding. Soon every surface was damp. The mist-like rain coated her skin, soaked her jacket, wet her new hair, making it go flat. It would frizz when it dried, she thought as she stamped home, wrapping her coat tighter around herself. But then what did it matter? What did any of it matter anymore?

*

'I'm a water baby,' she would repeat to strangers.

How she loved the beach, the sea, squealing as the waves swept in, tiny legs racing to get away before the water caught her.

She would beg us to go there, even in winter, not understanding why the pebbles were deserted, why the sea was a stubborn grey.

The beach had always been a magical place, full of fun and ice cream and games and laughter. Of endless summer: sandy toes and the taste of vanilla. Of her blissful smile as she pulled my hand and dragged me into the shallows. As she wiggled her toes deep into the wet sand and squealed as the water washed around her ankles, sucking and pulling at her.

The thought of the beach had always made my chest lighten, my mood lift.

It was different now.

Chapter 9

Thursday came around again and Maria found herself staying in her bed, the sheets unwashed, another launderette visit skipped, the room not aired, a thin layer of dust on the bed frame, dried watermarks on her bedside table. Her book was still in the same spot, the photo in the frame stood as if accusing her. Who would notice if she simply stayed in bed?

She didn't run the bath, didn't light the candles or put on any make-up. She sat, curtains still closed from the evening before, the television on, with no idea what she was watching, a sort of background noise to the fog in her own head. She wasn't sure how much time had passed but she found herself reaching for the bag from the solicitor's, opening the envelope with the keys inside, ignoring the note, and turning over the cold, hard metal in her hand.

Albie's house: *her* house. She couldn't start to get her head round it. She'd never even seen it. How could she own something she'd never even laid eyes on? It was absurd, a joke. It made her feel as if the depth of their friendship had been in her head. How could she pretend to know someone really well when she'd never even been to his home, when he had hidden so much from her? What a fool!

The keys sat in her palm and she studied them. More time passed. She could stay here, the television long since frozen, a square on the screen asking her if she wanted to continue watching. She hadn't even noticed the absence of noise. She could stay, sit in silence, or she could go and use the keys. A tiny flicker of curiosity ignited inside her: she imagined a palatial house on a tree-lined avenue, bookcases stacked with books, a polished dining room table, a chandelier. Isn't that how millionaires lived? And Albie had been a millionaire. Her hand closed over the keys in a tight grip and she felt the same swell of hot rage and confusion fill her up as she thought for the hundredth time of the enormous secret he had hidden, that he hadn't trusted her with. Did she think it would have changed the way she viewed him? That she would have treated him differently? She released her grip, a red mark where the keys had dug into her skin.

Then why leave her it all? Why spring it all on her? Why... She pushed her head back into the headrest and squeezed her eyes shut. She was back to the endless cycle of questions.

She knew she couldn't stay festering in this chair forever and maybe it would be better to get it done quickly, to try and focus her energy. Getting up, she put the keys in her handbag and, without bothering to glance at her reflection in the mirror, she pulled on the first coat to hand and headed out, letting the door slam behind her.

She hadn't meant to head there – Albie's address was still a further ten-minute walk away – but she found her feet moving automatically, as if it were any other Thursday and they just knew where they were headed. The café looked busy, steam clogging the windows so the inside was a blur of animated faces. She could make out Pauline moving between the tables, vivid red lipstick on a mouth always smiling. She paused outside, biting her lip. This wasn't any other Thursday, though. Today, she was headed to Albie's house for the first time – and Albie wasn't even going to be there. She would need strength but how could she order the tea and marble cake? She placed a hand on the cold glass. She would get an iced bun and a latte with three sugars. Something different, something sweet to spur her on.

She didn't push open the door though, bit her lip harder. She would have to face the question in Pauline's eyes. She hadn't even told her what had happened to Albie – she wasn't ready to say the words to someone who had known him, someone who would react to the news. She didn't have the strength to see her own sadness reflected back at her. Her palm was damp on the glass and she removed it, slid it into her pocket. What was she thinking? She didn't need to do this today. She didn't need to go to his house right now. She would go home, put her nightdress on, try and get back into her book, try and stop thinking about him every second of the day.

'Hey,' a voice said from behind her, 'it's you!'

The enthusiastic greeting made Maria spin round and there on the pavement stood a grinning girl, her long hair clipped back behind her ears, a flash of silver as she turned her head.

'Are you going in?' Rosie pointed to the door.

Maria took a step back. 'I was going to, but no, I'm, no, probably not...'

Rosie tucked a strand of chestnut-brown hair behind her ear. 'You seem a bit distracted, are you alright?'

'Have you come straight from school?' Maria tried to direct the conversation away from herself. She couldn't allow this lovely girl to check on her once again – it should be her being the strong one, she was a million years older for a start.

Rosie nodded, her eyes dancing with energy. 'So where are you going?'

'Well,' Maria said with a pause, and then maybe because she had shared so much the other day she found herself telling Rosie, 'I've got the keys, to the house I told you about, the one my gentleman friend left me. I was thinking maybe I'd go over there... but I'm not sure anymore, I...'

Rosie's eyes widened as she cut her off, 'You haven't been there yet? Oh my god!' She let out a puff, energy exuding from every pore. 'God, I wouldn't have been able to stay away! Just imagine what it might be like. He might have a cinema room and, like, a hot tub and stuff.'

Maria found her mouth twitching as Rosie carried on, the girl's presence cheering her.

'He will definitely have surround sound, those bifold glass doors and probably an ornamental garden, maybe a fountain,' she practically shouted the last word. Maria couldn't help it as her mouth lifted into a smile.

'Don't get carried away,' she replied in a soft voice, 'Albie wasn't like that.' She stopped short. Albie hadn't been like that, she was sure of it, but now she doubted that line. Did she really know him at all?

'Well, if you want some company, I am totally available to check out the pad of a millionaire!' Rosie stood, eyebrows raised in a question.

Maria squared her shoulders, knowing she should find the strength to do this on her own, that it wouldn't be right for Rosie to be there, but then she couldn't help it: the thought of the young girl there by her side as she faced it was an overwhelming comfort.

'Actually, I'd love that.' The answer left her mouth before she could stop it.

'Awesome.'

The word made Maria's smile even wider.

'So where is it?' Rosie asked.

Maria pulled out the address from the solicitor's information. 'Not far.'

'Well, come on then, I want to see how the other half live,' Rosie said.

'I…' Maria looked back in the direction of her apartment and then at Rosie's expectant face – so innocent and excited – and she found she couldn't resist, feeling energy for the first time in days course through her. 'If you're really sure you want to come…'

Rosie was already moving ahead of her, chatting about her day at school. She talked all the way to the address and it was a tonic for Maria just to be in her company and concentrate on that, not on the task ahead.

They arrived at a wide road lined with beech trees, fallen leaves plastering the pavement. They moved down the street, past large Victorian houses with enormous bay windows until they stood outside the address. A communal bicycle rack and a few empty parking spots took up the space in front of a large block of apartments: 'HARWOOD HOUSE'.

This was it. And yet, this didn't seem to be a singular house.

She pulled out the sheet once more, realising immediately that she hadn't read the instructions fully. She saw it now, the line beneath stating 'Flat 6c'.

She frowned, looking at the paper and the apartment block and back. One flat? Did he own the block? Was Flat 6c an ironic name? Was it the penthouse? She moved slowly towards the large double doors of the entrance way, a list of names and numbers next to letterboxes in a grid, an intercom to the left.

Rosie swapped a look with her. 'Is this right?'

Maria took a step forward, scanning the list. And there on a peeling sticker were the faded letters: 'A.YOUNG. Flat 6c'.

Maria nodded. 'I think so.'

Rosie's face said it all, reflecting Maria's own confusion. 'Well,' she said, clearly forcing the smile onto her face, injecting some brightness into her voice, 'let's take a look.'

Maria pulled out the small set of keys, hands shaking, and inserted the larger one. The door clicked open and they stepped inside. The foyer had a large blue mat, scuffed linoleum and smelt of bleach and motor oil. Two lifts, their outsides brushed silver, were to her right and there was a wide staircase just beyond that. It was hardly a cosy entrance – the clinical grey-white of the walls and a poster asking people not to urinate in the lifts made her eyes widen.

Rosie was biting her lip as Maria turned to face her. 'What floor do you think he's on?'

The sudden movement of the lift doors startled them both and a woman wearing headphones stepped out. Rosie stepped inside before Maria could change her mind: 'Come on then.'

Maria just made it in time before the lift closed once more. There were only four floors with the flat numbers written next to the buttons. Albie had lived on the second floor. The lift juddered and they were off; Maria felt her stomach gurgle in anticipation. Rosie was leaning back against the wall of the lift, one crooked leg up – so relaxed. Maria realised how much she needed her here to face it all. Who else could she have asked? Who else did she have to turn to? That thought froze her to the spot as the lift doors pulled back.

Albie's door had been painted a deep blue, a yucca plant was in a pot to the side. Maria's hand shook once more as she placed the Yale key in the lock, pausing before she turned it.

'You can do it,' Rosie said in a gentle voice behind her.

Maria took a breath and twisted the key.

The air was thick, stale, a tangy smell of turps underpinning other scents that reminded her of Albie: orange, wood smoke, books. Maria squeezed down the narrow corridor into a living area, a kitchenette in the corner.

'It's quite…' Rosie appeared beside her and Maria was barely listening as she finished her sentence. '…small.'

An upturned mug and bowl on the draining board made Maria freeze. There were still breadcrumbs on a chopping board, the light still red on the washing machine, as if he had stepped out of this room just moments ago.

'Are you absolutely sure this guy was a millionaire?' Rosie asked, and with a few steps she was already on the other side of the room, standing next to a leather armchair, worn patches on the arms, a dent in the cushion.

Maria smiled sadly. 'Apparently so,' she replied, knowing she was nervous to find out more secrets about this man she thought she had known. How had she imagined his home? As she thought about it, she realised this *was* what she had pictured, not the millionaire's place with floor-to-ceiling windows, abstract paintings on the wall, all chrome and marble. She'd imagined this, a haphazard collection of framed prints by his favourite artists, shelves crammed with books and a ridiculous number of teapots – he once told her that he collected them – an altar pew against a wall laden with art magazines and old newspapers.

Next to a window – that definitely needed opening – a table was laid out with pots of paints, brushes and sketchbooks. A jam jar swilled brown with dirty water, a paintbrush left out on the side. Maria found herself staring at it. Albie had held that paintbrush, had used that water when he last painted. The loss of him overwhelmed her for a moment. She took a deep breath and forced herself on. Paintings were stacked up against each other under the table, some original works on the wall, either side of a cuckoo clock. Then she realised with a start: they were his works. His small signature in the bottom right-hand corner of a beautiful painting of a river at dusk: a purple wash of colour, languid ripples on the surface, so realistic she could see the movement of the water, wanted to reach out and touch it.

She moved slowly across to the table, fingering the sketchbook that laid open. It was a pencil drawing of the South Downs, stretches of rolling fields beneath a wide sky. The image made her swallow, imagining him walking there, his flat cap on his head, a stick in his hand. He had been so full of life, it was cruel to think he had been robbed of the years ahead. The sketch was stunning too. How she wished again that she had asked him to show her his art. Like everything else, he had hidden this incredible talent.

Rosie was quiet, standing silently in the corner, watching Maria as she moved around the room, picking up and putting down things at will.

'It's all yours now then,' she said.

Maria paused, placed a gaudy teapot back on a shelf. 'It is.' She knew she wasn't ready to face what she would do with the flat. There were too many reminders of him today: the paintings, the notes in his illegible writing, a book on walking left spine up, a biro without its lid, all overwhelming her.

She moved out of the living room. There were only two more doors off the corridor, one a small, neat bathroom in avocado green with only a bath, a shower attachment connected to the taps. A sink, a flannel folded neatly over the side, beneath a shelf containing a toothbrush and toothpaste. *His* toothbrush. The other room must be his bedroom and Maria couldn't help but feel a strange embarrassment flood through her as she lingered outside: it felt wrong to be entering such an intimate space without him.

Rosie appeared in the corridor behind her, nodding an encouragement as if she knew Maria was undecided. Maria turned and stared back at the door, an innocuous cream door with a brushed silver handle. One push and she'd be inside, yet still she waited.

'Go on,' said Rosie in a soft voice from behind her. 'That must be where he's keeping all the precious stones and suitcases of money.'

This light-hearted comment was what Maria needed to take that final step, her hand reaching for the handle as she twisted it and stepped inside.

What she saw took her breath away.

*

She would stop and talk to anyone. And even when people were cold and distant, she would persist until they melted.

We were walking by the arcade when she spotted a policeman talking to a policewoman, their car parked some way off.

'Mummmmmeeeee, it's a lady.' She pointed to the policewoman, who spotted her, smiled and came over.

'Hello,' she said, bending at the knees and talking to her. 'Would you like to try on my helmet?'

She nodded, watching in wonder as the woman removed her hat, her brown hair flat, and placed it on her head.

Grinning, she spun round to look at me in the oversized hat, 'Mummy, look I policeman.'

'You look very important,' the policewoman said, smiling. 'And are you going to be a police officer when you grow up?'

She spun back round to answer, shaking her head so the helmet slipped down over her eyes. 'No,' she said from under it in an earnest voice, 'I'm going to be a witch.'

Chapter 10

It dominated the wall above the wooden double bed, the colours vivid against the plain magnolia walls. A beautiful portrait in oils of a woman sat in a high-backed chair, her hand resting on her arm, a half-smile on her face as she stared at the painter. The resemblance was uncanny: the portrait was of her.

She must have let out a noise because suddenly Rosie had joined her.

'Are you alr— Hey, it's…' she was staring at the wall opposite too, '…you.'

Maria nodded dumbly. 'Albie never painted portraits.' He had *told* her that, said he preferred landscapes and still lifes, said they were less problematic than people. She had moved around the side of the bed, drawn to the image, unable to drag her eyes away. He had flattered her, that much was clear, her grey hair glossy, her blue eyes bright, her skin smoother – fewer crow's feet and lines across her forehead.

He painted her.

'He hasn't finished it,' Rosie pointed out, looking at a patch on the bottom left, clothing yet to be painted, a sparse canvas background needing filling.

Maria studied it carefully, unable to respond, simply soaking up every last detail, feeling tears prick her eyes so the colours blurred together. He would never finish it now.

The thought was so overwhelming she found she couldn't stay standing, lowering herself onto the edge of his bed, eyes still roving over its surface. Why would he hang something half-finished? Another question to swirl and bump up against the others in her mind. Finally, she dragged her eyes away from it, soaking in the painful realisation that she had meant so much to him. He had left her all this, displayed a painting of her over his bed. She imagined him then getting in and out of bed, her face the very first and last thing he would see. She felt herself burn with heat. She thought of the things she would say to him if he were here, imagined herself reaching for his hand, revelling in the rough skin, paint caught in the edges of his squared-off nails.

Closing her eyes, she pretended for a moment that he was there, felt a warmth flood her body.

Rosie had asked her a question but Maria wasn't concentrating, caught up in the past, in the memories she had of him. Had he ever tried to tell her what she meant to him? Why hadn't she shared her own feelings? Why had she held back? He had been so understated she had missed the signs, or maybe she couldn't imagine someone like him feeling like that about her. It had been so many years and she had long lost her faith in men. And now, it was too late.

Looking around the room, she let the details soak in: a flat cap and trilby hat on a stand, a neat line of brogue shoes, shiny from polish, a cactus on his dark walnut dresser. She didn't want to clear any of this away, she wanted to curl up in a ball on the top of his bed and sleep there, to pretend for a second that he was in the room next door, sat in the leather armchair, that he would join her soon.

Her eyes fell to his bedside table: a lamp, an ashtray, his watch, reading glasses, some cufflinks and a small red alarm clock competing for space. She almost missed the piece of paper. It was folded in two, largely hidden by the ashtray – a souvenir from the past as he had told her he'd given up smoking years ago. For a brief second she doubted that fact – had he lied to her about the small things too? But then there was no evidence the ashtray had been used, no lingering smell trapped in the room.

She reached for the piece of paper, unfolding it and smoothing it out. Then she turned it over in her hands – it felt wrong to be rifling through his belongings, this might be personal.

'Read it.' Rosie's voice was gentle but determined.

Maria bit her lip, 'But what if it's…'

'Personal?'

Maria nodded, looking up at Rosie, who in that moment seemed so wise for her years.

'Nothing's personal now, it's all yours.'

Rosie moved across to sit next to her. *Gosh, she's a cheeky thing,* thought Maria. *She's also right, though.*

Maria thought then of the slip of paper, the note about the keys. Perhaps this was something more: an explanation, a reason. She felt her fingers itch, needing to know, desperate for more. Carefully, she turned the paper back over, reading the heading spelt in large sloping letters in a green fountain pen.

Wish List

She frowned – not a letter then. The page was crammed full, a list of bullet points and small ticks next to half of the list.

For the local RSPCA charity:
- *Donate a generous sum* ✓

- *Volunteer once a week* ✓

For St Joseph's Primary School:

- *Provide them with a year's worth of stationery* ✓
- *Help re-paint the children's nursery* ✓
- *Buy flowers for the playground* ✓

For the library:

- *Purchase the staff a new coffee machine* ✓
- *Volunteer for readings once a month* ✓
- *Donation of books* ✓

For the youth centre:

- *Donation for a football table, ping-pong table and jukebox* ✓
- *Offer help for monthly drop-in sessions* ✓
- *Mentor a youth* ✓

Rosie was reading the list over her shoulder and Maria realised the words were blurring as tears glistened at the kindness of her beloved friend. He had told her about the furry cat, Mr Pickles, that he'd adopted, who had promptly run away on the second day. He had mentioned Troy, a young boy who lived on a nearby estate, whom he regularly met, Albie's pockets always filled with cigarettes that he had confiscated from him. Maria had some sympathy for this teenager – she had once been a smoker, another bad habit from a lifetime ago. She remembered the day Albie had appeared in the café splattered in magnolia paint after helping out at the school. His grin as he told her about his favourite story – 'The Odd Octopus' – he read at the library.

'How was the Octopus odd?' she had asked in a bemused voice.

'Ah, you'll have to come to the library next Tuesday and sit on the mat with the kiddies to find out.'

Why hadn't she gone to the library? Why hadn't she sat on the mat and listened to his voice, the long drawn-out r's, his eyebrows moving as he read from his favourite book, revelling in the delight on the faces of the listening children? She had cried off, 'My hip! I'll never get up.' What she wouldn't give to go back to the café and change her answer. The tears fell now, into her lap as she held the list away from her body. What a stupid woman, to waste time, to say no.

'I can't believe… I didn't…' Her words were choked as she wiped at her face. Rosie sat next to her, a quiet companion, letting her cry, letting her get it out. Maria felt Rosie rest a hand over hers.

'I'm sure he knew you cared. He left you everything for a reason, you must have been very special to him.'

Her words gave Maria a sliver of comfort, enough to smooth out the paper once more and continue to read. She took in the rest of the list that had yet to be ticked.

For Keith:
- *Buy him a coffee and sandwich every day* ✓
- *Help him re-connect with his family*
- *Pay for him to get a haircut*
- *Make sure to smile and stop to chat every time you pass him*

For Timothy:
- *Find him and thank him for saving my life*
- *Take a trip to the sea together*
- *Donate to a charity of his choice*

For Pauline:
- *Splash out on a makeover for the café (state-of-the-art coffee machine, new fridges and stove, get rid of those tablecloths!)*
- *Buy her a gift – a spa day maybe? Check with Maria*

For Cathie:

- *Make amends and say sorry for not forgiving her*
- *Try to make up for lost time*
- *Treat her to a trip to Paris and try frog's legs and snails*

She read as fast as she was physically able, her mind racing. She knew Keith, a local homeless gentleman – Albie had mentioned him in passing, that he liked his coffee with milk and two sugars. She'd heard about Timothy too, he had saved Albie's life when they were students. They'd lost touch and Albie, on more than once occasion, had tried to track him down. Why hadn't she asked more? Why had she never probed? She wanted all the answers and now it was too late. Pauline, she knew well – Albie had always fallen into such easy conversation with her on their Thursdays at the café and Maria had let him, barely chipping in, but enjoying listening to them both. She bit her lip at the suggestion that he should 'check with Maria', as if she would have been the one to advise him.

She frowned at the other name though: Cathie. He had never mentioned a Cathie before. She was sure of it, she could recall all their conversations and Cathie had not been a name to pass his lips. Yet the name seemed familiar. She felt a rush of heat course through her and realised it was jealousy. She would most definitely have remembered her name if Albie had told her it. She wondered who she was, a small dread settling in her stomach. Paris: the city of love, romance. He had promised to take Cathie there. What would *Cathie* think of all of this?

Then she remembered where she had read the name: the solicitor's pack had contained a few addresses and she thought Cathie had been one of them. So who was she? Maria would have thought more about it, but the next bullet point made everything else leave her mind. Her own name, written in the green fountain pen, in his hand.

For Maria:

> • *Take her to The Ritz for afternoon tea – for some proper tea and cake!!!*

The Ritz?! She couldn't begin to imagine the grandeur. She would have had to have worn her Sunday best. Probably a hat. She thought of her wardrobe – nothing in it would suffice for somewhere so fancy. She would have had to go shopping for something new, something she hadn't done for years, something she had once enjoyed a lifetime ago, when she had been someone else entirely.

'It's you!' Rosie said, interrupting Maria's thoughts. And then of course bringing her back to this room, this list and the very fact that Maria would never be planning an outing with Albie to The Ritz. She'd never get to go there.

'Oh, you never went. But look,' Rosie said, shifting closer to Maria, 'look at the next thing on the list.'

Maria forced her eyes down.

> • *Paint Maria (don't give up – actually finish it this time! Even though it's impossible to truly capture her beauty)*

She felt her heart beat faster, her cheeks tingle. Such kind words. She looked up at the painting over his bed, at how he had viewed her. How could she have missed it? How could she have wasted so much time? Looking down, she continued reading quickly, needing to know it all. The next line shocked her.

• *Go to the grave with Maria and plant some tulips*

She must have made a noise because Rosie was asking, 'What?'

Too stunned to say anything, Maria couldn't even look at her. She didn't want to read anything more about it either. It made her stomach ache with fresh pain. She didn't want to think about the grave, couldn't. And the fact that he had known how hard it might be made her even more muddled. She looked down and read the final bullet point next to her name, wanting to distract herself from the thoughts piling on top of her.

This time she definitely gasped out loud, the noise loud in the tiny room.

'What is it? What?' Rosie asked, peering down quickly as Maria folded the paper in two once more.

'It's nothing,' she said, her voice high and quick.

'Of course it is or you wouldn't…'

'Really,' Maria insisted, hastily opening up her handbag, secreting the folded paper inside.

'But, you…'

Something in her expression made Rosie's words fade away.

Maria's handbag felt weighty with the list – and that last bullet point – inside, as if it were more than just a single slip of paper. She sat there dumbly on the bed, seeing the last line in her mind, repeating it in her head. Her fingers itched to open her handbag once more and check: it couldn't be possible, had she really read it right?

*

I had to take her into work for leaving drinks. Michael had been at the company for twenty-five years and had secured us our first TV advertising campaigns. They were presenting him with a plaque and the room was packed with people in the industry, many down from our London office and one or two across from New York.

I had dressed her in a velvet dress with an enormous bow around the waist that she said made her look like Sindy. She was a sociable child and I hoped she would just sit quietly while I circulated.

I'd had a great evening, chatting with the CEO in our London office, hints of a bright future for me. He'd breathed cigar smoke in my face and squeezed my waist and I'd smiled and let him.

His wife had joined us after a while – a striking woman with a Roman nose and a high forehead, dressed in a taffeta dress with a beaded bodice. She talked at me: the intricacies of a recent whist evening and her latest charity do at The Savoy, her expression forbidding.

My daughter had appeared at my side, eating a pineapple chunk on a stick. 'Go now,' she said, tugging on the hem of my dress.

'And who is this?' the CEO had asked, ruffling her hair.

His wife looked down her nose at this small child in a velvet dress and then back at me.

My daughter glanced up at this woman and then, with no warning, she told her, 'Your dress is really pretty.'

And I watched in amazement, my heart swelling, as this haughty woman cracked the first smile of that evening.

Chapter 11

For a moment she considered going to the beach, imagined herself walking along the promenade, the breeze through her hair, sand to her right, the sun setting on the horizon, a boat idling by. But she dismissed the thought as quickly as it came, knowing she didn't have the strength. She would catch a glimpse of the pier, be forced to remember a past she had been determined to put behind her. She would be forced to walk away.

Yet she needed to go somewhere with space – she realised she had been bottling up so many emotions since Albie had died. She had been so furious with him for leaving her, with no warning. And then the dogged thought that he had been lying to her, hadn't trusted her enough to tell her about his heart condition, his wealth. That he hadn't thought she was worthy of that information. So much festering anger stored up inside her that now she wanted to go somewhere she could let it all out. Now she had all this new information to absorb: the list, the apartment, how he lived.

Queen's Park was large and anonymous, she thought, heading towards the park. As she walked around the pond, the water glistening in the weak sunshine, ducks causing gentle ripples to echo across the surface, she felt her muscles relax, her shoulders drop. It was deserted at this time, the odd jogger or parent bundled into a thick coat, pushing a fur-lined pram, and she was able to think as she strolled, reflecting back over everything she'd discovered.

The wish list had been burning a hole in her handbag ever since she'd read its contents, the last bullet point burnt into her mind. The list had seemed so typically Albie, and explained how he filled his days. He had always seemed so busy, plans spilling out of him, people he'd come across, and she had enjoyed basking in the stories he'd told, living vicariously through him. She thought of her own week: a single task to be ticked off every day, her only connections brief and professional. How small her world had become, not that she deserved anything else.

She stopped short on the path, someone tutting just behind her as an elderly man skirted round her, his Jack Russell yapping indignantly as they passed. She had only ever lived for Thursdays, she realised. Everything else in the week had always paled into insignificance while she had been waiting for the other days to pass. How wrong that he had gone, someone who had filled his days with such thought and purpose.

He could have bought a mansion, moved abroad, owned a dozen holiday homes around the world, spent lavishly, flashed his wealth. But he hadn't done any of those things, hadn't boasted about it, used it to make others feel awkward or lacking. He'd lived a humble life in a one-bedroomed flat, spending the money on other people. Why, she wondered. Why had he felt that he needed a list? Was it just generosity?

He'd always insisted on paying for their weekly tea and cake, exasperated if she ever got there first, and she saw now that maybe this was his small way of sharing his good fortune. She had always assumed it was just him being a gentleman but now she could see it ran deeper than that. She thought back to all the ticks: all the ways of making things better for people he came into contact with. What a way to live! That was Albie though, seizing opportunities. She recalled that very first Thursday in the café. She'd been sat quietly, nibbling at a toasted teacake, and suddenly there was a scrape of a chair and he was sitting down right in front of her, introducing himself.

'Can I join you?' he'd asked, barely pausing for her to do anything but nod.

She remembered she had wiped at her mouth in alarm, assuming she was covered in crumbs and butter, feeling wrong-footed by this shift in her routine. She hadn't known what to say, readying herself to get up and leave. He had asked her whether she would like to share a pot of tea with him. She was about to say no, but there had been something in those navy eyes, something in the friendly way the skin creased round their edges that stopped her.

She had said yes. He had ordered a pot of tea, 'And a slice of that lovely looking marble cake, with two forks.'

Just like that: two forks. And when the plate had been set down he had pushed it between them, as if it was the most natural thing in the world.

'I'm Albie,' he'd said and offered her a fork.

She had taken it.

'Maria.'

She moved to a nearby bench, with an inscription on a plaque stating that Margaret had always loved to sit there and watch the world go by, and she wondered then if Albie might have liked something to mark his passing. Surely others would want to pay their respects? She imagined his full life, the people he had touched. He hadn't left instructions for anything like that, the solicitor simply stating that he requested a cremation and directions as to where he wanted his ashes to be scattered. That request lay heavy on her chest as if he had deliberately chosen the spot for her and not him.

The world suddenly seemed smaller and greyer, a cloud skidding across the sky, plunging the water in front of her into semi-darkness. She reached into her handbag and smoothed out the piece of paper once more, reading again all the bullet points he had never ticked, wondering again what had led him to create this list. All those people who would never benefit from his kindnesses. She felt a familiar surge of sadness, her own grief always so near the surface now, and a terrible emptiness. Where should she go once she had circled this pond? What should she do with this new knowledge?

She traced the next bullet point with a finger: Keith. Albie had clearly taken some time to get to know Keith, with frequent deliveries of sandwiches and coffees. What family did Albie refer to? What had happened to Keith, she wondered. She thought of the brief glimpses she had had of him, sat on a filthy sleeping bag in a doorway in Kemptown, a plastic cup for loose change in front of him, a mop of dark brown hair, weathered skin. He didn't seem old to her, was there a mother somewhere hoping he would get in touch? Let her know he was safe? Did he have siblings who had lost touch? What if no one helped him? It seemed worse now that she knew this might be the impact of Albie's death, so much worse even than herself just losing him. The sun reappeared behind the stray cloud and as the sunlight beamed down, highlighting the family of ducks waddling determinedly to the water's edge, the thought struck her: she must finish the list. The sunshine beat on the back of her head as she re-read the list, Albie's wishes. This was how she could honour him. This was, she knew with certainty, how he would have wanted her to honour him. All these people wouldn't miss out because Albie had died, she wouldn't let that happen.

She stood, her knees cracking with the effort, a hand out to steady herself. She folded the list in two and placed it in her handbag once more: so precious, a road map of what she now must do. She looked out across the water, at the reflection of the sky on the smooth surface, felt as close to Albie in that moment than since the day he died. All the anger and hurt she had been harbouring ebbed away, a poison leaving her, every bad feeling replaced with this new desire.

'I'm going to do it for you,' she said aloud, lifting her handbag onto her shoulder in a decisive move. A woman pushing a pram looked over at her, but Maria didn't care. She set off for home, a bounce in her steps, a small smile, the first in days, forming.

'For you, Albie Young.'

*

Her first day at school. I kept a photograph on my desk for years. Scruffy hair tied up in bunches, wide light-brown eyes, a shirt untucked already, knobbly knees underneath an oversized skirt I wanted her to grow into. She had wanted to wear the uniform in bed the night before, had compromised by leaving it laid out ready at the foot of her bed.

In the morning she had looked up at me in awe as I had tried to teach her how to do up the tie. Then she had stood just outside the gate on the pavement, chin jutted out, the shiny, new brown leather satchel over one shoulder as she'd posed for my photograph. The expression on her face: a mixture of excitement and abject fear.

My girl. I had taken her hand and started that first walk to school, trying not to squeeze too tight, trying not to show her that I was as nervous as her.

Chapter 12

What do you dress in to impress someone for the first time? She spent far too long deciding, pulling out skirts, trousers, shirts and rejecting all of them. At one point she found herself holding up a floral summer dress with a pie collar before reminding herself with a loud scoff that it wasn't a day out at the Queen's Garden Party.

She didn't want to appear too formal, too stuffy: the dress went the same way as the rest of her clothes. She picked out a pair of cotton trousers, barely worn, a crease down the middle, and a soft grey cashmere jumper. She filled up a thermos with strong coffee, made two sandwiches and wrapped them tightly in cling film. With a last look at herself in the small mirror by the front door, and a *you can do this, Maria*, she set off.

She was almost there, nails biting into her flesh as she approached the doorway, could only glimpse the edge of a blanket from this distance. She had half-hoped he wouldn't be there, that she could turn around and go home, console herself with the fact that she had tried. It was bad enough when strangers spoke to her but to initiate the contact was entirely new for Maria.

'Maria…'

Rosie seemed to appear from nowhere in front of her. Maria felt herself sag with relief, putting off this moment for a little longer.

'You were miles away, everything alright? I've been worried about you.'

Maria seemed to always forget how much energy Rosie had until she was standing bold as brass in front of her, all bright eyes and confidence. 'Oh, I'm...' Maria drew into a doorway, out of the way of people in the busy street. 'I was going to meet someone from the list, someone Albie had helped. I'm, a little nervous.' She coughed, embarrassed perhaps to be admitting this to Rosie, someone younger who she should be advising, not the other way round.

'It will be fine, more than fine, people want other people to connect with them.'

'I hope you're right,' Maria said, wanting to be emboldened by the words, not convinced they were true. She had learnt how to push the best of them away in the past.

'I could come too, if you like?'

'Thank you, you are kind but I know I need to do this on my own, to find the strength.'

'Look,' Rosie said, tugging on a stray strand of hair. 'Remember, it was what your friend Albie wanted. All those things on the list.'

Maria blinked, imagining as she often did her own name in sloping green ink on the list, the bullet points underneath it. She didn't want to think about those now. If she couldn't even take this small step...

'So that should give you some courage. Just imagine him: he'd want to be here still, doing his list...'

Maria swallowed, knowing there was truth in those words. The list, something Albie had cared about and wanted to complete for whatever reason. What had been driving him to do those things, she thought for the hundredth time.

'You're not convinced.' Rosie laughed, and the sound, light and teasing, snapped her back into the present, glad Rosie had seen her, grateful to draw some strength from someone else.

'I am. You've been a help, as ever,' Maria said, her voice low and soft.

A small dog stopped then, yapping at the space next to Maria, the owner apologising as she waved the distraction away.

Squaring her shoulders, Maria peeked around the corner of the doorway: the blanket was still there. 'OK,' she muttered, almost to herself, 'Wish me luck.'

'Good luck.'

She marched off, hearing Rosie's response caught on the breeze behind her. Taking a breath, she moved down the street towards him, knowing that this meeting was fraught with potential disaster. For a start she didn't want to seem like some lady of the manor lording it over him, patronising him. She'd hate him to see her like that. She didn't want him to be offended, or embarrassed. These thoughts almost forced her to turn around and scuttle away again. But she drew strength from Rosie's words, reminding her of the folded piece of paper in her bag: this was what Albie had wanted to do and that was how she should do it. This wasn't Maria doing it, it was Albie. She could draw on his strength. She had seen him with strangers – a wide smile, an easy word – instantly watching them relax. She had to channel that skill, that warmth.

He was sat in the doorway of a recently closed furniture shop. A large tartan bag, a rolled-up duvet cover and three or four blankets around him. He had a cap on his head, long brown hair sticking out of the bottom, and was wearing a scuffed pair of trainers and a bulky black Puffa coat. She took a breath, preparing herself.

Keith.

How often had she walked past? Not seeing a person but seeing only their homelessness. The sleeping bag, carrier bags, cup of change, bulky clothing, uncombed hair, weather-beaten cheeks hiding the person underneath. The person with family, friends, unique traits: a story. She felt herself flooded with a shame. It shouldn't have taken Albie's list for her to notice this person who she had walked past countless times. Pretending his situation had nothing to do with her because he was a stranger. Albie hadn't thought like that.

'Excuse me,' she stuttered at first.

Keith looked up at her, a weathered face dominated by bushy dark eyebrows that shifted upwards slightly as she stood there, thrusting out the thermos flask.

'I got you coffee, he said you liked it with milk and two sugars, but I wasn't sure if they were heaped teaspoons so I brought some more in a bag in case you wanted to add, and I just assumed that is about the right amount of milk so I'm sorry if it's too milky, or not. I could go back and get some more if it isn't right…' She knew she was babbling, words tripping off her tongue in a desperate attempt to make this first connection.

Keith struggled to his feet, towering above her so that she had to crick her neck to look at him. 'Kind of you,' he said, his eyes crinkling in the corners as he took the thermos from her, 'I love it with milk.'

He didn't sit back down but stayed standing as he twisted the cup from the top of the flask.

'And sandwiches, I made sandwiches. He didn't tell me if you were a vegetarian so I've made egg. I hope you like it. I've done it with butter, not mayonnaise, which I always think makes it taste better, but I didn't have any cress and I do think cress makes all the difference so I'm sorry, next time perhaps. I know he liked to bring you them every day… Well, that's what I've assumed from the list…'

Keith had been about to put the coffee to his lips but Maria noticed he had frozen midway through the action.

Her words trailed away as he lowered the cup.

'He didn't... who didn't... are you talking about Albie?'

Keith's eyes narrowed as Maria bit her lip and nodded.

The air between them seemed to instantly chill as Keith took a step backwards. 'Sent you, has he? Feeling guilty, I suppose? I haven't seen hind nor hair of him in two weeks. I should have known it was all a bit too good to be true. I thought we were friends, you know...'

Maria was alarmed at the sudden shift in his demeanour. His face seemed to shut down as he glanced off into the distance.

'Oh, oh, you don't... no, of course you don't...'

He didn't know. Of course. She should have realised he wouldn't know. Who would have told him? How could he know? She realised with a sinking heart that she would have to be the one to tell him.

'Keith, Albie is... Albie died,' she said, quickly. The first time she had said those words aloud.

A range of emotions flickered across his face: shock widening his eyes before they darkened with hurt, his eyebrows dragged down as he looked at her. 'I... how...'

A film of water and a single teardrop.

'They told me it was his heart: the final moment happened in his sleep.'

Keith nodded slowly. 'That's g—' He didn't finish the sentence but sat down in amongst his blankets, spilling a little of the coffee onto the pavement.

'I'm sorry,' Maria said, knees creaking as she joined him on the floor, 'I hadn't thought you wouldn't know, so insensitive of me. He really did care about you.'

'And you are...?'

'Oh, I'm sorry. I'm Maria. I'm, I was...' she corrected herself, 'a friend of Albie's.'

Tears had left tracks on his cheeks as he twisted to look at her. '*You're* Maria,' Keith said, emphasising the 'you're' as if he knew exactly who she was. It made her frown in confusion.

'Albie told me about you, so he did.'

'Oh.' Maria felt her face heat up. She fiddled with the tassel on the blanket beneath her. 'Oh, he did, did he?'

Keith chuckled softly, a small choked sound. 'He thought the sun shone out of your… you know.'

Maria plaited the tassel, feeling her own eyes sting with tears. She found she couldn't reply.

Keith was silent now, resting back against the glass door, a faded 'CLOSING DOWN' sign behind its smeared surface. 'I can't believe he died. He was so…'

'I know,' finished Maria when he couldn't find the words.

They sat back together in the small doorway, people passing them without glancing down. Boots, trainers, heels clacking past, jeans brushing the ground… Someone threw a cigarette butt nearby. Everyone moving quickly, distracted, busy: no time to stop, no time to notice.

Eventually, Keith spoke. 'How did you know he came to see me?' he asked, wiping his face with the back of his hand.

Maria rummaged in her handbag and drew out Albie's Wish List, handing it to Keith.

He was quiet as he read the words.

'The ticks are all the things he'd done so far. I wanted to keep ticking it, finish what he started,' she said, filling the silence, worried for a moment that Keith would be hurt or angry reading about Albie's desire for him to reconnect with his family. Maria still wasn't sure what family Keith had lost touch with.

'So, he wanted me to get a haircut,' Keith roared with a short sharp bark of laughter. He didn't seem offended, fingering the end of one of his strands of hair as if in thought.

'The thing is, he left me some money,' Maria went on. 'He didn't really seem to spend any on himself. I think he wanted to spend it on others, help them...'

Was that true? What had driven Albie to be so generous? Had he always been that way or had something happened to make it so?

'...so I hope you don't mind my offering, but if it would suit you, I would dearly love to introduce you to a couple of people I know.'

The other thoughts subsided as she waited for Keith to respond, concerned he might not react well.

Keith handed her back the list and took a sip of coffee. 'Well,' he said, a slow, sly smile on his face, 'I haven't checked my diary but I don't think I have any prior engagements booked in.' He gave her another low chuckle that warmed her stomach. Finishing the coffee, he twisted the cup back on top of the thermos, offering her his hand as he stood. She took it, grateful for the help, as she made it to her feet.

'Show me the way, Maria,' he said, in a mock bow.

Smiling, they set off, and for the first time since Albie had died she realised she didn't feel quite so alone as she moved through the streets with someone else by her side.

*

I was waiting for her at the school gates, watching the other children leave in clusters. Heads bent, swapping stickers, yo-yos out, high, excited squeals. Someone was doing hopscotch over the chalk squares and I was still watching them when she appeared in front of me, front tooth missing, enormous grin.

Behind her stood a young, male teacher I had never met before.

'This is Mr Mitchell,' she'd announced, her small hand tugging the hem of my jacket.

'Hello.' I'd smiled, holding out a hand to him.

Mr Mitchell took it, a bewildered expression on his face.

I frowned at him. 'Did you want to discuss something with me?' I shifted my handbag up my shoulder, feeling overdressed in my trouser suit next to this perky PE teacher in a polo shirt, a whistle looped around his neck.

'Oh, I…' Mr Mitchell's mouth opened a little wider and he looked down at my daughter as if she would provide the answer.

She was grinning up at him, an eager expression on her face.

'Mr Mitchell's not married either, Mummy,' she burst out.

'Oh… I…' Poor Mr Mitchell turned crimson, the blush spreading immediately up his neck.

I stifled a horrified laugh and pressed my lips together. 'How nice,' I said.

My daughter looked from me to Mr Mitchell and back again.

'Well, I best be getting this one home,' I said in a faux cheery voice. 'Lovely to meet you, Mr Mitchell.'

He started mumbling and pointing with his whistle.

'I asked him,' my daughter insisted as I pulled on her hand – she was not willing to go. 'Mummy, you could marry him,' she said, as she dug in her heels. She was surprisingly strong. 'You're hurting my arm.'

'Sorry.' I eased up, keen to get away before this got any worse. A bright idea struck me, 'Let's go and get a Slushie.'

She left without a backwards glance.

Chapter 13

It didn't take long for them to reach her hairdresser's and she was so grateful to Nina for quickly disguising her surprise with a beaming smile as she stepped forward.

'Maria, how can we help?'

'I was wondering,' Maria asked, 'whether you had a spare appointment?'

Nina checked the diary by the till, 'Mandy's got a slot in fifteen minutes if you don't mind waiting?'

'It's not for me actually,' Maria said shyly, feeling a little silly.

'It's for this mop,' Keith interrupted, saving her the explanation.

Nina's eyebrows disappeared beneath her thick brown fringe and then her expression settled. 'Well, Mandy is quite the expert with mops,' she said, causing Keith to let out one of his chuckles. 'Take a seat. Can I get you both a drink? Tea, coffee, juice?'

'No, that's alright, love – Maria saw me right.'

'A tea, if it's not too much trouble,' Maria said, moving to the squishy leather bench by the door.

'Of course, and there are magazines for your perusal,' Nina said.

'Ah good!' Keith brought his hands together. 'I do like to keep up with my celebrity gossip.'

Nina laughed as she turned. 'I'll go and tell Mandy she's got you next.'

Keith picked up one of the magazines on the table in front of them and did seem to enjoy looking at the glossy photographs, lingering in particular over the recipe pages at the back. Maria felt a flash of guilt. He must be starving, the way he was devouring that photograph of a mushroom risotto with his eyes. He looked up at her, a smile on his face.

'Needs more Parmesan,' he said, surprising her into silence, before returning the magazine to the pile.

Maria could see why Albie had liked Keith – he had the same easy manner, the same desire to make light of things. She had always taken everything very seriously and was grateful to be around someone who seemed able to laugh at it all. That was what Albie had done every Thursday, taught her that the world didn't have to be as serious as it seemed in her mind. But then Albie didn't carry around the same burden she had lived with. A gloom descended over her and she was relieved to see Mandy standing before them.

'Maria, how lovely! I hear you have brought someone with you?'

Keith stood up, his hands behind his back, as Mandy appeared to be inspecting him, a long look from his feet to his face.

'Well, you're a bit of a state,' she announced finally, her nose crinkling, one long pink talon tapping her teeth.

Maria sucked in her breath but fortunately, Keith burst out his bark of laughter. 'I was going for a devil-may-care vibe,' he said, removing his cap and holding it in his hands.

'Well, it is certainly something. Shall we go and fix it?' she said, holding out a black gown that Keith attempted to wear as a coat. 'Oh, for goodness sake,' Mandy tutted, removing it. 'I see I'll have to do everything.' She fussed around him, forcing his arms in and standing on tiptoes, tying a bow at his neck.

Keith followed Mandy in like an obedient child as she sashayed into the salon and deposited him in front of a large mirror.

'I'll wait here,' Maria called.

'Don't be silly, this was your great plan, get in here!' said Keith.

Mandy drew up a black stool and beckoned to Maria. 'Come and see me work my magic on someone else. It's good to see you again, Maria,' she said and her magenta lips flashed her a smile.

'It is, I'm...' Maria took a breath, ashamed to remember how she had behaved on her last visit. 'I'm sorry about before, I was... a bit...'

'You weren't yourself,' Mandy replied in a firm voice. 'Everyone's allowed a shitty day and I've had a decade of you being wonderful so please don't say another word or I'll hit you with my paddle brush.'

Wonderful, Maria reflected, feeling her body glow with the compliment. Keith didn't say a word, just looked between the two women, most likely wondering what on earth was going on.

Nina returned with a teacup. 'Thank you,' Maria said in a grateful voice.

'Nice to see you,' Nina replied before slinking away.

Maria settled on the stool with her tea, noticing a woman with a blonde beehive and a fake tanned face glancing across at them. Normally, Maria would have worried what she thought but now she rolled her shoulders back, proud to be seen with Keith, feeling Albie standing at her side.

'So!' Mandy said, talking to Keith in the mirror as she picked up strands of his hair, 'We'll get you shampooed and you can have our new conditioning treatment, which should do wonders. You've got a lovely colour hair, you know – they'll be no need to use any dye.'

'Steady on,' Keith said, two hands placed over his head, 'just a haircut, woman! I'm not here to have my hair turned black, I'm quite happy with my greys – says I've lived.'

Mandy smirked at him. 'As you say, sir. Now, follow me, you can tell him all about it.' She led him off to the row of basins, where Maria could hear them chatting, the conversation punctuated by Keith's low chuckle. Maria reflected that she didn't think she'd seen Mandy smile that widely in all her visits to the salon.

It was a lovely hour, the salon warm, Mandy and Nina exchanging banter with Keith, other customers chiming in, the low sound of the radio in the background, a lady opposite in rollers reading a magazine, a gentleman getting a trim next door. Maria felt cocooned in the safety of others busy and bustling around her and lost herself in the moment. It was a second before she realised Mandy was calling her name.

'You ready for the big unveiling?' she asked.

She had placed a tea towel on Keith's head and he looked like a rather stroppy shepherd. 'Is this quite necessary?' he asked, but he couldn't stop the smile twitching on his face.

'We're going for drama, Keith,' Mandy insisted, picking up two combs and beating with a makeshift drumroll on the back of his aluminium chair. 'Ready? I give you your brand-new look!' she announced as she whipped the tea towel from his head.

Maria couldn't help the gasp that left her mouth.

Keith was completely transformed. Gone was the long brown hair replaced by a slick, modern look: short sides, a fuller fringe, soft grey at the temples. The hairstyle was perfect, his face brought into sharp focus, the stubble on his cheeks now there by design.

'You did look like Leonardo DiCaprio in that film where he gets eaten by a wolf, but now you're Leo in *The Wolf of Wall Street*.'

'And that's good, is it?' Keith asked with a laugh, turning his head to the side and checking out the back.

'Very good, you're a darker, swarthier version of him with even better hair,' Mandy said, standing back, her pink taloned fingers placed on her hips.

'Alright, don't get yourself carried away!'

Mandy hit him on the shoulder with her comb as Keith twisted left and right once more, taking in his reflection.

'You've certainly done a good job,' he admitted, spinning round to look at Maria. 'What do you think?'

Maria found herself nodding enthusiastically. 'You look, you look brilliant,' she said, surprising herself with the confidence in her voice: *look at you, Maria, appraising men's hairstyles!*

'Albie would have liked it, you think?' he asked, turning his head from side to side.

'Albert? You mean Maria's mysterious gentlemen friend,' Mandy cooed, an elbow in Maria's side.

Both their faces must have betrayed them as, after a loaded pause, Mandy's hand flew to her mouth. 'Has something happened?' she asked.

Maria nodded slowly, as Keith confirmed, 'Albie died,' in a gruff voice, saving Maria the pain of repeating it.

Mandy's hand fell, her mouth hanging open in a horrified circle. 'Oh, you poor, poor thing!' she said, immediately enfolding Maria in a hug, her enormous bosom crushing into her back. She smelt of cigarettes and coffee and hairspray, but Maria was grateful for the warm reaction, for the arms encircling her. She couldn't remember the last time someone had hugged her like that, and she wanted to cling on.

'Oh, I'm really sorry, Maria, I know he was a special man.'

'Thank you, he was,' she said, giving Mandy an awkward pat.

'Well, I'm always here if you want to talk,' Mandy replied, drawing back. 'You're not any old customer, Maria, you know, we've been worried about you these past couple of weeks.'

'You're kind,' Maria said, her toes curling with embarrassment. She hadn't realised anyone would notice that she hadn't been herself – she'd always felt invisible.

'Nonsense! You've always been a brilliant listener, always asking, caring. Someone needs to take care of you for once.'

'Hear, hear, and I've only known you two minutes!' Keith grinned.

'Sounds like this Albie's brought you two into each other's lives,' Mandy said, glancing at them both in the mirror. 'That should be a bit of a comfort, I expect.'

The idea gave Maria a jolt: the thought that without Albie's death she might never have met Keith, that things were happening to her – good things – because he had died. It was hard to get her head around.

'Not sure Albie would have seen it like that, he wasn't one for signs or the such-like,' Keith added. 'I remember one time, it was absolutely chucking it down and Albie took me for a pub lunch. Well, we were a few ales down and Albie's eyes had started crossing and I'd told him that the universe had brought us together, the rain forcing us inside, or some kind of hocus pocus and he'd roared with laughter – he had this big rumbling laugh – and he just told me that he was pretty sure God wouldn't have wanted us to go into a pub with sticky tables and a broken toilet.'

Maria felt her face split into a wide smile. That sounded just like Albie. How lovely to hear more stories about him, how she craved them now he was gone.

'God, he could be funny,' Keith said, wiping his eyes. 'He was a pretty special man.' A cough then to disguise the catch in his voice.

'Very,' Maria agreed.

'Can't believe he's gone,' Keith said quietly, his new short hair making him look more boyish, vulnerable, as he met Maria's eyes.

'Me either.' She stood slowly from her seat, 'I think I better go and pay before you set me off.'

Keith nodded, perhaps relieved when Mandy ruffled his hair and commented, 'I'll just use some product, it's got sea salt in it...'

Maria headed to the till, leaving the two of them pretending to be reading the price list as she heard them laugh and tease, needing a moment with just her thoughts. It had been a strange day, telling people about Albie, realising that she had been carrying around the knowledge on her own, relieved to have said it aloud, shared it.

Mandy gave a throaty laugh and Maria glanced back over to them, wondering if talking to people in the mirror made it easier for her, a sort of version of avoiding eye contact, the protection of a mirror and her role as a professional helping her to open up. Or whether Mandy just found it easier to make connections. Maria marvelled at it, Albie had had that skill in spades.

'Come on, Keith,' she called, trying to be that person for a moment, testing it out on herself, 'I want to show you off.'

She paid, realising this was the first money she'd used that was Albie's, and felt a flush of pleasure. It did feel good to help people out in these small ways. She wanted to ride the wave and she found herself fussing over Keith in the street, trying to persuade him into a shopping trip. He relented outside a charity shop around the corner and found a T-shirt, a jumper and a suede duffel coat with a fake fur lining, padded for warmth. He left with a carrier bag of his old clothes and she insisted on adding it to her launderette pile on Wednesday.

'I'll get them back to you,' she said, trying not to turn her nose up at the sad state of the clothes inside. 'And now you look so smart, how about we grab a bite?'

Keith held both his hands up. 'As long as you promise nothing too fancy, no Michelin stars... You millionaires... Can't be trusted, you know.'

She could tell from the lightness in his voice that he was enjoying his day, both of them doing something for the man they had loved and admired.

'Jacket potato and cheese?' Maria said, knowing exactly where to take him.

'Perfect.'

'I know just the place.'

The café was empty, an elderly couple just putting on their coats to leave. Pauline was wiping at the tables and glanced up as Maria pushed inside, her shoulders back as she introduced Keith.

'Table for two!' Maria couldn't keep the hint of joy from her voice – it seemed wrong to sit alone in this café where she had spent so many happy afternoons.

She could tell that Pauline was itching to find out who this man, this good-looking, younger man by at least twenty years, was, meeting her eye as she fetched her pad and pencil, a waggle of her eyebrows as she headed over to their table. What did she think? That Maria had a toy boy? What did they call women with younger men? Some kind of jungle cat? A cheetah! Ha, that was her! Maria felt herself bubble with a delighted giggle at the preposterous prospect.

'Pauline, this is Keith, a new friend. We both knew Albie.'

'Knew?'

It was then that she realised she would have to tell the third person that day. She lifted her chin, took a slow breath.

'He died… Albie died. Two weeks ago. I'm sorry I didn't say anything before, I just… well, I didn't know how.'

Pauline blinked, wiped at her fringe, ash blonde tendrils sticking to her temples from the steam of the kitchen. 'Oh… Oh, how sad. I was worried. We did comment, seeing you of course – he never liked keeping you waiting…'

Maria nodded sadly. How true that was: Albie, forever the gentleman, horrified if he was more than a minute late.

'…He was such a wonderful man.'

'He was,' she agreed in a quiet voice.

'He always asked after my grandchildren, my health, all of that. Always listened to the answers, remembered the details. There ain't a lot of people do that, you know?'

Maria nodded, her good mood ebbing away with the reminder of what they had all lost.

Pauline couldn't seem to stop, clearly needing to remember more: 'There was one time I'd got a hacking cough, one of those stubborn ones you can't shift, and he'd appeared the next day with a cough syrup, just placed it on the counter with no comment. It was so thoughtful.' Her eyes filled with tears. 'What a shame, a real shame! Sorry, look at me goin' on. You sit down and welcome, Keith, a pleasure to meet you.'

'Thank you.' Keith placed a gentle hand on Maria's shoulder and steered her to a table. She was grateful that he was taking control, floored for a moment by another memory of Albie, 'He'd be so pleased you sorted me out, Maria. He was always on at me and look at me now.'

Maria looked up at Keith, at this transformed figure in fresh clothes, a designer haircut and stubble, and a smile on his handsome face. With a start she realised what an outward change he had undergone in just a few short hours. All thanks to Albie – and *her*.

Pauline followed them over to the table, handing them a menu. 'You order what you like on the house. For Albert.'

Maria felt grateful tears spring up. She had felt more emotions in one day than in the last year of her life. Albie's death had triggered so much. To think she would normally be sat in her apartment on her own with only a launderette visit to break up the monotony.

They ordered lunch and Maria found herself pushing the food around the plate as Keith told her stories about Albie, and she learnt more about the man she had so admired.

Pauline joined them at the table, plates of carrot cake set down in front of them. 'Fresh today,' she explained, handing Maria a fork.

Keith sipped at his cappuccino, taking a forkful of cake. 'Wow!' he said, a hand covering his mouth. He swallowed, looking at Pauline. 'This is the best carrot cake I've had in a long time. I always thought a soft cheese topping was compulsory but just a drizzle of lemon and a sprinkle of demerara really works.'

Pauline raised a neat eyebrow at him. 'You sound like you know your baking.'

Keith shifted in his chair, his voice lower, a hand lifted to rake through his hair, before stopping once he realised the long strands had gone. 'I used to work in a restaurant in London. A long time ago now.' He looked up at her with solemn brown eyes.

'London, eh?'

Keith's eyes slid away from them both as Pauline sat back in her chair. 'And what do you do now then?'

Maria gave Keith a panicked look. What would he say? He seemed such a different person from the man huddled in the doorway only a few hours before – would he want to hold onto this illusion a little longer?

'He's currently seeking employment,' Maria interjected, biting her lip and hoping Keith wouldn't mind.

He gave her a relieved smile and Maria returned it.

'That's right, I'm looking. It's been… a bit difficult.'

'I'm sorry to hear that,' Pauline said, distracted by the sound of the bell, a group of women pushing inside, one on a mobile, one with a baby in a sling, another chatting to a friend. The small space was suddenly filled with noise, discussions of where to sit, scraping of chairs, laughter. Pauline left to help them and it seemed the spell of the last hour or so was broken.

'Right,' said Keith, placing his palms flat on the table in front of him. 'Well… Thank you for everything, Maria. I'm so pleased you found that list, that we met. Albie was right about you.'

She was too shy to ask exactly how and too sad to find the words back. She felt the energy she had needed to face the day leaking away, and there was only ever a limited supply these days.

Keith picked up his carrier bag and went to say goodbye to Pauline. Then he returned and before she could fret or worry what to do next, he reached out and with one arm pulled her into a hug. 'Thank you,' he whispered.

'It's nothing,' she mumbled into the suede of his new coat, alarmed to see a tear stain as she pulled away. She was like a full-on waterworks these days. Albie's death had opened up this well of unshed tears.

Keith left quickly and she felt her heart lurch as she watched him walk past the glass of the café, a hand wiping at his face. He had loved Albie too.

She waved a goodbye to Pauline, left a generous tip, knowing Albie would have done just the same. Then she pushed back outside and headed home, alone.

• *Pay for him to get a haircut* ✓

*

We had headed up to London, her first trip there, and the start of a love affair with the place. The top deck of a double-decker bus, her tiny face, one large open mouth as we moved through busy streets, out along the sparkling Thames, the Houses of Parliament, Big Ben… these familiar landmarks she had only ever seen in books. Right here in front of her. I loved listening to her commentary.

Off to the Tower of London to see Beefeaters and look at the dungeons, admire the Crown Jewels. She had been convinced she would meet the Queen – 'If the flag is up, she's at home' – and had looked at me appalled when I had admitted that might not happen. 'But she lives there,' she had stressed as if the Queen was simply waiting for her. She had even brought the Polaroid camera so that we could take a photo with her.

We had eaten at a restaurant cloudy with smoke, bouncing on her chair as I tried to distract her with her new Magna Doodle. She could spend hours at home drawing and sliding the little bar along, but today it held no interest, wanting to keep going, keep seeing everything.

'London is huge,' she had said, eyes round.

I could see the future, a girl bright with energy desperate to explore. London was huge and suddenly in that moment I just wanted to be at home with her, listening to one of her favourite stories on the cassette player and plaiting her hair. I didn't want her to know about this big, wide world yet – I loved our world together in Brighton, just us.

Chapter 14

She'd never been to Devon, so she had booked a room in a B&B in Barnstaple for the night before to be fresh in the morning. Sitting in a small downstairs room for breakfast, just one other solitary guest shaking cornflakes from a box, she tried to imagine what he would be like, the man who had saved Albie's life. It was this thought that had driven her to pick up her landline, search for Timothy's name, track him down to the furthest reaches of Devon. Curiosity had given her the confidence she needed. This trip spanning half the country had been the furthest she had ventured in more than thirty-six years.

The bus was leaving in less than an hour and she wanted to finish her breakfast and make herself presentable, her stomach leaping at the thought of meeting a perfect stranger. She wanted to make a good impression.

She had tried not to think of Albie's other request, convincing herself it was a different beach, a different sea. Still, the thought of all that water, the sight of the horizon in the distance, made her hairline bead with sweat, her palms damp. She pushed unpleasant thoughts to the back of her mind and tried to focus on what she had to do: meet Timothy, thank him for saving Albie. Maria thought she might burst with the intrigue: what had happened?

Timothy had hinted at his lack of mobility on the telephone and when she arrived off the bus in the heart of Lynmouth, he was already waiting in his wheelchair by the drop-off point. He had combed-back steel-grey hair, a long face and deep lines around a generous mouth. He was sitting impossibly straight in the chair, chin jutted upwards, meeting her gaze.

'Maria,' he said, his voice booming across the space.

She stuck out a hand, immediately tongue-tied.

'Would you mind giving me a steer?'

He directed her along the pavement crossing a babbling river, water coursing between stones and boulders, a line of deckchairs stacked on a grassy verge beneath them.

'Hardly any tourists at the moment. Thought I could show you what Lynmouth has to offer.'

Maria was happy to be pushing him from behind, feeling more able to chat to a stranger without the intensity of eye contact. She found herself relaxing as they moved past shops selling trinkets, fudge, buckets and spades. Gulls screeched overhead, swooping across the sky thick with clouds. A large plastic ice-cream cone almost blocked their path and Timothy was nearly deposited in the road as Maria navigated round it.

'Nice driving,' he chuckled as she just kept him on the pavement. 'I thought we could head down to the beach further along here. It's out of season so always a lot nicer and dogs are allowed on it. I like to live vicariously through other people's pets since Monty, my Labrador, died last year.'

'Oh...' Maria stopped short. *The beach.* She felt her scalp prickle, gripped the back of the wheelchair, her knuckles turning white. 'If it isn't a problem, I was rather hoping we could stay inside. I'm quite spoilt for beaches.' She laughed, trying to make light of her unusual request, glad he wasn't looking directly at her.

'Brighton,' Timothy said, not missing a beat, 'I should have thought.' He swiped a hand through his hair, angling his head to the side to speak to her. 'Of course, we can go to a café in Lynton, an excuse to ride the Cliff Railway at least. They do excellent cream teas, if you like that, Maria.'

She felt a swell of relief course through her, that he had been so easily distracted and hadn't picked up on her nerves, or her desire to change his plan.

'That sounds wonderful, a proper Devonian cream tea.'

'We can fight over which comes first on the scones, the cream or the jam,' Timothy said in his booming voice. 'It's the cream obviously but some foreign folks are strange.'

Maria laughed, happy at how easily the conversation was flowing. 'I'm not here to start an argument, cream it is.'

'Excellent!' He clapped, making her jump, and pointed in the opposite direction. 'Steer on, we need to go left here,' he called out from in front of her, 'towards the harbour. See that pub, The Rising Sun? It's just around the corner there.'

Maria directed them over a bridge further along the river, skirting a harbour crammed with fishing boats tilted at an angle on the mud at low tide. Seaweed clung to the walls and the smell of salt hit her hard. She tried not to breathe it in, focused on pushing Timothy, distracting herself with a string of questions about the village.

Don't think about it, don't think about it.

'Oh, for years now… there was a flood in the fifties… busy in the summer… used to be a shop that sold the best pasties…'

Passing the pub, they rounded the corner, Maria's eyes firmly in front of her, aware of the sea to her right, grey and forbidding. In the distance across the water lay Wales, as Timothy was pointing out.

She nodded and sped up, pushing him along the road and past an information centre, glad of his running commentary.

Don't think about it, don't think about it.

They stopped at the bottom of a cliff face, a strip gouged out, tracks running up the length of it. A green carriage was ascending slowly, as one was descending from the top, cables working on some kind of pulley system.

'They're powered by water.' Timothy pointed to the lower green carriage, where water cascaded out of the bottom, as Maria craned her neck to see a second carriage.

'Two cars attached to each other. Once the top one becomes heavier, it starts to descend and the bottom one goes up. It's unique – well, there's one in Portugal but we don't like to shout about that.'

He paid for two tickets from the booth and they waited, the first passengers for the next trip up.

'How clever,' Maria said, marvelling at the engineering, staring at the passengers out on the small balcony of the carriage as they moved slowly to the bottom of the cliff face. A bell clanged and they filed out, Maria steering Timothy onto the empty car.

It filled up and they started to move up once the doors closed, the sound of the water gushing from below, the cables cranking as they rose higher. Looking out through the glass windows, she could make out the stretch of dull sky, cliffs opposite, cars winding around the road that seemed to cling to its side. The village was lost somewhere below them, its roofs and streets insignificant from this height. Maria was glad to arrive at the top and push Timothy out, her stomach lurching.

He directed her to a café on the high street, opposite a hall that was running a market to raise money for the RSPB.

'Shall we pop inside?' he suggested, pointing to the building. 'They have an excellent second-hand book section in there and I rarely come up here…'

'Of course,' Maria said, glad to be on the move, doing something. Timothy was more forthright than Albie, so she couldn't make too many excuses.

The hall was full and scattered with tables crammed with jewellery, scarves, pottery, locally made honey, cheeses and more. People manned stalls, some on stools, others standing. They moved their way around, Maria glancing up at the wooden stage at the back of the hall, realising there was no way of them getting the chair up the small stairs.

'It must be frustrating,' she remarked, knowing Timothy was looking over at a high-up stall that sold walking sticks, tweed hats and wellington boots.

'At times,' he said, cheerfully distracting her with a stall offering free chunks of tablet fudge to passers-by. They bought a bag each, the sweet, indulgent taste filling Maria's mouth.

'What a treat!' she said as she pushed Timothy out through a side door and into the second-hand books section. The smell of dust and air freshener mingled as they entered the labyrinth of shelves, browsing the titles and remarking on those in front of them.

'I used to talk to Albie about books. He loved thrillers and books set in World War Two…'

'He was a reader?' Timothy asked, his voice raised in surprise.

'Oh yes! We shared a similar taste in books,' she said, wondering whether that was strictly true. Certainly, she devoured every book he suggested, wanting always to share in the experience with him, swap thoughts, soak up *his* thoughts.

'Surprises me. The Albert I knew couldn't sit still long enough to read a book – I was always trying to civilise him.'

'Well, I suppose the older one gets…'

Maria thought back to when she was younger, in that other world she tried not to mull on too much, when she had been a keen tennis player, in between rushing from meetings to events to networking parties to home. That had all ended after that day… She had lost her taste for tennis, knowing her partners and opposition might have heard what had happened, that she might be forced to let them into her life – and the heartbreak that governed it. She had taken up running instead, sometimes out for hours pounding the streets in any weather, running to try and force her mind blank. Then one day she had stopped doing even that, she hadn't run for years.

'Maria… Maria?'

She realised Timothy had been trying to get her attention for some time.

'I'm sorry, I was somewhere else.' She blushed.

'Shall we head off and have that tea? I know you don't have too long…'

The café was on a corner of two roads, two enormous glass-fronted windows making the place light and airy, even on the dreary day. Seaside prints lined the walls in bright turquoise, yellows and greens, and Maria's eyes slid past them, not wanting to think about that today. A waitress in a black peaked cap ambled over to take their order and move a chair out of the space Timothy needed.

'Thank you, thank you,' he said in a hearty voice, clearly trying to put her at her ease. How frustrating it must be to have to constantly ask for furniture or things to be moved simply so you could sit down like any other person.

The cream teas arrived, small pots piled high with delicious, thick-looking cream, others with bright red jam packed with strawberries. The dough was warm to the touch as Maria sliced it open and laughed as Timothy watched her.

'I remember what you said,' she said, reaching for the cream and allowing him to relax.

'Excellent, excellent.'

'Wow, these are good,' she said between mouthfuls, hand over her mouth so she didn't spray crumbs. The cream smooth, the jam sweet, the scone warm.

'These would be my last meal,' Timothy agreed, loading his up so that Maria thought the whole thing might topple. 'You can never have too much clotted cream.'

A companionable silence descended as they ate, the room filling up with other people, a clash of delicious smells – bread, cheese, herbs – wafting from the kitchen at the back.

A man of similar age arrived and made his way over to the table, greeting Timothy warmly. *A local firmly at home*, she thought as he roared with laughter and the promise to meet soon.

'Used to play squash with him, good man,' Timothy said by way of explanation.

'How long have you had to use a wheelchair?' Maria asked, realising for an active person the limitations must be tiring.

Timothy patted the right wheel. 'A year or so now. I was struggling to get around – denial, I suppose – and then I realised I had stopped leaving the house, which wouldn't do at all.'

'Has it changed things?'

Timothy thought for a moment, his gaze steady. 'You learn to ask people for help more. It's made me a little nicer perhaps.' He chuckled as he forked his chip. 'Worried if I'm not, people will stop pushing me around.'

'I'm sure not,' Maria laughed.

'I don't like being on a different level though, people talking over you like you're a child.' His expression changed, his mouth turning down as he spoke.

Maria didn't know what to say, appreciated her own luck, no need for a replacement hip or a walking stick. She hadn't done enough in her life to warrant getting things replaced; she hadn't done nearly enough. She had a thought then – Albie had wanted them to donate to a charity, perhaps Timothy would be keen to donate money to a cause that would help the disabled?

'It's why it's nice to be sat opposite you now,' he said, popping the last of his scone in his mouth.

'And tell me more about how you knew Albie,' Maria said, keen to change the subject to cheerier things – and keen to know more about her dear friend.

'Albie was my best friend at university in Exeter. He used to come and stay in the summer here, worked at The Rising Sun for a while in fact, but we lost touch soon after we started work.'

'A falling-out?' Maria asked, after swallowing.

'No, nothing like that,' Timothy said, shaking his head. 'I worked abroad for years and we were both pretty hopeless pen pals. This was before email and Facebook, of course. My granddaughters are always talking about FaceTime. They go to another country and call you as if they're in the room next door. But I thought of him often, wondered what he was up to. I heard he never married…'

An eyebrow was raised in question and Maria felt a little warm, one hand covering the other, 'No… no, he never did marry.'

For a second a name flitted across her mind: Cathie. Who was the mystery woman? Had Albie planned to marry her?

She realised with a slow horror that she could feel tears build within her. She mustn't cry in front of Timothy. She coughed and covered her hand with the other one. 'I found this list,' she said suddenly, 'I think I mentioned it on the phone, let me show you.'

Reaching into her handbag, she could feel herself return to normal, focusing on the reason she had come. *For Albie.* She smoothed out the sheet of paper and handed it across the table.

Timothy patted his mouth with a linen napkin and took it from her.

• *Find him and thank him for saving my life*

'Oh, for goodness sake.' Timothy lowered the list, rolled his eyes at her. 'Anyone would have done the same. I'm no hero.'

'Well, Albie clearly thought you were,' Maria said with a small smile.

'He was terribly embarrassed about it at the time, I suppose it was rather hairy.'

'So what happened?' she asked, pouring him a top-up of tea from the pot.

'We'd been drinking – a few beers at lunch, you know the way, we were students with time to kill.'

'I can imagine,' said Maria, fondly imagining a younger Albie, cocksure and tanned in a pub in Devon.

'Well, the wind was up and Albert had recently believed himself to be quite the proficient surfer. He'd been swanning about that summer, working in the pub and going out any chance he could. Most people don't tend to surf in Lynmouth, they head down to Croyde, Woolacombe, those places. Anyway, the waves were looking pretty dicey that day and Albert was gripped with the desire to get out there. He tried to convinced me too but I was having none of it, beer going to my head, said I'd walk with him and watch for a while...'

A beach. Surfing. The ocean. Maria clutched the handle of her teacup as her head span and tried to focus on his words.

'Well, I went along and he was doing well. It was choppy and fairly wild but he was up and looking pretty good, then before I knew it, everything changed...'

She tried not to imagine him in the water, on a surfboard, young, unaware of the dangers, the waves crashing over him. The waitress walked by and Maria wanted to grab her and say something, stop this story in its tracks.

'...One minute he was up, the next he had fallen and disappeared beneath the waves. I'd seen the board shoot up and realised it might have hit him.'

Albie trapped under the waves, breathless, in trouble... The tea was bitter in her mouth.

'Well, he didn't surface and I didn't think he was just messing about, and I realised then I was practically seeing double, the alcohol catching up with me, so I rushed in after him, shoes and all, didn't want him drowning.'

Maria felt the room swim in front of her as she lowered the cup with a shaking hand, rattling as it hit the saucer.

'So you see, not so much a hero as a drunken, overconfident fool...' Timothy seemed to notice Maria's blanched face and stopped. 'Are you alright?'

'It's just rather warm in here,' she said, placing one hand over the other in a rhythm. She thought then of a way to move their talk away.

'Albie wanted us to donate to a charity – it was on his list,' she added in a quick rattle. 'I was hoping you would be able to suggest one?'

She didn't want to think about Albie in trouble under the water – she couldn't.

If Timothy was surprised by the sudden shift in conversation he didn't show it, simply screwing up his forehead as he thought. 'Well, I know around here, the RNLI has done some excellent work and is always needing funds.'

The Royal National Lifeboat Institution: saving lives at sea. Maria swallowed. 'Excellent, well that's settled,' she said, her bright voice belying the nauseous swirling in her stomach. 'Look, they have board games in here, do you play them?'

Timothy glanced to where she indicated. 'No, I haven't tried them, but look, they've got Scrabble, I see. My granddaughters have got me playing it on my mobile and they swap messages with me on there, it's rather sweet. Look…'

He pulled out his phone and tapped in some digits. The screen was filled with a jumble of letters like a mini Scrabble board.

'I'm currently winning by over 50 points. I managed to get the X onto a triple letter tile and you know what that means!' He waggled his eyebrows, which made Maria feel lighter.

'The youngest one has a pretty good vocabulary but she's a terrible cheat…'

He beckoned the waitress over and asked her to fetch the board, ordering them another pot of tea too. Maria felt her shoulders relax as the past topic faded away, the awful images of the sea ebbing away with it.

'Got to stay hydrated if I'm going to be on my best form,' Timothy said, tapping the side of his head.

The game was a wonderful idea, the conversation flowing naturally, punctuated by exclamations of frustration or cryptic sentences: 'Oh, I seem to have every vowel going!', 'Are you allowed "e.g." as a two-letter word?' Maria felt herself sink backwards into the comfortable leather seat, the room thinning out as they played on.

Timothy was enthusiastically telling her stories from his university days with a twinkle in his eye – 'Albert was always a terrible liar and would appear at seminars first thing, dressed in whatever he had been wearing the evening before, and would bang on and on to the tutor about car trouble when everyone knew the halls of residence were less than a five-minute walk away.'

She laughed along, enjoying hearing about a younger Albie, an Albert who drunk ale in the daytime, took up hobbies every month, stayed up late, trying to get Timothy to appreciate jazz. He wore a burgundy beret for a time and smoked rolled-up cigarettes and that image made her clutch her sides.

'He would speak in a French accent to women, it was horrifying.'

Maria laughed at the image but couldn't help a niggling question spilling out of her as she dabbed at her mouth with a napkin.

'Did Albie ever mention anyone called Cathie?'

Timothy sat back in his chair, brow furrowed, eyes moving left to right as if scrolling through a selection of images. Maria felt all the breath suspended in her body. Cathie who Albie had wanted to take to Paris. Was she about to have her answer? Did she want it? For a second, she wished she could cram the words back in her mouth, stop time so that she could stay in this blissful ignorance a moment longer.

'I can't recall anyone of that name,' he said finally, throwing an apologetic look back at Maria. 'I'm sorry, I'm pretty hopeless with names.'

Maria felt her shoulders drop, the tension leaving her body in one breath. 'Oh no – no, it wasn't important.' Perhaps Cathie wasn't the great love she had imagined if Albie's best friend had never heard of her? She realised she was hoping.

'Your turn, Maria. Maria…?'

'Oh, I'm sorry, I was somewhere else.'

Timothy had a wonderful energy that filled the small space and she could well imagine him rabble-rousing with Albie. His voice, louder, brasher still, contained a twang of the West Country and it made her heart ache to be reminded of the connection: how she missed Albie's voice, his infectious chuckle.

The time flew by and suddenly they were heading back down on the Clifftop Railway, watching as Lynmouth came into view: the rooftops huddled together, the snaking river slicing through the streets, boats dotted in the harbour. The bus was a few minutes late and Maria suddenly stood self-conscious again, wondering how to say goodbye.

But Timothy made it easy, holding out two arms so that she could give him a hug. 'You get yourself a mobile so we can play on that Scrabble app I showed you. I absolutely insist on a re-match,' he said, giving her a warm smile.

'I will,' she promised, knowing then that she would keep her word. She wanted to keep up this connection, this other link to Albie. 'Although it was quite a drubbing,' she added, gratified to hear his bellowing laugh.

The bus sighed next to her, the doors opening with a hiss, and Maria moved away, one hand on the railing to steady herself. After showing the driver her ticket, she moved down the aisle, sliding into a seat by the window. There was only one other passenger heading back to Barnstaple too and the bus was soon moving away from the kerb. Timothy raised one hand in greeting, chin jutting out proudly once more as he spun around and wheeled slowly back up the road.

She put a palm up to the glass, cold on her hand, as they climbed the twisting road out of the village. Who would have thought her meetings with Albie would land her here, making new friends, seeing new places and at her age too? It was Wednesday – she should have gone to the launderette, watched her clothes spinning in the machine. She closed her eyes and rested her head back on the seat. Who cares, she thought, filled with scones, tea and spent laughter, I can do that any old time.

*

I was sat in the front row, more nervous than I think I had ever been before. I'd done everything I could to be there. My boss had been a nightmare about it and I didn't want to anger her, but I wouldn't have missed this for the world. Her first play! And there was no one else, only me, and I couldn't let her down.

Women like me didn't all work but I loved my job, loved my freedom. And I wanted to show my little girl that women could be independent, driven, passionate about what they do.

God, my little girl. The thought made my palms clammier. Would she get it right? Would she freeze? I imagined her terrified and alone somewhere nearby, filled with nerves – it made her own heart ache.

The music started up, the clang, clang of a slightly out-of-tune upright piano, and there was a general hush in the audience. The seat next to me was free and I put my handbag on it and tried not to bite my nails.

Oh god, would she forget her lines? Would she…? There she was!

I felt my bottom clench tightly on the seat as my tiny daughter edged onto the stage. She was dressed as an enormous oversized pumpkin, her little green hat all squiffy, her thin arms poking out of the sides of her round orange body.

'Once upon a time there was a wood...'

There was a hush as she seemed to tail away and I realised she was staring at the front row seats, staring straight at me.

'Mummmmmmeeeee, you came!'

Laughter rippled round the room and I nodded, embarrassed, not wanting to say anything. She wasn't quitting: 'Did your stupid boss let you out then?'

Louder laughter and now I was hoping the floor would open up and swallow me whole. Oh god, she must have heard me being rude about Karen on the phone to Lucy.

'Mummmmmmeeeee, I'm in the play!'

My five-year-old daughter continued to chirrup away to me from the stage, her desperate teacher standing helplessly in the wings, holding back a banana and an apple who were waiting to go onstage for their lines.

Chapter 15

Lynmouth had been wonderful, an escape to a different world, an unexpected little bubble away from her life. Discovering more about Albie, or Albert as Timothy had known him, felt brilliant and devastating in equal measure. How could she not tease him about the things she'd been told? Not see his face break into that wide smile as she explained how she had tracked down Timothy, got back in touch. Working through this list seemed bittersweet, making her feel close to Albie and at the same time moving her further away, creating new experiences he wasn't around for.

Then there was this other figure from his past: Cathie. Timothy hadn't known her, what did that mean? Maria knew she had been avoiding contacting Cathie. A large part of her could fool herself into thinking that Albie had cared only for her – what if meeting Cathie finally extinguished that hope?

She had an address, it was part of the pack the solicitor had given her. She couldn't avoid this moment forever. She wrote a brief letter, introducing herself and her connection to Cathie and asking to arrange a meeting. As she licked the envelope closed, the glue wasn't the only ugly taste in her mouth: was she about to change everything?

Suddenly exhausted, she decided to take a soothing bath. But as she lay trying to relax, the water cooling, she could barely summon the energy to hold onto the bars and get herself out. Waves of grief struck her at the strangest moments. This morning she had been thrown when she had turned the last page of her book – a book Albie had recommended, a novel set in 1940s Cornwall – and somehow the fact she had finished it, and couldn't even discuss it with him, made her realise that life was just marching on without him. That books were being read, television shows being watched, people were moving on with their lives and Albie was one step further back in the past. Her heart ached thinking about it.

Staring at the list again, she realised she was simply re-reading the last lines: the lines under her own name. She felt a familiar lurch in her stomach as she thought of his suggestions, knowing she wasn't ready, might never be ready. But she knew she needed to clear out Albie's things.

She couldn't shift her mood as she closed the apartment door behind her, her tote bag scrunched up in her hand.

'Crap!'

Maria's hand froze on the door handle. Someone was huffing and swearing somewhere below.

'Shit!'

Maria bit her lip, not wanting to interact, just wanting to get out, buy some things and scuttle back to the safety and quiet of her apartment.

'Oh, for…'

A loud banging, more shuffling, a small voice speaking high and fast, a sigh.

Her neighbour appeared, auburn hair askew, cheeks red, a baby strapped to the front of her chest, dragging an empty pushchair up the stairs, three carrier bags stuffed with food in her other hand. 'Owen, come on, come on!' she called to her toddler, who was clambering up behind her. 'Hold on, be careful.' Her voice was strained as she gave Maria a panicked look: 'Owen, this lady needs to come down the stairs, speed up…'

'I saw a spider.'

'OK, not now, just come up…'

The toddler was sat on the middle step, staring at something.

'Ant spider!' He pointed excitedly, glancing up at his mother.

'Sorry,' the woman said, red-faced, setting down the pushchair and the bags near her front door.

Maria nodded, not knowing what to do or where to go in the small space. She had never introduced herself before. 'It's fine,' she replied.

The woman had moved back down the stairs to scoop up the distracted toddler who, once moved, started to wail, 'Want to see spider! Ant spider!' The tears came as Maria skirted round them both, his cries echoing off the bare walls of their apartment block. The woman sighed as she soothed him, looking almost close to tears herself. 'I'm sorry, darling, just get in, OK? I need to make you lunch.'

'Ant spider,' the boy repeated as Maria stepped down the stairs and away from them. The baby started to cry, the woman swore again and Maria felt guilty for the relief she felt as she pushed open the double doors to outside.

Even after all these years a child crying still made her insides ache.

Walking quickly, head down, the wind nipping at her face, she thrust her hands inside her coat pockets, cross that she had forgotten her gloves. Moving down the road, she ran through the brief shopping list in her mind: a few essentials, nothing more. It would ensure she could hibernate for another few days. She forced down the guilt that this was not what Albie would have been doing, that he wouldn't have hidden away.

'Maria… Maria!'

She wasn't sure how long the voice had been calling her, but suddenly there she was: Rosie, jogging to keep up with her.

'Hey,' Rosie said, puffing a little, her breath forming clouds in the air. 'Maria, how are you? How are you getting on?'

Rosie seemed to appear whenever Maria was having a bad day. She half-wished she wasn't standing there, looking at her in that open, honest way. Maria wasn't the woman Rosie saw, the kind, elderly old lady – she shouldn't waste her time on her.

'I'll walk with you, if that's alright. I'm heading this way. Soooo,' she said, barely taking a breath, mouth chewing on gum between the words. 'Where are you off to? Something else to tick off the list?'

Maria mumbled something into the collar of her coat.

'What's that?'

'I was just saying, not today,' she repeated, embarrassed to have been caught out.

'Oh. Well, that's alright, how have you found it? Have you ticked a lot? Want some company with any of them?'

'Oh, no, that's alright, I'm just… making plans for one… I need to, um, sort a few things…'

'Cool,' Rosie said, blowing a large pink bubble. It popped and the gum disappeared back in her mouth. 'Which one?'

'Oh,' Maria blustered, caught in her lie. 'The trip to Paris, I still need to hear from the mysterious Cathie,' she added, her voice strained. 'He always wanted to take her there, he said,' her tone high, trying not to betray her feelings to Rosie. 'I wrote to her but I haven't received a reply.'

'You should try again,' Rosie said in that carefree way of hers, clearly not realising the cause of Maria's jittery mood. 'I've been there on a school trip,' she went on, the bubble briefly back. 'It was awesome, we went to that glass pyramid thing and lived on crêpes and éclairs. Tess threw up on one of the Bateaux Mouches – that's a boat – it was gross.'

'Nice!' Maria said, unable to stop herself, smiling at Rosie's energy, lifting her out of her black mood.

'Yeah, our teacher couldn't speak French very well and he kept asking the boat person for "la bucket" – we were wetting ourselves.'

'Well, I might avoid boats but it would be lovely to see the Eiffel Tower and the Louvre, and to walk along the Champs-Élysées people-watching sophisticated Parisians.' Maria was surprised to find that she had thought about it, realising on one level she had been looking forward to the trip, the chance to see the city. On the other hand, meeting Cathie might unravel everything.

'That sounds ideal,' Rosie sighed, pulling her school coat tightly around herself. 'That list is brilliant. And you deserve a treat too, he's got you doing hard work on it!'

'Hardly.' Maria laughed, already feeling lighter, her step more confident, her shoulders rolled back.

'Well, I think it's awesome what you're doing, really awesome,' Rosie said, grinning and balancing along the edge of the pavement.

'Be careful,' Maria warned, seeing her so close to the road, the cars whooshing past.

She noticed they were standing outside the newsagent.

'I'm OK,' Rosie said, 'I better go now. You take care, OK? I'll see you soon.'

'I'd like that,' Maria replied, finding that she was smiling. 'I really would.'

Rosie waved goodbye and Maria watched her as she walked away, rounding a corner up ahead. She had her hand held up in a wave and a man walking past frowned as she lowered it. Ducking her head down, she pushed open the door to the newsagent and stepped inside.

It was dark for the time of day, one strip light flickering above her, another needing a new bulb on the other side of the room. Mr Khan was stacking shelves to her right, his face lighting up as he saw her.

'Good to see you, Mrs. I will be two minutes, do see my new royal selection.'

Maria gave him a half-wave and started loading up her basket with essentials: bread, milk, butter. Seeing Rosie had made her feel stronger, her miserable mood evaporating as she planned the rest of her day.

'Have you seen the new Meghan tea towels?' Mr Khan asked as he helped her lift her basket onto the counter.

'I haven't,' Maria said, watching him pull out a white tea towel with an enormous caricature of Meghan Markle in the middle – not a terribly good likeness.

'They are bestseller – two for £5!'

She noticed a few others displayed behind the counter: one with Meghan in a blue pencil dress, one clutching Harry's arm and another with her inexplicably playing tennis.

'Would you be interested?'

There was something about his warm smile, the encouraging look in his eyes, that made her nod along. 'Why not? You can never have too many tea towels. Mine are getting a bit ragged,' she lied, glad to see his face break into an even bigger grin. 'I'll have that one, and um... Tennis Meghan,' she said, pointing behind him.

'Absolutely. She is a fine princess. And she is a great wife to Harry,' he said, folding the tea towel up on the counter as if he had first-hand experience of spending time with her.

'Yes, she seems very nice,' Maria agreed.

'And you, Mrs, you seem a little better now. Spring is coming, the blossom will be out.'

Maria handed over money. 'That's true,' she said, having mixed feelings about the changing seasons that marked time moving on.

'I will have new mugs ordered soon, some of Eugenie the Princess.'

Oh no, Maria thought, realising there would be no avoiding that purchase.

'Well, I'll look forward to that,' she said as Mr Khan hastened around his counter to open the door for her.

'You take care, Mrs, always a pleasant thing to see you.'

Maria couldn't help her mouth twitching as she left, huddled into her coat once more, surprised again by the cold. Her hands immediately freezing, she wondered whether Keith had somewhere to stay that night – it was so cold to be out on the streets with just a sleeping bag and some measly blankets.

The outing had restored her energy and after depositing her things, placing the tea towels in pride of place over the bar on her oven, she turned, picking up her gloves from the table by the door, and left once more. No more wallowing in the apartment, people were relying on her now.

*

The kids would often stay out late. Brighton was safe and I got on well with my neighbours, who knew to look out for her too.

She was currently around at Polly's house because Polly had two space hoppers and I'd banned them from our flat, it was just too small for that level of bouncing. They had devised a game – the fastest to bounce down Polly's street – and I laughed as I went to get her, an elderly lady sat on a chair outside her front door, smiling at the noise they were making.

'They're getting better,' she told me as I folded my arms. 'One of them nearly went head first into that Morris Minor,' she added, pointing to the car.

'It's getting dark,' I called to her, 'Let's head home, I've made a shepherd's pie.'

She came careering towards me, the space hopper round in her arms, her little face peeking over it. 'Mum, Mum, watch! I'm soooooo fast. Polly and I are going to be in the Guinness Book of World Records. Come oooooonnnnnn!'

She's a cheeky thing, I thought, as I joined the old lady in her doorway, smiling as my daughter, the great love of my life, hair flying, enormous grin on her face, bounced past me.

Chapter 16

The moment she saw him in the doorway, she felt ashamed: she had planned to drop off his coffee and sandwiches every day. Albie wouldn't have missed a day. It was self-indulgent to mope about when others relied on her. She vowed not to do it again.

'Hi Leonardo,' she said weakly as she held out the thermos. Would he be angry? Weary of broken promises?

Keith frowned briefly as he took the flask, before remembering the morning in the hairdresser's and chuckling. 'Alright there, Maria? I'm still not sure who he is.'

'He was in *Titanic* years ago.'

Keith looked horrified, almost spitting the first mouthful out. 'That baby face!'

His appalled expression made her laugh as she settled herself without thinking on the blankets beside him.

A woman on her mobile paused, head swivelling as Maria made herself comfortable.

Maria was tucking her handbag neatly under her arm and Keith was smiling at her over the cup – 'You'd make a terrible bag lady, far too neat.'

He'd been writing in a lined notepad, the scrawl illegible from this distance and without her reading glasses.

'It's a diary of sorts, keeps me from getting too bored,' he said, following her gaze. 'I've been trawling for work again but most places want an address, won't take a chance.'

'How about the Job Centre, couldn't they help?' Maria asked.

Keith nodded. 'They could, they were helpful, but' – he looked at his shoes – 'I don't want to get a handout, I don't want money for nothing, I want to work. Anyway, don't want to waste their time, there are others far worse off.'

Maria couldn't help an exclamation.

'There are,' he insisted firmly.

Maria couldn't help but feel that Keith was punishing himself for something. And more than anyone, she knew what that was like. 'Is there… is there anyone you could go to? Friends, family?' she suggested tentatively.

Keith swerved the conversation, his smile wide, his words firm, 'How are you getting on, Maria?'

She let him change the subject. 'I'm… I'm…' She would normally have said she was alright, not wanting the spotlight on her, not thinking she deserved anyone's sympathy, but there was something about Keith's open face and the reminder of the person that connected them that made her more honest. 'I miss him,' she said matter-of-factly. She put a hand up to her chest.

He nodded slowly. There was nothing else to say. He sipped at the coffee and as she stared out at the street, she could feel the cold of the pavement despite her clothing and the blankets, a sharp breeze around her ankles. How did he abide living like this? No one should have to sleep outside in the wind and the rain.

'So,' Keith said, leaning back against the wall, 'tell me what's next.'

She frowned, not sure what he was getting at.

'The list, Albie's list, of course! What's next? You been to The Ritz yet?'

Maria felt her cheeks heat up. 'Don't be stupid! Me at The Ritz?'

'He wanted it.' Keith shrugged. 'Show me…'

Maria reached into her handbag and pulled out the folded piece of paper, one corner holding the smallest tear. 'I've slowed down a bit, I suppose. It just seems…' She didn't finish the sentence. What word was she searching for? Overwhelming? Intimidating? Unachievable? She didn't want to think about the last part, the lines under her own name.

'Who's Cathie?' Keith asked, his face open and enquiring.

'I…' Maria felt an uncomfortable pain in her stomach at the name. Who *was* Cathie? 'That's a good question.' She laughed, trying to sound light and untroubled but aware the laugh was high-pitched and too loud.

Keith hadn't noticed anything amiss, still scanning the page, 'Well, that's a good one,' he said, finger stabbing at one of the bullet points.

Maria leant towards him. He smelt of wood smoke and the sea, and she tried to push away the thoughts edging in. 'Oh, I'm not sure…'

- *Splash out on a makeover for the café (state-of-the-art coffee machine, new fridges and stove, get rid of those tablecloths!)*

'What's there not to be sure about?'

'Will it seem a bit rude? Pauline might be offended, she might think I don't like the café as it is.' And she *did* – it was where she met Albie, after all.

'Maria,' Keith stopped her, lowering the list, 'this is what Albie wanted, that's all you need to remember. And what's a few new tablecloths? She won't be offended, I'm sure. She didn't seem like the easily offended type. I'll come with you and we can ask.'

Maria wrung her hands. It would be nice to tick something substantial off the list. And Keith was right, these were Albie's wishes and despite his secrets, despite everything that had happened since he'd died, she had trusted him. The thought that she had trusted once before flitted across her mind but she pushed it away. Biting her lip, she nodded once. 'Alright.'

'Right, well we can ask and then you can tell me what colours and whatnot. I'm no good at interior design but I do know a thing or two about painting and decorating so I can source the stuff you'll need.'

'I could get the cash out for the paint and things.'

'Great, great.' Keith nodded, lifting up his pad and pen. 'I'll make a list. You're going to want sandpaper, a primer coat, paintbrushes, of course...' He tapped his teeth with the pen. 'She'll probably have a ladder, but we should ask—'

'And I'll pay you for the work, of course,' Maria said hastily.

Keith stopped tapping the pen and rolled his eyes at her. 'Quit trying to pay me for everything. I'd love to do it for Albie and it's better than moping around in this doorway for another day. And if there's that delicious carrot cake in it for me, I'm there.'

His words seemed genuine and Maria felt a warmth flood through her for this lovely man, along with renewed curiosity as to how someone like him had ended up alone in this doorway. What had happened that Albie knew needed fixing?

They finished planning what they'd need, Keith guessing quantities. Then he got to his feet and helped her up. As ever, he towered over her. 'We'll need to get on and ask Pauline.'

'Right,' said Maria, straightening her skirt as she stood, glad to be drawing on Keith's energy.

'Oh, and you can tick that one,' he said, handing her back the list.

'Which one?' Maria glanced down at it.

'Stop and chat to Keith, of course.' And as Maria gave him a small smile, he threw back his head and laughed.

*

She'd been begging me to take her for a perm for weeks but I didn't want her to ruin her beautiful hair. She had clattered through the flat, her hair crimped and tied back with a scrunchie, blue eyeshadow inexpertly applied, clip-on hooped earrings and a lurid off-the-shoulder top in hot pink.

I hadn't meant to look quite so surprised, my mouth a rounded 'O' as she appeared, her roller skates tied together, her bright blue leg warmers balled up in her other hand.

'What?' she'd asked self-consciously, biting a lip. At least there was no lipstick yet, I'd thought.

'Nothing.' I'd stared back down at the sheaths of paper in front of me – a presentation I was working on for the next day, my owl-like glasses resting on top.

She tugged at her ra-ra skirt. 'It's just a roller disco, Polly's mum's taking us.'

I forced myself to smile at her, no lecture or words of advice. 'Alright, that sounds like fun.'

I didn't want an argument tonight. Sometimes it was so intense, just me and her, and I knew I shouldn't crowd her. I had a daughter who opened up to me, who let me inside her teenage world, and I didn't want to ruin that.

'I thought we could go shopping tomorrow. That new single by Madonna is out and I know you've been wanting it.'

She seemed to relax then, moving across, dumping her roller skates on the armchair to pop a clumsy kiss on my head. 'Thanks, Mum. Yeah, that would be awesome.'

I looked up at her, my baby girl growing up right in front of me. For a second, I felt tears threaten. Coughing, I looked back down, a graph, a sheet of accounts. 'Great,' I said, 'Like the earrings.'

She blushed, suddenly looking ten years younger again. 'Thanks,' she mumbled, touching the left one briefly.

The doorbell buzzed and I had already lost her, roller skates scooped up, denim jacket flung on.

'Bye, Moooottttthhhhhhheeeeerrrrr!' she shouted as she left the flat.

I heard her footsteps stamping down the stairs.

'Bye,' I whispered. 'I love you.'

Chapter 17

Keith was there early, surrounded by carrier bags of supplies, dust cloths, paint pots and more.

He handed her an envelope. 'The money I didn't spend.'

She wanted to thrust it straight back into his hand. It felt like his money as much as hers: it was Albie's. But she knew he wouldn't accept it, so she put it in her bag with a muttered 'thank you'.

Pauline headed towards them down the street, a wide smile on her face, her ash-blonde hair still damp from a morning shower. When they had asked her the week before she had cackled at Albie's list: 'He always hated our tablecloths, they were the height of bleedin' fashion in the nineties.' She had agreed to the makeover immediately and together, they had planned a colour scheme, going online and choosing various bits and bobs. Keith had offered to source the rest.

'You've got it all, brilliant. You're a diamond!' Pauline said, clapping her hands together.

They carried the things inside and Pauline instantly fired up the kettle. Moving tables and chairs to the kitchen, they cleared the room in record time. Maria set about folding up the dreaded tablecloths, feeling nostalgic at the red-and-white checked pattern, the very tablecloths over which she had looked at Albie.

Amrit arrived then, a welcome distraction, sweeping her now blue-streaked hair back into a ponytail before shaking Keith's hand. 'Alright, Maria?' she said over her shoulder. 'Love the dungas!'

Maria grinned as she stood up in some oversized denim dungarees that Keith had picked up for her from a charity shop – 'I feel like a proper painter now.'

Amrit threw on a long-sleeved shirt and headed into the kitchen to find Pauline.

Keith was watching her go, a small sad smile on his face, his thick eyebrows drawn into a frown.

'All OK, Keith?' Maria stepped across to him.

'Just, ah, it's nothing, she reminds me of my son. He was always dying his hair crazy colours. I sometimes wonder what colour it is now, or whether he grew out of that…'

Maria waited, not wanting to break this tentative glimpse into Keith's life. 'Do you not see him?'

Keith turned away, picked up the ladder. 'He doesn't want to see me.' His voice was tight as he adjusted the ladder, refusing to catch her eye. 'Can't say I blame him, I wasn't the best dad. Too wrapped up in myself, and didn't like him pointing that out. We had a row. I said things I didn't mean…'

'We all do when we're angry,' Maria said gently, her heart going out to this man, the hurt clear in his eyes.

'But I was his dad, I should have done better by him.'

'I'm sure, if he knew…' Maria knew what it felt like to feel you'd let someone down. She had been punishing herself for the same thing for most of her life. She felt the familiar swirl of nausea even after all these years as her mind flitted back to that same face. She placed a hand on her stomach, concentrated on the man in front of her. What would she want to be told? How could words ever suffice? 'Well, I think he'd be lucky to know you,' she said softly, tugging at a loose thread on her dungarees. She knew it wasn't enough but hoped it might be some comfort to know not everyone viewed him in the same way.

Keith turned and looked at her. 'Hey, I know what you're up to, Maria,' he said, waggling his finger and reaching to plonk a paintbrush in her hand, bringing her back to the café. 'Don't think I don't remember: "Reconnect with his family." You're as bad as that Albie, you just want me for your ticks.'

She would be offended had he not given her a reassuring grin and a quick squeeze of her shoulder. 'Let's paint this room, eh? Then maybe you can fix me up.'

Maria nodded, knowing that was enough for now. A son. She couldn't imagine Keith being a bad father, he was such a joyful, positive person with so much energy. She wondered how he had ended up estranged from his family and living without a home. She knew she shouldn't push him, he would open up if he wanted to. And she hoped she could help him, not just because of the list but because she had really started to care about him too. This thought came as a surprise, realising in that moment that she liked these connections, that Albie had given her permission perhaps to finally make them.

Pauline appeared in the doorway, her hair hidden beneath a knotted coloured scarf. 'Right you lot, let's make this place bloody sparkle!'

Keith did the majority of the work, lifting the ladder onto his shoulder and sticking masking tape all along the ceiling and windows. He never stopped, dipping the paint roller over and over again as Amrit, Pauline and Maria stopped for tea and a fast-diminishing plate of brownies.

Amrit took delivery of an enormous chrome coffee machine, which would have looked more at home in NASA than in a Brighton café, and Pauline spent a good twenty minutes running her hand along the gleaming surface. 'Oh, it's got two steam arms!' she exclaimed, eyes wide. 'I always wanted to froth milk with them. I'm going to make a new range of flavoured cappuccinos.'

'Gingerbread?' Amrit asked hopefully.

'Hazelnut, gingerbread, salted caramel… I'll do 'em all,' Pauline replied, clapping her hands together.

Gradually, the room took shape. Gone were the holes in the walls from old pictures, the stains from a former spillage, the scuff marks on the skirting boards. Replaced by walls in a wonderful shade of duck egg blue, crisp white blinds at the windows, new lampshades in a soft gold.

Maria stood back, watching the delight on Pauline's face, Amrit and Keith laughing as they stood in front of the finished walls, overalls and faces spattered with duck egg blue. They both loved music festivals and Keith was telling her about the time he had gone to Glastonbury and got so close to the headliners on stage, he'd been able to smell the sweat. Here in this café, dressed in overalls, decking the place out, no one would ever see Keith as a faceless homeless person, someone to scuttle past, ignore. He had a natural authority, directing everyone to paint or sand or scrub. He was Keith: formidable, funny and bright.

'One last thing,' he said, pulling out a bag, 'Maria, I think you should do the honours.'

They had taken their time to select the perfect set and Maria pulled out the new tablecloths with a dramatic flourish: white stiff cotton with intricate cut-out edges.

'Oh, ain't they perfect!' Pauline said. 'Not a gingham check in sight. Albie would be so relieved.'

They finished as the sun was setting, the newly painted walls tinged with a warm orange light. Pauline brought them all mugs of chicken soup and warm bread fresh from the oven. The smell filled the room as Maria broke the warm dough in her hands, looking around at everyone eating, content.

'I think Albie would love the new look,' Pauline said, smiling round at the prints on the walls, the sparkling coffee machine, the freshly painted walls, the scrubbed, sanded and polished counter top. 'The customers aren't going to know what's hit them. I can't thank you enough.'

Maria batted the words away, 'It wasn't me! It was all him.' She felt a mixture of emotions inside, knowing they had done something wonderful, the joy on the faces of the others obvious, but also a silent goodbye to the café she had so loved, the room she conjured in her memory every time she thought of a Thursday afternoon with Albie. For a second, she thought she might begin to cry, the emotion building in her throat.

Amrit waved them a goodbye, jolting Maria from her thoughts. 'Have fun,' Maria called after her, watching her leave for a nearby pub to listen to a live music set with friends. Pauline started clearing away their bowls and plates. Keith was at the sink washing up before she could even ask. Maria finished her tea and wandered over, marvelling at Keith's ease as he loaded an industrial-looking washing machine.

'You seem to know your way around.'

Keith murmured something Maria didn't catch, noticing Pauline watching him carefully.

'Well, you two will want to be getting home,' she said with a clap of her hands, looking out at the darkening day. Moving across the room, she started to pull down the new blinds.

Maria flashed Keith a look, knowing that Pauline still wasn't aware of Keith's circumstances. She felt a stab of shame: shouldn't she offer Keith a place to stay? She didn't have a spare room but she imagined her sofa would be better than the alternative. She wrung her hands as the words froze somewhere inside her. Someone entering her flat, another person, for the first time in years and years. She would have to talk to him, the awkwardness of moving around him. And what if he reacted badly to the offer? Would he feel patronised? Would she threaten the budding friendship? Her mouth opened a fraction and then snapped shut.

'Yes, yes, best be getting going,' Keith said in a loud voice.

Maria felt a deep sadness at the way he swallowed down any disappointment at leaving the warm cocoon of the café, as if he had somewhere to go.

She wouldn't give him away.

'Keith, if you wouldn't mind, could you help me get this stuff back?'

'Course.'

Pauline moved across to Maria and without warning, bent down to give her an enormous hug, her hair tickling Maria's nose, her rose-scented perfume consuming her. 'What a wonderful day. Thank you.'

Maria felt a delighted joy as she extracted herself from Pauline's embrace, scooping up her handbag. 'It looks brilliant,' she said, taking a last glance around.

Pauline grinned. 'Come back in soon and see me.'

She nodded.

Keith was packing the ladder and paints away in a storeroom as he called a goodbye and Pauline began the process of locking up. Maria waved and left the café, her bones weary from such a long day. As she moved down the pavement she thought of the transformed space, the old café, the café she had always associated with Albie: gone. The thought made her stop, a fresh wave of grief forcing her to place her hand on a lamppost, catch her breath.

Glancing over her shoulder, she saw the lights on, remembered Pauline's expression as she had drunk in the wonderful changes they had made. She thought of Keith still in there, the new people in her life who were only there because Albie was gone. It was a strange and confusing thought, that the list was forcing her to move on, to change things, to move her further away from her old life: the life that contained Albie. Yet she knew he had wanted those changes, had planned to make them himself. Even that last one, the one attached to her own name. She swallowed, watching the café windows descend into darkness as she turned for home.

*

I met her outside Woolworths, her cheeks stuffed full of penny sweets.

'Mum,' she said, wriggling out of my grasp as I went to kiss her.

She had grown up so much recently, a pre-teen who was quick to anger, wail, laugh, blush.

'Hey, you need me for my money so you have to let me kiss you!'

She looked around and grinned, 'Shurrup!'

We headed to Tammy Girl, a shop crammed with rows of glitzy clothes: skirts, dresses, dungarees, tops, hair scrunchies, jewellery, shellsuits and more. Her heaven.

It was a big day.

She disappeared into the cubicle, surreptitiously taking in three bras with her. I wasn't allowed inside.

Moments later, there came a whispered, 'Muuuum...'

The woman outside the cubicles glanced across at me.

I moved outside the curtain. 'Are you alright?'

The whisper again, 'I can't... I'm a bit... tangled.'

Frowning, I tried to swallow down the giggle that threatened, 'Do you want me to take a look?'

'No, I… yeah….'

I pushed inside and saw her in the corner of the cubicle, one arm twisted behind her, her blue top dangling half-off, swatting at the clasp of the training bra that seemed to be tangled round her and her top in the most extraordinary way. I couldn't help the quick laugh that escaped me.

'Mum,' she pleaded, twisting once more. 'Help!'

'How did you even…?' I giggled as I released her top, moved the straps around, undid the clasp.

'I tried to put it on over my top and then sort of wiggle out of it like the girls do in PE but it got stuck,' she explained.

I looked at her, standing there in the white bra, my little girl on the cusp of adulthood.

'Quite ambitious for your first time maybe?'

She nodded solemnly, 'Yeah. Yeah, maybe next time.'

I gave her a quick squeeze and felt a hand poking my kidneys.

'Mum, stop it!'

I chuckled all the way out of the cubicle.

Chapter 18

The library session was starting in under an hour and Maria was already fretting over it. She had two frightening things to do today and she wasn't sure which one she was dreading more.

She had offered to read that morning, taking Albie's spot as a volunteer. She had loathed reading aloud in school, remembered English lessons on her feet, following the text with her finger, her mouth dry as she stumbled over simple words. She had always loved books but only in her head – others seemed to make it seem so straightforward, even doing different voices for different characters. What would the children think of her halting, quivering narration? Why had she offered?

Reaching a hand up, she pushed down the label scratching at her neck as she left her apartment, counting the minutes till the dreaded moment. Distracted, she moved down the stairs, meeting her neighbour flying out of her door. She was rushing to take a bin bag down the stairs to the communal area, her baby once more strapped to her, calling behind her to her toddler, telling him to stay put in the hallway while she was gone. 'Don't touch anything,' she shouted. 'Oh sorry!' She almost collided into Maria.

Maria should have offered to stand there with him for the two minutes his mother was away, but it was one thing to be directed to help people by Albie, quite another to find the confidence to push into someone else's life uninvited.

'That's alright,' she said, feeling useless, marvelling at the way in which this woman seemed to juggle everything. She returned in the blink of an eye from dumping the bin bag, taking the stairs two steps at a time, calling, 'Owen!' and his reply, 'I wait here.'

And then Maria was out in the street, walking quickly, when it occurred to her that she could have asked her neighbour to join her: her toddler might have enjoyed listening to the stories, and it might have afforded her a moment's peace. But Maria dismissed the thought as quickly as it came. She couldn't just impose on people, the neighbour probably had plenty of friends and places to go – not everyone was lonely like her. She didn't need Maria barging her way into her life.

The library loomed large in front of her and Maria took a long, deep breath. Mothers with prams, some holding the hands of older children, were filing inside. A colourful poster in the window announced 'Storytime: Starts 11 a.m.' Maria gulped, her palms slipping on her handbag. It was warmer than she had thought and she felt hot and bothered in her thick coat.

Moving inside, the air smelling of books, glue and dust, she approached the curved desk, waiting patiently as a woman with tight grey curls systematically worked her way down a towering pile of books, stamping the insides and moving to the next.

'Hello,' Maria said, the word barely loud enough to alert the woman. 'I'm Maria,' she continued, slightly louder, 'I'm here to read a story.'

The woman didn't stop stamping. 'You're Maria,' she replied. 'Diana. Good of you to volunteer. Was sorry to hear about Albert. Nice man, the children loved him. I'll be with you shortly.' Every sentence was punctuated with a ruthless stamp, making Maria jump.

When she finished, she moved around the desk, stepping in front of Maria, her walk brisk. 'Well, they should all have arrived by now, we'll get you started. The books are in a pile on the table there. I'm sorry about the first. Apparently, *Aliens in Underpants* is rather amusing, not quite my taste but there you are.'

Maria bit her lip as she took in the small circle of people, stepping over abandoned bags, moving round folded-up pushchairs to a small table in the corner where she was meant to be seated.

'Everyone, this is Maria, a volunteer today who will be reading. Let's make her feel welcome.'

There was a smattering of applause and Maria, cheeks reddening, wanted to turn and run.

'Hello,' she squeaked and allowed herself to be ushered towards a large beanbag-style pouffe in front of a radiator.

She immediately regretted not removing her coat but everyone was looking at her now and she had already sat down on the pouffe, sinking into it so that she had little hope of being able to get up again. She would keep it on, she thought, as she reached for the first book with shaking hands.

Fifteen expectant faces looked up at her. One boy at the back was standing up, dressed as a tiny dragon, pointing to something on the wall behind her. His mother mouthed an apology.

'Right,' Maria said, opening the first book, feeling dizzy with nerves, the words swimming in front of her, a green alien in red frilly knickers with four eyes making her think she was seeing double for a moment. 'A pleasure to be here,' she croaked. 'I'll just begin, I think.'

Taking a last look at the faces in front of her, the children staring, some of the mothers smiling at her, others on mobile phones or staring off into space, she took a breath and began.

'There once was a girl who lived in the forest far away from anywhere…'

The thirty minutes passed quickly, her voice growing more confident as she went on, gratified to hear the tinkle of laughter from the children, their earnest expressions as they listened intently to the stories. The books were fun and bright and she found herself wanting to make them exciting. She pictured Albie with his energy and charisma and tried to channel it that day for these children. She did silly voices, waggled her eyebrows, forgot her nerves, the expectant faces and the heat pumping from the radiator behind her and lost herself in the story, in the moment.

Diana ended the session and there was loud applause and lively chatter as mothers moved their children away, some kissing the others goodbye, others agreeing to head out for a coffee. The room was buzzing with noise and life.

'Thank you, that was great,' a woman in a headscarf with kind brown eyes remarked as she passed.

'Nank you,' her girl said, smiling and tugging at her mother's skirt.

'My pleasure,' Maria replied, feeling at the heart of things for once.

The library emptied and Maria finally struggled to her feet from her precarious spot.

'Well, that was a success,' Diana said, stacking up the small pile of books to return to the shelves. 'You're a natural,' she announced, which Maria felt was a compliment coming from such a no-nonsense sort.

Maria found herself agreeing to return the next month, swapping book recommendations with Diana, who kept thrusting different things into her hands. She finally made her excuses and left, knowing she couldn't put off the second terrifying thing she had to do that day a moment longer. Maria felt her earlier nerves return, the library trip now seeming a walk in the park compared to the task ahead. She thought then of the list safely tucked away in her handbag, trying to draw strength from the fact that this was someone else's wish.

It had started to rain and she was grateful that she had remembered to put her umbrella in her handbag. The air smelt damp, daffodils bunched underneath the trees, the colour cheering on such a grim, grey day.

The youth centre was set back from the road, the entrance a flaking blue door. A couple of teenagers were leaning against the rail on the steps going in as Maria loitered on the other side of the road, staring at the façade. It seemed a world away from anything she had known and she was nervous about meeting Troy, this young boy who had no doubt looked up to Albie. How would she be able to tell a child about his death? What words would comfort him? How could she ever come close to replacing him? She wavered, watching the teenagers move away. Maybe she should head home, think about it more, write him a letter, allow him a moment to process the news on his own terms.

She had just about made up her mind to leave when a familiar figure stepped out of the door of the youth centre. Rosie. She noticed Maria on the other side of the street and started with surprise before crossing the road, barely glancing left or right. Maria looked around worriedly for cars.

'Maria, what are you doing here?'

'Oh, I'm… well, I was meant to be…' She felt silly and tongue-tied.

Rosie brushed a piece of hair behind her ear as she waited for Maria to get the words out.

'…I'm trying to find someone. Troy.'

Rosie looked apologetic. 'I don't know him. Does he hang out here?'

Maria nodded. 'Albie used to come here to see him, he told me he met up with him regularly.'

'Oh!' Rosie cocked her head to one side. 'Well, you need to get in there then.'

'I do.' Maria was still stuck to her position on the pavement.

'But you're... afraid?' Rosie guessed, the words slow.

Maria dipped her head. 'Albie mentored him. He, he won't know what's happened...'

'I see,' Rosie said, her voice filled with sympathy. 'That's sad. It's good you're here.'

Maria looked up at the young girl, trying to draw strength from her words.

'I know I'd want to know,' Rosie said with a single shrug.

'You're right, of course you're right.'

'Look, I've got to get going, but you're definitely doing the right thing,' Rosie said, touching Maria's arm. Maria stared at her hand, warmed by the reassuring gesture. She nodded then, knowing this young teenager was braver than she would ever be.

'You're right. I'll do it. I'll head in there now.'

'Fab,' Rosie said, grinning at her. 'Look, let me know how it goes, yeah? You'll be alright.'

Maria bit her lip, wringing her hands.

Will I be?

'Go on!' Rosie laughed.

The sound was so carefree, Maria wished she could view the world in such an untroubled way. She had to admire Rosie's positive spirit, living in the moment, living with no regrets. Unlike Maria, who seemed to be filled with regret. She thought then how she wanted someone else by her side in that moment: Albie. His easy confidence, his kindly eyes. He would place a gentle hand on her back, steer her inside, pay her a compliment she would bat away. Why had she not thanked him every time? Paid *him* a compliment?

She watched Rosie leave and then, taking a deep breath, she crossed the road and headed up the stairs to the blue door. The entrance smelt of bleach and rubber-soled trainers. A corkboard just inside the foyer was covered in posters – adverts for a band, youth choir, the numbers for Childline and Samaritans, information about the sexual health clinic, all criss-crossed over each other. Glass panels in a set of double doors to Maria's right showed a peek of the main room: a carpeted space containing a table tennis table, football table, a couple of sofas, and milling teens. She could hear the beats of a song she didn't recognise pulsing through the doors, a shout and the echoes of laughter.

Her palms felt slippery as she approached the door. No one glanced her way as she pushed inside, heart hammering, the hubbub louder, the music all around her. She bit her lip, loitering as the door closed behind her. The room smelt of burnt popcorn and two teenagers were lounging on bean bags, a large television playing a soap opera above their oblivious heads. She scanned the room, wondering what Troy looked like, trying to pick him out from the crowd from the small details Albie had given her.

A young man approached her, a red tartan shirt over ripped jeans, an enquiring look on his face. 'Are you alright?'

'I…' She could sense a couple of nearby teenagers looking her way. 'I'm looking for someone,' she told the man in a soft voice. 'A boy called Troy. Troy… I'm not sure of his surname, I'm afraid…'

'Troy…' The man rubbed his chin, a tiny red cut where he must have caught himself shaving. 'I haven't seen him in here for a while.'

He seemed distracted, then called out to the group nearby, 'You lads seen Troy recently?'

Shuffled feet, shrugs, a string of nos.

Maria felt her shoulders drooping. 'Oh… Well, it was kind of you to ask.'

The man was already moving away as he added, 'Kids come and go from here, I'm sure he'll turn up.'

'I'm sure he will,' she whispered, taking a last look around the room.

She pushed back out into the foyer, feeling deflated. Had she really thought it would be that easy? What should she do now? She should have asked the man to leave him a note, or she should have left her number. Glancing back towards the room, the man in the tartan shirt was now at the table tennis table, picking up a bat.

'Scuse me.'

A large boy with ginger hair, black cargo trousers and a T-shirt with a skull and bones on it joined her in the foyer. Maria felt the adrenaline rise, gripped her handbag close to her chest.

'You wanted Troy?' He kicked at the floor with his trainer.

'Oh,' Maria said, her grip loosening.

'He hangs out at The Level,' the boy muttered the words, glancing back at the door as if embarrassed to be seen talking to her.

Maria looked at him blankly, not sure where he meant.

'Skatepark,' he added quickly, almost certainly about to bolt.

'Do you know him?' Maria asked, desperate for any information.

'Yeah, yeah, Troy's alright. Been a bit screwed in the head after finding that old man dead, the one who sorted us with the football table and stuff. Messed up, that.'

Maria's mouth fell open, her voice emerging a whisper. 'Troy, Troy… He *found* him, found… Albie?'

The boy tugged on the bottom of his T-shirt, 'Yeah, man. He had a key to his place and the old man didn't show up where they normally met so Troy went to find him.'

'Oh my god!' Maria couldn't hide her horror. The poor boy, no one should ever have to go through that experience let alone a child, someone who had cared about him too. She didn't have the words, she simply stood in shocked silence.

'So yeah, he's a bit off at the moment but he hangs out down there a lot so, you know, maybe he's there taking some time.'

Maria nodded dumbly, picturing Troy walking into that apartment, calling out Albie's name, moving down the hallway, finding him cold. She shivered despite her layers, wrapping her arms around herself.

'So yeah, hope he's OK. Tell him Gunnar says "hi", alright?' The boy gave her a nod as Maria came to.

'I will. I will… Thank you Gunnar. Of course, I'll go and try there now.'

She wandered outside, knocking her shoulder into the doorframe as she left, surprised by the change in temperature, the cold snapping at her, the bottom of her coat flapping in a sudden gust of wind. That poor boy. What a thing to go through. She knew she must find him. Must somehow try to make it right.

Pushing into a newsagent opposite the centre she approached the counter and got directions for the skatepark that wasn't far away. As she walked, mind racing, she just hoped he was there, that she could talk to him.

The skatepark was set under an underpass, a large concrete space with small ramps and rails set off the main part, walls graffitied in livid colours, a group of kids in hoodies, boards resting against their knees, one smoking up a rolled-up cigarette. Another group were doing turns on the slope of the underpass, their speed amazing her, the sound as their trainers slapped on the ground, one boy hopping off to break his fall. Maria couldn't help the gasp that left her mouth.

A couple of boys, one so tall he could be mistaken for a grown man had it not been for the lack of facial hair and the baby cheeks, turned to stare at her. She did look ridiculous, she realised, standing there in her corduroy skirt, sensible brown ankle boots and woollen coat, clutching her leather handbag to her like a shield. *Try to look confident,* she reminded herself. She was here for Albie, for his friend, and she had to find the boy who had found him. The desire to meet Troy had increased tenfold with that knowledge. Jutting her chin forward, she met the tall boy's eye.

He looked a little alarmed, then with a smirk called out, 'Alright, Grandma? You lost your way to the bingo?'

His friend spat some of his canned drink on the floor, erupting into laughter.

Maria took a step towards them both: 'I was wondering if you knew Troy?' Her most polite voice, she held his gaze as he assessed her from top to bottom. She must have passed because he hollered over his shoulder in the direction of the underpass, 'Troy mate, your nan's here.'

A tall black boy in an orange hoodie looked up from the group. 'I don't know her,' he called back, flipping up his skateboard with his foot.

As she moved towards him, it felt like the longest walk, watched by the other boys, the skatepark falling silent. She pulled at the collar of her coat as she headed across to the group. *Stay confident. They're just kids*, she reminded herself.

'Troy? Are you Troy? I'm, I'm a friend of Albie's,' she said, her voice growing in confidence.

She could see now that he had cropped hair, a silver stud in his left ear. Troy turned back to the group, two of the boys looking at him before their eyes slid away. Maria could feel their awkwardness. *Had he told them what he'd found?*

He shrugged. 'Albie's dead.'

The harsh words made her catch her breath. She took another step forward. 'I know. I heard you…' she tailed off, not wanting to talk to him about this in front of others. Troy seemed to stiffen, darted a look at her. 'I just wanted to talk to you, if that's OK?' Maria tried to smile, tried to convey her desire.

He shrugged once, not saying anything. His bulky clothes were no doubt designed to make him look bigger, older. Some of the others were a good few years older than him, she realised.

He span round, his eyes narrowing as he spoke, 'Look, I don't know who you are but I don't want to talk about anything, alright?'

Maria held both her hands up, desperate to conciliate. What could she say? He had rounded his shoulders and turned his back on her again. The other boys had taken his lead and started to talk amongst themselves and one set off on his skateboard. It signalled the end of the conversation.

But Maria wasn't ready to give up just yet.

She reached her hands out, almost grazing his shoulder, before he turned back to her: 'Go, alright? Just go.'

Her hand was suspended in the air between them and with tears building in her throat, she lowered it. She paused, not knowing what to do next, not wanting to just give up but recognising the anger, the sadness, the determined desire to block out others, from her own experience. Of course, he was hurting. She didn't know how to respond, how to make it right. Albie would have known but then she wouldn't be here if he hadn't left her, hadn't left them both.

'I…'

Another boy with greasy shoulder-length hair took a step in her direction: 'He's told you once, alright?'

The words were clear: you're not welcome.

She left after that. What else could she do, she thought as she crossed the concrete, eyes at her back, whispers following her. As she headed home, she turned it all over in her mind. She wondered what she could have done differently.

Back home, she stared at the list as she sat in her chair. She thought of Albie mentoring that boy, thought of the times he had spoken about him with teasing affection: his frustration when he had realised Troy was skipping school, his excitement when Troy had complimented him on one of his paintings, and the fond way he had shown Maria text messages with a series of photos – faces with different expressions, a big thumbs-up.

She couldn't give up, she thought, as she got into bed that night. He had meant a lot to Albie and Maria needed to try to help him. It wasn't for ticks or anything like that. She thought of the expression on his face when he had talked: a hurt, a deep sadness, an anger. She knew that look, she knew it so very well. She knew that he would try and push away anyone who cared. She plumped her pillow and closed her eyes, concluding that was the wrong thing to do, push people away. Because you ended up alone. Very, very alone.

She showed up again, and again.

Sometimes he was there, sometimes he wasn't.

She showed up with sandwiches and chocolate bars, apples, hot tea in a flask, bottles of water. Some of the other skaters started to greet her warmly when she appeared. Troy would look up, scowl at her, his brown eyes filled with animosity as a few of the older kids gathered round her, accepting treats and 'ribbing' her: 'That's taking the piss, Maria'.

It was a different world, far removed from her tiny flat, her quiet existence. She loved their energy, the jokes, the slaps on the back, watching them focus as they leapt and jumped on the thin pieces of wood. She looked forward to going, thought about them when she was away from them, planned things to bring them.

She kept appearing, at the same time in the afternoon, wearing the same hopeful expression as she scanned the concrete for him. She would watch them all, admiring the skill: the skateboarders' skinny arms bare in baggy T-shirts, baseball caps shielding their eyes from the sun, as they twisted and leapt and rolled.

After a few weeks, finally Troy sidled over to her and silently took the proffered Crunchie bar. 'You don't give up,' he grunted, sitting down on the cold stone and biting into the chocolate. He ate the whole thing and Maria simply stood there, too afraid to push him, too afraid to say anything, to break this tentative peace. As he wiped the crumbs from his chest, she noticed his thin arms underneath the faded orange hoodie he seemed to live in. He then stood up, tugging at his trousers that always slipped down. He didn't meet her eye as he ambled off, a quiet voice calling back, 'See you tomorrow, yeah?'

She grinned quickly, then wiped the smile from her face as the other kids looked over, nodding solemnly, a hand in a half wave, 'See you then, Troy. Same time.'

*

A man was going to take me out: Paul, from the London office. He had liked me since we had met to discuss our latest campaign. He used to be married too and I had felt a little frisson when we went to shake hands at the end, our hands touching.

My new flares and an orange patterned shirt that I'd been told by my friend and neighbour Tiffany was all the rage completed the look – and I was embarrassingly excited about the prospect of a night out.

Sarah had agreed to sit in the flat as a babysitter – I didn't feel too bad saying yes as she was just next door. She had insisted, the whole street seemed to want me to find love again. They all knew how Steve left me, his name mud in Brighton. Not that he'd be back here, too busy shacked up with his secretary in London like the cliché he was.

'Mummmmmeeeeee.' She appeared at the door, Sindy hanging from one hand, blanket from another. 'Your hair is pretty,' she said as I turned. I had put a hairband in it, was wearing it big and curled, like a Charlie's Angel.

'Thank you, darling,' I said, my heart swelling as ever at her barefooted appearance, my gorgeous urchin. So grateful to have her: she would always come first, no matter how amazing the man.

A knock at the door. 'It's on the latch,' I called and I heard Sarah push her way inside.

She loved Sarah, turning immediately to go and talk to her about the cobweb she had seen and how Mummy had let her give Sindy a bath.

'Mummy hair pretty,' I heard her say to Sarah as I moved through to the living room, smiling at the scene as Sarah was kissing the top of her head.

'Thanks, Sarah,' I called as I picked up my keys from the side table.

'Hmm… Not so much from the back,' I heard a tiny voice add in a cheeky voice as I shut the door.

I laughed all the way down the stairs.

Chapter 19

The church was half-empty and the vicar raised two neatly pencilled eyebrows as she greeted Maria in the doorway. 'Great to see you, great,' she said in a voice that implied every member of her dwindling flock was precious.

It was a hot day: people lounging in parks, playing Frisbee, eating ice lollies, jogging, juggling, carrying windbreakers, deckchairs, towels as they headed to the beach. Very few had chosen to spend it in the cool, dark building, dust dancing in the air as the sun filtered gently through the stained-glass windows.

Keith had joined her for the service. She had kept her promise and had been dropping coffee and sandwiches to him every day for weeks now. She always looked forward to their chats and sometimes they would go for a walk or head to the café. He had offered to accompany her to church, perhaps realising that she had been avoiding it, that she might need someone to give her the strength to face it. She thought briefly of another church, less than two miles away, which she hadn't visited in thirty-six years, of the yew tree in the corner, what rested below its branches, and then she pushed those thoughts back down deep inside her.

The service began, the pews sparse, self-conscious voices wobbling over the hymns. Keith had a surprisingly good singing voice, she thought, as he stood next to her, holding a hymn book open for them to share, bellowing out the words to 'Dear Lord and Father of Mankind'. His words bounced around the walls, breathed life into the space. She couldn't help smiling.

'What?' he whispered, nudging her, 'I always liked that one.'

She felt the warmth of him at her side, grateful that he was there with her. Staring around at the familiar scenes on the stained-glass windows, the shiny plaques set into the walls, the embroidered cushions hanging from the back of the pews, her body relaxed. She let out a deep, contented breath.

The sermon was short and energetic, the vicar walking up and down the aisle as she addressed them, connected with them, making eye contact. She felt Keith straighten in the pew as at one point, the vicar appeared to talk directly to the pair of them, and for a second, she felt close to giggles before she swallowed the silliness. It had been years since she had done anything with a friend. She thought then of all the times Albie had asked her to join him in activities and she had refused, not wanting to get in the way, be a bore. Why had she always assumed he was just being kind?

Soon they were drifting outside, surprised by the sudden warmth compared to the church's cool interior, one hand shielding her eyes as they struggled to adjust to the brightness. They sat down on a stone bench in the shadow of the church and watched the slow procession of the remaining congregation, Maria resting her head back against the cool stone, feeling glad she had gone. The vicar emerged, pulling the door shut, locking it with a key from an enormous jangling bunch of them.

'Great to see you, Maria,' she said as she passed them, not a hint of reproach for her absence. Maria just hadn't been able to face the place, not since Albie had died.

'Lovely service,' Keith remarked, which made the vicar beam.

Keith looked relaxed and healthier: pink in his cheeks, his eyes bright. Maria wished she could do more as she placed one hand over the other, building up to ask him.

'You remember Albie's list…' she started tentatively.

'Yes.' Keith sighed as if he had been waiting for this.

'Well…' Maria coughed, her fingers plucking at the cotton of her skirt. 'It mentioned that you were estranged from your family and I was wondering if…'

'I'm not ready,' Keith said quietly, 'can we change the subject?'

Maria, more than anyone, understood and she stood up and stretched. 'I'm getting hungry, how about we get some lunch?'

A momentary pause as Keith's eyes filled with worry. 'I can't…' He held out both hands as if demonstrating the shortage of cash.

'On Albie,' Maria added hurriedly, kicking herself for being insensitive. How could Keith afford lunch? 'A Sunday roast, there's a pub around the corner that was advertising them. I haven't bothered with a roast in years.'

'Bit warm for a roast?'

'It's never too hot for a roast,' Maria replied, glad to see he was relenting.

'Well, why not?' he said, standing and linking his arm through hers. 'I'd like that.'

They left the church, Maria quickly shifting subjects, keen to show that she didn't want to make him feel uncomfortable, or that she was only spending time with him because of Albie's list. Pointing to a woman walking a Labrador on the other side of the road, she said, 'Labradors are lovely looking dogs, aren't they?' and felt pleased to see Keith's whole body relax as he responded with a grateful nod and fell into step beside her.

They didn't speak on their way to the pub, walking slowly in the heat, the air warm, the distant chime of an ice-cream van passing, shouts and squeals from behind a wall – a garden of children, a birthday party perhaps. Finally, they arrived, a chalkboard outside advertising a Pork Roast with Crackling. Maria felt her stomach grumble, looking forward to sitting down, all this walking more than she was used to.

'About earlier,' Keith said, quietly stopping her with a hand before she stepped inside.

She turned to look up at him, his face largely in shadow, the sun bright behind him.

He was looking over her shoulder, not quite able to meet her eye. 'I will talk to you about it one day, you know. Keep asking.'

She nodded at him. Patting him on the arm, she said, 'Come on, let's get out of this wonderful sunny day and eat our body weight in roast potatoes.'

'The lady knows best,' he replied, his voice light, his face untroubled.

*

A friend in Tesco told me she'd heard from her cousin that Steve was married now and had twin boys. They lived in Cumbria and he worked for her dad, doing something in farming. It hurt – the idea of Steve and his new family. It shouldn't have: it had been years with no news but the pain felt as fresh as the day he had walked out.

I'd left the supermarket with an empty trolley and was late for school pick-up.

I was quiet on the walk home, responses late, distracted. She didn't say anything, she didn't seem to notice anything was amiss. She was obsessed with Hubba Bubba bubble gum and I let her buy two packets in the newsagent on the way home, reaching into the small freezer for the dinner I hadn't bought earlier.

I hadn't eaten mine, pushing the food around the plate and trying to imagine what Steve would look like now: did he still wear leathers? Did he have streaks of grey in that black hair? Did he love his twin boys with a fierce passion?

I hadn't heard the kettle. She pushed the mug towards me.

'Mum.' Her look was solemn. I stared vacantly in her direction and then down at the drink in front of me.

She had made me a tea.

She half-rubbed, half-patted my back, 'There you go,' and my heart lurched for my child who saw everything.

It must have had at least five sugars. I spat the mouthful back into the mug as discreetly as I could. 'Thank you, darling,' I'd said, knowing it had been done to comfort, to help. My heart swelled with the enormous love I had for her.

Thank god, thank god I had her.

And a red-hot anger fired through me that he would never know this incredible, generous, loving girl.

I had so much to do the next day, so many meetings lined up, but in that moment, I just wanted to gnash and wail and throw things.

Cumbria.

I'd never been and now I struck it from my list of places I wanted to visit.

Twin boys.

Works for her dad.

'I just need to do a little work,' I said, picking up my briefcase in the hope I could disguise the emotion building inside me.

She just looked at me, watched me leave the room, twiddling a strand of her hair round a finger, a sure sign of nerves. I couldn't meet her eye as I pushed my bedroom door shut.

'I'll come through and say goodnight soon,' I said in a high, unnatural voice before dissolving onto my bed, face into the pillow.

I didn't want her to see me crying. This wasn't how it was meant to have been.

Chapter 20

Troy looked awkward in the doorway of the café, removing his baseball cap as he searched the room, a nearby couple looking up at him enquiringly.

Maria waved from her spot at the table, nerves butterflying in her stomach that he had agreed finally to meet her here. She felt self-conscious about the scrutiny of the other teenagers at the skatepark and this was where she felt their shared link to Albie meant something too, where she felt comfortable enough to talk in more depth, get to know him better.

She had gone for her blow-dry that morning, Mandy asking her why she seemed so jumpy. Maria had told her why: that she wanted to make a really good impression.

'He'll love you, Maria,' she had said, touching her shoulder. 'You're kind, non-judgemental, easy to get on with.'

'I don't know about that,' she had replied, seeing her face smiling stupidly in the mirror opposite at the compliment.

'Just be you,' Mandy had said, adjusting her leopard-print hairband and picking up her hairdryer again. 'And he's a teenager so don't be worried if he hardly says two words – they don't.'

That last sentence had made Maria blink, the familiar ache in her chest as her brain moved automatically to a place she tried to avoid. She nodded once, trying to swallow down the grief that was building in her body. How many years would have to pass before it stopped hurting?

'Seeing anyone?' Maria had asked, wanting to be distracted by one of Mandy's amusing diatribes about the useless men of Brighton. Instead, Maria frowned as she watched Mandy go scarlet to the roots of her recently peroxide-dyed hair. 'Maybe, early days, not sure.'

She had clamped up after that, which was most uncharacteristic. Normally, Maria was treated to a blow-by-blow account of the man under scrutiny: what his hobbies were, what he did for a living, passing judgement on his clothing to his family situation to his ex-girlfriends. This was unheard of, Mandy's eyes sliding all over the place, refusing to rest on Maria.

'I'm just going to book in this next customer,' she mumbled, scurrying to the counter and a waiting woman with short auburn hair.

Nina glanced over from her customer next door, mouth half-open as if she was about to share something, closing sharply when Mandy returned. Still, Maria had been too distracted by the meeting ahead to think about it too deeply, and Mandy's love life was her own business so if she didn't want to tell Maria anything, that was fine by her.

When she returned, Mandy had launched into a loud review of a new restaurant a few doors down: 'New management, not sure about the menu. It's a bit too exotic for me, I just like a decent burger, hand-cut chips, you know, and it's all tapas, and I've never been a huge fan of sharing my food neither…'

Maria had let her speak, not pushing the other topic and grateful to have the time pass in this way. Mandy seemed to talk particularly quickly, not letting Maria ask any questions but leapfrogging to the next conversation, desperate to move on. Nina stood nearby, quiet and watchful as Mandy finished Maria's hair. Maria had rushed off with a hurried goodbye, nervous about the meeting ahead.

The stench of cigarettes struck Maria as Troy sat down, scooting sideways into the chair. She had chosen a different table for them, not able to sit at the one she had always sat at with Albie. The smell of smoke reminded her of another afternoon in that café, when Albie had shown her a lighter, white with a black skull and crossbones, which he'd confiscated in his attempt to get Troy to give up the habit.

'The old man hated me smoking,' Troy said, as if he had read Maria's mind. 'Bad habit though, going to give up again soon.'

'It's hard giving up a bad habit,' she said and was rewarded with a grateful smile. 'I should know, I used to be a smoker too. God, sometimes I miss it.' She surprised herself with the admission.

She clearly surprised Troy too as he snuck her a small smile. 'Smoking? Really? Want one?'

'No!' She laughed, blushing. 'Anyway, I don't anymore. That was years ago. Now…' she said quickly, not wanting to think about those times, the other parts of her old life, 'what can I get you?'

Troy looked longingly at the counter piled high with iced buns, Eccles cakes, muffins and scones. 'I'm alright, I'm not hungry.'

'Well, I'm having a raspberry muffin, and it's all on Albie so go on,' she encouraged, knowing he was just being polite.

'S'OK.'

Maria raised one eyebrow, a trick she hadn't done in years, one that had always caused a reaction, a bark of laughter or a roll of her eyes depending on her mood.

'Chocolate cake then, thanks,' he mumbled into the table.

Amrit appeared at that moment to take their order, expertly not reacting to Maria's newest table companion. She had only ever come here with Albie and this was just the second person she had brought into their haven since his death.

'One muffin and one chocolate cake, please. And I like your hair!' Maria commented, noting the fresh new silver streaks, like a very attractive badger.

'Something for the summer. Thanks, Maria. Won't be long.' She noticed Amrit couldn't resist a curious glance back as she left the table.

Maria stared back across the table, which suddenly seemed like a desert to cross.

'It's just been re-decorated earlier this year, it was Albie's idea!' She tapped on the table. 'He'd hated the old tablecloths, thought the place could do with a bit of love.'

'Cool.' Troy nodded.

'All the furniture is new. Faux leather seats, I think.'

She realised Troy hadn't seen the café before the transformation, wouldn't notice any difference. She also knew that as a teenager he probably didn't have a lot to say about soft furnishings. She suddenly longed for Amrit to return to fill the silence for her.

Troy looked around the room, humouring her: 'S'nice.'

She swallowed down her nerves. This was ridiculous, she was the grown-up and yet it had been years since she had talked with a teenager. She felt the grief of it as that thought sunk in, the pain sometimes winding her when she least expected it.

Distracting herself, she looked across at Troy. 'I've never asked how you first met Albie?'

Troy crossed and re-crossed his arms on the table, trying to get comfortable. Was he as nervous as her, perhaps? Up until then their meetings had been sporadic, her dropping by the skatepark, snatching a few moments with them. This was different: just them, sat across from each other, Albie's absence like a third seat at their table.

'Sorry, is this a little like an interrogation?' she said.

'Nah, it's alright. Nice to talk about him, you know. Sometimes all I can see of him is that day…'

Maria realised with a hideous lurch that he was talking about the day he had found Albie, cold and inert in the bedroom of his apartment.

'I'm so sorry,' she said, reaching out to touch his forearm, the touch a surprise to both of them. This was much more Albie territory: being a comfort to others, a support.

'He dropped his mobile outside the youth centre,' Troy began, clearly not wanting to dwell, 'I chased after him. He made a real fuss about it, like I'd done this incredible thing, asked me loads of questions, about the youth centre, home, and there was something about him that made me talk, you know?'

Maria nodded and smiled, she did know: Albie had the remarkable ability of making people open up.

'Well, he gave me a bit of a hard time about not being in school, guessed I'd lied about my age, but not many people gave a shit, sorry…'

'It's fine!' Maria smiled, remembering briefly the days when she swore like the best of them, all those years ago. How she'd had to watch it once her own child picked up on everything.

'And it was kind of cool, you know, then asked if I minded if he came to see me, check out the youth centre. I didn't think he'd do it, you know, but then he came same time the next day…' Troy looked up then, met Maria's eyes. 'Kind of like you, you know, not quitting, like, but showing up again, reminded me of him.'

Maria blinked, impossibly moved by the comparison.

'Albie signed up to mentor me and it was good, you know, he seemed to understand. And we hung out. Fuck, I miss him. God, sorry.'

Maria smiled again, more sadly. 'I miss him too. So much.'

They sat then in a more relaxed silence, both thinking of the same man, the same person who had touched both their lives.

Amrit brought over their cakes and this seemed to prompt them out of their reverie. Maria noted Troy's enormous slice of chocolate cake with satisfaction, the double layers of chocolate buttercream icing, the sprinkles on top.

'That looks good,' she said, pointing her fork at his plate.

'It does. Only birthday cake I'll be getting,' he said, casually slicing into it.

Maria set her fork down, a horrified look on her face. 'Your birthday? It's today? I had no idea. Happy Birthday!'

Troy shrugged, a small embarrassed look down at his plate. 'Doesn't matter.'

'Of course it matters,' Maria scoffed, picking up her fork again. 'Birthdays always matter. Well, until you get to my age and then you want to start counting backwards…'

She couldn't help but pause and think of Albie then, how he'd never see another birthday. She hadn't even known when his birthday was, had never thought to ask. All those uncelebrated days in the years she'd known him. She should have asked, should have bought him cake, got him a present. So many 'shoulds'…

'How old are you?' she asked, not wanting to make that mistake again.

'Seventeen.'

'Oh, that's a big one. Anything special planned this evening?' Maria asked.

His expression made her want to take the question straight back.

'Mum's a bit busy.' His lips sealed close and Maria kicked herself for walking into such a minefield. She knew from Albie that Troy had a difficult home life, younger siblings and a dad who'd left them when they were young. Why had she not treaded more carefully? This was her problem: thoughtless, careless, bumbling into things without stopping to reflect – Albie wouldn't have made such a mistake.

She noticed a small pad sticking out of one of the enormous pockets that ran down Troy's trouser leg. Desperate to move the conversation on, she asked, 'What's that?'

He drew out the pad. 'S'nothing really,' he said, covering it with a defensive hand. 'Drawings.'

'Can I see?' she asked, holding out her hand.

Troy shrugged and handed it over. Maria had wondered whether it was some kind of diary but the thought that this young boy walked around with a pad of drawings made her heart lurch.

She opened the first page. They were good, really good. Vivid colours, cartoon-like pictures, reds, blues, greens, thick black lines. She turned the pages, discovering more sketches, some scribbled out, some calligraphy, different fonts spelling out different words.

'What does this mean?' she asked, pointing at the sheet.

'YOLO,' Troy said, peering over at it, 'means You Only Live Once.'

'Albie would have loved that sentiment,' she remarked.

The briefest pause before Troy grinned. 'Yeah, he would've.'

Maria continued to absorb the pages.

'It's just doing lettering, practising, you know,' Troy said, a little self-consciously. 'Albie set me up with an apprenticeship on Saturday mornings at Electric Lady. Adam's the owner, got me doing these…'

'They're brilliant,' she said, examining the next page: a dripping rose, blood from its thorns. She could see the petals, the shape of the flower, smell its sweet scent. 'Do you want to be an artist?' she asked, turning the page, not looking up, lingering now over the picture of a man: flat cap, large brown coat, a twinkle in his eye, a broken nose. 'Oh!' she said, taken aback, a stutter to her voice. 'It's just like him.'

Troy couldn't help the pleased twitch of his lips. 'I want to be a tattoo artist,' he said softly, as if saying it out loud might make it real. 'That's what I'm doing at Electric Lady, it's a tattoo place.'

Maria didn't want to tear her eyes away from the picture of Albie, something about the stoop in his walk, the light-hearted expression. Troy had the same gift; they had shared a real talent for art.

'You can have it, if you like,' he said, dragging Maria back to the room, the noise of the café, Troy looking at her.

'Oh no, I…'

'You can keep it,' he repeated, his eyes not quite meeting hers.

'I couldn't, it's yours, it's…'

She saw his shoulders fall. Why was she saying no? Out of embarrassment? Did she not think she deserved it? He had offered it and she snapped back, her usual response.

'That would be wonderful, I'd love it. But…'

Troy took the pad back, neatly pulled out the page with Albie's image on it. 'There you go,' he said, thrusting it towards her and sliding the pad back in his pocket.

'Thank you,' Maria said, eyes still roving over the image on the page. 'I'll keep it on one condition.'

Troy looked up, eyes already narrowed in defensive suspicion.

'If you sign it for me,' she said firmly, rooting in her handbag for a biro. 'Then it'll be worth millions in the future.'

A tiny laugh, short and deep, came out of his mouth and Maria felt a moment of satisfaction to have been the cause of it. He signed his name in the bottom left of the drawing and then handed it back. She took it reverentially, placing it between the pages of her book so it wouldn't crease.

'It seems wrong that you've given me something when it's your birthday,' she admitted.

'You gave me the cake, it was sick.'

'Was it?' Maria asked in alarm.

Troy frowned. 'Yeah.'

'Oh dear,' Maria said, wringing her hands and looking towards the kitchen. Should she tell Pauline? She didn't want to upset her but she probably needed to know.

Troy's eyebrows had drawn together, a twinkle in his eyes. 'That means good.'

'Oh,' Maria exclaimed, a hand on her chest.

The short, deep laugh came again. Then, without much warning, Troy slid his chair back. 'Look, I better be going, but thanks for the cake, yeah?'

She had wanted to ask him more about being a tattoo artist, about his other hopes and dreams. She wanted to know why it would be the only birthday cake he would have that day. She wanted to make this day special. Wasn't that how mentoring worked? And yet she found herself nodding, half rising out of her chair, thrown by his desire to leave so soon.

He didn't let her draw out a goodbye, gave her a low wave, nodded at Amrit as he skirted round the adjacent table to the door.

Maria watched him go, sloping past the window of the café, head down, hood up, movements cat-like. She wondered where he was off to now, how he spent his days, how he would spend his birthday.

Pauline approached the table with a tray and a cloth. 'Who was that then?' she asked, stacking the plates and cups on the tray.

'Someone Albie was mentoring,' Maria explained.

Pauline looked up. 'That man was a dark horse, wasn't he…?'

For a second Maria couldn't help the thoughts: Albie had been a dark horse. The wealth, the secrets – and Cathie, of course.

'…Plans for the café,' Pauline continued, 'mentoring the local youth… What next?' She laughed, setting the tray to one side and wiping the table down with a cloth.

'Funny you should say that,' Maria said, dismissing her previous thought and turning to her with a small smile, 'How are the next couple of weeks looking?'

Pauline paused, gave Maria a puzzled frown.

'Can you take a day off?'

*

Our little flat has a balcony overlooking the sea and I love to sit out in the evening as the sun sets, smoking a cigarette, holding a glass of wine.

One evening before bed, sat curled in my lap in her cotton nightdress, she had looked around the balcony.

'We don't grow anything. In Polly's house she has a big plant called yucca, which is funny.'

She settled in my lap as the sun was sinking, oranges and pinks ribboned across the sky.

The next day I brought home seeds, pots, a bright red watering can, a bag of soil.

'What's that?' she asked, looking curiously in my basket.

'You'll see.'

We planted them in clay pots, sat in the corner of the balcony. Barefoot and earnest, she watered them every day, religiously, just before her own breakfast.

She asked after them, she talked to them, she sang.

'Mrs Finchley told me that's how plants grow big,' she'd said, continuing to tell the pots about how Worzel Gummidge had swapped his head that

day, how there were nine planets in the solar system but maybe more in others, how Polly was her best friend but she liked Katie too.

Then, hearing a cry one morning, I rushed out, hair damp, one stocking on, one crumpled in my hand. 'What is it?'

'Yellow, a yellow flower,' she said, eyes bright with excitement.

She tended to those tulips as if they were the most precious things in the world – and cried when they finally died.

I can't look at flowers without thinking of her, without thinking of the wonder on her face that made her beam when she first saw them blossom. I can't look at them without feeling an ache so deep in my soul, I wonder how I will bear the pain of it forever.

Chapter 21

She had looked up a few different places in an hour or so radius of Brighton, baulking at the prices and then reminding herself that this was not her gift and frankly, Albie could afford it. She phoned her chosen spa and booked them two spots for a whole day, the woman on the phone running through each option: did she want a hammam massage with herbs in their new cedarwood barrel sauna? Did she want the lunch inspired by the principles of Ayurveda to optimise digestion? Did she want…? Maria said yes to every question, feeling the excitement build inside her.

Pauline had offered to drive them. Maria had wanted to take the train but Pauline was so no-nonsense that she found herself agreeing and met her at an allocated time outside her apartment.

'Sorry about the crisp packets,' Pauline said, brushing at the seat. 'I'm a proper car slut, can't keep 'em clean. Did you bring flip flops? I like the new look though!' she added, glancing across at Maria. Today, Maria was wearing loose clothing and trainers. She'd removed the tags that morning, fretting over the ironed creases in the fabric, gasping at the price of fashion these days.

'Flip flops?' Maria said, putting on her seatbelt, 'I don't own flip flops.'

'Didn't think so, so I chucked in a spare pair for you, but they might give them for free – I heard some fancy places do that. Mint?' Pauline offered her a tin of travel sweets dusted with sugar.

'Oh, lovely, thank you,' Maria said, taking one, the powder sticking to her fingers. She tucked her bag under her legs. The car smelt of wet fabric and prawn cocktail, a faded air freshener dangling from the mirror, its smell long gone.

'S'good,' she said as they pulled into the traffic, her mouth full.

'So,' Pauline said, twiddling the button on the radio, 'journey time's just over an hour. Tell me exactly what we're doing, I could not be more excited.'

The drive went by in no time, and before they knew it, they were arriving. The spa was part of a hotel, a pebbled driveway sweeping around the front of an enormous cream Georgian manor house, pillars either side of the heavy oak doors. The car crunched across the gravel, Maria straining her neck, admiring every detail of the grand façade. Bay trees in terracotta pots stood in uniform lines, impeccably manicured hedges, a polished marble floor as they stepped inside. The scent that struck her was immediate: beeswax polish and money. She felt self-conscious as she moved across to the polished wooden Reception desk, pulling on her hooded top, more suited to a gymnasium than a swanky hotel. A young man with slicked-back blond hair looked up with a smile, not seeming to bat a professional eye at their attire.

Pauline was giving a low whistle behind her, distracted by double doors to the left opening onto an enormous restaurant with soaring flowers in the centre of every table.

The man directed them both to the side entrance to the spa and they traipsed round, peeking at a freshly-cut lawn with what looked to be a labyrinth at its centre, a couple sat on a bench overlooking the scene.

'Cor! This is alright, isn't it?' Pauline whispered reverentially, pushing through the double doors, a discreet glass sign on the right of them announcing 'The Waterdale Spa'. The smell of chlorine hung in the air as they squeaked across to another reception desk manned by a smooth olive-skinned girl. 'Welcome to The Waterdale Spa,' her voice whispered, satin-smooth and reverential. Maria felt an overwhelming urge to bow.

They were handed an enormous pile of pristine white towels, dressing gowns and (free) fluffy slippers and instructed to follow as the hostess pointed out the various doors: treatment rooms, resting area, relaxation lounge, swimming pool, changing rooms, sauna, steam room and more. The words were largely foreign to Maria, who had never been anywhere like this, so she let Pauline ask the questions, sort the timings. She just stared, awe-struck, as they moved, trying not to stumble as she peeked out over her enormous pile of fluffy items.

As she stumbled into the changing room, heading to a locker, she could see Pauline was already somehow half undressed, talking about the eucalyptus steam room and the cold shower experience. For a grandmother she had an enviable figure: willowy long limbs, a narrow waist. In comparison, Maria found herself looking around for a cubicle to hide.

'Oh, they've got an outdoor and inside sauna, you know,' Pauline read from a notice on the wall.

Maria grinned as she realised Albie had guessed absolutely right. This was the perfect gift for Pauline, she was absolutely in her element.

'I thought I'd get Shellac,' Pauline was saying as Maria continued to hunt for somewhere to change. She looked at her dumbly. 'For the toes,' Pauline waggled a foot. 'I've always wanted to get a gel manicure and now I can try.'

'Great,' Maria said, spotting a small changing room in the corner, trying not to stare at Pauline's royal blue bikini as she passed. Maria wouldn't dare to wear a bikini; Pauline was only a few years younger, but she carried it off effortlessly.

Maria got undressed and reached into her bag, pulling at the tags on her new black swimming costume. She'd had to buy it especially. It hadn't occurred to her when she had called to book, until the receptionist had listed what to bring. And of course, swimming pools, hot tubs… there was bound to be water. Now, she reminded herself why she had booked the spa: it wasn't about her, it was a gift for Pauline from Albie. Just seeing Pauline's wide-eyed reaction at the high-vaulted swimming pool area, the black-tiled bottom of the pool sparkling with tiny silver flecks, the sleek cushioned loungers that lined the room, Maria knew she had done the right thing by coming.

Pauline immediately stepped into the almost-empty pool, her ash-blonde hair tied in a high knot as she set off doing breaststroke. Maria sunk onto a nearby lounger, pulling out her book and taking the odd glance at the pool. It did look inviting but there was no way she was getting in.

Time passed and people came and went. Pauline swam towards Maria, her fringe stuck to her forehead, her cheeks flushed with the exercise.

'This is amazing. You ain't getting in?'

'I'm alright,' Maria said from the safety of her lounger.

'You're not going to get wet?' Pauline splashed at her, spraying the side. Maria lifted her knees up, just avoiding the droplets.

'How about the hot tub?' Pauline said, climbing up the ladder.

'Oh, I'm not sure…' Maria replied, glancing across the room.

'Come on,' Pauline said, standing dripping in front of her, 'Don't make me sit in there on my own.'

Maria could see she wouldn't be giving up. She put down her book and nodded, standing and wrapping the dressing gown firmly around her.

'Come on then,' said Pauline, padding across to the large circled pool, steam rising from its surface. Pressing a button on the side, it bubbled into life and she stepped into it, turning to hold her hand out to Maria. She took it, dressing gown abandoned on a chair nearby, a tentative step into the water. Apart from her baths she avoided water.

'Watch yer step!' Pauline said, sinking into the bubbles. 'Oh my god, this is bliss.'

The water was wonderfully warm and Maria reminded herself that it was just like an oversized bath. She edged her way into a sitting position and rested her head back, feeling the water tickle the bottom strands of her hair.

'That better?' Pauline asked, opening one eye to look across at her.

Maria couldn't stop the grin from her face. 'It's gorgeous,' she said, the jet streams of water gently pummelling the knots in her back and thighs. She allowed herself to rest right back against the side and close her eyes, savouring it.

'So, are we going to talk about him?' Pauline said after a while, both eyes still closed, head tilted back.

Maria gave her a sideways look, 'Who?'

Pauline opened one eye. 'Who do you think? Our amazing bene-factor, of course: Albert. I was always curious, were you two…?' She waggled her eyebrows.

Maria couldn't help a small giggle escaping. 'He was my friend,' she said simply. 'But I wish…' She settled back against the edge again, sighing deeply.

'Oh, I think I see.'

'I don't know he ever felt the same way,' Maria said hurriedly, not wanting to presume. 'He mentioned a woman, Cathie. He wanted to take her to Paris...' The information burst out of Maria in an embarrassed rush.

'Cathie,' Pauline repeated.

Maria nodded, 'I wrote to her. To tell her. She didn't reply.'

'Didn't she? Well, well there ain't no rivalry there...'

Maria looked up at her, her breath seeming suddenly stuck in her chest. Pauline was giving her the strangest look. Did she...?

Maria couldn't help asking, her eyes widening, 'Did you know her?'

'Cathie was Albie's sister! Thought they'd had a falling-out a while back, he mentioned it in passing. I was telling him about two of my sisters – they don't speak, they had a massive falling-out over a casserole dish, one of those nice ceramic ones. Someone smashed it or didn't return it, I forget, and it all exploded. Families, eh?'

Maria wasn't focusing as Pauline continued. Sister? Cathie was Albie's *sister*? How had she never known this? And he'd told Pauline, but not her.

All the worry she'd had, the imagined romance, the years of a lost love, gone. Maria couldn't help a silly smile forming on her face.

Pauline noticed and started to laugh, 'You dolt!'

Maria imagined her face becoming crimson, feeling luck that she could blame it on the heat of the water.

'And this!' Pauline threw an arm around, saving Maria from more detail. 'Lavish spa days, renovations... what else has the man got you doing?'

'He had this whole list – a wish list, he called it – and I'm working my way through it.'

Pauline was silent for a bit. 'What a wonderful way to live. I wonder why he created it.'

Maria opened her eyes again, realising she had been asking herself the same thing. He was generous – he had shown that in all her dealings with him – but the list did seem to go above and beyond generosity. As if something else was driving him to complete the bullet points. Why did Albie feel he had to live in this way? Was it simply that he wanted to help others or was there a deeper reason behind it?

'I'm not sure,' she admitted finally, 'I wish I knew. And I wish I could show him the list still lives on even, even after…'

Maria was glad to be in the water, glad her face was already wet.

Pauline stretched out her legs, brushing Maria's in the water. 'Oops, sorry. You know, it's inspired me really. You can't help but be affected by all that goodness, it's bound to rub off. We're running an afternoon cake sale for the Macmillan Cancer Support charity – Keith's agreed to do the baking for it. In fact,' she said, 'I've offered him a job. We need someone else in the kitchen who knows what they're doing, I want to stay front of house nowadays…'

'Keith,' Maria repeated, her voice brimming with joy. 'Oh, but that's brilliant.' She felt her face stretch into the most enormous smile. Keith finally had work, someone had given him a much-needed chance.

'Yeah, and I offered him the bedsit above the café. Seems he's had some trouble recently with accommodation,' she said, a sly glance across.

Maria bit her lip.

Pauline cackled. 'You could have told me you hauled the man in off the street…'

'I didn't…' The water sploshed as Maria started.

Pauline batted her away. 'I'm joking, I'm joking, I knew something was up, he kept appearing in the café with the same clothes for a start, so I asked him outright and he told me. I was relieved, no great secret that. For a minute I was worried he might have killed someone or something. He didn't *seem* the killing type. So, he lives there now. He's keeping the place tidier than any previous tenant. He asked me if he could borrow coasters from the café. Coasters, for god's sake, man's a neat freak.'

Maria felt herself relax, laughing at Pauline's exasperated expression. How wonderful that Keith now had a roof over his head, not damp and cold and ignored on the streets of Brighton. She hadn't seen him in a while and was delighted that was the reason.

'The Albie Effect, isn't it? I've gone soft,' said Pauline, sinking deeper into the water.

The Albie Effect, Maria reflected, feeling the warmth all around her and now in her too. How true. He was making everything better still, touching the lives of others even now.

They stayed in a happy silence and before Maria knew it, an olive-skinned girl was standing in front of them in her dazzling white uniform informing them their treatments would begin in five minutes.

With her skin shrivelled from the water, Maria stepped out of the hot tub and into her dressing gown.

'Treatments!' Pauline announced with an excited clap.

The massages were utter heaven, lilting music playing as fingers pressed and squeezed her flesh. Aromatic oil was rubbed into her back and shoulders and Maria soon forgot to be embarrassed about her rolls of flesh or the wrinkles on her skin, too carried away by the ecstasy of being pampered. When she stood, she was dizzy, skin and hair damp and smelling of the orange-scented oil they'd used.

Pauline looked at her groggily, clearly feeling the same way. 'Not sure I'm going to be able to stay awake for the rest of the day.'

They had their toenails painted side by side, Pauline selecting the same bright coral for them both and Maria getting a tiny glimpse into what her life might have been like with a best friend. They talked more over the healthy lunch, Pauline telling her all about her childhood in East London, her mum a midwife, her dad a plumber who loved to fix up anything with a wire so their whole terrace house was crammed with broken electrical goods; her first husband who lost all their money buying a holiday home in Spain that didn't exist. She talked and Maria listened and laughed, swerving questions about herself and diverting the attention back to Pauline.

Pauline offered an enormous tip to the receptionist, asking if she could track them down some cake.

'It's a special lunch designed around the principles of Ayurveda to help aid digestion and leave you feeling restored and energised,' the receptionist explained in a zen-like tone.

'That is great but I have a medical need for a sugary treat,' Pauline said solemnly, marvelling at the speed with which the girl produced two enormous slices of Black Forest gateau.

'So…' – Pauline cut into the cake – 'what about you, Maria? Apart from Albie, has there ever been another man in your life?'

'Albie wasn't…'

'Oh, pfft,' Pauline said, angling the loaded fork at her. 'Any fool could see the man was head over heels for you.'

Had he been? Maria wondered, the cake dry in her throat as she swallowed. *Had she really missed the signs?*

'I was with someone once, a long time ago,' Maria admitted, cutting into her cake, and tried to change the subject by asking another question.

Pauline sat back, cake half-eaten in front of her, eyes narrowing a fraction.

'Never mind that, Go on, tell me a bit more about this mystery man.'

Maria swallowed; she hadn't spoke about him for over forty years. 'It was a very long time ago now,' she said, trying to wave it off, surprised by the stick in her throat.

Pauline wasn't fooled. 'Doesn't matter how long ago, things still hurt.'

How true.

For a moment Maria was tempted to share everything: the whole sorry story. Lay it all out. She had spent a lifetime keeping it inside. But something stopped her: habit, and fear, of course – fear that she would threaten this precious new friendship if Pauline knew everything.

'He was my first love, I suppose,' she said, offering something small. 'It started well, he was good fun. He had a motorbike and loved taking me to the pictures and wanted to be a radio disc jockey. I thought we'd get married.'

Pauline had tilted her head to one side. 'Sounds exciting.'

'He *was* exciting. The centre of it all, lots of energy, great fun, brave. I introduced him to my parents back home in the Peak District. My mum didn't like him, said as much to me and he called her a bully to her face. I loved him for that, for being the person who saw her for what she was and also for being the one to say it when I'd never been able to…'

'I didn't much get on with my mum either,' Pauline admitted. 'Sounds like someone good to have in your corner. What happened to 'im?'

Maria licked her lips, thoughts racing through her mind. She didn't want to tell Pauline the truth, found it lodged inside her.

We had a child.

We had a child and all the things that had made him fun, all those traits, weren't much good when Maria had needed someone to rely on, to share the load.

We had a child and he walked out when that child was eleven months old.

'It just fizzled out, he left and I wasn't much interested in men after that…' Maria mumbled, knowing if she told Pauline the truth there would be more questions, questions she had never been able to face.

She was slumped in her chair, drained even from these admissions, more than she'd ever really shared before. Only Albie had learnt the whole truth. She had spent months kicking herself for the way it must have changed his opinion of her.

'Well, that doesn't sound so strange, although it still doesn't explain what you're punishing yourself for.' Pauline appraised Maria.

Maria swallowed her cake in one abrupt mouthful.

'I'm right, aren't I?' Pauline continued as Maria started to splutter on the sponge. 'Water over here,' she called out to the receptionist as she rubbed Maria on the back until she'd stopped coughing. 'Alright, Maria, alright, no need to keel over,' she added, getting up and tightening the belt of her robe. 'You win. You're off the hook, no more grilling from me… for now.'

Pauline was true to her word; she didn't ask her another question all the way back to Brighton, just played the radio, sang along and offered her mints. Maria rested her head back on the seat, the tension leaking out of her. It might have ruined things and she was used to keeping secrets. With the fresh air outside flooding the car, her body feeling relaxed and pampered, her skin soft and her feet encased in the brand-new spa slippers to protect her brand-new spa pedicure, she just enjoyed the ride, imagining her life had always been like this and wanting to keep hold of this feeling for as long as possible.

*

She ran into her room the moment she was home, her sobs barely muffled by a ballad from The Carpenters spilling out of the cassette.

I waited a moment, not wanting to push straight in.

'Do you want me to get out the SodaStream?' I called.

No answer.

This wasn't good. She'd been pestering me for weeks to buy a new cylinder for that machine: 'It doesn't make the drink fizzy otherwise!'

I couldn't wait any longer, knew she didn't like me going in without her permission: the worn sign sellotaped to the door warning people in bright purple felt tip to 'Keep Out'. I was the only other person who lived here.

Ignoring the sign, I opened the door.

'Mum, no…'

She was face down, half-on, half-off the bed.

'Hey,' I said, rushing over, unable to do anything else.

The bed sagged as I sat next to her and reached out a hand to place on her hair.

She let me, not hiding the fact she was crying, letting the sobs take hold so the bed shook with them.

The day darkened, the room in shadow, and I waited there, hand on her hair until she stopped: small sobs hiccoughed out and then silence, just slow, gentle breathing.

The words when they came were muffled.

'What's that?' I asked.

'It's stupid,' she said, her voice broken with sadness and anger.

'I'm sure it's not.'

She sat up, wiped at her eyes, not quite able to look at me, her fingers plucking at the maroon duvet cover.

'They called me a bastard.'

'Who did?'

'The girls at school. They said I didn't have a dad so I was a bastard...'

I felt shock and anger stop the words in my throat.

'...Liam told Tyler that he liked me and now Ali won't talk to me because she likes Tyler and then they all said they think that...'

I was barely listening now, heat rising in me at this exhausting explanation of a crowd of mean girls. 'That's horrible, they're not your friends,' I said, furious on her behalf. 'How dare they.'

'They are,' she replied miserably. Then sat up straighter, 'They were.'

'Well, they're not even using the word right,' I said huffily, arms crossing my chest.

She gave me a sideways look, 'Whatdya mean?'

'Well, a bastard is someone who doesn't have any parents. And you have me.'

Her mouth twitched. An almost smile.

'And you do have a father. It's not your fault he's a selfish ass and left us.'

We sat side by side as I breathed through my nose with things I wanted to say to this group of girls. But instead of saying anything else I felt an arm snake round my waist, a head drop onto my shoulder, 'Thanks, Mum.'

I drew her tight into me, 'I love you so much, do you know that? More than two parents, more than two hundred bloody parents!'

I could feel her body relaxing as I held her.

'If you want me to hire someone to beat up those girls, I have connections. I'm a very powerful woman these days,' I said, raising an eyebrow.

She let out the smallest giggle.

Relief flooded through me, perhaps this wasn't too bad.

There was a pause and she cuddled in tightly.

'Can we use the SodaStream now?' she whispered.

I laughed, the sudden bark of sound snapping us apart.

I stood up and held out my hand to her, 'Absolutely.'

Chapter 22

She had bought a mobile phone the day before. The nice man in the shop had sat her down and explained text messaging to her and she had got the hang of it. He had even taught her about the little funny faces – called 'emus' or something like that – and showed her where they were. She'd left the shop clutching the box to her chest.

Troy had written his number down on a spare scrap of paper as she had wanted to be able to contact him. She couldn't wait to return to her apartment and send him her first text message. She had also asked the man in the shop to connect her to the *Words with Friends* app and she had invited Timothy to their first game.

The half-an-hour wait for a response from Troy seemed to last an eternity, checking the phone, waiting for the little envelope icon, the satisfying 'swoosh' sound. Then the answer came through: *c u then.*

An excitement moved through her body. There was something important she wanted to do. She grabbed her handbag and set off out again, knowing exactly where she was headed.

He arrived the day after. She buzzed him into the building and greeted him with a shy smile as he appeared outside the apartment door.

'S'nice,' he said as he shuffled inside, looking around.

It seemed strange to see someone else in her home, and with a jolt she realised it was the first time. That thought winded her for a second. No other living soul had seen inside her home. The all-familiar gaping loneliness threatened to overwhelm her for a moment and she had to stop to catch her breath.

It *wasn't* nice, she thought, as she looked as if through his eyes at the dated place: peach curtains that she'd never changed, Artex ceilings, dull pictures, a smeared mirror, cheap pine furniture, mismatching cushions. Perhaps she would give her own apartment a makeover like the café. Albie would like that, she reflected, with a sense of longing.

'So you got a mobile,' Troy said, seeing her holding it in her hands.

'I did. I already spend far too long on it. I've started playing *Words with Friends*, do you know it?'

Troy shook his head.

'I'm being rather badly beaten by Timothy, he's very good at adding letters to the ends of high-scoring words. Anyway…' Maria took a breath, knowing she was prattling on. 'I've got something I want you to have,' she said shyly, handing him a slim, rectangular gift wrapped neatly in bottle-green paper and a tartan bow, 'a belated birthday present.'

Troy backed off.

'Hey, there's no need, honestly, I shouldn't have said anything.'

'I'm glad you did,' Maria insisted, placing it firmly in his hand. 'I hope you like them. Happy Birthday.'

With an embarrassed shrug, Troy angled his body away from Maria and slid a finger along the paper in a neat line. Ever so gently, he took out the present and handed the paper back to Maria. He stared at the artist's set, taking it in. Maria had asked the attendant in the shop for the very best and had been pleased with the purchase. It was a large collection in a shiny wooden box, all the colours lined up in perfect order: pinks, purples, yellows, greens, blues; the colours bold, the tips perfect.

'These are watercolour pencils, so you can add water to them and turn them into paints. And felt tips, of course, and those are fine liners. The lady in the shop told me they are very good quality, perfect for fine work like your sketches.' She knew she was babbling again but Troy wasn't saying anything. She pointed at the pad inset into the case. 'A new pad for when you fill your last one. It's for your drawings, they're really good... And there's more,' she said, beckoning him.

Troy looked a little dazed as he dumbly followed her into the living room. Albie's mentorship had been all about trying to get Troy to spend some time on things he loved. She'd had the idea a few days before and had been so excited to think of his face. A sudden wave of worry washed over her: had she got it wrong? Would it be met with silence? Would he hate it? She wrung her hands as she stood in the doorway for a moment.

'I know you and Albie sometimes painted together and I hoped you might want to carry on so I did this...'

She waved an arm to the wall, where she had set up a small desk under the window. Sunlight sliced across the surface, over tubes of paints, a wooden palette, a cup for water, a collection of fresh paint-brushes and pastels lined up in neat rows. She had even bought a stool from a refurbished furniture shop around the corner.

'It's somewhere for you if you want to use it, anytime. I won't pack it away... It's your space...'

In a small A5 frame propped up on the desk stood the sketch he had given her of Albie. 'To motivate you,' she said, seeing him stare at it.

Troy didn't say anything and Maria bit her lip, the clock ticks sounding louder, the apartment waiting quietly. He moved forward, one hand reaching to touch the edge of the desk, lowering the artist's set. She watched him pick up a tube of paint, a paintbrush, turn them over in his hands. Still, he said nothing.

'I just thought…' She couldn't bear this silence. Had she done something wrong? Had she been presumptuous? Maybe he had a perfect place to draw and create. Maybe she was overstepping.

'It's…' He placed the paintbrush he was holding down carefully. 'I…'

'Maybe it was a silly idea. I know you barely know me but you see Albie and you, well, I know he would want you to…'

'No, it's not that,' Troy said, his voice a little gruffer than Maria had heard it before. Was that a hand up to his face? Was he embarrassed? Was she embarrassing herself? 'S'amazing,' he mumbled so quietly she might have imagined it.

'Oh.' The relief was huge. He didn't hate it. She hadn't embarrassed herself, in fact, she wondered whether he was rather choked with emotion.

He seated himself onto the stool and continued to study all the items in front of him.

'You could stay now if you like, I don't mind at all. I was just going to read. I could make us tea – do you drink tea?'

Troy shook his head, 'Nah.'

'Of course. Well, as I said, it's here anytime…'

'I drink water,' he said, looking up at her quickly.

Maria beamed, almost tripping to get to the kitchen cupboards, to turn on the tap. 'Water, perfect, lovely, that's great to hear.'

She brought him a glass and he was already bent over the pages, with a smattering of pastels, pens and more on the desk. He was focused, barely glancing up as she placed it down next to him. Retreating to the armchair, she picked up her book. It was the first time she had read for more than a page or so, the first time she'd properly read since Albie died. Somehow here in the small apartment, Troy sharing the same space with her, she felt herself unfurl. Relaxing back into the cushions, she enjoyed the sound of Troy's brushstrokes, his steady breathing, the angle of his head as he worked. Hours passed before he seemed to leave with a reluctant look back at her.

'You come again soon,' she called as he passed her, clutching the glossy artist's set to his chest as if it were a newborn baby.

Then, with barely any warning, he reached over and placed one arm around her shoulder, squeezing her quickly. 'Thanks, yeah.'

He was gone before he could see that the gesture had made her cry.

*

I'd liked Darren but he'd wanted a fresh start, the space you could buy in Australia – the life for kids, outdoor space, the beaches, the warm sunshine. 'Everyone's more relaxed, got a healthier work-life balance. Come with me.'

I didn't go. He stuck around for four months more trying to convince me that I could do it but she was happy. Her life was here, her school, her friends. I couldn't uproot her to the other side of the world, it would be selfish.

The day he left, I took the day off work, curling into the tightest ball on my bed, knees to my chest, and let myself sob for the life I'd let go. He'd always been so kind, showing his love for us in practical ways: never had more shelves been put up, more cups of tea been made. I wept for the life I could have had: the exhausting work would've been over, I could've stepped off this treadmill I'd put myself on, I could've share the parenting load once more. Three was nice.

The doorbell went and I wasn't quick enough, had dozed off, soggy tissues scattered in balls around me, eyes red raw. She didn't say anything, just climbed onto the bed. I felt the mattress give, smelt cherries as she lay down next to me, one arm over my body like I'd done countless times to her.

She didn't make a joke, make light of it: she'd liked Darren too.

She snuggled right in, close to me.

I let out the smallest sob, reaching for her hand, feeling it grip me tightly, nails smooth with varnish.

'Thanks, Mum,' she whispered.

I squeezed my eyes tight, feeling the ache in my chest for all the love.

'I choose you,' I whispered back.

I would always choose you.

Chapter 23

Since finding out that Cathie was Albie's sister Maria had felt the jealousy drain away, replaced by an urgent desire to make the Paris trip happen. She had applied for a passport, her old one long-gone, lapsed when she had no need to travel anywhere, no one to travel with. The photo showed a somewhat startled Maria: eyebrows lifted, wide blue eyes blinking in surprise at the flash of the photo booth. It was the first photo of herself she had seen in almost forty years.

She still couldn't believe that Albie had hidden this other secret from her. A sister! Someone who had grown up with Albie, who had known him as a young boy. Had he loved trains? Jigsaws? 'Snails and puppy dogs' tails'? Had he been a gentle boy or a whirlwind? She was sure she once asked him about family and he'd given the impression that he too was on his own. It was something she'd always felt they'd had in common yet in the wings was a sister.

As an only child Maria had often watched in baffled awe at the easy relationship between siblings. In her class at school, she had befriended twin sisters and had always watched in slack-jawed amazement at the overlapping excited chatter, the light punch to an arm, the rolling eyes, the energy of them. Had Cathie and Albie been like that, she wondered.

The list had mentioned a need for Albie to 'make up for lost time'. How long? What had happened? She hoped Cathie would perhaps give her more of an insight into why Albie felt he needed to live his life through the list.

She wrote another letter, and a third. She included her address, landline and new mobile number in each missive. She received no replies. She had to try one last time. So, one evening, fortified by a sherry or two, she went on the Internet on her mobile phone and booked two tickets on the Eurostar, leaving the following weekend. Then she scanned numerous hotels before selecting the perfect place and booking two single rooms. She wrote down all the information on a single sheet of paper and added a brief note: *Albie never made it, but he wanted you to.*

And how, Maria wanted to know why: why Paris? Why did he want Cathie to go there?

Two days later, she received a text message simply stating that Cathie would meet her at St Pancras International an hour before departure. Maria stared at the words for almost a full minute. She sent a large yellow smiley face back from the box of little pictures.

Almost immediately, she was in a spin. She had to make plans: work out a walking route – nothing too much in case Cathie didn't want to spend all day on her feet – and things to do, research the city more thoroughly. Her phone had maps, even of France. The man in the shop had mentioned it, she remembered. She returned to see him and he taught her more about how to go 'online' and use the Web. There was a little button she could press and the whole Internet was just there. She could look up a hundred details: the best restaurants, the exhibitions, the nicest hotels. All sat in her living room!

Then she panicked over her attire: what does one wear to Paris? She scanned her wardrobe. Parisians were famously chic. She conjured up images of women in narrow-waisted dresses, flared-out skirts, elegant heels, expensive hosiery, blood-red lipstick and a sultry scent to boot. She wanted outfits to match the fabulous setting; she was also desperate to impress Cathie, this mysterious sister with whom Albie had been so keen to reconcile. She rarely spent money on clothes, and she took good care of the few items she owned, but today, she was keen to splash out.

Idling along the High Street, she felt her enthusiasm waning, the faces on the various shop assistants unwelcoming. She stared down at her drab attire and started to doubt the need for anything new. Who would care now? She was just an old lady in their eyes, she was well and truly past it. Stopping to rest on a bench, she made the decision to head home: she would make do.

A woman walked past the bench, two teenage daughters in tow, both trying to drag her into different shops. Maria gave them a weak smile. 'Muuuum, pleeeaasseee!' she could hear as they disappeared into the shoe shop nearby.

She felt a dull ache in her stomach, then glancing up, she saw Rosie leaning against a shop front. Maria held up a hand in greeting. Kicking back against the stone, Rosie bounced over, 'Hey, Maria, you shopping?'

Maria could see her confusion: no carrier bags weighing her down.

'I wanted to, but nothing here is really… me. I'm just not young enough for half these clothes.'

'Rubbish, you could totally rock it!' Rosie scoffed, batting this comment away with a hand and joining Maria on the bench. 'What kind of thing do you want? I could come with you and help you look, if you like.'

'It's for Paris, so something suitable for that.'

'You're going,' Rosie grinned. 'Brilliant. Come on, I'll help.'

Maria felt embarrassed to be relying on Rosie yet again but it was such a comforting thought to have someone with her as she walked into the bewildering array of shops that she agreed immediately.

'I love shopping!' Rosie announced, standing up and beckoning Maria with a hand. 'And of course, you need fabulous things for Paris.' She steered Maria into a nearby department store. 'Right, let's get started.'

Maria felt energised, pulling various items off the rail, stroking the soft fabrics, barely glancing at the price tags. When she was unsure if something suited her, she would look to Rosie for her opinion on it.

'You should try it,' Rosie would often say, making Maria add it to the growing pile. 'You should wear brighter colours,' she said, as Maria held up a red linen dress. 'That's gorgeous.'

Maria twisted towards the full-length mirror, her eye drawn to the red. She wondered if Albie would have liked it, remembering his compliments she had always batted away: 'That's a lovely colour on you, Maria', 'You always look so elegant', 'That dress is wonderful', 'People will wonder what you're doing, sitting here with me'. She swallowed down the regret, glad Rosie was here, chivvying her into the changing room.

Maria felt like a celebrity trying on different dresses, skirts and shirts, emerging from the changing rooms to spin in front of Rosie, who clapped and whistled. A nearby shop assistant glanced across curiously as Maria headed back behind the changing cubicle curtain.

With Rosie's encouragement, Maria spent most of the last three months of her pension on different outfits, choosing a pair of soft pink suede pumps and changing into them there and then for her walk home. Albie's money wouldn't be used for this, this was all hers, her own vanity – she wanted to look good for Paris, for Cathie.

A week later, she was standing in St Pancras in a new tan knee-length coat, her small wheeled suitcase by her side, handbag tucked tightly under one arm. She was proud of herself after a train and tube journey to get here. She hadn't been to London in more than twenty years and it seemed even more vivid and busy than she remembered. St Pancras was a bustling, bright space. A young girl was playing a glossy black piano nearby, her long brown hair reminding Maria of Rosie, and a friend leant against it, laughing in delight. Shoppers clutching carrier bags stepped around Maria; a man with a briefcase strode past, jabbering into his smartphone. It was extra-loud and extra-bright – and Maria felt her stomach swirl with nervous anticipation.

As Maria stood outside the ticket collection booth of the Eurostar at the allotted time, she panicked that the text message had been a hoax and Cathie wouldn't be there at all. Maria glanced at the large clock overhead and bit her lip. She had sent a photograph that morning so that Cathie could recognise her. Cathie had sent one back in return, in her nurse's uniform, her work badge still on the lapel. Surely if she wasn't planning on coming, she wouldn't have sent it?

The woman from the photograph approached, the same height as Maria but a good few years younger, wheeling a silver suitcase behind her. Stopping in front of Maria, she held out her hand. She didn't look all that similar to Albie, maybe the same shaped nose, similar dark blue eyes, but her expression was foreign, the mouth set in a hard line as Maria took the proffered hand to shake.

'I nearly didn't come,' she said, 'But…' She left the sentence hanging.

Maria didn't feel self-assured enough to say more than, 'Well, thank you. Shall we…?' Maria nodded her head towards the Departures and Cathie silently followed.

As they waited to show their passports at check-in, Maria was trying to work out how many years apart Cathie and Albie had been. She certainly looked in shape: dressed almost entirely in slimming black, only a sheer grey scarf breaking up the colour. Short cropped hair, dyed blonde, accentuated a thin neck. Maria complimented her on her silver stud earrings, not wanting to seem as if she was staring. When Cathie smiled a shy acknowledgement, a twinkle entered her eyes and Maria saw the connection to Albie for the first time.

It was awkward as they queued for coffees and sandwiches for the train, Maria insisting on paying for everything. 'It's on Albie, it's all on Albie,' she said, feeling as if she had eight fingers on each hand, spilling change, searching for the envelope with the tickets, her handbag suddenly seeming to contain a hundred secret compartments. Cathie looked on, refusing sugar, a spoon, a cookie. Maria was so desperate to please, couldn't seem to stop herself offering anything in sight. She must calm down.

'So, you say he left a list, after he died…'

Maria nodded. 'A wish list. Things he wanted to do – for other people. That was how I found out about you.'

Cathie didn't say much else and Maria didn't know how to handle this strange situation so followed her lead. Her new suede pumps were a little tight and she wanted to kick them off and rub at her feet, but she stayed standing in the holding area in silence because Cathie didn't seem to want to sit down. She was fidgeting, patting at her hair, avoiding Maria's eyes. Finally, the clock ticked to their departure time and they boarded the train in silence.

Oh goodness, Albie, what have you done? Maria thought as she stepped inside. How would she be able to spend two whole days with someone so frosty, so polar opposite to Albie? She gave Cathie a nervy smile, distracted then by their surroundings.

Maria had never been on the Eurostar, the first-class carriage roomy and smelling of leather and lemon scent. 'This is exciting,' she said, finding their seats and pleased to see the table in front of them.

'We can have a picnic,' she carried on, forcing her voice to be jolly, trying to channel Albie's easy manner. God, how she wished he was here – it would be so much easier if he were here, directing, fussing, taking control.

Cathie didn't reply and Maria sank into her seat, barely noticing the soft leather, the comfortable armrests, still fretting over this tense start. As Cathie sat down opposite, Maria noticed her surreptitiously wiping at her eyes and realised then that perhaps Cathie's seeming coldness was more complicated, that perhaps she was struggling with something. She thought then of Albie's list, his desire to make amends. This weekend was important.

Cathie had opened her book and Maria tried to follow her lead and bite down the questions, but she couldn't help it. If she didn't ask, she might burst.

'I'm so glad you decided to come,' Maria said, the carriage moving from light to dark as the train moved through the English countryside to the Channel.

Cathie placed her book spine up on the table, fiddled with her earring. 'I'm sorry you had to write me so many letters. I…' She straightened in her chair. 'It's been a long time, I wasn't sure how to react.'

'I had no idea Albie had a sister,' Maria said, 'I thought you were a glamourous ex-girlfriend, or a wif—' She stopped short then, worried Cathie would be offended Albie had never mentioned her.

'Younger sister. Albie was six years older than me,' she said in a tight voice.

'I had no idea.'

Cathie tilted her head to one side, her lips pressed together. 'We hadn't spoken in years. I only heard he had died from a letter sent from his solicitor...' She bit her lip, head turning towards the window that was a blur of greens and greys.

Maria didn't ask about the letter, could see the emotion moving across Cathie's face.

'I'm sorry,' she said, gratified that Cathie looked back at her with a sad smile.

The rattle of the approaching drinks trolley came as a relief.

'Would you like anything?' Maria asked, and then added, 'To hell with it, we're going to Paris.' She had often drunk wine with girlfriends when she was younger – those days were a distant memory – and for a second, she wanted to feel the same sense of connection. She ordered a half-bottle of red wine and tried to relax as Cathie nodded for a glass.

The wine was rich and smooth and Maria rested her head back and tried to relax as Cathie reached out to drink her glass. This was really happening, she was on the Eurostar heading to a glamorous city she had never dreamed of visiting, with a woman she had never met before. She had travelled to France once, almost fifty years ago, on the ferry – she and her partner had spent a week in Bordeaux. It had rained and he had grumbled about the lumpy bed and the lack of 'normal British food' for the whole week until she'd wanted to pelt him with Brie. That was a lifetime ago, before her passport had lapsed and she had holed up in Brighton. Paris, in her mind, was the epitome of elegance and now she couldn't wait to see the sights through Albie's eyes: the Eiffel Tower, the Arc de Triomphe, imagine his sad expression in front of the fire-ravaged Notre-Dame.

Cathie seemed to soften a little as the train raced through the tunnel and into France. She showed Maria a photo of her two Morkie dogs, who her neighbour was looking after while she was away: 'That's Napoleon: he's just had an operation on his leg, so brave. And that's

Pickle: she hero-worships him.' Maria told her she was considering adopting a cat. This made Cathie smile and Maria leant back, feeling her muscles relax into the seat.

'Trains do remind me of Albie,' Cathie mused.

She shared a story of a train journey with Albie when he was eleven and she was five. They had been heading to an elderly aunt in Bristol from Devon and, delighted by the lack of parental supervision, Albie had eaten an entire tin of travel sweets on the journey. On arrival, he had promptly vomited on the elderly aunt's shoes. Cathie had smiled rather ruefully at the end of the story, perhaps feeling strange to be telling a story from so long ago, about someone with whom she had been so close and yet whom she hadn't seen or heard from in decades. Maria didn't push for more, not wanting her to feel overwhelmed.

The train station was buzzing with busy commuters, jabbering into mobiles, following signs and arrows to platforms, the Metro, toilets, taxis. Maria and Cathie found the taxi rank and dived gratefully inside the first car. Maria had printed her itinerary sheet in the newsagent the day before – Mr Khan had insisted on waiving the 10p charge and Maria had left with a Prince Harry figurine in shorts that mostly resembled Paul Scholes – and directed the driver in broken French. She had spent the days before the trip trying to learn certain phrases – it had been years since her French O Level and her skills were rusty, to say the least.

The hotel was a white-fronted terrace house, window boxes spilling with bright purple flowers, iron-wrought balconies outside the floor-to-ceiling shuttered windows in a faded rose pink. In the front courtyard, people sat chatting, smoking and eating around small circular tables, vases of spring flowers at the centre.

'It's perfect!' Maria stared up at the house, a cornflower-blue sky soaring above them, sunlight flashing on the windowpanes.

They agreed to meet an hour or so later in the foyer and Maria gave Cathie an awkward wave as she pushed into her adjacent room. The single bedroom was compact but luxurious, a speckled grey marble bathroom with a freestanding bath making Maria immediately want to run the gold taps and immerse herself in a luxurious bath. She crossed the room eager for fresh air, and as she opened the balcony doors, a breeze immediately made the cream chiffon curtains billow. The smell of thyme filled the room and she turned to unzip her suitcase and select something to change into.

She had planned a meal in a restaurant overlooking the Seine, a route mapped out that would pass the Eiffel Tower. She chose charcoal linen trousers and a loose white shirt, her pink pumps completing the outfit. Applying some eyeliner and a slick of coral lipstick to which Rosie had given the thumbs up, Maria grinned at herself in the mirror, feeling more and more alive than she had done in months, perhaps years. As she examined her reflection, she reminded herself that she must try to discover the story behind this trip, the reason Albie had chosen Paris and wanted to make amends with his sister.

They walked, the air punctuated with horns from boats, the gentle lap of the river, strains from street musicians, chatter from people in restaurants and cafés lining their route. It felt easier to talk to Cathie as they walked, not needing to make eye contact, able to be distracted by the sights. As it turned out, they had plenty in common.

Lights danced on the water as they stopped on a bridge, its rails crammed with hundreds of padlocks – some with initials scored in, or hearts and private notes scribbled on. Up ahead a couple were posing either side of their padlock, their hands together, forming a heart shape.

Maria looked away, reaching to tilt one towards her. 'What a wonderful thing to do,' she exclaimed, reading some initials on the metal surface.

'They take them down every few years, I read,' Cathie said, shattering Maria's romantic illusions that the padlocks would stay in place for eternity. Would she and Albie have scrawled their initials on one, she wondered for a moment. *Silly woman*, she chided herself. *Of course not.*

They both sucked in their breath as they stood, necks craned, underneath the Eiffel Tower – a towering architectural beauty under the azure sky. 'It's so much bigger than I thought,' Maria said, eyes roaming.

Cathie simply nodded, walking up the stairs and away. Maria felt her stomach drop: where was the thrill, the excitement?

Cathie was waiting for her on the terrace across from the tower, looking back towards the famous landmark, her eyes covered in a thin film. Maria joined her, both hands on the wall in front, waiting.

'I'm sorry,' Cathie said, giving Maria a sideways look, 'I'm nervous, I think. I know how much Paris meant to Albie, I know why he wanted us to come here together…'

Maria pressed her palms into the cold stone. Was this it? She desperately wanted to press for more but didn't want to shatter the moment.

Cathie took a breath, looked back out at the sparkling lights of the Eiffel Tower illuminating the inky blue night sky. 'Our mother had always wanted to come here, that was why it was so special to him.'

'Did she never take you?'

Cathie pressed her lips together, shook her head. 'And when she got ill, she couldn't travel. Albie was so heartbroken, always talking about Paris, talking about how she had never gone.'

Maria felt a lump in her throat for Albie and his regret. She was hit with the uncomfortable realisation that she knew what it was like to wish desperately you had done something differently.

'I had promised him we would go one day together, that we would take the trip our mother never did…' Her eyes filled with tears at that moment and Maria wondered what had happened that meant Cathie had broken her promise.

'Let's go and have dinner,' Maria said kindly, realising Cathie was wrestling with emotions, knowing she shouldn't push her anymore.

Maria had booked a table in a restaurant that looked out over the water. The kitchen was filled with sizzling sounds, the clatter of pans, and the most exquisite scents drifted into the dining room. They ordered quickly, a starter of onion soup with fresh, warm bread, and Maria picked the next dish.

'I'm sorry to do this, but Albie would have insisted…' She attempted to order their main courses in French, Cathie frowning as she spoke in stuttered, formal starts.

Albie, you better be right, Maria thought as the waiter emerged soon after with steaming bowls of snails.

Maria looked amusingly at Cathie. 'He added it to the list so…'

For the first time Cathie really smiled, straight teeth glinting. 'Why couldn't he have told us to eat eclairs? Well… Wish me luck!' She lifted the fork to her mouth, a glistening snail stuck to the prongs, and popped it in, chewing slowly before swallowing and reaching for her water glass. 'Actually,' she said, laughing, 'they're really quite good.'

Despite their rubbery texture they were delicious, dripping in butter and garlic. Maria couldn't help enjoying every mouthful. Albie, yet again, had surprised her.

The restaurant was filling up and was now busy with customers breaking fresh bread, perusing the menu, their faces glowing from the tea lights scattered on the tables. The waiters moved back and forth purposefully, the smells from the kitchen clashing, the windows steaming up. Maria felt relaxed and grateful to be in this lively city. A place that only a short time ago would have terrified her. Normally, she'd be at home in the quiet of her apartment, sat in her armchair completing a crossword or a chapter of her book, with just the tick of the clock and the hum of traffic in the distance for company.

'So, I have a full day planned tomorrow,' Maria said, bringing her knife and fork together on the plate. 'I thought we could walk into Montmartre, have a *chocolat chaud…*' She attempted the accent, feeling herself flush, and Cathie laughed. 'Try that café TripAdvisor told me is the best in the city – TripAdvisor was very helpful. And then perhaps in the afternoon we could head to the Louvre, they have a lot of Impressionists and the *Mona Lisa*, of course. I can't believe I'm going to see the *Mona Lisa* in the flesh.'

Cathie had fallen quiet at this and Maria was overcome with worry. 'Unless you want to do something else…?'

'The Louvre,' she repeated, her hand shaking as she raised her wine glass to her mouth. 'He had always wanted to go there, she had—' Cathie broke off, blinking rapidly, stopping herself breaking down there and then at the table.

At that moment the waiter interrupted them with the dessert menu.

'No, *non, non merci*. Just the bill, please,' Cathie said.

Maria wasn't sure what was so wrong with her suggestion. What had gone on between Albie and Cathie? How could it be related to the Louvre? Maria and Cathie had been fine, getting on in fact, and this abrupt change in mood saddened her. The muscles in Cathie's neck were tense as Maria paid the bill, waving away Cathie's feeble protests to contribute: 'Albie insisted.' Maria knew it must be tied up with the reason she and Albie hadn't spoken. She went over the conversation, confused as to why a visit to the Louvre would so upset her.

All the way back to the hotel Cathie sat and stared silently out of the taxi window and she barely looked at Maria in the tiny, creaking lift to their floor. Maria bade her a brief goodnight as they stood awkwardly in the corridor. 'Good n—'

The door slammed shut before Maria could finish the sentence, frowning as she slotted her hotel card into her door and stepped inside.

She had left the windows open and the room was cool, filled with voices, a motorcycle engine, music from outside. Suddenly Maria realised she didn't want to be on her own, fretting over things going wrong in the restaurant.

She headed next door to a small restaurant, now emptying of people, and ordered a glass of pudding wine. How different this trip might have been if she had come here with Albie, she thought as she swallowed the liquid, syrupy and sweet. She wallowed in these thoughts before pulling out the wish list, now creased in twenty different places and the writing so familiar:

• *Make amends and say sorry for not forgiving her*

With a last mouthful she knew she had to find the strength to do this for Albie, to get to the bottom of the rift between him and his sister. Clearly, Cathie had loved him once; when she told the occasional story about their childhood she was admiring and indulgent of her brother.

The next day Maria broached the subject almost immediately as they sat having buttery croissants in the morning sunshine in the hotel courtyard. 'About yesterday—'

'I don't want to go to the Louvre, I… I can't, I'm sorry.' It was as if Cathie had been waiting. She looked into her *café au lait*.

Maria paused for a second before reaching to place a hand over Cathie's. 'That's quite alright, and you don't have to explain, but…' Maria took a breath.

Be brave, Maria, for once.

'…Please don't doubt if I am here as your friend. I want to get to know you better.'

Cathie exhaled and sat back in her chair.

Maria, her whole body tense, waited.

'It's just… that was their place. Albie and her. I can't…' Cathie dabbed at her mouth with a linen napkin.

Maria tipped her head to one side, holding her breath, wanting her to continue.

'Our mother loved art, was a brilliant artist herself. Albie inherited her talent. I can't draw a thing, not even stick men, but I always loved watching her draw and paint. And she taught both of us. I was hopeless, but Albie fell in love with it all too, was the willing student…'

Cathie was staring out across the courtyard now, eyes somewhere else, rooting through a past only she could see.

'I remember she saved an age for this enormous glossy table-top book, thick with pictures of her favourite paintings. She knew everything about Monet, Degas, she could tell you how long it had taken to paint the sunflowers, what colours were used and how, the brushstrokes, everything. And she dreamt of going to art galleries, seeing those paintings first-hand. Albie, Albie always said they'd go. Even after her diagnosis, breast cancer, he still said it to her, but he was never around, too busy with his damn business…' Cathie's voice had changed, hardened, her eyes focused somewhere over Maria's head as she replayed moments from her past. 'He made excuses, and she was always so damned accepting of them…'

Maria frowned, not recognising this Albie who could let people down, who would put a business first, not without good reason.

'I should have stood up to him but he was my big brother... I...
and then when I didn't... when I...'

Maria was leaning forward, willing Cathie to explain more.

'I couldn't... God, he never forgave me...'

Couldn't what? Maria was lost. What did Albie never forgive? What
could be so terrible that it caused him to never speak to his younger
sister again? She was desperate to know but Cathie had already moved
on and she didn't feel confident enough to interrupt and ask.

'And now, trying to send me there without him, well—' Cathie
came to an abrupt halt, her chest rising and falling.

Maria calmed her with a hand. 'The Louvre was my idea, it wasn't
on his list. It had been my thought, I knew Albie loved art. But we don't
have to go, we can go anywhere else. He just wanted you to experience Paris. We could go to that wonderful bookshop, the Shakespeare
something, I saw it in that film *Julie & Julia*.'

But something had changed and she couldn't seem to fix things.

Cathie swiped at her eyes. '*He* should have brought me here, *he*
should have forgiven me years ago. What I did was hardly worse than
how he drifted in and out of our lives in those last months.' The anger
in her voice was unmistakable, betraying years of the same thoughts
eating away at her.

Maria felt her shoulders sagging, hope sinking. What had she
imagined? That she could fix a long-running feud with one trip away?
That the magic of Paris would heal the hideous rift that had opened
up? That she, a perfect stranger to this woman, could sweep in and be
the great heroine? She didn't have the power to fix anything, she was
foolish to even try. She didn't even know what she was trying to fix.
And anyway, some things couldn't be fixed, she thought, shaking her

head, not wanting the memories to flood in, the familiar lurching pain that accompanied them.

'He never forgave me, and god, I was so sorry, I was so sorry. And I hated him for not forgiving me, and now I can't even tell him that I forgive him. He's robbed me of that. We messed up, we both messed up. I should have been there… I didn't get back in time…'

Time for what?

Maria froze in horror as Cathie started to cry, and looked over her shoulder for someone else, someone who could comfort to take over. There was of course no one: an idling waiter and two men playing backgammon, lost in their game, not remotely fussed by a weeping woman nearby. Just Maria. She felt helpless, believing for a second that this was too much for her to handle. Then she found her confidence, unstuck herself and rubbed Cathie's back. 'There, there, it's alright, I'm sorry, I'm sorry. It's alright, I'm sorry.' She left her hand there as Cathie juddered to a stop, shoulders still, face hidden, her breathing slowing.

Cathie lifted her head, reached for a napkin and dabbed at her eyes and nose. 'I missed her funeral, I missed our own mother's funeral,' she explained, 'and I didn't even have a good reason, not really. I was away with a boyfriend. I can't even remember his name now, so meaningless…'

Cathie had missed her mother's funeral. That was what she had been alluding to, the reason Albie had been so furious with her.

'But I was angry and she'd gone and he hadn't been there, he hadn't done what I'd done, looked after her, he hadn't seen what I'd seen, how ill she got right at the end, when the cancer had spread through her body…' Her voice trailed away.

A nearby waiter approached and then turned quickly on his heel.

'How awful, I… I'm so sorry,' Maria said, knowing that even after all this time, the hurt never really went away.

'We never spoke. He wouldn't listen to me, didn't want to hear it. He was so stubborn, suddenly the virtuous son…'

Maria flinched at this description of the man she so admired: a different man then, someone who had made mistakes.

'And that only made me angrier, the times I'd *begged* him to get back home, to be with us, to see for himself.'

Maria bit her lip, forced herself not to defend Albie.

'I trained to be a nurse, maybe after Mum I was trying to… I'm not sure,' the words were spilling out now, Cathie lost somewhere in the past. 'He was still off being a big shot, waiting for me to apologise, but I… couldn't. Then the years just… passed. So many years. And then the letter came. From the solicitor.' Cathie's chin dropped to her chest and she sat there, balling up the napkin in her hand.

There was a long period of silence and Maria felt her heart go out to this woman, the pain etched on her features. She found it difficult to reconcile herself with the new knowledge: that perfect, unblemished Albie could ever have been at fault. And yet here was his sister with their sad story. A whole life he'd missed out on: his baby sister. She swallowed down words, just realising she needed to sit there, to be still and listen.

They had a quiet day. They walked to the bookshop, enjoyed the smell of the second-hand books, browsing the shelves, settling themselves in enormous armchairs and sipping coffees. They wandered through the streets, idling in parks, simply taking in the city with no real aim. It was better than Maria's busy itinerary.

Perhaps the breakfast had been a release as Cathie seemed more relaxed, laughing at Maria as they walked past Cartier.

'How can you never have heard of it!' she exclaimed.

Maria, glad to be teased, simply shrugged.

They ended up boarding a Bateau Mouche on a whim, moving over the blue-grey water of the Seine, feeling the wind whip their clothes against them, push and pull at their hair. Watching people walking past on the paths next to the river, stopping for selfies, sitting on benches. They saw couples kissing, people walking dogs, the tips of cathedrals, apartment blocks, hotels. The sun played hide and seek above them, turning the water varying shades around each bend. Maria closed her eyes and felt the rays on her face.

They stopped in a patisserie to order the most delicious light macaroons in pastel shades and exclaiming at the taste, Maria insisting on buying more to take back with them. *How could she have got to her eighth decade and only now be tasting something so delicious?* She paid for them with another note, handing the bag to Cathie.

'Albie always said he had a sweet tooth,' Maria said as they left the patisserie, thinking of all the marble cake they shared.

'How long were you together?' Cathie asked as they stood on the pavement, about to plan their next move.

Maria felt the macaroon sticking in her throat as she swallowed. 'We weren't, we weren't together. I used to see him, once a week, on Thursdays.'

Cathie frowned, two lines appearing between her brows. 'On Thursdays.'

Maria nodded. 'In a café. We shared a pot of tea and a slice of cake every Thursday for four years.'

'You weren't his partner? But I assumed, all this…' Cathie waved her arm around, the patisserie bag dangling from her fingers.

'It was what he wanted to do with you. To make amends. He had written it on his list, he was working his way through it. I'm still not exactly sure why. But he died before he could take you—'

'Did he give you the list when he died?'

'No, I found it. He left me his apartment and it was on his bedside table, half-complete.'

'His apartment,' Cathie said, eyebrows shooting up. 'He left it to you?'

'Well, he left me everything…'

A car roared past, almost blocking out her words.

'He left you… everything,' Cathie interrupted.

Maria stopped, about to explain more about the things Albie had put on the list, about all the good he had done, at her determination to continue what he'd started. She realised she hadn't told Cathie a great deal, that she might have assumed the list had been instructions about Paris and this trip.

'Everything…' Cathie repeated slowly, '…to someone he saw once a week.'

Maria nodded, smiling at the madness of it without thinking.

'But the business, the apartment, he must have been wealthy.'

'He was…' Maria nodded. 'It was such a shock.' As she spoke, she had a fleeting worry that she was being insensitive. 'I had no idea,' she added hurriedly, concerned that the topic of money could be a sticky one. Certainly, Cathie's face had changed. Her expression stony, arms folded over her chest: 'I can't believe it. Everything.'

Maria felt herself tense. She now saw that the words contained another meaning, that Cathie's eyes had been narrowing. 'Well, I suppose, I'm not sure…' Maria felt wrong-footed, her tongue too big for her mouth.

'And I've been brought along on this all-expenses trip to rub it in, I imagine. His gold-digging girlfriend showing off, in her fancy clothes, splashing his cash about, paying for meals and boat rides and—'

Maria felt as if she'd been slapped, took a step backwards, blinked rapidly. 'No, that's not what—'

Cathie's fists had curled up, her voice high and fast, 'When he knew how we struggled, he… to a total stranger. To…'

Maria couldn't speak, too shocked at this burst of anger.

'God, I have to get home!' Cathie said, sticking her hand up for a taxi, stepping off the pavement so that a motorcycle had to swerve round her. 'I want to leave.'

Maria nodded, devastated, not sure whether to follow her into the taxi as it pulled up, but not wanting her to just leave. Eventually she got in the car, gulping at this sudden turn of events.

They sat in silence back to the hotel and in the cramped lift to their rooms. Heavy-hearted, Maria packed her suitcase and left her room, not knowing if Cathie would even wait for her. But she was there, sat in the foyer of the hotel, determinedly reading her book.

'You'll be wanting to pay the bill,' Cathie said waspishly.

Maria stood there, not sure what to do, what to say. She didn't have the words, didn't know how to fix things, and felt a mixture of emotions: confusion, anger, pity. She paid the hotel bill wordlessly and waited for the taxi to the station sat on the other side of the foyer. This was ridiculous and yet she couldn't seem to cross the floor to mend it.

Cathie didn't meet her eye as they made their way to the train station. Maria sat alone all the way back to St Pancras, as Cathie had moved the moment she had been handed her ticket, heading straight to the second-class carriage without a word. Maria watched her go, wondering how it had all gone so wrong, the memories of their shared time together already fading. If the money had been left to her just to fritter away, she might have understood, but she didn't want the money, she wanted to do what Albie had been doing with it. A small part of her felt angry at Cathie's accusations: she didn't want to have to explain things to her. Why should she? Why should Cathie call her a gold digger? It wasn't right. Or was Maria angry because there was some truth in it? Did she enjoy this new role? Her new-found freedom? Had she been splashing the cash? She bit her lip and stared out of the window, the darkness of the tunnel reflecting her hopeless mood.

She didn't see Cathie in London as she alighted the train and walked away from the station onto the tube escalator. She pictured the list in her handbag. After all this, could she really tick this trip off the list?

*

'Whatcha doing, Mum?' She was standing balancing on one leg in the balcony doors, a Walkman tucked into her stonewashed jeans, headphones around her neck, her hair tied back with a bright pink scrunchie.

'Nothing!' I laughed in suspicion. 'What do you want?' I asked, opening one eye from my deckchair in the corner and realising she was still there, still balanced on one leg.

'Nothing. I'm just watching yooooooooou.'

'Well, don't. Go and find something else to do.'

'Whyyyyy?'

'Because there are better things for you to be doing.'

'But I like it.'

I closed my eyes, swallowing the laugh down. 'You're a very odd girl.'

'Genetic, innit?'

'Cheeky.'

A shadow passed over my body and I opened my other eye. She was standing on one leg again directly in front of my deckchair.

'Seriously, go and find something to do.'

'But I was doing something else and I got bored, Mother of Mine.'

I struggled up into a sitting position. 'Right, how can I help? You are clearly not going to leave me alone or stop standing on one leg until I can assist. Are you after food?'

'Nope.'

'Milkshake?'

'Nope. Let's go to the beach,' she suddenly shouted, making me jump. 'Come on.'

I was surprised. Normally, she never asked me to do things with her, had been so busy recently with her new set of friends. I felt a buzz of warmth in my stomach, a reminder of the tiny girl who had wanted her mummy by her side at all times, who had screamed at nursery drop-offs, flailing her little arms as she wept her name.

'Go on then,' I said.

She finally lowered her leg and a grin split her face open. 'Let's get 99s and go swimming.'

'Actually, that sounds perfect,' I said, getting up from my chair.

And it was. A perfect day. A stroll to the beach, the seagulls gliding past, the squeals of children splashing in the waves, the heat of a mid-summer day, the feeling of the sand between her toes, my daughter's soft singing as she lay on a towel next to me, listening to Bonnie Tyler on her beloved Walkman. Just the two of us for a precious while.

'Cool.'

'Cool.'

'And maybe a donut?'

'I thought you didn't want food?'

'Well, a donut isn't really food, food, is it?'

'Whatever you say,' I said, grinning, as I watched her race back through the doors of the balcony, calling 'Come on, Moooottttthhhhhheeeeerrrr!' behind her.

Chapter 24

Maria was sitting on the bus stop bench opposite the skatepark, waiting for Troy to appear. She felt guilty for having been in Paris, was concerned he was punishing her for abandoning him so soon after promising him the use of her apartment. She'd texted him twice but hadn't got a reply and she was worried. She almost gave up and stayed at home but she knew he didn't have anyone else looking out for him and she didn't *want* to give up. Anyway, it was a distraction from her own thoughts that had been chasing her on a loop these last few days.

Timothy had started a new word game with her, had opened it with 'MARTYR', the Y hitting a double-letter score, but she hadn't mustered the energy to reply. All this time, she couldn't shake the things Cathie had said to her, examining them from every angle, wondering at them, picking out each sentence and turning it over in her mind. She'd started to believe some of it, she knew on some level she hadn't deserved Albie's attention in the first place.

Then there was the list and the things it had triggered. The trip to Paris hadn't gone as she'd hoped or imagined. She had failed to see that dredging things up from the past didn't always go well. Sometimes it was best to let them lie. Perhaps she should give it all up, stop chasing things that had nothing to do with her? If she hadn't happened upon the list, she wouldn't even have known it existed.

A figure was moving down the road, speeding up when she was close. 'Maria, how was Paris?' Rosie asked, beaming at her, her school pigtails flying, making her look even younger than she was.

Maria couldn't rouse a smile in return and Rosie's face became full of concern. 'Oh no, was it rubbish?' She sat down next to her, sticking out her legs, tights laddered, black school shoes scuffed.

'It was, well, it didn't quite go as I'd planned.'

'Does anything?' Rosie said in a soft voice.

Maria looked startled for a minute: such a grown-up thought out of her mouth. 'I suppose not,' she replied with a sad shrug.

Rosie rotated her ankles as she sat there in silence.

'I wanted to help heal a rift between two people but I think I just made things worse,' Maria admitted in a dull voice.

Rosie picked at a loose thread on her jumper. 'You can't always fix everything.' She pulled on the thread so that it lengthened. 'But it's nice that you tried. That counts for something, you know.'

Maria stared at her shoes: sensible leather lace-ups today, no rose-pink pumps. 'Maybe.'

Rosie nudged her. 'It's true. You care, no one can say you don't.'

Maria looked out at the road, at the skatepark where the teenagers gathered in small pockets. She could hear someone's phone playing music.

'I took Albie's sister to Paris – he'd wanted to go with her. But it all went so wrong, she got so cross about the will, about the trip, about… I'm not even sure what… and now I don't know what to do next,' she admitted, feeling the hopeless hole inside her open up once more.

'Look,' Rosie said, her voice strong. 'If she got upset with you about things that is her problem, she is projecting onto you.'

'Perhaps,' Maria mumbled, marvelling at how wise this teenager could be.

A bus pulled up at the stop and a woman holding an umbrella stepped off. The woman gave Maria a concerned look. 'Are you OK?' she asked.

'Fine.' Maria nodded, embarrassed. Was it really that plain to see?

The woman moved away, one last glance back before she rounded a corner.

'Honestly,' Rosie said, as if there'd been no interruption, 'she'll come round.'

'You seem so sure,' Maria said, wishing she had the same confidence.

'Of course,' Rosie tutted, rolling her eyes, 'I'm very wise.'

'You are.' Maria smiled, feeling her heart lift.

Rosie scooted closer and rested her head briefly on Maria's shoulder. 'You'll be alright,' she said simply.

Maria felt a tiny shock at the connection and found herself touching the spot where Rosie had rested when she pulled away. It threw her so much, she forgot to say goodbye to the young girl as she headed off. Then Troy was standing in front of the bus stop staring at her.

'Y'OK?' he said, body hunched over, the orange hoodie rolled up to his elbows.

Maria nodded, relieved to see him. 'Troy,' she said, struggling to her feet, her bottom practically numb from being sat on the bench for so long.

'Are you waiting for me?'

There was hollering from the skatepark. Troy stared at the ground. 'I wanted to see how you're getting on. I texted you.'

He looked over his shoulder at the nearest group of boys, some of whom were looking back at him. 'I'm fine. You should go now, yeah.'

Maria frowned, not wanting to be fobbed off. She couldn't admit that she wanted the company too, was glad to be talking to him. 'What have you been up to? I'm sorry I haven't been at the apartment much, everything's still waiting there for you…'

Troy wasn't looking at her, scuffing his trainer on the ground. There were sniggers coming from the park, someone wolf-whistled.

'Have you been using the paints?'

'Oi, Troy!' came a shout from behind.

He glanced behind him again. 'Look, I haven't, alright?'

Maria straightened, tried to play her disappointment down. 'Well, there's plenty of time.'

'I don't have them, OK?'

'TROY, mate.'

He rolled his eyes. 'Oh, for— I really need to go.'

Maria didn't trust herself to reply, aware of the boys staring, Troy's mood changeable, his fists clenching and unclenching. Why didn't he have the paints? He had seemed so thrilled when she had given them.

'Well, if you wanted to come back to my apartment sometime, or we could go to the café perhaps for some food—'

'I don't need your fucking charity, alright?'

'It's not…' Maria felt hot tears build in her eyes. She didn't want this to become another confrontation. 'It's not… charity, I just hoped we could see each other again.'

She didn't understand Troy's anger, his scowl as he stared at her. This wasn't how it was meant to be. Why was everything going wrong?

'What's the point? You'll just leave like everyone else when you get bored.'

Taking a step towards him, Maria raised a hand. 'I wouldn't, that's not—'

More calling, Troy was fidgety. 'It's just better like this, alright?'

Maria could see it was a losing battle, that he didn't want her here. 'I'll go,' she whispered.

'Good, alright… yeah,' the confidence had seeped out of his voice but he didn't make any attempt to follow her as she moved away.

She didn't want him to see how upset she was. He had been through enough, she knew that. She shouldn't have expected so much. What had she imagined? That one visit and a box of paints and he'd be her new best friend? It didn't work like that. She trudged along the pavement, the sounds of the boys in the skatepark fading as she crossed another road. She couldn't stop replaying his face when he'd seen the desk, clutching the artist's set to his chest. Had that all been fake? Had she imagined it?

The thought of returning to her silent apartment seemed too grim and she found herself walking in another direction, her legs aching as she turned the corner and saw the familiar steamed-up windows, the figures moving behind the glass.

This place had always been a comfort, she thought, as she pushed open the door. Admiring the new look, the chic blue of the walls, the bright white of the tablecloths, the tiny pink spray of flowers in the centre. The place was humming with life and the smells of herbs, coffee and frying sausages were comforting. She could hear the clatter of the kitchen beyond, heard the tapping of the till. She looked around and realised not a single table was free, the room was so packed with customers. Albie would have loved to have seen everyone enjoying themselves, admiring the new fresh look of the place.

Excusing herself, she squeezed between tables, lingering near the counter. Pauline was busy serving a customer, while Amrit was bent over a row of hot drinks, tapping chocolate powder on top of them. She could make out Keith through the hatch to the kitchen and tried to catch his eye, but he was focusing intently and didn't see her.

Amrit moved past her: 'Hey, Maria.'

Keith looked up from his spot in front of the grill. 'All good, Maria?' he called, flipping chicken fillets over on the surface, charcoal stripes on top.

'Yes, thanks. I…'

He took a ticket down from the shelf in front of him and read it. 'That's good, good,' he said, glancing behind him and calling, 'Amrit does that say sweet potato or normal fries?'

'Sweet,' she called back, nudging a shelf closed with her hip before re-entering the main room. 'Sorry, Maria, it's rammed.'

'I can see, that's wonder—'

Amrit had already walked past, pulling out a pencil from her hair, a notepad from the pocket of her apron.

Pauline was tapping things into the till, a harried expression on her face. She didn't seem aware Maria was standing there.

Maria looked around at them all: busy, distracted. A couple got up to leave from the table she had always shared with Albie. Maria stared at the empty chairs, the table piled high with empty glasses and plates, their dirty cutlery left on top, screwed-up napkins to the side. She could sit down, she could order something.

How could she be surrounded by people and still feel lonely, she thought with a sinking heart as she found herself drifting back to the door, opening it and stepping outside. Barely noticing the cool wind that buffeted her from every angle, walking away from the comforting place and the people who didn't have time for her. She would just be in their way: a nuisance. She wasn't being useful anymore, they were perfectly fine without her. What had she imagined? Maybe Troy was right and she was treating everyone like they were charity.

She walked, pounding the pavement, not really thinking where she was headed, just not wanting to stop, furious thoughts from the last few days urging her on. She had been stupid to think things were different now, that she had people in her life. She didn't deserve all the wonderful things that had been happening recently, that wasn't her life, and she had been silly to think it. After so many years, why would her luck suddenly change? She had deviated from her routine and got hurt.

She was in front of the building before she even knew it, moving up in the lift and removing his key from her purse. His apartment smelt musty – the abandoned piles of his belongings from a previous trip where she couldn't decide what to do with them. She had made it a mess and now she wished she hadn't touched anything in the first place. She'd just made it worse.

She made everything worse.

Stepping into his bedroom, she moved to pull at one of the curtains, jamming it halfway along and giving up. Her own face looked down at her as she sank onto his mattress, the duvet folded up in a square, pillows plumped in a pile. Before, she had stripped the bed, removed the grey and blue quilt, the navy sheets and covers, had paused for a second to smooth at the pillow where his head had rested. Now, the stark bed made the room seem cold and unfamiliar.

She sat there in the semi-darkness for a while, not getting up to turn on the light or move to make herself something in the kitchen. She glanced at the bedside table, the bare spot where she had first seen the list. It seemed to have only brought misery into her life recently: Cathie, Troy, even the café. It had been better when she had stayed in her apartment, not engaged in life, all alone. At least then she knew where she stood, didn't alter her expectations of how her life would be.

She felt exhausted as she lay back against the duvet, the material crackling without its cotton cover. Staring up at the ceiling, she tried to recall Albie's face, tracing his features in her mind. What exact colour had his eyes been? Had he parted his hair to the left or the right? She blinked a tear away. Why hadn't she paid more attention?

He had meant so much to her and she had never even told him that. She needed him now, his strength, his low chuckle, his loyalty. He had always been interested in what she had to say, had always listened to her, an animated look on his face even when she was telling him about the launderette being closed, or the tea stain on her TV listings. How much time she'd wasted not telling him things. She thought of the list again, of reading her own name at the bottom. She thought then of what Albie had wanted to do for her and it finally made the tears come.

*

I found her old Sindy doll in the purple flares and orange flowery top hidden in the back of the wardrobe, with a puzzled expression as I recalled that she had told me she'd thrown her out. Too old for dolls, I'd thought sadly at the time.

She had been trying to hide the fact that she still wanted to keep her.

I held the plastic doll in my hands, a doll she had played with for countless hours, a doll that had been a comfort when she'd had nightmares, a companion when she was bored.

I clutched that tiny doll, wanting to smile, wanting to remember all the times I had seen her with it, lying on the back seat of the car on a long journey, Sindy tucked next to her, or abandoned on the floor when I called for dinner, or sat at the table when she'd had to do her homework.

That doll was still here when she was not.

I picked up the doll and walked across the room, throwing her in a small wastepaper basket as I left.

Chapter 25

She returned to her apartment in the darkness, wandering the streets as couples and friends moved in and out of Brighton's restaurants and pubs. Laughter, music, chatter, life: she felt as if she was seeing it all through a thick pane of glass, always with her nose pressed up against it, looking in.

She'd lived much of her life that way, she realised, had allowed herself to become this person. She deserved to be this alone. It hadn't always been like that though and memories forced her to stop and catch her breath, one hand resting against a lamppost, the steel cold to her touch. She thought back to the days when she had an unstoppable energy for life, had woken every day feeling positive and focused. She'd been quick to laugh, to tease and be teased. Albie had been able to draw that person out, through his gentle probing over their tea and cake, his amused glances, his passion as he shared his thoughts. She had found herself opening up, laughing without muffling it with a hand and her stomach aching some days from it.

Another wave of regret washed over her: at all they had lost. She had transformed when she was with him, but she never had enough confidence to thank him for that change, enough confidence to reach across that narrow gap and clasp his hand.

And now she was letting him down.

It was late, very late, and in the window of the first-floor apartment she could see a grey silhouette. It was the woman with the children, the room lit up behind her. She had tied her hair up in a knot on her head and was swaying slightly from side to side, a child in her arms, head resting on her shoulder. Maria could make out the woman's mouth opening and closing as she smoothed the child's head. Next to her stood an ironing board, the iron propped up and an enormous pile of washing beside it.

Maria remembered those early days of motherhood: the bone-aching tiredness, the knowledge that even though your head hit the pillow you might have to wake and get out of bed again in an hour, a minute, another few hours. Always on someone else's schedule. The insistent wail of someone you and only you are responsible for. The fact that the next day might be the same again. The lonely feeling you can have despite being with children, the need for another adult to hear you, to share the burden.

Steve had left her after only eleven months of being a parent and, for the most part, she had enjoyed doing it alone. She had been doing it alone anyway. He had barely contributed, not interested or engaged in their home life. He would only ever complain, about the disturbance, the mess, the noise, the break in his own routine.

She had thought they would do things as a family: long walks along the promenade, both holding pudgy hands, watching their child run ahead, learning to kick a ball, to fly a kite. He had promised her a lot when she was pregnant, stroking her stomach and talking nonsense to her bump.

His disinterest began almost immediately: a refusal to share in the night feeds, comments about a woman's role, long evenings out at the pub, leaving her there to rock and soothe and cry silent tears into her small child's hair as the loneliness consumed her. His leaving had hurt though. And then there was no one to share in the difficulties and the triumphs: the first word, walk, day of school. The anger built too, at the fact that he could leave something so precious and never look back.

Maria looked up again at the window. The woman had stopped swaying and soothing. Perhaps the child was now asleep. Suddenly her neighbour glanced in her direction and Maria found herself starting, looking away. She didn't want to be called a nosy busybody, she didn't want trouble. Keeping her head down, she let herself into the apartment block.

What if she took her something the next day? Made her a meal perhaps? She had always been quite good at shepherd's pie, hadn't bothered to make it recently but perhaps she could take the woman something for her freezer, something to keep her going. The thought chased her up the stairs, towards her apartment. Then the truth hit her: the neighbour was just a stranger. She wouldn't want an old woman fussing about, making her feel as if she couldn't cope.

Charity, Maria thought, Troy's words cutting deeper inside her. Why did she think she could help?

She removed her key, passing the other door, hearing a cry from inside. Was it the baby in her arms who had woken, or the other child in another bed? Was there anyone else there to help? She blocked out the sound as she dragged her feet up the last set of stairs: it was none of her business. She headed to her door, slotted the key in, opened and closed it firmly. *Forget it, Maria, haven't you learnt your lesson already?*

She lay in bed, drifting in and out of uneasy sleep, and morning light began to edge around the bedroom curtains, straining to get inside. The room was now an orange-grey colour, her belongings taking shape. Another day. She knew she wouldn't get any sleep now and reached for her book on the bedside table, pausing for a second as her eyes took in the familiar photograph. The gentle throb of the start of a headache. Mouth dry, her water glass out of reach. Opening the book, a folded piece of paper fluttered to the floor: the list. She had left it there and forgotten.

She stared at it for a long time, seeing his distinctive slanted writing in that green ink, and felt there were things she should have ticked, progress she should have made. But it wasn't as neat as that, she knew, it wasn't as simple as ticking off deeds. Staring at Cathie's name, then Troy's, she wondered for the millionth time what had happened, why it had gone so wrong.

Then there was the last part of the list, about her. Why had Albie added her name, and at the end? What might it have been like had he lived long enough to do these things with her? Regret filled her.

'For Maria,' she read in a whisper, 'Go to the grave…' She folded the piece of paper back up without reading more.

She had never been back to the graveyard.

She imagined it now, the gravestone standing in the shade of a yew tree in the furthest corner of the graveyard. How tall would that tree be now, she wondered. Would it still be there at all? Would its leaves still scatter on the ground below? Was the gravestone now crooked, green with moss crawling over its surface, a signal to everyone that it had been forgotten? Was it ignored by passers-by?

She had let that person down so badly and now she had allowed the grave to be neglected too. How could she visit with tulips? Even if it was what Albie had wanted, how could she? Perhaps if she had him at her side, holding her hand, transmitting his warmth and strength to her, she would be able to push at the lichen gate, move along the twisted paths between other people's loved ones, kneel in front of the grave, and start the process of cleaning it, restoring it, making her own amends. Finally.

It had been more than thirty-six years. She hadn't dared visit since the day she had watched them lower the coffin into the ground, that terrible mound of earth piled up next door to the gaping hole. The first handful thrown on top, the noise as it struck the wood. The hands on her shoulder, the watery eyes, the sobs from others, the curious glances in her direction. The blame she had felt as they had watched her, waiting for her to react.

She had simply stood, inert, unable to feel anything beyond the icy block that had become her heart since that moment she had been told the news. She hadn't cried that day, didn't remember the words spoken to her, didn't remember leaving the graveyard. She hadn't realised then that she would never visit. She used to walk past, see the spot in the distance, the grass a little raised compared to the others. She would take flowers, clutched in a tight palm, and linger outside the railings. Then, she would turn around and return home, knowing she didn't have the strength to set them in a pot, to read the words etched in the stone. If she didn't visit the grave, perhaps she could convince herself none of it had ever happened.

And suddenly the months had passed, then the anniversary of the day it had happened and still she stayed away. She stopped walking past, stopped buying those bright yellow tulips, stopped going to things, stopped seeing friends that reminded her of the days before it had happened, stopped answering the phone, stopped seeing family, stopped leaving the house. It was amazingly easy to disappear into the new, small life she had created for herself. She moved, not far, but gave no forwarding address. No more Christmas cards, no more annual reminders of how other people's lives were moving on, news of their children – holidays, achievements at school, exam results, places won at college and university.

Sometimes though she would still be floored, caught out on the street by an old acquaintance, someone she had known before it happened. They would call her name with a half-wave and then a quick dash across the road. 'Maria, how have you been? I've been trying to reach you… so and so told me you still lived in Brighton, I was worried you'd moved away…' Gradually she started to shop in the evenings, nip out in sunglasses in summer, large hats in winter, and cross the street if she saw a face she recognised. Over the years, the instances became fewer and fewer, the faces that passed her growing unfamiliar, her world smaller and smaller.

Then Albie had stepped into it, had joined her without ceremony, sat down opposite her at that tiny table in that café and started to chat. She hadn't meant to engage him, hadn't meant to let him make her laugh or buy her a slice of marble cake, but somehow she hadn't been able to help herself. When he had looked at her, it was as if he could see the person she had been, had used to like. She wanted him to keep looking at her like that.

Now he had gone and she was brought back to her bedroom with a devastating thud.

She placed her book back on the bedside table, the list folded safely inside, and settled back under the duvet, ignoring the brightness in the room, the heat from the sun outside. She didn't want to tick things off anymore, didn't want to be reminded of his writing, the things he had done for others, the things she needed to do. She just didn't want to face it all. Turning her face into her pillow, she forced herself to shut her eyes as the tears silently fell. Outside, she could hear the sounds of the world moving past without her.

*

She spent almost the whole summer on a lilo, paddling lazily on this bright pink inflatable thing that I had bought to use as a mattress for sleepovers. Friends seemed to gravitate towards her, girls liked her. She would make them laugh, do wicked impressions of their teachers and had a mum who let her stay out until dark.

Her hair was long, thick, and she backcombed it to make it really stand out. She wore a swimsuit with a belt and treated Brighton beach like her personal playground, shoulders brown from the sun. Skinny as a rake, she would lean against the kitchen counter and tell me all the gossip from her group, hands waving around, never still as she spoke in the fastest voice. I couldn't keep up, but I loved to listen. Loved that she shared so much with me. Glad it was just the two of us, our special bond. I hadn't missed Steve in years. How he had missed out!

She glowed with charisma and charm, chatted happily to children her own age and adults, used perhaps to my company. I hadn't been half that confident when I was her age and my mother had been determined for me to settle down quickly, not to waste my time with college or qualifications. As she talked – about how they were going to burn their files after O Levels and dance around the fire on the beach – I laughed at her youth, her energy, excited for all that she had to come.

Except, it never did.

Chapter 26

The water was cold, her skin more shrivelled than normal – her toes, fingers, palms white and spidery blue veins livid on the surface of her hands. She didn't know how long she had been in the bath but today was Thursday and as if on automatic, without a thought for the last few months, she had run the taps. Stepping into the lavender-scented water, it had hit her once more: this ritual no longer brought her any pleasure. It would simply be the only thing she did that day.

The thought of the emptiness gaping before her froze her in the water, until it gradually turned from hot to tepid to cold. Goosebumps appeared on her skin as she stared blankly at the tiled wall opposite, droplets of condensation snaking slowly down the ceramic, pooling on the lip of the bath. How many Thursdays had it been now – and would she feel the same every single Thursday from now on?

She moved and the water sloshed against the side as she reached for her towel, clutching the rail in the bath to help steady herself. Gingerly towelling herself dry, her features obscured in the steam in the mirror, she thought of the bare cupboards, the fridge with its paltry offerings. She could get dressed, head out, and yet… She took her dressing gown from the back of the bathroom door, shrugged it on, its familiar smell a small comfort as she padded softly back across to her bedroom, the bottom of her hair curling from the damp. Propping up her pillows, aware of the yawning silence, she rested back against the headboard, tucking her cold feet under the blanket bunched at the foot of the bed.

She must have dozed off, her stomach aching with hunger, her mouth dry. Reaching for the water glass, she realised it was empty, but she couldn't face the interminable walk to fill it up. Every task seemed so gargantuan, so insurmountable.

The phone rang in the lounge, shrill and sudden, then stopped. Maria didn't feel a flicker of curiosity: a cold caller no doubt, a stranger pestering her for something she wasn't interested in.

Her book sat on the bedside table, as if confronting her. She didn't need to see the list inside to know that the only things left to tick off were under her own name. She didn't deserve to be on it at all. Albie hadn't known the truth about her, hadn't known what kind of person she truly was – if he had, her name would have disappeared sharpish, she was sure of it. The last item was impossible, something she couldn't imagine, and didn't want to think about.

Now that the list was all but over, and everyone was getting on with their lives, Maria had lost her purpose: that momentary zeal that had brought her such temporary joy gone. And the list hadn't always been the great success it should have been. She had been so determined to honour Albie and yet she had managed to mess things up. She thought again of Cathie and Troy: would Albie be pleased with how she had handled things, despite everything? She closed her eyes, exhausted by her thoughts and by the heavy weight of grief.

Noises in the stairwell outside woke her: a baby's wail, the insistent voice of a small child. She could hear the clump of items on the floor, an adult voice tired and pleading before a door opened and closed somewhere beneath her, then the sounds muffled by another wall.

How many other people were moving in and out of their lives in this block without talking to others? Albie had been a rarity, someone who had actively sought to help strangers – people he had no previous connection to at all. She marvelled again at his good nature, his generous spirit. Now she had put the list to bed that generosity had ended, and his light had truly gone out. The thought was so bleak she found a tear escaping, leaking down her cheek, to be absorbed into her dressing gown. Another hour and she would have been walking to the café to meet him.

She thought then of the last Thursday they had met: nothing had marked it out as particularly unusual. Albie had been sat at a table, a pot of tea in front of him, poised with a fork for cake. He had his back to the door and she remembered his head turning as she entered, his face lifting, eyes crinkling with the wide smile he gave her. He had stood up immediately – he always stood when she arrived – and he had reached over to kiss her lightly on the cheek. He had always greeted her like that, his skin brushing against hers for a second, his hair sometimes damp, as if he had taken a shower recently.

'You alright, Maria? You look nice, that scarf's very pretty,' he'd commented, pulling out her chair for her.

She'd batted away the compliment, secretly thrilled as she'd spent an age selecting that exact scarf, and had dusted her eyelids with the same pinkish hues.

They'd immediately shared their news, Albie telling her about his visit to the library. 'One of the children there asked me to read *The Very Hungry Caterpillar* again, he likes the way I go "Munch, Munch, Munch" apparently. I've added it to my CV.' He had laughed, a building rumble that seemed to always make others want to giggle too. The only time she ever laughed in almost forty years was when Albie made her. 'You should come next week,' he'd tacked on.

How she wished she had said yes. She thought then of all the other times he had asked her to join him: 'You should get yourself to the youth centre, come and see the changes', 'You could join me on the phones, the RSPCA always love a volunteer', 'We could go and check out that exhibition if you like', 'There's a new Thai restaurant opening in Kemptown, do you like Thai, Maria?', 'Troy would love to meet you one day, I'm sure'. Always her answer had been the same: no, no trouble, no bother, no, no, no, no, no.

Why had she always answered in that way? Why hadn't she just once seized on the opportunity to spend more time with him? Why had she imagined he was just being kind? Why had she really not wanted to be any trouble, a burden, a charity case? She knew now that he had cared for her deeply: what he had left her, the list, the things he had written, *that final line*.

What a waste, she thought, the tears thicker now, cheeks damp with them. What a waste. Her fault, all that time, those opportunities: gone.

It should have been her: no one would have noticed or been affected if she had gone. Instead he had left this enormous Albie-shaped hole that stretched out and touched countless lives. As she had worked her way through his list, she had seen first-hand the good he had done, felt the warmth from others as she put them first. It had felt amazing and wonderful and for a second, she convinced herself the connections were real, lasting. That he had managed to change her too.

Now though, in this silent apartment, with the ticks checked off, it seemed that it was over, that she had been wrong and that her joy had been fleeting. But glimpsing it had almost made it worse. She hadn't exactly been happy in her previous life, but she had grown accustomed to the lack of action, the lack of anything much. Now, she felt the absence of anything meaningful keenly, because for a second, her days had been full with the joy of others, full of Albie's life and laughter.

She shuddered, sinking deeper into the pillows, her chin lowered to her chest. *Another Thursday*, she thought, *another Thursday with an Albie-shaped hole.*

*

We'd been fighting those last few weeks, always the same argument over and over. Her pushing to stay out later, to head out two nights in a row, and me saying no, setting a curfew.

'I'm sixteen, an adult,' she'd say.

But to me she was still my little girl. My little girl who never fights with me.

Last week I raided her room when she was out shopping, searching in the back of her drawers, under her bed, for I didn't know what. Her diary was shoved between the frame and the mattress of the bed, more girly than she was currently trying to be, decorated with stars drawn in biro, hearts, her own name scribbled in different fonts. I stroked the pictures on the front, so tempted to open the pages and read the things she didn't share with me, but I replaced it where it lived. I trusted her and there was a small part of me that simply didn't want to know.

This was when I wished I had a partner, someone else to share the load. How I loathed Steve on days like this. I felt terrible – I'd stay on late at work and she'd get back from school on her own, or go to a friend's, and by the time I'd get in, weary from the gruelling day I'd had, she'd be in her room, listening to her cassette player, not wanting to talk.

I left her notes, directing her to the new pack of Findus Crispy Pancakes, or the bowls of Angel Delight she used to love, that I would've made the night before. Does she still love it? I didn't produce her a sibling; I wasn't there waiting with a batch of homemade muffins ready to hear about her day. But I knew she was proud of me. She would often tell me so, asking about my job, listening carefully about the latest campaign I was working on. I didn't want to give it up; I would tell myself it was because we needed the money – and that was true – but I also needed it, I needed to be me, not Mum/chauffeur/cleaner/fan. Just me.

And yet. Sometimes, I wasn't even sure who her best friends were – the same girls I used to hear about playing with their Barbie dolls or sat round screaming over the hundredth round of Hungry Hippos? Or a different crowd? Did she spend too much time with boys? With people who weren't a good influence? I'd try to grill her during those precious hours in the weekend together, but she'd never offer up as much as she used to. When she was little, I would know every tiny thought that would enter her head: she would blurt it, embarrassingly and truthfully. Of course I missed that, instead hearing those monosyllabic replies, her eyes rolling. And if we were getting on, I wouldn't want to probe or push, just thankful I had my wonderful girl with me: her wit, energy, zest for life making me feel excited about the future, as if anything was possible.

How did a mother balance along this fine line? There she would be in the hallway, telephone cord wrapped around her fingers, having leapt on it on the first ring. The mumbled conversations, arrangements scribbled in ink on the backs of her hands. I'd try to peek, try to find out. Sometimes she'd even tell me. I wouldn't push, guilt stopping me from being stricter. Would any of it have happened if I'd been stricter?

Chapter 27

It was another day before she noticed the single sheet of folded paper that must have been pushed through her letterbox. She picked it up without a thought, assuming it would be a leaflet, a flyer – junk. Her name was written in bold on one side and with a frown, she unfolded the sheet.

'Mrs. Your art stuff got taken. I'm sorry I swore at you. Troy.'

She read the words, then re-read the words over and over. The artist's set, someone had taken it from him. Maria thought back to the day at the skatepark, and the angry curl of his fists. She had misread it, assuming he was angry at her, bothered by her, when in fact he had been ashamed. Someone had stolen the present she had given him, the precious gift he had clutched to his chest. Her heart ached now that she replayed his expression, the defensive scuff along the ground, as if he couldn't bear to look at her.

God, it didn't matter. She could buy him another one, it was replaceable.

A noise outside made her open the door, hoping perhaps to see him standing there, too embarrassed to knock. When had he delivered the note? Had she walked past it this morning? Yesterday? She had lost track of the hours, the days, had simply been existing in these four walls, curtains drawn, windows closed, time blurring.

It was the woman from the apartment on the floor below, the sound of a car seat banging against her door as she rooted for keys in her bag, her child tugging at the hem of her sweatshirt.

'Mum, Mum, Mummmmmeeeeee, Mummummum.'

The neighbour looked up at the sound of Maria's door opening and caught her eye, managing a wary smile.

'I'm sorry, he's hungr—'

Maria said it before she'd really thought through the words, 'Do you want some help?' She found herself moving out of her apartment, padding down the small staircase between them in her slippers and dressing gown, not even embarrassed to be dressed in that way. 'Let me,' she said, holding out a hand for the car seat.

'Oh, that's alright, you're OK…'

Maria recognised the dismissive gesture, the false note of cheer. She had been like that, she had refused offers of help, outings, opportunities.

'Well, let me get the door for you at least,' she said, gently pushing open the door and allowing the woman to scrabble inside.

The baby in the car seat, alerted perhaps by being put down, started to screech and the harried woman wiped a hand through her unkempt auburn hair, the roots needing doing. She was pretty, Maria thought: smooth skin, a beauty spot just above her lip.

'Mummmmmmeeee, raisin biscuit, raisin biscuit!'

'In a minute, let me just—'

'Egg on toast. Raisin biscuit. BANANA MILKSHAKE!'

'Yes, OK, I've just got to…'

The woman seemed to dither between removing her little boy's jacket, plugging a dummy in her baby's mouth and placing her own handbag down. Then she seemed concerned with ensuring Maria was alright, 'Thanks for the help. And I'm sorry about the noise, he's been a bit off today… he's normally fine.'

The baby started screaming again, dummy ejected, and the toddler began chanting, 'MILKSHAKE, MILKSHAKE!'

'Look, why don't I make the young man his lunch while you take care of the baby?' Maria found herself saying, almost an out-of-body experience.

'No, no, we'll be fine. I just need to…'

Maria could barely make her out as the baby's wail intensified.

'…Sorry…' The woman flushed as she scooped the baby out of the car seat, her sobs gradually soothed as the woman made light circles on her back. '…Sorry, right, I can hardly think.'

'Mummmmmmmmeeeeeeeeeeee.'

'Honestly, I could do with the company,' Maria said, hoping the woman wouldn't take offence at her offer. She suddenly felt a desperate urge to help, to do something for this frantic woman who seemed distracted and exhausted and alone.

'Want eggs on toast,' the toddler repeated.

'Oh god, I don't have any eggs,' the woman said, almost on the verge of tears.

'EGG ON TOAST, THANK YOU MUMMY, THANK YOU, PLEASE.'

'I've got some eggs in the apartment,' Maria said, praying that she was right, ready to pad back up the stairs. 'Let me get them.' Here was something she could do now, right now, to help. So what if she was still wearing her dressing gown, hadn't looked at her reflection in days? She had a renewed purpose.

'EGGGGGSSSSS.'

Thank goodness for the four eggs she found in a carton on the side, about the only food she had left. Her own stomach rumbled as she returned.

'If you've got bread, I can make us some eggs on toast. I need to eat something too so it's no trouble.'

The woman only lingered for a second, jiggling the baby in her arms, her toddler tugging at her, still repeating, 'EGG ON TOAST, EGG ON TOAST' on loop. 'If you're sure, I don't want to bo—'

'I'm absolutely certain, I'm starving. Right, young man, do you want to help me whisk the eggs?' She was talking, acting, as if something else, someone else, had taken over her.

Amazingly, the toddler fell silent and after a momentary look at his tired mother he was clearly too fascinated to refuse the offer.

'And what's your name?' Maria asked him as he sidled over.

'That's Owen,' his mother answered.

'Come on, Owen, let's go and make eggs.' Maria ushered him into the kitchen and helped him up on the chair, swiftly navigating around the space, which was almost an exact replica of her own kitchenette.

She found the items she needed and soon she was showing Owen how to whisk eggs. There was a slightly tense exchange when he insisted on holding the remaining two eggs and had almost dropped them, but Maria had wrestled them back from him by showing him how the toaster worked and the crisis had been averted. The woman had settled on a bar stool at the counter, her baby drinking from a bottle.

'This is really kind,' the woman said, still sounding a little embarrassed.

'Honestly, you're doing me a favour, anything to avoid putting on the laundry and I don't have any fresh bread so this suits me very well. I'm Maria, by the way,' she added with a small smile at the woman.

'Cara,' said the woman, looking up from staring at her baby.

'No, I'm Owen,' the toddler said, glaring at his mother, making Maria laugh.

Maria set a plastic plate on the table and filled a plastic beaker with water. 'Does he want the eggs chopped up?'

Cara looked momentarily horrified. 'No, no, he likes to do that.'

Maria couldn't help laughing at her expression. 'I remember that well. My girl used to hate it when I took the yogurt lids off, she threw so many on the floor.' Maria slid a plate across the counter. 'I'm sorry if they're not any good, I didn't time them.'

But Cara just looked delighted that someone else had cooked something for her.

Then they sat together and ate their eggs. Maria wasn't used to company anymore, didn't fill the silence with questions. It didn't feel awkward though, Owen providing some commentary to fill in the gaps and Maria simply enjoying being in the presence of someone else, and someone who she thought might actually feel the same.

The baby started straining and squawking as Cara jiggled him on one knee, eating her eggs with one hand.

'How about you let me tidy up here while you go and play with this one?'

Cara finished the last mouthful. 'Oh no, honestly, I couldn't...' she said, swallowing quickly, hand over her mouth.

'Of course you can,' Maria scoffed, 'it would be my pleasure.' She wouldn't let Cara refuse.

Maria watched as Cara fussed over Owen, wiping his hands and face before he raced out muttering about his cars. A sudden memory of her own child at that age: a ball of energy diving from one activity to the next.

Cara paused, biting her lip, clearly not sure what to do.

'Go,' Maria said, giving her a gentle push. 'Please.'

Once she had finished washing up their meal, scrubbing at the plates and saucepan, wiping at the crumbs, she discovered some Marigold gloves under the sink. Hearing the noises next door – 'Look, Mummy, it's a digger, a lellow digger' – Maria quietly snapped them on. She started to scrub at the sink, the draining board, counter tops, the table, the windowsills, neatly tidying as she went, discreetly moving a dead basil plant to one side before watering it. She wiped at the top of the oven and all the while she enjoyed the ache in her hands and her arms as she worked, enjoyed the harder beat of her heart, the sounds from the other room: the excited burble of the baby, the exclamations from Owen, delighted at spending time with his mother.

Cara appeared in the doorway, eyes round as she looked around the room. 'Oh wow, you've transformed the place. I haven't got anything much to pay you with, but…' She moved across to her handbag.

Maria batted her hand in the air. 'Don't be silly, it took two seconds. It's the least I can do, and anyway, you gave me the bread…'

The woman laughed. 'That's not exactly a fair exchange.'

Maria didn't say anything, thinking then of Albie. She knew the list had given her permission to engage again. In helping others, she was honouring the spirit of his wish list, remembering all the wonderful things he had done. Since Paris, she had doubted her own memories at times, had found herself skirting the things Cathie had told her, not wanting to believe that the Albie she knew could have been the young man Cathie had described.

'It feels good to be able to help others. Recently, I've been thinking about that more and more.'

Cara stood thinking for a moment, not responding. Then a slow smile lit up her face, lifting her features so that for the first time that day she didn't look as tired. 'Well, I think you're a very special lady.'

Maria felt a lump forming in her throat. How wrong Cara was. She looked down and picked up the egg carton to hide her mixed emotions. 'I'll be getting back to the apartment, but I really enjoyed chatting with you.'

'Owen,' Cara called out, 'come and say goodbye and thank you to Maria.'

The toddler appeared momentarily in the door. 'Bye, bye, please.'

Cara shrugged. 'Close enough,' she said, sounding lighter already.

An idea grew as Maria left the apartment, smiling at Owen, who gave her a toothy grin and a distracted wave. She had almost completed Albie's list, but what if she added items of her own to it? What if the wish list continued?

She could add Cara to it: she could do a weekly clean for her, offer to babysit, offer to help her out. The plan started to take shape as she thought of the other things she could do.

She washed, got dressed, and felt more herself for the first time in an age. She glanced at the note Troy had left her: she would text him too. It felt as if a weight had been lifted from her chest, as if she could breathe again. She hadn't realised the fug she'd been living in, and as she pulled back the curtains, she noticed a bright blue sky, wisps of clouds.

Mr Khan looked up as she entered the newsagent with her carrier bags. 'Hello Mrs, we've missed seeing you in here, did you get away?'

She was touched he had noticed her absence, wondered why she always assumed people didn't care. People kept surprising her. Placing the items for a couple of shepherd's pies on the counter in front of him, she replied, 'I did, I'm back now though.' She felt pride inside as

she said the words. The list would live on, and she would be the one
to make that happen.

*

*I hadn't gone into her room, felt strange pushing open the door, knocked
without thinking. No one answered, of course.*

*There were clothes strewn on the floor: neon pink legwarmers, her
favourite T-shirt, all bundled together where she had flung them. Trainers
kicked to the side, her cherry lip gloss abandoned, blue eyeshadow still
open, the applicator on the carpet. Before, I would have sighed, told her
off for being so careless.*

The silence was overwhelming.

*I couldn't believe she wouldn't be bursting in, accusing me of messing
up her stuff. Couldn't believe she wouldn't be sitting cross-legged on the
floor, trying to perfect her latest bold look. Couldn't believe she wouldn't
be playing her cassette player at full volume, tapes scattered over her bed
as she crooned to Blondie.*

*I moved slowly across the room and lowered myself onto her bed. I just
sat there, sat dumbly staring ahead, as the sky turned from blue to navy
to black. I just sat there.*

Chapter 28

She had stared at the list long into the night, reading about the things Albie had done, thinking about the ways the list had reached out and touched so many lives, and her idea just grew and grew. The next morning, she was overwhelmed with wanting to tell someone who had known him, to share the seed of her idea, and found herself pushing open the door to the café. This was always the space that reminded her of him, reminded her of the happy hours she had taken for granted, foolishly imagining they would last forever.

'Maria,' Pauline chimed from her spot behind the counter.

Maria focused, back in the present, lifting her hand in greeting.

'It's lovely to see you. Keith and I were just wondering where you'd got to, thought you might have gone away again, Paris gave you a taste for travelling…'

Maria felt her face become red as she thought of how Paris had ended. She hadn't liked to dwell on the things Cathie had said about her, or on the Albie Cathie had described, clashing in Maria's mind with the image of the man she carried around with her.

'No, I've been here,' Maria replied, approaching the counter, which was piled high with delicious-looking treats: macaroons, muffins, fresh bread rolls, croissants.

'Well, I wanted to get hold of you, see if you wanted to come to the cinema with me. Meryl Streep's in something new and I love her, but I ain't got a number for you.'

'Actually,' Maria said in a shy voice, rummaging in her handbag, 'I do have a mobile now.' She pulled out her new phone, held it up.

Pauline clapped her hands together. 'You've joined the twenty-first century! About time, brilliant, write your number on this!' Pauline flung her a napkin and took a biro from behind her ear, before turning to serve an approaching customer.

Maria stared at the napkin blankly.

'All OK?' Pauline asked, twizzling a paper bag and handing it to the man.

Maria nodded, pen hovering.

'Maria?'

Maria looked up, eyebrows drawn together, 'I just realised I don't know my number.'

Pauline chuckled. 'Amrit,' she called over her shoulder.

Amrit appeared in the doorway to the kitchen, biting into a hot cross bun. 'Yep?'

'Can you work out Maria's new mobile number, you're good with technology,' Pauline said, taking coins from the customer.

'Sure,' Amrit replied as Maria handed it to her, and watched as Amrit tapped numbers and scrolled, until only seconds later, she was scribbling the digits down on the napkin. 'And I've saved it in your address book, Maria, under "ME", so you can bring it up when you need it.'

She handed the phone back and Maria smiled and nodded.

'Thank you.'

Keith emerged from the same doorway, apron round his waist, a tea towel flung over one shoulder. 'I thought I heard your voice,' he said, immediately stepping forward and planting a kiss on Maria's cheek. She felt wrong-footed, eyes widening. He seemed to stand taller than she remembered, his gaze level and confident. She marvelled at the changes in him, pleased to see the wide smile, healthy complexion: he looked wonderful.

'Hey, I don't pay you to flirt with the customers,' Pauline said, coming over and punching Keith lightly in the arm.

'Maria's no ordinary customer,' he said, 'So where did you get to? We missed seeing you in here.'

'Oh, I've been…' Where had she been? She had been hiding away, assuming these people didn't care or wouldn't notice. How silly, she thought as she stood looking at their open, interested faces. Why did she imagine she was so invisible to others?

'I was hoping you'd get here so I could take a break, it's like slave labour around here,' Keith grunted, unable to keep the smile from his face.

'I could pay a slave a lot less,' Pauline scoffed, pushing the till closed with her hip.

Maria pointed at the chalkboard suspended over the counter. 'You've got some new specials.'

Pauline glanced up, unable to keep the respect from her voice, 'That's this genius here, he knows a million recipes, that one.'

Keith grunted again, a blush building from the collar of his polo shirt.

Maria scanned the menu: 'Homemade Artichoke and Pancetta Soup', 'Tagliatelle with a Prawn Gorgonzola Sauce', 'Homemade Lemon Meringue Pie'. 'It all sounds delicious,' she said, stomach rumbling at the thought.

'Well, whatever you want, it's on me,' Keith said, leading her to a table. 'I wouldn't have this job without you, Maria.'

That sentence jolted her, ready to protest, to downplay her part. Yet she couldn't help but be suffused by a good feeling: she had contributed a meaningful change in Keith's life. 'You did this for yourself,' she said, knowing that was absolutely true.

Keith handed her a knife and fork wrapped in a napkin. 'Without Albie and you, though, I'd still be in that doorway, wasting my life away.' For a second emotion crossed over his face, his brown eyes filming over. He coughed and looked back at the kitchen. 'Well, I better get on, don't want to get fired. Enjoy your food.' He gave her shoulder a last squeeze.

Maria nodded, not quite trusting herself to reply. His words had triggered something inside her, strengthened her resolve: she would keep Albie's list alive by making it her own, the good that could come out of it growing, touching lives in ways she hadn't even begun to imagine.

She had the tagliatelle, the sauce creamy, the enormous pink prawns coated in cheese. She couldn't remember the last time she had eaten something so delicious.

'Genius, isn't he?' Pauline said, scooting opposite her for a moment, 'I am so pleased we found him, and he's such a gent, the kitchen staff love him…'

Maria dabbed at the side of her mouth, 'Albie was always complimentary: he saw something that others just walked past.' For a second she felt a familiar wash of sadness threaten: it had taken Albie's death to bring Keith into her own life.

At that moment the bell went and Maria was surprised to see Mandy push inside, a zebra-print headband in her curly blonde hair, and glance around the room as if she was expecting someone. When Keith passed by the window of the kitchen, Maria saw her lick her lips, pat at her hair.

'Maria,' she gushed, spotting her.

Mandy took a seat, not quite meeting Maria's eye but seeming focused on the door to the kitchen.

'Are you alright?' Maria asked, frowning at Mandy's jittery behaviour.

'Fine,' she mumbled, then came to, looking at Maria. 'Sorry, yes, fine, thanks. You look nice. Nina and I wondered where you'd got to. She wanted to update you about her latest find – seems that coin might be Roman after all, she might be invited to speak at some conference…'

'How wonderful,' Maria replied, feeling another flood of warmth that others had also noticed her absence. How foolish she'd been to cancel her appointments, to shut herself away.

Mandy ordered a coffee, and when it came nursed it for the longest time. Maria glanced at the clock above the counter, wondering why she seemed so jumpy.

'Any more dates with Harry Potter enthusiasts – or in general?' Maria asked, waiting for Mandy's latest woeful tale from the Brighton dating scene.

'Oh!' Mandy said, sitting up and patting her hair again. Keith was standing in the window of the kitchen. 'No,' she mumbled distractedly, 'no one on the scene right now… I'm… taking a break from online, like a detox.'

Maria had never known Mandy to halt her search for a partner. 'That sounds…' She wasn't sure what it sounded like, confused until Keith was standing next to their table and Mandy's expression was different, lips parted, eyes wide. *Ah!* Maria thought.

'You alright, Mandy?' Keith asked, arms crossed, flour streaked on his forearms.

Mandy straightened in her chair. 'Well, thanks, thanks for asking,' she gushed, a sparkle entering her eyes.

Maria chuckled inside, recognising that reaction: it was the way she had looked when Albie had talked to her. She remembered that feeling: giddy, as if there was only him in the room, in the whole world really.

'I need to get back in and see you for the mop,' Keith said, swiping one hand through his hair that was a little longer around the ears. Speckles of white dust settled from his fingers.

Mandy tinkled, a high laugh Maria hadn't heard before. 'You do that. Anytime.'

'In the meantime, I'm about to take my break,' Keith said, reaching to undo his apron.

Mandy's eyes opened a little wider. 'Oh really? Is it your break now?'

'Same every day.' He grinned at her.

Mandy started to blush to the roots of her hair.

'Want a walk or something? I could do with stretching my legs.' He folded up his apron in his hands, waiting for her response.

Mandy stared up. 'Great, yes, why not?'

Keith turned and popped his apron under the counter, 'Great. Maria? Care to join us?'

Mandy stared at her hard and Maria swallowed down a laugh. 'No, I'm alright, thank you. I, um… I have plans.'

Mandy's shoulders dropped a fraction, a clear relief that she had him to herself.

'You two enjoy yourselves,' Maria added with a smile, as Mandy stood up expectantly.

'We will,' Keith said. 'You take care, Maria. Come back soon, alright?'

'I will.' Maria enjoyed watching Keith steer Mandy out of the café with a light hand on her back.

Pauline moved across, clearing Maria's plate away. 'Love is in the air, eh? She's been in here almost every day.'

Maria looked up at her and let out the giggle she'd been holding in. 'They'll be no escape for him.'

Maria was still laughing to herself as she walked back home, full of pasta and coffee and walnut cake. Keith had seemed like a different person, or perhaps the old Keith, the real Keith: confident, friendly, teasing. She could see Mandy and him together. Mandy had always been bright and positive, caring and thoughtful: he could do a lot worse. The sun warmed her back as she moved back down the street, her mobile now crammed with her friends' phone numbers, ways of connecting with people.

She headed to the lake, wanting to enjoy the warmth of the day. Timothy had been away on a tour of Scotland and was back, thanking her for the large donation she had made on his behalf to the RNLI, ramping up their games so that her mobile buzzed with his attempts. It was like Scrabble and Timothy was horribly adept at it. He was winning this game by a clear 34 points. She loved their connection in this way: the chance to play, to use her brain, to see herself improve but also to share the odd message in between, Timothy checking in on her, telling her news from Devon, asking her for news from Brighton.

The park was largely deserted, a woman with two young children playing football, a Springer Spaniel trotting by on a lead, a man jogging, earphones in, utterly focused as he passed her. Maria skirted the water's edge, ripples from a lone swan coursing through the water, the surface glittering. The air smelt of a distant bonfire and freshly cut grass. She headed to the bench she had sat at before, the plaque gleaming from a distance.

Taking a seat, she closed her eyes, tilting her head backwards so that she could feel the sun on her face. As she opened her eyes slowly, a figure was haloed in the beams of light.

'Rosie,' she whispered, smiling slowly at the girl standing in front of her.

'You were lost in another world.' Rosie laughed, her school skirt rolled up at the waist, her tie loose. 'Budge up.' She threw herself down next to Maria, sticking her legs out in front of her. 'God, I love this weather.'

Maria smiled, closing her eyes again. 'I know, it's wonderful.'

'So,' Rosie said after a moment, 'how are you getting on with that list?'

Maria opened one eye. 'I finished it,' she admitted.

'Everything?' Rosie said, the surprise in her voice.

'Everything,' Maria nodded, reflecting over all the things she'd done. 'It's done such good, it's been an amazing thing to witness.'

'Don't be so modest: *you* made it happen,' Rosie reminded her gently.

'No, Albie did that, I just... I carried it on for him.'

'So, what was The Ritz like?' Rosie asked, curiosity in her voice. 'Fit for the Queen? Everything made of gold?'

'Oh,' Maria said, squirming in her seat, 'I didn't go. I did—'

'You did everything on the list for other people, didn't you? Not yourself?' Rosie's voice was stern.

Maria didn't know how to reply to that: it was the truth.

'You so haven't finished the list then,' Rosie said, nudging her in the ribs.

'I...'

'You need to do all of it – even the stuff for you. You know that.'

Maria looked at Rosie, feeling emotion build inside her. 'It's not as easy as that,' she protested, her good mood evaporating fast, replaced by panic as she thought of the bullet points next to her own name. Rosie didn't understand, she couldn't.

Rosie stopped her, 'You just said the list has been good. Right?'

Maria nodded reluctantly. Why was Rosie always so forthright? Always straight to the heart of the matter?

'So,' Rosie continued, 'surely you can trust that Albie might have known what you needed to do.'

Maria felt a lump build in her throat. 'Maybe, I… I'm not sure I'm ready,' she admitted, realising as she heard the words aloud that she was still afraid. Finishing the list would make things so… final and she wasn't sure she could do that. She wasn't ready to say goodbye.

Rosie was quiet for a time, watching the lake. A second swan had joined the first and they glided past gracefully, apparently effortlessly – Maria knew that under the water their legs were circling furiously. People made things look so easy, were we all pedalling furiously under the surface to stay afloat?

'You are ready, you know,' Rosie said, touching Maria's arm. 'And I know you'll finish it. You will.' She stood up and paused, Maria shielding her eyes as she stared up at her. 'I needed to tell you,' Rosie said, looking out across the water, 'that I'm going away now, I wanted to say goodbye.'

Maria stood, 'Leaving?'

'I've got to,' Rosie said, her voice light. 'Places to go, you know.'

Maria didn't want to ask where she was headed.

'But look, I'll be thinking about you,' she said, stepping towards Maria, leaning down to wrap her arms around her, and give her a warm hug. Maria could feel the tickle of her fine hair, her solid grip. She smelt of cherries. Maria blinked back the tears as she stepped back to take a last look at her.

'Thank you for everything you've done for me,' Maria said, knowing that without this sparky teenager, she wouldn't have been able to face some of the things she had done. She had been with her every step of the way.

Rosie paused, head cocked to the side, as if she could read Maria's thoughts. 'You'll be absolutely fine without me, you know.'

Maria straightened, righted the handbag on her shoulder. 'I know,' she admitted quietly. 'But, oh, I'll miss you.'

'So, you promise you'll really finish that list?' Rosie grinned.

Maria nodded. Two women jogged past, one turning her head as Maria dabbed at her eyes.

'Good. Look, I'm rubbish at goodbyes,' Rosie said.

'Me too.'

And then suddenly that was it.

Rosie turned, waving quickly, not prolonging things. Without warning, she was gone, running around the edge of the lake, away before Maria could say anything else. Maria watched her leave, ponytail bouncing, as she moved to the other side of the water, then the glare of the sun blinded her as Rosie disappeared on the other side.

Maria stood up, remaining still in the same spot for a moment or two longer, thinking over their exchange. It had been a strange few months, she reflected, as she turned to walk away in the opposite direction. But Rosie was right: she would complete her part of Albie's list, and she would make it her own too. She pulled out her mobile phone, knowing now was the moment. Wanting to complete her first addition to the wish list, she typed a message into her phone, ready to start a new chapter in her life.

*

I stared for an age at the photograph on the fridge, both of us huddled in enormous winter coats, faces mostly obscured by faux fur-lined hoods. She had a pink nose and the most enormous grin. She had her arms wrapped tightly around me and for a second, I could feel her squeezing me as if she were still here.

Chapter 29

Troy had responded to her text and had appeared at her apartment a couple of hours later. She had pottered around, fixing them snacks and drinks, pleased to have him back. Troy seemed to like her lemon drizzle cake, so she had had one baking in the oven, the sweet but tangy scent filling the air. The first lemon drizzle she had made in over thirty-six years: a recipe that reminded her of her own daughter, who had loved it.

He returned almost every day that week, even for an hour or so. Maria started to suspect he was checking in on her as much as choosing to draw. She loved him being there, watching him hunched over the stool, total concentration on his face, the tip of his tongue out as he drew careful lines, selected colours; the gentle scratch on paper, a frustrated sigh. Sometimes the quick balling up of paper that Maria would rescue later, unable to see the mistake.

Today, she had texted him again asking him to come over.

She had been using the Internet lots, getting ideas, losing hours trawling the pages and discovering new things. She was collecting Wikipedia pages, images, YouTube videos: recipes she wanted to show Pauline and tattoo sketches for Troy. She had also turned to it to help add things to Albie's list, to help get ideas of her own, and she stayed up late concocting plans, before finally falling asleep.

Today would be the first time she would be doing something new and she felt excited as she read the words written out in different coloured ink, her handwriting more rounded than Albie's above.

• *Adopt a cat*

She wanted to help an animal and had decided to adopt. When Troy arrived straight after her text and she told him her plan, he agreed to help with her search. She pressed the button on the phone and slowly tapped at it, accessing the website of a local cat rescue centre. Troy peered over her shoulder. It was the saddest website containing thumbnail pictures of homeless cats. After five minutes scrolling down the page Maria wanted to adopt them all.

Troy was staring silently behind her at the tiny pictures. 'There are so many,' he commented finally, a tinge of pity in the sentence.

Maria handed him the phone. 'You choose one.'

Troy took the phone reverentially, his face solemn as she handed him this task.

'I don't want a young cat, I want an older cat,' Maria added firmly as Troy started to scan down the pages. 'Need to still be here for it.'

'Don't say that,' Troy said quietly, briefly glancing at her.

'It wouldn't be fair on a kitten,' Maria said firmly, 'I won't be around forever.'

Troy swallowed, didn't add anything, just carried on scrolling down. 'She's ten years old,' he pointed out.

'I want a cat that no one else wants, one that has waited all her life for someone to notice her.'

'He's eleven, one ear,' Troy said, pointing at the thumbnail of a cat.

Maria thought it was the ugliest cat she had ever seen: a ginger cat with a scar on his nose, a bent-down right ear, but his expression as he stared solemnly into the camera moved her. 'A him...' She looked again at the photograph, feeling certainty flood through her. 'Yes, I like him. I'll call him Albert.'

Troy filled out the necessary forms for her, asking her various questions.

'Are you away from home a lot?'

'No.'

'Do you have regular visitors to the residence?'

'Just you,' Maria said happily, noting the tiny smile as he continued to read.

'Are you a smoker?'

'No.'

He booked for someone to contact her about a home visit and check. She felt the stirrings of excitement build in her that she would be rescuing a cat and giving it a good home for the last years of its life. That she would always have company too, something to care for and nurture.

Troy left with a promise to see her soon. He still refused to accept another artist's set to take away, but borrowed some fine liners and a pad, always returning with most of the pages filled. She was in awe of his industry, his creative designs. The bud of an idea had been forming there too – she had added it under his name on the list. She needed to take a trip to Ms Leonard to set it in motion.

Maria felt a fire within her. For the second time since Albie died, she felt her purpose, her future, but with more certainty than ever before. The list had changed her life again and Albie continued to work his magic from the grave.

As she collapsed into bed, her phone beeping and humming with messages from Pauline, Keith and Troy, she felt deeply grateful that Albie had walked across that café on that day to sit with her. She stared at her own name on the list, knowing something had changed, that perhaps she was ready, finally, to tackle what she had been avoiding.

*

What did I miss the most? It wasn't the things I expected. It was the noise that was gone: the sound of her moving in the room next door, or singing to her cassettes. It was her head on my shoulder crying over That's Life! *It's her endless chatter about girls at her school, names I kept forgetting. How I wished I'd listened closer.*

Sometimes it was the panic that I can't remember any details. As if all my memories were suddenly reduced to the photographs and home videos. I was sure I'd eventually forget the exact shade of her brown hair, the name of that boy who'd bullied her in Year 6 – Luke, or was it Thomas? – the way she pronounced 'carefully' wrong, the way her face screwed up when I'd given her 'the talk'.

I wonder which details I made up, re-painted in a new light – the main one perhaps that I'd been a good mother.

Chapter 30

She hadn't expected to hear from Cathie, had tried to forget the words that had stung in Paris. An answerphone message that she was heading down to see her the following day threw Maria into a spin. Was she coming to accuse her of worse things? Could Maria refuse to see her?

The following day, she dressed carefully in cropped navy trousers, a white shirt and a thin grey cardigan. As she was brushing powder onto her nose, she started at the sound of the buzzer: Cathie was early.

The greeting was strained as Cathie appeared in the doorway to the apartment and lingered half-in and half-out.

'You've done something nice to your hair,' Maria said, indicating the new colour, Cathie's cropped hair now a mid-brown.

Cathie held a hand up to her head and said thank you with a self-conscious flush. Would she have responded in that way if she planned to shout at Maria? Trying to relax, Maria stepped back to invite her inside. She had hoovered and laid out biscuits on a small plate all ready.

'I booked us tickets for Sea Life – I think it's the biggest aquarium in England or something like that,' Cathie gushed.

Maria tried not to let the surprise show on her face: fish? Was she going to throw her to the sharks? 'Is it really?'

'Well, I'm not sure but I thought it might be nice. I've parked the car outside if you wanted…'

'Of course, there's no time like the present,' Maria said, scooping up her handbag and following Cathie down the stairs, past the pram abandoned outside the apartment below.

Cathie drove almost in silence and Maria wondered whether she would simply ignore how they had left things after Paris. She snuck a sideling glance at Cathie: her eyes remained on the road ahead. Maria's palms felt slippery on the leather of her handbag.

They turned into the car park and Cathie took forever shifting backwards and forwards, backwards again to squeeze into a spare parking spot.

Maria hadn't realised how close the aquarium was to the beach and her heart beat that little bit faster, the desire to turn around and head home overwhelming. Could she say something? Fabricate an excuse?

A few months ago, she wouldn't have thought twice but today, sitting next to Albie's sister, her one connection to him, her one chance to learn more about him, she just couldn't say the words. She would head inside, she wouldn't look up, she wouldn't think about it.

She walked quickly – Cathie finally seemed to loosen up just as Maria was clamping down. *Just get inside and then relax*, she thought as she stared at her feet on the pavement, almost tripping. Pushing through the doors, trying to silence the sound of the rolling waves in the distance, the squawk of a seagull overhead, she could finally focus on what Cathie was saying.

'I'll get the tickets,' Cathie said, moving across to the counter as Maria waited, the world coming to once more. The foyer was largely empty, a mid-week day out of season, with just some pre-school children up ahead, surrounding a harassed-looking teacher and one or two older people reading information about our seas from large boards covered in photographs. Maria could see one of a turtle, its neck trapped in the plastic wrapping from a pack of cans, one eye doleful and despairing.

'Shall we head in?' Cathie handed her a ticket and gave her a small smile.

Maria recognised the gesture as one of apology and returned it, able to concentrate now she was inside and the beach out of sight.

They moved through an enormous room lined with tanks, information about the various creatures on display below. In the centre of the room stood an enormous tank, like an indoor pond, that contained huge stingrays, moving rhythmically along the floor. Cathie was peering down at them, admiring their speckled backs, their graceful motion.

Maria was distracted by a nearby array of tropical fish, the colours vivid against the blue of the tank. The atmosphere was soothing, the air cool, with the gentle slap of the water from the bigger tanks, the hum of a nearby air-conditioning unit.

Almost an hour went by, meandering around the various rooms and watching children, noses pressed against the glass as they pointed and squealed. Maria had learnt a great deal about marine life. She would have shared it with Albie, had she been seeing him – he would have enjoyed hearing about it, she was sure. He had always loved the *Planet Earth*-type documentaries, had instructed her to watch the latest David Attenborough series and she had duly circled them in her TV listings guide. She felt a pinch in her gut that they would never get to discuss it.

Stood next to an enormous tank, reef sharks gliding past inches from the glass, Cathie finally took a deep breath and spoke about it all. 'Maria, I've been meaning to come and see you since Paris. I behaved appallingly. There's no excuse, I'm ashamed and so sorry.' She inhaled loudly, the words that seemed rehearsed now out in the space between them.

Maria could have been petty, resisted the apology, acted defensively or even shrugged it off. But she felt nothing but relief, a weight she hadn't even realised she was still carrying lightening. She looked at Cathie, the lines deep on her forehead as she waited in anticipation of how Maria would act.

'I really didn't mean to rub anything in,' Maria said, 'I was as shocked as you to discover what Albie had done.'

'It was none of my business, his money is his money and he had every right to give it to whomever he wanted. I was jealous, I suppose, and it made me say horrible, unforgiveable things.'

Maria held out a hand, placed it on Cathie's forearm. 'Not unforgiveable.'

They moved through to another room with two ancient-looking turtles. One gave Maria a wary look as she passed him.

'These guys might even be older than me,' Maria chuckled, wanting to distract Cathie, make her realise the past was the past.

Cathie, however, still seemed preoccupied, barely glancing as one of the turtles stepped out onto its artificial bank right below them.

'I still can't believe he isn't here,' she said, both arms resting on the lip of the enclosure.

Maria joined her, wanting to be a comfort. 'He is living on in the things he did though.'

'How do you mean?' Cathie asked, turning to face her, an overhead spotlight giving her skin a strange green hue.

'Well, the money, *his* money, I wanted to explain it in Paris... You see, he spent it on other people. He did so many good things with it, they were all on the list. In fact,' Maria had a thought, 'you need to see something. Shall we get out of here?'

Cathie nodded, clearly happy for Maria to boss her about. Perhaps it reminded her of her youth, of following around a brother older by six years. Maria felt strangely overprotective suddenly, imagining a young Albie there by Cathie's side, wanting to protect.

They left Sea Life, Maria so focused on where she was headed that she barely thought twice as they pushed their way back outside and was confronted with a glimpse of sparkling sea.

'Let's get the car,' she said, her voice steady as she turned in the direction of the car park.

She directed Cathie through the streets of Brighton, the traffic slow with roadworks, the temporary traffic lights finally clearing for them to turn down the familiar tree-lined road, 'This is it, park here.'

Cathie switched off the engine and stared at the building opposite.

'Come and see what he did,' Maria insisted, stepping out of the car and pulling her cardigan tightly around her.

Two girls sat on the wall outside the Youth Centre, staring at Maria and Cathie as they ascended the stone steps.

'Hello,' Maria said brightly. One girl chewing gum looked as if she might have swallowed it.

'Y'alright?'

Maria pushed inside. 'So,' she said turning to Cathie, 'he kitted out this place. He bought them a football table, pool table, jukebox, he re-did the carpets, had the walls painted. Look at them.' Through the glass of the double doors they could see teenagers standing around the tables, playing, laughing, jostling. 'And he didn't tell anyone, he just got on and did it. I only found out because of the list he left.'

'Did he not want a plaque or something?' Cathie asked, looking around the foyer.

'Gosh, I can't see Albie being fussed about all that.' Albie would have loathed having his name up and lauded for it. He had been so keen to keep his good deeds to himself, he hadn't even shared them with Maria.

Cathie raised an eyebrow. 'When I knew him that was *all* he wanted. He got a bespoke named desk plate for his office, this ridiculous triangular object, like one of those things that separates the food at the supermarket, and he kept it on his desk with his latest title. He used to make up things like "President" and "CEO".'

Maria frowned at this foreign idea. 'I can't imagine Albie having that kind of ego,' she said, baffled by this insight into a young, ambitious brother – a stranger to her.

'I used to tease him for it. Me with my nursing, I was never going to be earning the big bucks. I used to call him Lord Albert to annoy him.'

Maria shook her head, reflecting on the strangeness of how different people could see the same person.

'It's great that he changed in that way. I wish I'd…' Cathie tailed away and Maria genuinely wished she had seen Albie as she had known him: generous, humble, selfless. She wondered what had changed in his past to make him that way, she had always assumed he was just… better.

Before she could ask, a familiar face appeared in the rectangular glass of the door. 'Maria!' Troy said, moving into the foyer, with another boy of the same age trailing him.

'Oh, hello.'

'Were you looking for me?' Troy asked, a worried look on his face. 'Is everything OK?'

Touched by his concern, Maria smiled. 'Oh no, I was just showing Cathie here the things Albie did. Cathie, this is Troy, Troy, this is Albie's sister.'

'Cool,' Troy said, enthusiastically nodding his head. 'He was a legend.'

Cathie gave him a tiny smile. 'I'm just hearing all about it.'

Troy's face lit up as he turned to Maria. 'You had the home check yet?'

'No, not yet. I'll let you know when they do.'

Troy's friend was still hovering nearby, and Troy turned to him: 'This is Maria, she's gonna adopt a cat, man – I helped her pick him out.'

'Hello,' Maria said, giving the boy a smile. He had long hair that fell to his shoulders and a raven tattoo on his neck. 'That must have hurt, I wouldn't have the courage,' she said, pointing to the artwork.

The boy put one hand up to his neck in a self-conscious gesture.

'I really like it,' Maria added.

The boy's hand dropped, his mouth lifting.

'He's going to let me do one on his leg when I get qualified.' Troy beamed.

'Sick,' Maria said, which made Troy bark with laughter.

Cathie was watching this exchange in bemusement.

'Well, we've got to get going. See you around, Maria, and nice to meet you,' Troy said to Cathie and Maria puffed with pride at knowing this polite, lovely boy. Albie had done so well to encourage him, she just hoped she could make a difference too. He deserved good things.

'Lovely to see you, Troy,' Maria said and watched them walk out. Then, turning to Cathie, 'Shall we get going too? I know exactly where we should head next.'

*

I hated thinking of that last evening. Another row, the same one, sparked as easily as all the ones before.

'You need to be back here by nine.'

'That's so early, Polly's mum lets her out till ten.'

'I don't care what Polly's mum does, you need to be back here by nine. I don't want you out in the dark.'

'No one has to leave then! I'll look like a baby.'

'I don't care how you look, you need to be back.'

She had pouted at that, hands clenched into fists.

'I don't have to let you go out at all...' I'd raised my voice with those words, annoyed because this argument was eating into my evening and I needed to work on some figures for a campaign, the numbers blurring on the page in front of me. But these words always worked.

'You're so strict, it's not fair.' She'd stamped through to her room, slamming the door.

I'd rolled my eyes, left her to it, and she emerged from her room an hour later, dressed and ready to join her friends. Had I even told her I loved her when she left?

God, I loved her.

Chapter 31

It was quiet, the post-lunch rush already thinned out. Pauline was wiping down a table and looked up as Maria and Cathie moved inside. 'Hi Maria. Amrit's off for a couple of days so it's just me. I'll be with you shortly.'

'No rush,' Maria said, moving to a table near the kitchen, Cathie following in her wake.

Peering through the hatch, Maria saw Keith leaning against the table, leafing through a recipe book. 'Keith,' she called out, 'come out here, there's someone I want you to meet.'

Keith looked up, one eyebrow raised in surprise and closed the book. He emerged from the kitchen. 'Who is this new bold Maria and what did you do with my rabbit-in-headlights friend?'

He gave her a quick kiss on the cheek and she felt herself blush. Was that what she had been like? A rabbit in headlights? Maria thought back over the last few months: he was right, she supposed, she was more confident now. She felt more... herself. It was the other Maria who hadn't been her, she realised.

Keith held out a hand to Cathie. 'Pleasure to meet you, any friend of Maria's—'

'Lovely to meet you, this is a nice place. I love the soft blue colour...' She indicated the walls.

'It's been recently refurbished,' Keith explained. 'Maria must tell you, it's quite a story.'

'That's why I brought Cathie here, I wanted to show her. This is Albie's sister, Cathie.'

Keith didn't say anything, just stood looking dumbly ahead, his hand dropped to his side. Maria shifted her weight, worrying about his reaction. Had he met Cathie before? Was something wrong? Then, without warning, he launched himself at Cathie, enveloping her in a hug, her face pressed against his shoulder. 'Albie's sister!' he repeated, squeezing her close, her face startled, eyes wide. 'Albie was... Albie changed my life,' he said simply.

Cathie bit her lip, the raw emotion prompting her eyes to fill with tears. 'I... we hadn't spoken for a while.'

Keith nodded sadly. 'I'm sorry to hear that, I understand only too well.'

Cathie looked up sharply at the sentence, relief passing across her face as Keith moved to fuss over them, clearly not judging her.

'You two take a seat. Let me make you something, Albie's sister,' he repeated, pulling out a chair, grinning like a lunatic. 'I can't believe it. You know you do have his eyes... Have a seat, have a seat, a total honour,' he added, pulling out a napkin with a flourish.

It was as if Cathie were the queen, Maria reflected, giggling at the scene. It was wonderful to see Keith's reaction, such an outpouring, reminding her once again what an impact Albie had made, how many lives he'd touched.

'I've got some delicious seafood soup left over from the lunchtime rush, today's special. Let me get you some, do you like fish?'

Cathie nodded mutely, perhaps still processing everything.

'Excellent,' said Keith, almost manic, 'you wait here, I'll go and prepare it. Some for you, Maria?'

'Lovely,' she nodded.

'Albie's sister!' Keith said to himself yet again as he moved back towards the kitchen, tightening his apron as if going into battle.

He returned with bowls of soup and hunks of fresh white bread, the outside crisp, the insides wonderfully warm and soft, the fragrant smell filling the small space. Pauline had cleared the final tables and had joined them for a moment, greeting Cathie with a squeal and immediately presenting her with an Appletiser on the house: 'For Albie'.

They swapped stories, Maria pointing out the changes in the café and telling Cathie about the first time Albie had edged his way across the room to sit with her: 'He just pulled up a chair opposite as if we were old friends.' She felt the familiar pain in her chest, a sort of delighted agony, as she spoke about him, as she remembered tiny details: his broken nose, his kind dark blue eyes, the scent of talcum powder when he moved past her.

Keith was smiling as she related the tale and started to tell Cathie his own. 'He did the same for me. Just appeared in my doorway with a coffee and a cheese baguette. Sat down on my mat and started telling me about this news story he'd just read – something about penguins in knitted jumpers, I forget exactly, but it really tickled him.'

'Doorway?' Cathie asked, her brows drawn together.

'I used to live on the streets,' Keith admitted, his chin tilted a little as if he needed to hide the fact it hurt him to admit it.

'Oh… But you don't now?' Cathie asked.

'Nope.' Keith spooned a mouthful. 'I live above here, landlord can be a pain but at least I have a bed.'

'Hey!' Pauline said, whacking him on the upper arm, 'The landlord's a bloody delight.'

Keith roared with laughter, rocking in his chair. 'Yeah, well it'll do for now.'

Maria settled back, feeling comfortable as ever in the presence of her friends, the café filled with their laughter and chatter. This place would always remind her of good times.

Pauline disappeared again, clattering around in the kitchen, doing a stocktake. Cathie seemed to relax, complimenting Keith on his soup, dabbing the corner of her mouth with her napkin as she took a breath, shared her own memories of Albie from when they were children: building wigwams in the woods behind their house, writing short stories that he would read to her at bedtime.

'I adored him. He would cart me around on his shoulders and I would constantly bring him things I thought he'd like: rocks, sticks, once a dead bee... It's funny,' she said, her voice breaking a moment, 'I've spent so long focusing on our falling-out, I haven't thought of these things in years, haven't allowed myself.' She dropped her head at that, her chin on her chest, the regret obvious as she fell silent.

Keith was quiet too, staring at his empty bowl as if it contained the answer to some complicated question.

Maria frowned, not wanting to probe too much in front of Cathie.

Cathie took a breath, surreptitiously wiping at her eyes. 'I won't be long,' she said quickly, her chair scraping as she got up, headed to the bathroom in the corner.

Maria watched her go and then turned back to face Keith.

He remained still, lost somewhere else as Maria gave him a small smile. 'You alright, Keith? You seem very quiet.'

He looked up, pain etching his eyes. 'It's just brought it home, seeing her.' He tipped his head towards the bathroom, his voice soft.

'I don't want to be like that with my boy. I don't want to not know him, not hear from him.'

Maria's heart ached at the words, his loss clear. She couldn't imagine anyone being cross with Keith, not wanting to hear from him. To her, he was a warm, generous soul, but she knew he hadn't always been like that, and he was the first to beat himself up over his past.

He squared his shoulders, looking up at her. 'I'm going to get back in touch, I'm not going to take no for an answer. I have to tell him that I love him. In our last row I said such stupid, hateful things and I don't want to be filled with this regret. It ruins people.'

Maria was moved by Keith's serious expression, the worry in his eyes. 'I'm sure he'll want to hear from you,' she said, placing a hand on his arm. 'And if you get in touch and it doesn't, well, if you need company, or someone to talk to… I know only too well what it is to live with regrets.'

Keith's eyebrows lifted at the admission, Maria hastily looking away. She had never shared her own sorry story, this was the closest she had come to letting it slip.

Keith's mouth opened and Maria felt the room stop, the sounds fade away as she waited for his questions. Was a small part of her relieved that she might finally try talking about it?

'Well,' Cathie said from behind her, making Maria jump.

Keith's mouth snapped closed.

Maria felt a mixture of feelings at the interruption. She breathed in deeply, slowly, trying to ignore her pounding heart. She wouldn't have to share it with him today, but something told her from his watchful look that this wouldn't be the last of it.

*

I stopped seeing friends, I pushed people away. It didn't take much. No returning calls, a few angry words in passing, a refusal to leave the house, constant excuses and gradually they ebb away.

I became the talk of our street, our house of flats: pitying glances, tipped heads, whispers behind hands. God, I hated them all with their normal lives: the rows with their children, their partners' foot rubs, their holidays.

Sarah, my friend and neighbour who had spent countless hours gossiping with me, meeting me every week to watch the latest episode of The Two Ronnies *on our rubbish television – the only good thing on any of the three channels she'd said. She had set me up on dates, delighted when Darren had lasted a couple of years before he'd left me for Australia, and had brought a Viennetta and pretended to be horrified when we finished the whole thing. She was the last friend to go; she clung on for a while. It took a lot to tell her to leave and I moved out of our building to make sure of it.*

It is surprisingly easy to shed the people in your life when you are determined to do so, and I was.

Chapter 32

It was lovely to have made her peace with Cathie and Maria was gratified to receive a text message almost immediately: *Lovely to see all the places that meant a lot to Albie.* She'd promised to return again soon, invited Maria to her house in Margate too. She had photographs from their childhood – she was going to scan some and send them. A tiny Albie, Maria thought with a small smile. She imagined a cheeky boy roaming the fields of the West Country, pudgy legs, a wide grin.

Beneath her apartment she could make out some distant crying and found herself dressing quickly, moving into her kitchen and collecting up various supplies. She removed the wish list from its new home in the top drawer of her bedside table and started writing on it. This was something that would make a difference, she was sure.

She appeared at the doorway downstairs, holding a mop and bucket filled with various cloths. 'Right, you are absolutely not to argue with me but I want you to sit down on your sofa while I take care of things for you,' she said, feeling authoritative.

Cara's mouth was half-open, Owen clinging to one leg, a muslin over her shoulder, a baby in her arm tugging on the bottom of her rather lank hair.

'Oh… I…'

Maria put up a hand. 'In return, I'll have a cup of tea and maybe a biscuit.'

Cara looked worried, raking at her hair. 'Oh, I don't think I have biscuits.'

'Biscuit,' said Owen brightly, and suddenly ran away.

'That absolutely won't be a deal-breaker,' Maria assured her.

'I think I have a Snickers bar somewhere though,' Cara said.

Maria laughed. 'You're more in need,' she said, eyeing up Owen, who had reappeared covered in flour.

'Mummy, I made a snowman.'

'Oh god,' Cara said, racing to the kitchen. Maria followed, trying to hide her laughter as Owen presented them with his snowman, which seemed to consist of a large pile of plain flour and a carrot on the floor.

'He melted.'

Cara's mouth twitched and Maria bustled inside. 'Well, if I start in here, then I'd love to play with the little man,' she said over her shoulder.

'No, honestly, I couldn't…'

Maria placed a hand on Cara's upper arm. 'I really do want to, please let me.'

Cara seemed to weigh things up, the baby now crying in her ear, Owen running down the corridor, announcing that he had a 'lovely surprise' for her.

Maria gently shoved her out and, after a moment's fretting in the corridor, Cara moved through to the living room, where Owen was bouncing on the sofa playing 'trampoline'.

'Mummy, I flying.'

Maria ran the taps, snapped on her Marigolds and set to work. Cara had turned on some music next door and she found herself humming along as she swept and scrubbed and mopped. Her back ached, but she enjoyed transforming the place, gratified to peek through the door to see Cara laughing as she sat on the carpet next to Owen and about ten thousand small cars, the baby dozing in a rocker nearby.

She joined them once she'd finished, bringing two coffees through on a tray.

'Biscuit,' Owen asked hopefully and Cara rolled her eyes and got up to go to the kitchen.

She returned holding a plate with three Hobnobs in the centre. 'I ration them,' she explained as Owen picked up two. 'Just one!' And when his lip wobbled, she said, 'You get nothing if you take two.' He returned the second to the plate quickly.

Owen had finished his biscuit and clambered into Cara's lap. Placing both hands on either side of his mother's cheeks, he looked at her: 'I share yours.'

'I know what that's code for.' Cara laughed, breaking off the tiniest piece of her biscuit, which Owen immediately demolished.

Maria nibbled on hers, enjoying being around a little one and all the energy a child his age brought, enjoying his wonder over the small things, his solemn introduction to his row of cars, and finally, the small hand in Maria's as she got up to leave.

'Let's make a traffic jam.'

So, she stayed a while longer, ushering Cara off to take a shower while she watched the children.

Cara was quick, returning in tracksuit bottoms, her hair wrapped in a towel, but her cheeks were flushed pink and she seemed to have more energy, less tension. Maria wished Cara had more help – it was lonely and hard, this stage of motherhood. She thought back on her own experience, not used to staying with the thoughts but this time forcing herself to remember: the showers with the door open so she could check on her daughter enclosed in a play pen; the anxiety of the early months, bent over her cot as she slept, needing to hear the breaths, see her chest moving; the worry when she got ill, or cried out. The amount of stuff required to just leave the house, the roll of a stranger's eyes if her daughter cried in a public place.

She finally got up to leave after Cara finished feeding the baby and was putting down Owen for a brief nap. He had given a sleepy 'Bye, bye' and a wave as he was carried through, his tiny head resting on Cara's shoulder, to his room.

Cara returned as Maria was packing her things away in the kitchen. 'Thank you so much, the place looks amazing. I can't believe you did that for me,' she said in a low voice, careful not to rouse Owen.

Maria felt herself grow hot, feeling that she was getting far too much credit for a couple of hours out of her day. 'It's wonderful to do something small that makes a difference to someone else.' She wrung out one of the cloths and threw it in the empty bucket. 'A friend taught me that,' she added quietly.

'Well, thank you. I won't let you clean for me again but it has made a huge difference.'

Maria propped up the mop in the bucket, ready to make her excuses and leave Cara in her one moment of quiet, before Owen woke, before the baby demanded something else. 'I won't clean for you every week, but…' Maria took a breath, knowing the next sentence would cause a reaction. 'I want to hire someone who will.'

Predictably, Cara started to protest, her face a horrified gape. Maria raised a hand to hush her. 'Before you say no' – Cara fell silent, still staring at her as Maria continued – 'let me tell you about the lovely man who will be footing the bill…'

*

The job I so loved became exhausting: all the people to speak to, to manage. I lost the energy and what was the point of the work? I couldn't remember.

I started missing the networking events, became sloppy with the projects I handed in, forgot to fax people information on time, was short with the boss. It came as no surprise, after months limping along, to be let go. The old promises of promotion long gone, this woman wouldn't be promoted, this woman didn't even belong in this company. There wasn't a leaving do. If there was, I wouldn't have gone anyway. All those years, gone in a blink, and when I left, carrying only my handbag, I didn't even care.

Chapter 33

They were heading up on the train. Maria met him outside the station dressed all in black, a T-shirt with a small red logo on the chest, baggy trousers, scuffed trainers. The most unlikely couple, she thought, as she smoothed at her pale pink skirt, her cream jacket, feeling somewhat overdressed.

Troy looked her up and down. 'These were the only things I've got,' he said, a hand rubbing at his chin, clearly panicking as he saw her smart clothes and freshly washed and dried hair – Mandy's best work.

'We'll sort you something,' Maria said, tucking his arm into hers and moving into the station. 'Let's just get up there.'

She hadn't thought about his clothes, she realised as she collected their tickets from the booth, how thoughtless of her. He should feel comfortable but then they were headed to The Ritz, so she didn't want him to stick out and be made to feel awkward. Would he even be able to get in with trainers on? She didn't want that to ruin their day.

'I've never been to London,' Troy admitted, settling himself in his seat, bouncing once, twice with nervous energy.

'It's been almost forty years for me so that's almost the same.' Maria gave him a small smile, trying to make him feel more comfortable. 'I'm glad you're coming, I'm frankly terrified and I need the company. Albie and his grand plans, eh? He's laughing somewhere.'

That seemed to relax him a little and he sat back, head resting on the seat.

She had brought her book but didn't remove it from her bag, just watched as they left Brighton, the landscape changing as they coursed through the countryside, greens and yellows flashing past. She bought them drinks from the catering cart, her tea slopping as she stirred it with a plastic spoon, Troy taking small sips of his can of Coke, jiggling his leg up and down in the aisle. Slowing near the capital, the carriages flashed light to dark as they passed tunnels, bridges, large concrete buildings.

Troy was leaning forward, arms resting on the table in front of him. His mouth opened as they passed through a tunnel lined with vivid images, graffiti that she wouldn't even have noticed. 'Sick,' he said under his breath, which she knew now meant he was impressed. He had brought along his sketchpad and had opened it then to jot something down. He was always thinking, she realised, always creating. She couldn't wait to share her surprise with him later.

They had time before their booking at The Ritz. Staring at the complicated lines on the Underground map, they both looked at each other before Maria made the decision. 'We'll splurge on a taxi,' she said firmly, turning towards the exit for the taxi rank. 'Albie wouldn't want us to slum it, not today.' She knew with absolute certainty that he would have wanted to spoil them.

Troy looked visibly relieved. She hadn't seen him in this setting before, staying close to her side, one hand steering her by the elbow, pretending perhaps to be caring for her, while the frightened expression on his face reminded her that he was young and out of place. She felt fiercely protective of him, glaring at a man jabbing at a mobile who shoulder-barged him.

The taxi dropped them near Green Park station and they stepped out onto the street, pausing for a moment at the sheer number of people and cars, buses and taxis whizzing past.

'Right, let's get you something a little smarter, shall we? And I could do with something too, need to make Albie proud.'

Troy simply nodded, allowing Maria to usher him into a nearby clothes shop, watching him run a hand along a row of shirts, biting his lip as a young guy approached.

'Can I help you with anything?'

Troy shook his head quickly, almost scuttling back to Maria's side.

Laughing, she moved down the aisle, pulling out a simple black V-neck jumper, the fabric impossibly soft. 'How about this?' she asked, holding it up to her body.

'Your top is nice,' Troy said, mumbling at his feet.

'Not for me, you idiot, for you.' Maria laughed out loud and the shop assistant looked up. Maria had never called anyone an idiot, and she was gratified to hear Troy laughing in response.

'S'OK,' he said, letting her hand it to him.

'Don't be too effusive,' she sighed, moving along and pulling out a shirt, T-shirt, trousers.

'Woah, hold on!' Troy said, turning over the price tag.

'Come on, Troy, Albie would want us to dress up for the occasion.'

Troy's mouth twitched, his eyebrows pulled together before he apparently made up his mind. 'Alright. Is there a changing room, mate?' he asked the assistant, who pointed him to the back of the shop and a row of three curtained cubicles. 'I'm not doing a fashion parade for you though,' he added, taking the hangers from her and heading towards the back.

Troy tried everything on, peeking out from behind the curtain, pretending to be checking on her.

'Do you want me to take a look?' Maria asked and he nodded once, holding back the curtain.

He was wearing a pair of dark blue jeans, a pale blue shirt and the black V-neck jumper – he looked impossibly good-looking.

'What do you reckon?'

Maria looked him up and down: 'I think we're going to need new shoes.'

It was a different person who stepped into The Ritz with her a couple of hours later, Troy walking taller as he accompanied her across the polished, bright foyer, his new shoes tapping on the marble, an enormous chandelier overhead, a grand staircase sweeping away to their right.

'We have a reservation,' Maria said in an exaggerated whisper at the double doors to the restaurant.

Troy tugged on his collar, clearly unused to the new clothes.

'You look perfect,' Maria said as they waited, admiring the shine of his new black leather shoes, his old clothes and trainers stored in a large carrier bag in his hand. He stopped fidgeting and gave her a wide smile.

'Do follow me please,' the discreet voice of the maître d'.

Troy waggled both eyebrows as they followed the man, who didn't have a single hair out of place and was holding a starched white cloth over one arm. Maria felt the stirrings of a laugh inside her. *Albie Young, what were you thinking?* She thought fondly of the café back in Brighton with its old gingham tablecloths, the table – always scattered with salt grains – wobbling unless you folded up a napkin for underneath its leg, the paintings on the walls with stickers announcing their price. Here were landscapes in gilded frames, enormous layered chandeliers

– light gleaming from every perfectly cut-glass teardrop – crisp white tablecloths, polished oak surfaces, people in expensive suits, beautifully cut clothes. Maria felt relieved that they had gone shopping, her own new silk neckerchief perfect for the occasion.

They ordered the champagne afternoon tea and sat in a sort of scared silence as they soaked in the room.

'This is mental,' Troy whispered, leaning in towards her.

She bit her lip: 'It is a bit.'

Too frightened to raise their voices, they exchanged various looks as people moved past, chattered at tables. The waiter approached, practically hidden behind the most enormous tiered cake stand. He set it down in the centre of the table and departed.

Maria stared at the stand in front of them. Tiny sandwiches – cucumber and cream cheese, salmon, and egg and cress – cut in perfect triangles lined up along the bottom, enormous fluffy scones next to pots of thick clotted cream and the most delicious-looking strawberry jam, then miniature cakes of every variety – layers of delicate sponge, fillings in pastel shades, even a small, perfectly round marble cake. Maria couldn't look away. It was as if Albie had planned it. A beautiful patterned teapot with bone china tea cups was presented on a tray, a feast for the eyes.

The waiter reappeared moments later with an ice bucket on a stand, two champagne flutes propped inside, and opened the bottle with a loud pop, making them jump. He poured champagne into the two flutes, one hand behind his back as he talked them through the various items, 'And the champagne will compliment it, with notes of citrus and honey, as I'm sure you'll notice.'

Maria swallowed down a giggle and Troy listened intently, giving a solemn nod after he sniffed at his glass. He was enjoying playing the role.

They tried everything: an explosion of flavours in her mouth. The lightest sponge, the richest cream, the sharp tang of the champagne, the bubbles tickling her nose. It all tasted as fabulous as it looked, her stomach weighty with it all as she sat back.

'Wow!' she said, wishing she could let out a button on her skirt.

Troy licked a finger and grinned at her, reaching across and offering her the last miniature cake. Maria lifted a hand, even that required effort, and shook her head – 'I really couldn't.' She watched him pop it straight in his mouth.

They continued to admire people coming and going, feeling light-headed at a second glass of champagne. Woozy and full of food, Maria was grateful to get up and head outside, the breeze bringing her back to life.

She felt her shoulders relax as they stepped back onto the street, Troy immediately talking at full volume. 'That was mental. Fuckin' hell. I thought we'd get kicked out if we spoke too loud.'

His laugh was infectious and she found herself joining in. Afternoon tea at The Ritz was an experience but she knew she didn't fit into that glitzy polished world.

'Was there meant to be more than cucumber in some of those sandwiches? That was weird. Oh my god, I'm full though! Those puffy pastry things were amazing, hands down the best thing I've ever eaten. God, though…' He hunched over, laughing again. 'Can I take off these shoes now? They're rubbing my feet.'

Maria waited as he pulled his trainers out of the bag and slid them back on, the hole in his sock reminding her to get him some new ones.

'Come on, I want to take you somewhere else,' Maria said, feeling lighter as they moved away, out into the real world, with ordinary people.

She had practised using the map on her mobile phone and was directing Troy, stopping intermittently to check the little blue dot was moving in the right direction.

'It's along here,' she said, wandering down the road towards Piccadilly Circus, Troy blinking up at the enormous neon signs wrapped around the buildings, completely silent as his neck craned left and right, soaking it all in.

There were people everywhere: some on phones, some posing for photos, some moving past with briefcases and serious expressions, a huge crocodile of schoolchildren, weary teachers flanking them on either side, others clutching a million carrier bags stuffed with shopping. London felt like the middle of the universe, the bustle like nothing she had ever known. She craved the peace of Brighton, the slower pace, the open space. For a brief second, she missed the stretch of ocean before that thought was pushed down inside her again.

Passing through Leicester Square, Maria marvelled at the buzz and Troy stared up at the movie posters. 'This is where there are premieres of all the films,' he said, 'I've seen it on TV before.' They were right in the heart of things, right in the middle of the action.

'It's down here.' She directed him down a wide road, London buses sighing with relief as they stopped, taxis and cars meandering past, people jaywalking, skirting the stationary cars, horns blaring.

The National Portrait Gallery, grand in its Portland stone, soared above them, people checking their watches by the entrance, calling out to children rushing past. Troy seemed to have lost all words as he practically tripped up to the entrance. They seemed to be ticking off every London landmark. Maria thought of Albie chuckling somewhere at their bemused, overwhelmed expressions, as they caught each other's eyes and grinned in shocked bemusement.

Little them! In London!

She had wanted to take him to an art gallery, somewhere to inspire him, but realised early on that she had led him to a part of the gallery that was not perhaps the type of art that got him excited.

'There are a lot of old white men in tights,' he said, standing in front of yet another oil painting of a man in sixteenth-century garb. Maria couldn't help but giggle as she viewed the place from Troy's position.

'Let's go and see the Tudor room, they'll be some of Henry VIII in there,' she said, leading him to the staircase.

'Henry who?'

Maria rolled her eyes. 'You know, big king, broke from Rome.'

Troy continued to look at her blankly.

'He was the one with six wives.'

'Player!' he smirked and Maria hit him with her handbag. Troy put up both hands. 'What?! He was a lad!'

The portraits of the Tudors seemed to spark his interest, studying their expressions as they stood in front of each one.

'She looks like she's got a secret, doesn't she?' Troy said, pointing at a portrait of Anne Boleyn, a triangular headdress, a nipped-in waist, a knowing look on her face.

'She supposedly had six fingers.'

'Gross.'

'I'm not sure how true that was, Albie didn't believe it. We discussed a programme about her that dismissed a lot of the old myths. He was a fan, thought she was "a much-maligned woman" as he put it. I think he admired her.'

Troy had grown quiet as he watched her.

'What?' she said, patting at her hair self-consciously, wondering if she had something on her face.

'You really miss him,' Troy said simply.

Maria nodded slowly. 'Every day.'

He turned away. 'Me too, man.'

They moved through the last few rooms deep in their own thoughts, no more talk of kings or queens, just knowing they had been brought together today because of him. This was a different world and Troy was getting a glimpse of it. She felt a sudden guilt knowing they would be heading back on the train, that she would be snatching this away as easily as she had introduced him to it. Maria knew it was time to share her surprise with him.

'Can we take a seat?' she asked, moving towards a leather bench in the middle of a room punctuated with glass boxes filled with sculptures.

The crowd had thinned out and the room was largely silent, other than the sound of footsteps on the wooden floorboards loud in the space, people speaking in low voices, heads bent together as they read the information on the small plaques.

Troy sat, placing his carrier bag of clothes on the floor, a nearby attendant glancing up and then away.

'Troy,' she said, twisting on the bench to look at him, 'there's something I want to talk to you about.'

His face closed down, his eyes narrowed, fists curled in preparation. Was he so used to hearing bad news? She could see the defensive tightening of his muscles, a vein going in his neck.

'It's a good thing,' she said, wanting him to relax again, to trust her.

He softened a fraction, head tilted to the left as he waited, hands still curled tightly.

'So, you know that Albie left me things in his will?' she said, words slow and careful. She had thought about how she wanted to tell him, nervous that it wouldn't come out right.

Troy's frown deepened, 'Yeah.'

'Well, the thing is, I went to the solicitor the other day as I now need to make my own will' – she threaded her hands together – 'in case anything happens.'

'Are you alright?' he blurted, his panic palpable.

'I am, but I'm getting on and I want things to be clear if anything were to happen,' Maria said quietly.

He seemed to relax a little, his face clearing. 'Oh good, alright, sounds sensible.'

'The thing is…' Maria took a breath. 'I want to leave you his flat.'

Troy's eyes widened and both hands went up. 'No, no, that's alright, I'm fine, man.'

Maria's voice was firm, 'I want to know you always have somewhere to go, somewhere that is your own.'

Troy was shaking his head. 'No, that's too much. I don't need it, I'm alright.'

'I don't want to debate it with you,' Maria said softly, one hand on his leg. 'This is what I wish if I go and Ms Leonard will be in touch if so.'

'Honestly, I don't, I wouldn't…'

'I don't want to talk about it more,' Maria said, her tone no-nonsense, a new authoritative look, the parent, 'Albie would want it too.'

Troy's hands dropped into his lap and his head bowed. There was total silence for a while. 'You really want to do that for me.' The words were so hushed she might have missed them.

The solicitor had recorded all Maria's wishes. She had wanted to get her affairs in place, ensure that the people in her life now would still be looked after when she was gone. She had instructed Ms Leonard, Becky (she'd insisted), and had left money to Keith so he'd never have to be back on the streets, enough for Cara to at least hire a cleaner every week, Pauline to visit the spa whenever she liked, Timothy to take the cruise he had told her about. Charities, the church, tiny sums for people who had always been warm and made her life a more pleasant place: Amrit, Mr Khan (how much Meghan memorabilia might he buy, she wondered), Mandy and Nina, and finally, she had left Albie's art to Troy and Cathie.

'I want to do that for you. And there's more…' She took a breath.

Troy looked up, aghast, and the expression made her laugh aloud.

'God, anyone would think I was about to tell you I've shot your pet rabbit. Relax…'

But he couldn't relax, biting his lip.

'I've enquired about putting a small deposit down on that shop with the boarded-up windows on St James Street that's been closed for years. The owner is happy for it to be rented out and used as a tattoo parlour when you're ready.'

Troy's eyes grew so wide she could see the whites all around his pupils.

'Once you're eighteen, you can get a licence. I thought you could talk to Adam, see how long you've got left as an apprentice. I've every faith you're going to be a brilliant tattoo artist.'

Troy's mouth parted and he simply sat staring at her, processing everything she was saying.

'You are so talented and you have wonderful ideas and I know Albie thought so too. He would want to see you achieve your dreams. And it won't be easy,' she warned, trying to jolt him out of this catatonic state, 'and you'll have to work for it, but, well, what do you think?'

Troy was still dumbstruck, unable to form words or react to what she was saying. He finally came to and he simply wrapped one arm around her shoulder. 'You're amazing,' he said, pulling her into him. 'You've changed my life.'

Maria felt tears fill her eyes. She straightened and smoothed at her skirt. 'I'm not sure about that,' she said, voice wavering.

Troy was shaking his head slowly from side to side. 'A parlour. I can't... it's going to be...' His face split into the widest smile, two sets of bright white teeth, his eyes sparkling. 'Oh my god.'

'Oh my god indeed.'

'OH MY GOD,' Troy burst, laughing so loudly the attendant looked up from his spot, a finger to his lips. 'FUCKING HELL.'

They left before the attendant was out of his chair, sides aching as they propped each other up all the way to the exit.

*

She placed the photograph on the bedside table. There were others, neatly stuck in an album: not enough. Why hadn't she taken more?

This one was her favourite, stuck to her fridge for years, so familiar, so her. *She could stare at that photograph and remember what it felt like to have her face pressed so close, the wind biting at their skin, bundled into their thick coats, clutching each other as she held the small camera in her hand, her wrist bending as she pressed down on the button.*

'Look,' she'd said, holding it up in Boots, seconds after the album was back from being developed. 'This is a nice one. Love you, Mum.'

She didn't say it often, and certainly not in public, standing in front of the counter of Boots as a middle-aged woman handed back my change.

I took the photo from her and studied it, smiling. 'It is a nice one.'

'You keep it,' she said, rifling through the rest of the photographs, her laughter filling the space as she stumbled across some from a friend's fifteenth bowling birthday party. 'Look at Polly's face!'

I tucked the photograph inside my book and smiled as she continued to show me the rest of the album: grinning teenagers, energy spilling out of every single one of them.

Love you, my girl.

Chapter 34

She ticked '*Take her to The Ritz for afternoon tea – for some proper tea and cake!!!*' under her own name and stared at the words below. She didn't know why today suddenly seemed right, but she knew something had changed. Today was the day.

Perhaps it was the fact that she had found the source of her strength, knowing that others were relying on her: Cara, Troy, they needed her. She hadn't felt needed for thirty-six years. The last person who had needed her was lying in that graveyard.

Pushing the negative thoughts to the back of her head, she dressed carefully in jeans and a bottle-green jumper. She clipped back her hair and fetched a tote bag from the kitchen. She would need to stop by the DIY store and pick up some things on the way.

It was a cool, fresh day and people were milling around the streets, sitting out on tables outside restaurants, enjoying the unseasonable weather.

The DIY shop was dusty and dark as she pushed inside out of the sunshine. She bought secateurs, a packet of tulip seeds, soil and a cream ceramic plant pot. A cloth, spray cleaner for granite and marble, a nailbrush. She handed over her card at the counter, chuckling softly to herself as she remembered the last time she was in there buying weed killer she didn't need, when searching for a man she did. She left, her tote bag packed with her supplies.

Go to the grave…and plant some tulips.

Swallowing her fear, she set off in the direction of the church, wanting to walk there slowly, taking time to compose herself. Her stomach was leaping and gurgling with nerves. She gripped the bag tightly.

Rounding the last corner, she took a deep breath, seeing the spire up ahead, sunlight slicing across the roof, casting shadows on the ground beneath. The iron railings had been recently painted, she noticed, as she approached the lichgate. She licked her lips, wavering on the pavement. She could turn around. She could head home. She could walk past without looking back, like she had done countless times before, never allowing herself to glance inside, to think about what was resting in the corner.

No one else was around and it seemed the noise from the street behind her faded as she stared through the gap above the gate to the grass beyond. Marble gleamed amongst green grass flattened by footsteps, new rows that she couldn't remember had cropped up. It had been almost forty years. She could see the yew tree, bigger than in her memory, spreading its branches over a shady corner.

Her palms were slick as she pushed through the gate, the squeak as it opened, a sudden cold as the sun disappeared behind a cloud.

The walk to the headstone seemed to take two seconds and forever and suddenly she was standing there. It wasn't crooked or covered in moss as she had thought of it over the years. The words were still bold, engraved in black on the polished stone: ROSIE BIRCH, BELOVED DAUGHTER, 1968–1984.

Rosie. Her wonderful, beautiful, lively Rosie. Her eyes filled with tears and she sank to her knees on the grass, not caring about the damp, her knees soaked through within seconds.

Rosie. How could she be sitting in front of Rosie's grave? Maria's whole body shuddered with grief as she pressed her hands to her eyes and let the tears fall.

Her daughter, just a sixteen-year-old. She had failed to protect her own daughter.

The memories battered her as she knelt: Rosie as a baby, with downy hair and the softest skin; as a toothy toddler, careering down the promenade; as an awkward pre-teen, all braces and long limbs, awkwardly hiding behind a curtain of hair; as a teen, dancing to music blaring in her room, packed with her friends spilling off her bed and onto the floor, giggling excitedly, experimenting with make-up.

Her last memory: Rosie clattering down the stairs after their argument – the sound of heels she had only started to wear recently – shouting a stiff goodbye, heading out of the door to waiting friends, not wanting another lecture about a curfew. Maria, distracted by the work she had to do that evening, calling to her from another room, but too late for a response. She couldn't remember what she had called out. She should have told her to be safe, to take care, to be back at a certain time. That she was precious. She should have told her that she loved her.

She shouldn't have let her go.

She hadn't been able to go to bed, had waited up for her, annoyed because she had work the next day. Rosie could be thoughtless, too tied up with her friends and having fun to think. She had stood in the doorway of Rosie's room rehearsing the lecture she would give her: that there were other people in the world to think about. She'd been out too much. They'd already had the row that evening because of it. Yes, she was sixteen now, but she still lived under her roof. 9 p.m. Voices were raised. Doors had been banged.

Maria looked from her watch to the clock and back. No sign. Where was she? She would be exhausted for work the next day: she was an advertising executive and she wanted a promotion, had been working seventy hours a week. She wanted to be a good role model for her daughter, show her that hard work could pay off. That she could support a family as a single mother, have ambition, have it all.

Then the clock's hands crept round and a dread built. She had circled the tiny flat, dialling the numbers on the telephone, getting it wrong, swearing and starting again, finally disturbing the father of Rosie's friend. Something felt wrong. The hands crept round way past the allotted curfew: 10 p.m., 10.30 p.m., 11 p.m.

She had known it before the doorbell rang. The policeman was holding his hat in one hand, smoothing down his hair with the other when she had opened the door on him. Startled, he had rushed the words out: her friends had said she lived here.

He hadn't been old, no more than late twenties perhaps, younger than her certainly. She had made a noise, couldn't remember much else, but it had alerted her busybody neighbour, who had stuck a head out, ready to tell her to be quiet before seeing what the commotion was about.

They had tried everything he had said, someone had done CPR. They believe she had died when she hit the water.

The pier was dangerous.

The girls had gone to the beach, had been messing around on the pier. She had fallen from the end and her friends had alerted passers-by, but it had been too late.

The fall had killed her.

She would need to identify the body.

Did she have someone who could come with her?

That walk through the hospital seemed neverending: down in the lift, the steel grey walls closing in on her, the lack of windows, the false lights flickering on the corridor walls as she approached the sign for the morgue.

The policeman had stayed with her as she had made the identification. It hadn't been her – for a moment, Maria had imagined she would see another girl, another face, one she didn't recognise.

But it had been her. Pale, silent: dead.

The policeman had held onto Maria.

Did she have someone who could be with her?

Yes, she thought. She had someone: she had Rosie.

How could she be gone?

Maria had to sell their flat with its sea view that taunted her every day, the view Rosie had loved, the sight of the pier turning Maria's stomach. She had never been back to the beach since. She didn't move away, couldn't leave Brighton, couldn't leave her daughter there alone. And yet she hadn't returned to see her at the graveyard until today, hadn't been able to face her feelings. She couldn't overcome the terrible, crushing guilt that had forced her to move, to hide away, to quit the career she loved, to shake off her friends and remaining family, to hide in the back office of an accountancy firm until her retirement, to sit in the bland, silent, stale one-bedroomed apartment, no longer caring.

Until that afternoon in the café when a kind man with a West Country accent and an amused twinkle in his eye had forced his way into her life – and forced her to engage again.

She stayed next to the grave until her shoulders stopped heaving and her head began to ache. Then, taking the cloth and the cleaner, she got to work, spraying the gravestone, circling the cloth, watching the stone brighten, the words pop out. She clipped the grass underneath, ready to plant the seeds: tulips, as Albie had suggested. So thoughtful that he remembered that story: a small snippet she had offered up from her life with Rosie. Tulips would suit her, Maria reflected. Bright, bold.

'I'm sorry it's taken me so long to get here, darling…'

She talked as she worked and told Rosie about her ideas for the list, knowing that she wouldn't appear anymore, not now Maria seemed to have found the strength she needed to face things alone.

'I've adopted a cat. They did a home visit which went well, I think. I bought a litter tray, food. The cat will arrive soon. Troy's going to help me. He's so excited about him, made me buy lots of cat toys. You'd like Troy, he's imaginative, like you…'

She dug, making holes for the seeds, leaving neat piles of soil nearby. Dropping the seeds in carefully, she filled the holes, smoothed them, watered them. It was hours later by the time she stood, back aching, legs creaking as she stretched. The grave was transformed: neat and gleaming.

Go to the grave…and plant some tulips.

How she had wanted to ignore those words. Albie had seen what she had needed to do – and now, in the circle of sunlight and the slight breeze, the feeling of something brushing past her, she felt him nudge at her hand, felt a warmth at her side as he joined her staring down at her beloved daughter.

'Thank you,' she whispered to him, feeling the enormous boulder she had carried around for the past four decades start to slip from her shoulders. 'Thank you, Albie Young.'

*

Schoolchildren were everywhere, stood in huddles, shoulders shaking with their sobs as I moved through them to the church door.

She'd had so many friends. Of course she had, she was my Rosie: my brilliant, vibrant, warm-hearted Rosie, found washed up on the beach that she'd loved. Cold and pale and very alone.

I hated these children.

Where had they been that night? How could they have been so irre-sponsible? Why were they still here when she was not?

The service was a blur of tearful words. Sarah spoke about the times they had danced around the small flat, singing into hairbrushes, the time Rosie had given Sarah a makeover and practically burnt off her hair in the process with her crimping iron. She spoke about her love of bright pink bubble gum and her earnest concern that if she swallowed some a tree would grow in her stomach, her pride about her mum who loved her, who worked, who had done it all alone.

Sarah had smiled at me then, but I couldn't move my face, couldn't react. I just wanted her back. Wanted her here. I wanted to howl and tell everyone to leave, leave because this couldn't be happening. We couldn't be burying her. Not my Rosie.

The vicar talked about a better place, peace, the comfort of never growing old. I hated that, hated God for taking her from me. Why hadn't he taken me? Steve? Anyone else. Not Rosie. Rosie with a head full of dreams for her future, her desire to go to London, to study design, to live near Primrose Hill, to support her old mum in the years to come.

The service had ended, a hundred hands patting my shoulder and a hundred mouths whispering words meant to be a comfort in my ear. 'She won't be forgotten', 'A wonderful girl', 'Gone too soon'. God, I hated them all. Why couldn't they leave me, leave me alone?

She was lowered into a gaping hole, a mound of earth piled up next to it. I tripped on the way to throw the handful of dirt on top: someone held me up, steered me away. Someone was wailing, a terrible sound, a wounded, haunting sound. Someone who had lost everything, whose life would never be the same again. I was wailing.

Chapter 35

Troy had messaged, asking her to meet him here.

She was curious as she knocked on the apartment door – he'd instructed her not to use her key to come inside.

'This is all very mysterious,' Maria said as he opened the door to Albie's flat to her.

He looked energised, bouncing from foot to foot and his brown eyes bright. What had he done? She tried to crane a look over his shoulder.

'What are you up to?' She laughed, enjoying seeing this strange excitement on his face.

He opened the door a little wider – there didn't seem to be anything in the corridor, nothing out of the ordinary.

'So, can I come in?'

Perhaps he'd cleaned, or rearranged the furniture?

'I wanted to do something nice, for, you know, taking me to The Ritz and stuff…' he explained, allowing her to squeeze into the narrow corridor.

'You didn't have to, it was Albie's plan. It's always Albie.'

Troy scuffed a trainer on the ground, not quite meeting her eye. 'Well, it wasn't Albie what you've done for me, that was your idea, the parlour and that.'

Maria felt affection bloom for this boy in front of her, whose skinny frame had filled out, and who was even taller than when they'd first met.

'You don't need to do anything for me,' she protested.

'I just want you to see something.' Troy turned and moved down the corridor, lingering outside Albie's bedroom.

Curiosity piqued, Maria followed him into the room.

'It was on his list, wasn't it? That he never finished it, so I…' Troy's voice faded away as Maria looked around the room.

Everything looked the same, the bed still stripped and unmade, curtains pulled back, items packed neatly away in boxes. Above the bed, her portrait seemed to dominate the small space now that it was so empty of Albie's things. 'Oh! You…' Maria's eyes widened as she realised the difference.

Troy was biting his lip.

'…You finished it!'

Troy nodded. 'Do you mind?'

'Mind!' Maria repeated, staring back at the portrait. Troy had painted the area Albie had left blank in the bottom corner, adding her missing hand clutching the top of the chair. He had also filled in other details, she noticed: shading so that the light fell softly on the side of her face.

'He did most of it, I found some sketches and tried to copy what he wanted…'

'I love it.' She grinned, joy filling her every pore. 'You are so clever, you'd never know it wasn't by his hand. How wonderful, how lovely!' She felt tears prick her eyes – he had spent time doing this thing for her. 'Oh, he'd be so proud of you!' she said, moving around the bed to really take in the changes.

Troy seemed to relax, the energy sweeping out of him. 'Sick, Maria, man, I was so worried you might not like it.'

Maria was so busy looking over the details she almost missed his next sentence.

'I found something,' he said, moving around the other side of the bed.
'Hmm…?'

Troy reached across and lifted the portrait off its hook, laying it
gently on the bare mattress between them. 'It's on the back. Albie did
it. I found it when I took it down…'

Maria was confused, her eyebrows drawing together as Troy turned
the portrait over, face down on the mattress.

'What are you—' The question froze on her lips as she realised the
back of the portrait was covered with inky words, words written in
Albie's hand. 'Oh my…'

'He wrote it for you…' Troy said, backing his way out of the
bedroom and leaving Maria alone with the words.

They were crammed onto the surface, neat lines of writing, the
opening at the top, *My Dear Maria...*

'Oh my…' Maria whispered, not realising she was alone in the
room. As she lowered herself down onto the mattress to read, she
felt the whole world reduced to this space, to this letter she had been
waiting to read all this time. A letter from Albie, a letter that would
surely explain everything.

As she read, the tears slid from her face, dripping onto the mattress,
absorbed into the fabric. She read it quickly, having to wipe at her
face as the letters blurred before her. And then a second time: slower,
carefully. *Oh Albie*, she thought as she finished, as she re-read the way
he had signed it. *Oh Albie.*

She had said goodbye to Troy, hugging him tightly, thanking him for
his thoughtful gift and knowing exactly where she was headed. Reading
Albie's words made her next decision easier. She thought of the last line

on the wish list. The last bullet point, the one under her own name. She would go now and honour it.

Albie would have liked it, she thought, as she pushed through the door of the small, independently run shop. She had walked past it for years and had never thought to step inside. At first it had seemed silly to do it without him. It wasn't like it could end how he had imagined it. And yet it seemed wrong not to complete everything, to choose the very thing he wanted to get her.

The room smelt of cranberries and furniture polish, the walls were lined in rich cream leather and polished clear boxes displayed a plethora of jewellery, sparkling and gleaming under the spotlights overhead. A woman stood behind the counter, hair pinned back in a neat bun, smooth, dark skin, a bright smile.

'Can I help you with something?'

Did she imagine Maria would be asking for a christening gift for a grandchild, a new watch to replace her old, maybe a necklace for herself? She searched the woman's face, which remained open and expectant.

'An engagement ring, please. I'd like to view your engagement ring selection.'

• *'Buy the ring, propose to Maria…'*

Only the smallest flicker betrayed the woman's surprise at the request. 'How wonderful,' she said, moving to a cabinet on Maria's left. 'Will the gentleman be joining us?' She peered behind Maria as if some suitor would magically appear.

For some reason Maria found the sentence exceptionally funny and burst into an unexpected, loud laugh, startling the woman. 'No, no, he won't be joining us.'

Again, the woman remained perky. Maria wondered if she worked on commission.

'Well, this is our selection. We have different styles, different sizes of diamond, of course; we have white gold, rose gold, platinum bands and more. Do browse and I can answer any questions you might have.'

She stepped back as Maria peered into the cabinet, the rings spaced out on a dark blue velvet tray. Some were beautiful, the stones gleaming: three in a row, one enormous one, one raised in a clasp of gold, another band studded with tiny ones. It was quite an array and for a moment Maria was overwhelmed with the choice. She hadn't owned much jewellery. Steve, Rosie's father, hadn't bought her a ring, had said he was saving for something special. After he left when Rosie was only eleven months old, she was glad she didn't have a band to remind her.

What would Albie have picked for her, she wondered as she stared at the selection. She noticed one of the rings, a simple gold band with a beautiful solitaire stone at the centre. It was elegant, modest and just right. She motioned to the assistant. 'If possible, please could I try that one on.'

'We would resize it of course, they often don't fit, but the resizing is complimentary – and we offer an annual clean for a very small sum.'

'Good, good,' Maria said, watching in quiet amazement as the woman took a key and unlocked the cabinet, the glass sliding across, her hand reaching inside to pull out the tray.

'That one, please,' Maria said, indicating the top right corner.

'A lovely choice,' the woman said, giving her another wide smile. Maria knew she probably would have said that if she'd selected any one of them, but it made her feel better all the same.

She felt wobbly, this enormous decision that she should have been making with someone else. It wasn't so much the ring but everything it represented, what it meant to be purchasing it.

She held up the ring, the stone flashing under the spotlight, the platinum band bright and clean. It was a wonderful ring and Maria slid it onto her finger. It felt snug and strange and wonderful. Like it was made for her.

'Oh!' the lady said, her mouth a small 'O'. 'That hardly ever happens. It's obviously meant to be!'

She sounded genuine and Maria found herself smiling up at her. 'I think it is.'

Maria slid off the ring, reluctantly handing it back to the woman. 'I'd like it, please.'

The woman couldn't hide her surprise now – it was the fastest sale she'd ever achieved. 'You are a woman who knows her own mind,' she said, both eyebrows raised.

Maria straightened, ready to pull out her purse and pay. She wanted that ring back on her hand, she wanted that unfamiliar item on her fourth finger. She wanted to stare at it from every angle, admire the way it gleamed under the light, wanted to stare inside the stone at the tiny fragmented glass. She wanted to imagine Albie sliding it onto her finger, looking at it in wonder, in wonder at what it represented: engaged.

'That I do,' she said, drawing out her bank card. 'I've waited long enough.'

The ring came in a small square velvet maroon case, making it seem even more flawless, which the woman wrapped in a small bag, tied with a navy-blue ribbon. She insisted, wouldn't let Maria simply walk out with the ring. She gave her a leaflet about the care of her ring, a reminder to insure it and a card in case she wanted to make further purchases. Maria wasn't planning on anything else: Albie hadn't added 'Buy a tiara' to the list. She grinned at the thought and the woman tipped her head to the side.

'I want whatever you're on,' she said, passing the bag to Maria.

'High on life,' Maria replied, feeling for the first time in many years that this was really true.

Albie might not be here with her now but his list had shown her that he had really loved her, had truly seen her and loved her. This ring represented the fact that he had wanted to share his life with her and that thought settled on her chest and made her heart sing.

She left the shop clutching the bag, knowing where she had to go next, knowing where Albie had wanted to propose to her.

Chapter 36

He had wanted to make a new memory there. A happy memory. He had known she would need to be ready, need to have let go of the past. Perhaps that was why it had been the final thing on the list.

She took a breath as she approached the familiar street, one hand squeezed tight on the small bag from the jewellers, the other carrying a heavier bag. There were more people here, the road busy too with cars and cyclists. A moped moved past, engine sputtering.

She arrived, craning her neck to look up. Their old apartment in a Georgian block: a wrought-iron balcony, repainted in a royal blue. Rosie had loved to sit out on it and look out across the water, taking endless polaroids that she'd stuck on her walls with Blu Tack. She had loved the sea, the view. Her O Level Art project had been returned to Maria by the school and her final piece had been a photographic collage of that view, the blues splicing over each other, white card cut into tiny pieces recreating the reflections on the water.

This was Maria's first glimpse of this stretch of beach in thirty-six years. Sand and pebbles that she and her daughter had sat on, played on, lain on hundreds of times.

Further along there was now a large Ferris wheel like the London Eye dwarfing the beach, the outside of the old arcade more neon than she remembered, more stalls selling ice cream, coffees. The familiar sickly smell of sugared batter and warm dough hit her nostrils. Rosie had loved those bags of warm donuts, had struck up a friendship with the boy in the stall next to the arcade, who always added a few more for her. Everyone had loved her, drawn to her energy, her laughter, her confidence. She had been so impossibly full of life, forever trapped in Maria's memory as that bouncy schoolgirl who never grew old.

Maria felt her stomach swirl as she took the first step across the road to the wide promenade that ran along the beach. Someone passed on a skateboard, the sound of the wheels making her jump, and someone shouted for their toddler further up ahead. She made her way slowly to the pier, her shoulder suddenly shoved backwards as a man, not looking, bumped into her.

'You alright?' a young girl with long strawberry-blonde hair asked her.

Maria nodded, staring at her as if it was thirty-six years ago and nothing had changed, as if she might have been one of Rosie's many friends.

The wooden boards of the pier were dusted with a thin layer of sand and Maria stepped forward, noticing the cracks between them showing dark flashes of sand and water rolling in. Benches lined the middle of the pier with couples sitting and elderly people watching as she made her way down. Her legs felt wobbly as she moved, the larger bag knocking against her thigh, her heart hammering. *Rosie had walked here*, she thought, as people passed by, teenagers grinning into phones as they took selfies, the sea behind them.

She wondered whether Rosie had taken her camera that night, whether she had dangled over the side trying to get the perfect shot, the flash surprising her. Was that how it had happened? They didn't find a camera, they didn't find a bag. They had only found her, washed

up the next morning further along the beach, her dark brown hair
haloed around her pale face. The coroner had reported: misadventure.

This wasn't about Rosie and what happened, Maria reminded herself:
she was here for another reason, here to lay the ghosts to rest once and
for all, to embrace the future.

She found a quiet spot overlooking the sea, the many shades of
blue and green shifting in front of her. She had missed this: missed
watching the colours blend and merge, the clouds skittering overhead,
the elegant sweep of a seagull, the smell of salt, the long stretch of sea
to the horizon. She closed her eyes, the sun on her face as she thought
of those happy days on the beach, swimming in the sea, squealing at
the shock of it, of lazy walks along the pier, ice creams dripping from
chins, strands of hair whipped across their faces, laughter snatched
away in the wind.

Placing the heavier bag on the boards, she drew out the urn. She
had finally picked up the ashes from the funeral directors, encased in
a smooth cream tube. 'Biodegradable,' the director had told her, 'that's
what he wanted. Said you'd be along to pick him up and scatter him
somewhere beautiful.'

Holding Albie in her arms, she stared out at the ocean: this was a
beautiful place, this was a place he would have wanted her to come.
Timothy had reminded her that Albie loved the sea and this seemed like
the perfect place to say goodbye. Unscrewing the lid, she took a slow
breath out and then, tears stinging her eyes, she said her goodbye in
the wind and watched him billow and fall into the water beneath them.

It was a goodbye to Albie, but also to her fears and the pain that
had haunted her for so many years.

Then she opened the other, smaller bag and drew out the precious
box, carefully sliding the ring onto her finger. She pictured him there,

laughing as he grumbled about getting on one knee, the twinkle in his eye that always told her he was joking. The perfect gentleman, he would have got on one knee, she thought, turning to the space next to her. He would have looked up at her, his blue eyes serious for a moment as he used her full name. 'Maria Birch,' she imagined him saying, 'will you do me the honour of becoming my wife?'

She blinked, certain for a moment that she had heard those words, spoken with a West Country lilt, low and steady. She would have said yes, of course, she would have held his hand as he creaked back up to a standing position, one hand on his lower back. She would have watched in thrilled amazement as he pushed this very ring onto her finger. She would have felt her heart lift with the sure knowledge that she wasn't alone anymore. That someone loved her and she loved them. She hadn't believed her heart would ever mend and yet, standing on this pier, she could feel it healing, the cracks disappearing, filled with memories, warmth, laughter.

She stared across the water once more, rays of sunlight beaming onto the surface, pushing the clouds apart. She exhaled slowly, felt the ring on her finger and imagined him there, wrapping one arm around her shoulder and pulling her close. She had been so lucky to have been loved.

Chapter 37

My dear Maria,

If you're reading this then it means I am gone. I am sorry if this is the way we say goodbye. There was so much I had planned for us.

I always wanted a little longer, was greedy, but the doctors were pretty grim from the start. I've been glad of their honesty, insisted on it. And so I started to get my affairs in order. Was it a terrible surprise to discover the man you'd sat opposite every week had so many secrets? I so nearly told you, so many times, but I couldn't stomach saying the words aloud, I didn't want your face to cloud with pity and to have the endless questions about treatments and more. They told me my heart would simply give out. I wanted you to remember me full of life.

And maybe you didn't feel the same way, I was never quite sure how you felt about me. I didn't want to rush you, but I need you to know now that I was in love with you: hopelessly, horribly and endlessly in love with you.

I wasn't deserving of you, Maria. I had spent years focusing on all the wrong things, my savings account was full and for what? I had no one to share all that money with and I realised I was completely alone. I needed to be sure that I was worthy of you and so I started a project, a list that has brought me unimaginable joy – and peace. And my greatest wish for the list was to complete it, to finally feel worthy and lay myself out for you to see: to hear then what the most genuine, kind woman I know thinks of me in her heart.

I am not that man yet and I worry that I can never atone for the person I used to be. I was such a selfish ass, Maria, so wrapped up in my own brilliance, my own job, friends, life. I didn't think of others, didn't walk a mile in their shoes. Too busy chasing things that, I realise now, didn't matter a jot: money, success in business, connections to important people. As I got older, I looked around, realised it had done nothing to make me happy. I had started to make piecemeal changes, and then I sat down opposite you on that fateful Thursday and knew I had to do more.

I didn't see my own mother slowly dwindling in front of me and I let my little sister Cathie take on the burden of caring for her. I would be out at another meeting, another event or weekend with friends: always something, always someone else, and then it was too late and I was standing at my own mother's funeral, angry at her for leaving, angry at the world and at anyone else but myself. I lashed out, alienated myself from my own sister, my last real family and the one person who saw the real me. I didn't want the mirror held up to my face.

My mother was the most wonderful, caring woman, Maria, much like you: gentle, humorous, interested. You are always so alive with thoughts, devouring books, films and television programmes, challenging me, laughing with me. I have adored seeing things from your perspective.

I saw you still painfully reliving your own past, not allowing yourself to embrace the present or the future, and it made me want to forgive myself.

The first day I saw you sat in the café, this beautiful woman in a pale pink scarf and soft grey cashmere jumper, looking about twenty years younger than me, I felt drawn to you. Translucent skin, a rare but wide smile, cerulean blue eyes that slid away from my face when I found myself pulling out the chair opposite you – and every time after that if I paid you a compliment.

You would place one hand over the other, again and again, a nervous gesture that always made me want to reach across and still them with my own hand. I would think about it, waver, hover ready to do it, but I was too frightened that I would ruin things, that it would change everything and that this delicate friendship we had would be over.

It always seemed that you were on the verge of leaving, flighty and hard to pin down. At first, I thought you were a social butterfly – of course people would want to be in your orbit, you had places to go, people to see. Over time I came to realise that you had created a cage around yourself: a timetable of events, a small world in that apartment of yours which you so rarely seemed to leave and to which you never invited me.

What had happened to you? I wondered about it for that first year as we got to know each other, as we talked about everything and nothing, skirting the important things, both quick to make excuses if we strayed too close.

'Oh, my family,' I would say with a dismissive wave of my hand, my heart beating wildly in my chest. 'Nothing to speak of there.' How could I tell you what I had done? How I had behaved? That I had cut my own sister out of my life after she failed to show up to our mother's funeral, that I had used that against her to stay away, not wanting to confront my own guilt, and that I had failed them both by being such an absent son and brother? That I had put off making my peace with her out of my own stubborn pride. You would have looked at me differently and I couldn't stand that thought.

How proud I still am, wanting to fool you with my own worthiness.

I did ask you about family once and you had told me that you had had a daughter, Rosie, who was buried here in Brighton, and that you hadn't been back to the grave. You had covered your mouth with a hand at that admission and the surprise I'd felt that you had a daughter silenced my own tongue when I should have comforted you and made you feel less alone. What an idiot I was to let it go that day, to not dig deeper then. Worse still, for a second I had been jealous at the look when you spoke about her, the pain of your love, jealous you were talking about someone else in that fierce way. How horrible, to think that in that moment. So, you see, I am not so changed after all.

I would look forward to Thursday above anything else, especially to that easy way you would be sat at one of those tables with those disgusting red cloths, a slice of marble cake and a pot of tea waiting for me, with a triumphant look that you had beaten me to it and paid. How I hated it and loved it when you did that, but mainly it would make me smile on the way home, chuckle with a promise I would be early the following week.

Thursdays, when I would think of all the things I wanted to tell you and when really, I just loved looking at you, watching your rosebud mouth as you told me about a documentary, a radio play, a book that had touched you or listening to your soft laugh as Pauline chatted. You glowed bright in that dowdy space: elegant, timeless. What were you doing with a boy from the West Country who'd spent most of his life wrapped up in himself? You had the biggest heart, always thinking of others, wanting to please. But you also wanted to disappear, to not cause trouble, to not take up space. I wanted to shake you at times, force you to realise that you deserved all the kindness, that you deserved to take up room in this world.

You mentioned what had happened to her once – and how it hurt you. Do you remember?

You told me, in the simplest terms, how she had fallen, how her friends had run away, frightened, how a passer-by had tried to help her, how she couldn't be saved. You blamed yourself: she shouldn't have been out, it was late, you'd rowed that night about her curfew, you shouldn't have let her go, you should have known where she was, you should have paid more attention. The grief was etched on your face as you spoke. My heart broke for you then.

I knew you needed to forgive yourself, that this awful thing had destroyed you. I needed you to realise that it wasn't your fault, Maria, and that you were a brilliant, caring mother. Rosie would have been in no doubt that she was loved. But I could never find the words – I would buy that slice of marble cake and try to force myself to raise it. You would avoid talking about the past and I let you, because that look on your face, that awful sadness was heartbreaking. So many years, Maria, and still the pain was obvious. All I wanted was to make your eyes crease, to make you smile.

You always commented on tulips in the café – they seemed to make you smile for the briefest second before melancholy set in. You had planted them with her when she was young: yellow tulips, you'd mentioned briefly, and I wanted you to plant them for her, with me there by your side, supporting you.

I am working my way through the list in the hope that through it I can reach my dream: to see if I can win your hand. By the time you read this letter, I hope I have managed it, that I have changed and become worthy of you. I hope that we are together. I know that is all I could want.

I love you, Maria Birch, plain and simple. You are my everything.

Your Albie x

Chapter 38

She stepped off the pier and took her time walking along the promenade, an old familiar route, imagining for a moment a small hand in hers, a little girl hopscotching on the stones ahead, an older girl wobbling past on her first roller skates. She had loved the beach and Brighton with her girl: a team of two in this wonderful town. She breathed out, taking a last long glance at the sea glittering in the evening light. A cruise ship passed on the horizon, the only blemish as the sun sank lower in the sky, stretching her shadow on the ground in front of her.

She walked slowly and determinedly to the café, which was coming to the end of a busy day: some tables dirty with crumbs and plates, others newly scrubbed down, and only a couple of customers left. Amrit was sweeping in one corner and gave her a small wave as she arrived.

'Hold on, Maria, I'll be with you in two minutes…'

The table Maria wanted was free and scrubbed clean. She made her way over to it. Even though the scene was different, she still pictured the spot: the place she had been sat when he first moved across to introduce himself. She pulled out the chair and sat down.

Amrit appeared, vivid green streaked through her hair today, a pencil poised. 'Keith's got some good specials going today. There's probably some of his cherry Bakewell tart left, if I ask?'

'A slice of marble cake and a pot of tea, please,' Maria said, interrupting her.

Amrit blinked, didn't say anything, just a short nod and moved across to the counter to get things ready.

Keith must have heard her voice in the largely empty café and he emerged, an eager look on his face. 'Hey, Maria. I'm glad you came in, I've been wanting to see you. So, hey, you see… just thought I'd say you can tick me off,' he said, a hand through his hair.

Maria frowned up at him, his hands rubbing on his dirty apron.

'The list,' he added at her blank expression, his voice lowered. 'You helped me reconnect with my family.' He bit his lip and stared at the ground as he waited for her reaction.

'You got in touch with your son,' she said with a warm smile.

Keith nodded, the information bursting out of him, pride thick in his voice. 'He lives in Portsmouth, he's asked to see me. I'm… I'm going to be a grandad, Maria.' When he looked up at her she saw fresh tears in his eyes.

'That's… that's amazing.' Maria felt her heart lurch for him.

'Mandy's going to come along,' he added, chin up, swallowing. 'For support, you know.'

'Support, eh? That's what you youngsters call it, is it? How nice of her,' Maria said with an expression of feigned innocence.

Keith nudged her, laughing. 'Alright, I just wanted to say thank you, again, for everything. I feel like I've been given a second chance,' he said, his voice full of emotion, a short squeeze of her shoulder.

'I'm so glad, you deserve it,' Maria said, taking a breath as Amrit returned with the tray of tea and cake.

A large group of customers arrived so Keith disappeared back to the kitchen with a quick goodbye and Amrit set to taking orders, clearing the last of the tables, pushing a pair together to accommodate the group.

Maria stared at the slice of marble cake, the pot. She poured the tea carefully, stirred in the milk. Then raising the fork, she took the first mouthful of marble cake. It tasted sweet, of so many wonderful days with the best person she had ever known rolled into one bite. She closed her eyes, savouring the taste. She finished the tea and she finished the cake and then she left quietly, just a tip on the table, no more words.

She walked back to her apartment slowly and enjoyed weaving between the streets of Brighton: relishing others' joy as they passed her.

She felt bone-tired when she finally made it back, drained from the emotion of the day, from the relief of releasing all the grief, all the regrets that she had stored up over a lifetime. Pushing open the door, the engagement ring flashing, she dropped her bag and moved inside.

Entering the bathroom, she poured the last of her lavender oil into the warm running water. She fetched a large glass of cool wine and her book, removed her clothes and sank beneath the water, her skin warmed, soft. Her wine tasted like raspberries and a summer's day. She read, topping up the bathwater until she had finished the final chapter: a wonderful read, an Albie recommendation, so much came back to him.

She wrapped herself in her dressing gown and padded through to the kitchen, enjoying the slow process of cooking dinner. Filling her glass, she listened to the sizzle of the pan, smelt the charred meat. The memory struck her in that moment: a last meal, he had asked her once. She had said a Sunday roast, but perhaps it was this, she thought as she took the first bite – a thin steak that was perfectly done, pink in the middle, with homemade chips and peas.

Playing her favourite CD, she rested back in her armchair, letting the music flow round her, and closed her eyes, lost in the moment.

She allowed herself to sink into a past of memories: remembering the time Albie had given her a first edition of a book she'd mentioned she loved; remembering Rosie racing in to tell her she'd won the Singing Prize, that she was a Head of Year, that Tess was no longer her best friend, that Matt had been seen kissing Gemma behind the chemistry block and wanted to go to second base. Some of the memories caused her to giggle softly as she took another mouthful of wine, floating back in time once more.

She thought of her new friends: pictured Troy in a tattoo parlour lined with his original designs, customers leaving with intricate marks running up their arms; Keith and Mandy on a cruise ship to the Mediterranean, Mandy making him do the *Grease* duet in front of the other holidaymakers; Pauline sat on her stool knitting in the new-look café, her naughty cackle at something Amrit said; Cara putting her feet up, her apartment clean and comfortable as Owen played and her baby slept in her arms; Nina discovering something gold and wonderful on one of her trips out with her metal detector; Cathie watching the two dogs she so loved, laughing as she threw them sticks; Timothy playing backgammon outside a café as if he was in Rome and not Lynmouth. So many people crammed into the last few months and one person linking them all to her: Albie.

Buttoning up soft pink pyjamas, teeth clean, make-up wiped away, feet bare, she slipped beneath the fresh sheets and rested her head on the plumped pillow. She lifted her hand above her to stare again at the ring she had picked out, that he would have loved on her. *Albie*. Now, she let herself think just of him.

Albie on the first day he'd met her, Albie on the second Thursday when he'd reappeared and she hadn't questioned it, on all the Thursdays where he spoke about films, books, politics, his own life – Troy, the library, his childhood – and asked her questions. His West Country accent, the bump in his nose, the soft blue of his eyes that crinkled kindly when she spoke. Albie on the day she had shared her sad story, the serious way in which his eyes had filled with the tears she herself struggled to spill. *Albie.*

Sitting up in bed, she reached across to open the top drawer of her bedside table. She pulled out the list, staring at the many ticks, the bullet points, her additions on the dog-eared paper. Rummaging for a pen, she took a breath, staring at the gap at the bottom of the back page. Enough space for one more sentence. She removed the lid of the pen, resting the list on the surface of the bedside table.

Writing in a slow, careful hand, she added, '*To one day be with Albie again.*'

Then she closed the pen lid, placed it and the list back in her bedside drawer and reached to turn off the lamp. For a moment her eyes rested on the photo in the frame: herself and Rosie in faux-fur hoods, cheeks pressed together, pink noses, enormous grins, filling the picture. She blew a kiss at her beloved daughter and then switched off the lamp. In the dark, she scooted down, resting back against the pillow once more, letting her head sink in softly. No noise outside the apartment, nothing to disturb her. Taking a long, slow, deep breath, she closed her eyes.

A Letter from Ruby

I want to say a huge thank you for choosing to read *The Wish List*. If you did enjoy it, and want to keep up to date with all my latest releases, just sign up at the following link. Your email address will never be shared and you can unsubscribe at any time:

www.bookouture.com/ruby-hummingbird

I thoroughly enjoyed telling Maria's story and hope you were rooting for her and the rest of the cast. I wanted to write a book that would move my readers and put a smile on their faces. Albie's list has inspired me to look at my own life and wonder at the small ways I can help those around me. I think we could all be more Albie!

I hope you loved *The Wish List* and if you did, I would be very grateful if you could write a review. I'd love to hear what you think and it makes such a difference helping new readers to discover my books. I also love hearing from my readers – you can get in touch on my Facebook page or through Twitter and Goodreads.

Thanks,
Ruby Hummingbird

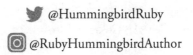

@HummingbirdRuby

@RubyHummingbirdAuthor

Acknowledgements

This book was a true joy and a privilege to write. Thank you so much to my editor Christina, who has boundless energy, enthusiasm and positivity. Your obvious love for this book has fuelled the process and working with you has been a pleasure from the start.

To the team at Bookouture: the other editors who have tweeted or messaged and the indomitable Kim and Noelle, I have felt welcomed by you all from Day One. Particular thanks to Natasha Hodgson for her excellent and thoughtful copyedit, Ellen Gleeson, Alexandra Holmes, Jane Donovan, Leodora Darlington, Alex Crow and Jules Macadam. I adore the detailed and unique cover and an enormous thank you to Sarah Whittaker for her work designing it. Thank you to the whole team for everything you do to ensure my book will be read by so many wonderful readers. To the Little, Brown Rights Team: Andy, Kate, Hena and Helena, thank you for talking to publishers in different territories and being so wonderfully passionate in your response to the book. I hope I can connect with readers around the world who will take Albie and Maria to their hearts too.

To Clare, my agent, for her constant belief in my writing and her no-nonsense approach when we discuss things. Thank you for always trying to get back to me so promptly with news and chat when there are a hundred other things going on. The Darley Anderson office is made up of some wonderful people and I want to thank Mary, Tanera, Sheila, Christina, Georgia, Chloe and Rosanna too.

Thank you to my extended family for such happy times and, in particular, my parents for their endless interest in my writing. To my husband and children, I feel incredibly lucky to have you around me every day.

And lastly, to the Jilly Cooper Book Club – an eclectic mix of passionate women – thank you for your support, and practical suggestions in response to my random research questions (from cat adoption through to the geography of Brighton). This book is dedicated to Andrea – a generous, joyful spirit. I am so grateful to have known her.

CPSIA information can be obtained
at www.ICGtesting.com
Printed in the USA
LVHW110900150520
655294LV00002B/50

9 781838 880927